Good Girls Gone Bad

Bad II the Bone Book 3

Anton Marks

All rights reserved. No part of this publication may be reproduced, distributed or transmitted in any form or by any means, including photocopying, recording, or other electronic or mechanical methods, without the prior written permission of the publisher, except in the case of brief quotations embodied in critical reviews and certain other noncommercial uses permitted by copyright law. For permission requests, write to the publisher, addressed "Attention: Permissions Coordinator," at the address below.

Marksman Studios

Marksmanstudios1@gmail.com

www.antonmarks.com

Publisher's Note: This is a work of fiction. Names, characters, places, and incidents are a product of the author's imagination. Locales and public names are sometimes used for atmospheric purposes. Any resemblance to actual people, living or dead, or to businesses, companies, events, institutions, or locales are completely coincidental.

Ordering Information:

Quantity sales. Special discounts are available on quantity purchases by corporations, associations, and others. For details, contact the above email address.

Good Girls Gone Bad/ Anton Marks - 1st edition.

ISBN 978-0-9562660-88

Copyright © 2023 by Anton Marks

❦ Created with Vellum

A big thank you to **James Bacon** *and the* **Dublin 2019 an Irish World Con** *and it's continued support of my work.*

Chapter One

Yacht Club, Docklands, East London

Yvonne 'Y' Sinclair looked at her reflection in the silver tray, and the image that looked back made her grimace. It was not that she didn't care that London was teetering on the edge of an existential crisis of good and evil – that was a given. This, on the other hand, had a far-reaching personal impact. That was why she promised herself this one thing. The next time she transformed from a dark-skinned black woman to a white-skinned brunette, the spell would give her something resembling a bust and an ass.

She felt inadequate, which was not good for her self-esteem.

Not good at all.

Y wasn't the only one having second thoughts about this mission.

"Reassure me suga. What the fuck we doing here?" Cleopatra Jones whispered the question with a Georgia twang she had never entirely left in Atlanta. It was low and distinct, meant for her sister's ears only. Yvonne knew this was coming. You had to admit, even for them, this was bizarre. And Bad II the Bone was intimate with what constituted bizarre more than most. The roles they played tonight had them dressed as silver service staff for a secret function that attracted a powerful cadre of London movers and shakers in the esoteric world. Their usual gigs involved bodyguard duties to the rich, famous, and sometimes disreputable. But ever so often, Mr Patel, the seer of Pakistan – *Mas P*, as Suzy Wong, the third member of their merry band, preferred to call him – had a job for them that was 'unusual'. Mr Patel was their business partner, who handled promotion, marketing and bookings for the Bad II the Bone Bodyguard Agency. No one knew how or why, but Mr Patel was plugged in, connected to the metaphysical forces that blew through the world, and only a few could feel and discern. When the man from Punjab was sent the warning and sensed the convolution, he divined a morsel of meaning that their alter egos, the Guardians of the Light, could use to fulfil their purpose. Y looked over to Suzy Wong, the diminutive Chinese Jamaican empath and wushu master, as she busied herself doling out champagne to excited attendees. While she diligently completed her duties, Suzy made sure she was close enough to the action to sense whether the Spear of Destiny that was on display was fake or real. It was good to know who was in possession of a powerful artefact like that. And how they might use it. And in this case, the Guardians were justified in being concerned. The new owner of the Spear of Destiny was a leader of a far-right political party, who had the favour of some influential and powerful people judging by the numbers that were attending the unveiling.

Y took in a breath and smiled.

"I know how you feel, but Mr Patel thinks there is much more to this than the unveiling of a powerful artefact."

Y came closer to Patra's triple earrings, smelled her perfume and said, "Keep aware and be patient."

Patra nodded and grimaced. Not feeling it.

"It ain't easy being around these Aryan looking, master race spouting, anti-Semitic posturing, black people lynching, motherfuckers. But for you, my sexy leader, I'll try."

Patra gracefully turned and strode away with her empty tray balanced nimbly in hand, a veneer of servility replacing her anger as she disappeared into the guests.

Suzy Wong stood at the table filled with macaroons and slices of cake. She was closest to the stage where the Master of Ceremonies was spouting on about the symbolism of the Spear. Suzy wondered if he understood the power coursing through the fibres of the ancient Roman weapon that was said to have been plunged into the side of Christ.

She doubted it.

Suzy could sense its power without even trying, but it was obvious that the majority of people standing there had no real respect for what was on display. They seemed more interested in their palates as they depleted the treats she was offering them from her table, with no one smiling or offering a single word of thanks.

She had changed from her well-proportioned and toned Chinese Jamaican self to a dark-haired chubby Romanian girl. The elite here were from a different European stock that looked down on the gipsy heritage the witch's spell had randomly conjured for her.

Why employ people like her if you had disdain for them? She thought. But Suzy answered her own question.

The dynamics of power always had someone you could step on to confirm your superiority. Politics was not her thing, but it was difficult, almost impossible, to be a daughter of

Jamaica and not be acutely aware of how the mechanism of politics worked. The island was just a smaller and more transparent example of what was going on here.

When the Master of Ceremonies came back on stage moments later and called for everyone's attention, Suzy had an idea of where he was going with this performance. She'd seen it done before. Looking over the two hundred-plus guests in black-tie and evening gowns, Suzy wondered how much money he would raise from what he was preparing to say next. She took a deep breath and felt the wave of apprehension and frustration emanating from her sisters - Y and Patra, across the hall.

"Ladies and gentlemen," he repeated with that same smoothness of a professional speaker. He had all eyes on him.

"The evening began with mystery, you were enlightened with some history, and now you're being tantalised with the power and the glory." His voice rose, and there was some applause and laughter. "And the night is still young. But before we lubricate you some more and ask for your credit cards, I would like to bring on stage the man with the vision, the power and the plan to make Britain great again, the Right Honourable Egerton Musgrave."

Applause erupted in the hall; everyone seated stood up and watched the tall, middle-aged, athletically built sandy haired politician bound onto the stage. He hugged the MC as he exited and strode to centre stage, preferring a discreet clip-on microphone to the standard handheld.

"Thank you, thank you," he said, his hands almost placating their excitement as he pumped the air with his palms. "Friends, benefactors, believers. You are here because of the vast resources you command and because you can wade through the fake news and discern the truth. We are a sinking ship, ladies and gentlemen, who could so easily save ourselves if we rid the country we love of the unnecessary dead weight that is drowning us."

There were nods, 'here, here's and boisterous Aye's.

"We have symbols that tell us we are ordained to lead this nation back to its greatness. The Spear of Destiny is one such symbol, but there are many more, and we will acquire them."

He strode across the stage, making sure everyone bathed in his passion. His eyes were lit, his voice tremulous with fervour.

"This is the beginning, and you, my people, are the pioneers. You are the chosen..."

SUZY STOOD RESPECTFULLY WITH HER ARMS BEHIND HER back at her station. Repulsed by what was being said, she repeated the mantra of calm instead of focusing on the hate and looked inwards. Abbot Wing Chung of the Kowloon Shaolin Temple would be disappointed.

Her mind had wandered to the past. Suzy's school days at Immaculate Conception High School in Kingston, Jamaica. Hands behind her back as she crept up on Sister Maria Lee, the only woman who knew of her gifts and actively encouraged their development.

"Penny for your thoughts," she had asked her geography teacher.

And just as they had done it many, many times before, Sister Maria said, "You tell me."

And Suzy would.

Using her gift to unravel how her teacher was not only feeling but her intentions had become second nature. Some people were like lighthouses guarding a stricken ship to safety, while others were like sirens – all beautiful voices and promises but luring the unsuspecting into the shore's rocks. Sister Maria was a lighthouse. But what Suzy was feeling now in this place of power, privilege, and hate was a swirling tornado of the yin and the yang that had suddenly appeared on her psychic radar. She smelt a whiff of leather and frankincense. She sensed a warm breeze of wisdom, age, and the fiery determination that made the hairs on her arm stand on end. This was a new addition to the room, and it was sudden and unexpected. Suzy held her breath and transmitted her disquiet to her sisters across the room in a split-second of discovery. She spun towards the direction where she thought the emotions were coming from, but she was too late.

Three suppressed shots rang out in quick succession.

Whup! Whup! Whup!

The politician crumpled as three high-velocity bullets broke the sound barrier, struck him and sent his body twirling backward like a failed ballerina to the floor. They were not killing shots. Shoulder, thigh and calf. Through and through. But that was enough to switch off civility and engage the prehistoric instinct of survival. The panic spread like a wave mixed in with the Pop! Pop! sounds of smoke canisters arcing through the air. Armed security tried to reach him, but they were moving against the flow of bodies, a look of perplexity on each and every face.

How?

Smoke drifted quickly through the hall, obscuring faces, making the mad dashes for safety seem like a staccato form of impressionist dance. Except, this art form was accompanied by a score of screams and panic. Egerton Musgrave lay on his back, losing blood as his life fluid fanned out around him, but he was still conscious. Conscious enough to see the little girl on her hands and knees moving around in his sticky blood, sobbing beside him. This was supposed to be a learning experience for his daughter, to connect her with the values that would make her a force in the world when she was older.

What had gone wrong?

"Daddy, you're hurt," his daughter sobbed. "You're hurt."

The MP looked up at his daughter; his eyes were misty and unfocused. His lips parted ever so slightly, and the little girl's ear came closer to his mouth as if she knew he wouldn't have the strength to speak.

"It's going to..." he paused and swallowed painfully, "... It's going to be alright. Everything's... going to be all ... right." His gravitas returned to his words but just for a moment. Because unknown to his little girl, who was too grief-stricken to realise it, his next moments were focused on the giant of a man looming over him. The man who had emerged out of the smoke as if he was a part of it, and it was a part of him. Who moved silently and precisely through the world of chaos he had caused as if he had switched off two of his five senses. From the politician's perspective, his assassin was blurry at the edges, but the handgun he had aimed at his forehead was distinct, a solid ugly thing that could take life without remorse. Egerton didn't want his daughter to see this. She was oblivious to the blur standing over her father. She held onto her father even when the giant interfering with his senses spoke, kneeling beside him. His daughter looked up at the giant, curious but not afraid.

"You're hurt too," the little girl said, staring at the giant's pitted and scarred ballistic mask.

"Yes," he said simply and used a finger size of a stick of dynamite to ruffle her blonde hair. He shifted his attention back to him.

"Kiss her and hug her every moment you can," the shadow man said. "And if you can take yourself away from your hate and lies, thank her. I would kill you right here, right now, but your daughter has saved you."

The shadow man stood and turned away, took a few steps, stopped and turned back to the Right Honourable Egerton Musgrave. He removed the ballistic mask as if it was an impediment to his vision. What had earlier been hidden was now clear, making the politician wish he had never seen that face. A face that would haunt him for years to come.

"Let's not meet again, Mr Musgrave," he snapped the ballistic mask over his face. "Because if we do, it will not end well for you."

His security team had responded mere seconds after the politician had been shot but were unable to fight the crowds going in the opposite direction to get to their client. Y and Patra were way ahead of the game and had given chase after the mystery assassin. Suzy hung back, leaping on the stage to comfort the wide-eyed little girl and sharing the bewilderment, having seen and felt something her perplexed preternatural sensors were still processing. Shaken, Suzy was trying to understand. As she hushed the traumatised child, she could still taste honey on her tongue and the smell of chaos and frankincense in her nostrils. Nothing about this assassin was normal and she caught herself wishing Y and Patra would not find him. They didn't have the luxury of her empathic senses but brief sensory snapshots psychically transmitted to their minds should help them understand her mixed emotions. Suzy was just as confused as the gun-toting security personnel who had just arrived, administering first aid and scooping up the little girl from her arms. They were confused because they could not understand how someone had slipped by their defences. And she was confused because the assassin did not feel like a killer. Suzy soaked in the chaos and waited for word from her sisters.

Y AND PATRA WERE MOVING QUICKLY THROUGH THE HOTEL but the assassin was quicker. They were following a trail of destruction left in his wake as the giant of a man bulldozed his way through the five-star establishment. A lobby door was smashed off its hinges, indicating their quarry had passed this way. He may have thought his penchant for brute force would disrupt his pursuers, but as jagged as the smashed doorway was, it provided a makeshift entrance as both Y and Patra dived through what was left of the solid wood door. They hit the ground, rolled, and continued running without missing a beat. They were both running side-by-side.

"Damn, this nigga is strong and quick," Patra noted with a tone of admiration.

"Abnormally," Y answered. "Where did he go?" Both women were running side-by-side without Patra answering; both sets of eyes fell on the double doors at the other side of the lobby swinging open and closed.

The hit man was heading through and up into the refurbished sections of the hotel.

The girls split up.

Patra had taken an alternate route hoping to cut him off, but Y was right behind him and still amazed at such a big man's athleticism and stamina. He moved like Mercury, his stride was powerful yet precise. And if Y would take her eyes off him for a moment, she would abruptly lose sight of him, only for the man to materialise yards ahead with his precise lope not missing a beat. Y's mystically enhanced muscles were pushing hard, but she could not catch up to him. She could feel the drag caused by the enchantment that made human onlookers see her as a white woman, not her chilled dark skin self. It was as if her innate talents were working in opposition to the enchantment that enshrouded her. The transplanted hex had not fully taken. Y removed the tattooed sigil from her wrist with her thumb, uttered an ancient Gallic trigger word and felt her false identity seep into the ether. Y had done the right thing. Her disguise was slowing her down. As she mounted the steps, her stamina improved like a fuel injection. She transformed into the curvy form she knew and loved so well. Bursting through the fire door draped in plastic ribbons, she adjusted to the thick carpets of a huge corridor, looking left... nothing. Then right, there he was, moving like he was skating and teleporting in short bursts simultaneously. He was impressive but they had to stop him. The corridor looked like it ran from one end of the building to the other. A transverse spiral column allowed access to the entire body of the building through passageways, escalators, stairs and laundry chutes. Y wondered where Patra had disappeared to, and instantly she could sense her sister's excitement in her stomach. Patra was up to something, and knowing her, she had bet on herself to do something crazy.

Y could only admire her free spirit, even when the stakes were high.

Patra had intuitively figured out a trajectory that would allow her to collide with their quarry. And fifty metres ahead, Patra burst out from a room and tackled the fleeing assailant. Y forced more power from her legs, wanting to get to them as quickly as possible.

It wasn't to be.

The man had brushed off Patra's attack like she was inconsequential, sending her toiling arse over heels into the adjoining wall.

Y kept going.

Patra sprang back from the wall landing on her feet like a

cat, defying gravity, almost aiming to smash back into the fleeing assassin. This time he didn't pay attention and moved with such rapidity it made Y gasp. The giant caught Patra by her neck and twisted his torso to look back at Y charging towards him. She was already committed, and the cry of frustration left her lips because she knew what was coming next. The giant held up Patra by her shoulders and observed her carefully.

Then said in a cultured deep bass, "Your energies are best directed elsewhere, Guardians."

The giant then hesitated and, with a shake of his head like he was dealing with a petulant child, flung Patra at Y. Y's reflexes were sharp but her strategic skills were sharper. She used her body to absorb Patra's momentum, knowing that even if she dodged her sister's impersonation of a human cannonball, that freight train of a man would get away. Y could see what he was planning to do and could only watch in a kind of numb admiration on the carpeted floor. Patra untangled herself from Y, both breathing easily after the superhuman exertion and both casually watching the giant steamroll his way to the end of what would soon be a plush corridor when the renovation was complete. Patra leaned on Y's shoulder.

"Dude doesn't know he's heading down to a dead end," Patra said matter-of-factly.

With equal casualness and a sardonic smile, Y said, "I don't think he cares."

Taking her eyes away from the spectacle, she bent to pick up what looked like the page from a notebook dropped by the assassin in his haste to escape. At the end of the corridor was a beautiful stained-glass window fifteen feet tall and ten feet across. It depicted the trade and seafaring heritage of the Docklands and East London, where the hotel was being renovated.

Both women stood listening to the thunderous echo of gunfire. Boom! Boom! Boom!

Without missing a stride, the giant had shattered the window and launched himself into the inky night of the London sky, seven stories up, glass shards surrounding him like the shattered wings of a Crystal Angel.

Chapter Two

Golds Gym, West London

*Sip a glass of cold champagne wine
the rug that we lie on feels divine.
And there's no, no, no, no Parallel ...For we two
Ecstasy the word of the night...*

Detective Winston 'Shaft' McFarlane mouthed along to the classic British soul of Omar and wondered if anyone in the known universe ran on a treadmill listening to 'there ain't nothing like this.'

He doubted it.

His taste in workout music may be dubious, but goddammit, it worked for him. Shaft looked down at the digital readout on his treadmill and smiled. He was making progress. His rate was nine, and his distance would be 5 km. He was halfway there, and he had plenty more in the tank. He had never been completely out of shape his entire life, but over the last few years, his life had shifted dramatically. And that was putting it lightly. His life had altered seismically in his professional and personal spheres, which had rocked and eventually toppled how he viewed the world. The very core of his beliefs were challenged and then discounted. Shaft learned and was encouraged by a very important woman in his life that he needed to be prepared, and this was one of the ways he knew well. And as usual, she was right. Yvonne and her friends were in tip-top physical condition, and he couldn't be seen around her without at least an appreciation for the merits of physical exertion. Although Y and her other sisters-in-arms, Patra and Suzy, were cheaters when it came to their extreme levels of physical conditioning. Shaft understood. The supernatural forces that had chosen them had also seen fit to imbue the ladies with the stamina and evergreen bodies of Olympians. The shit they had to deal with, required it. The stress he had to deal with because of the fallout from their exploits required that he be at the gym as many times throughout the week as he was able.

Mens sana en corpero sano – a sound mind in a sound body. Now that was true.

Shaft adjusted his headphones, the soft pads around his ears damp with sweat. He reached for his towel hanging on the arm of the Gymshark, and without missing a stride or reducing his pace, he dried his face. Immediately he planted his mouth and nose into the soft, fragrant folds of his towel, his headphones slipping from his ears. The sounds around him turned up, and he started hearing the grunts, the trickle of mobile conversations and the distant *clang* of weights being dropped on rubberised floors. Just as he was about to block out the gym world again, something more arresting than sounds made him take pause. He loved this perfume, and with his eyes closed, his investigative mind in sync, he could identify the wearer.

"Marilyn," Shaft said, feeling the presence of someone starting up the machine beside him.

"Detective McFarlane, are you trying to impress me?"

Shaft shook his head in amusement and reduced the speed of his treadmill to a walking pace.

"When are you going to stop calling me Detective?"

Shaft looked over to the woman on his right, who was in the process of matching her speed with his. She looked cheekily at his display.

"Not bad, you're getting some good distance in," Marilyn said.

"Thanks, I took your advice about pacing," Shaft said.

She smiled.

"I have to keep you fit. You do an important job, Detective."

It was Shaft's time to smile.

"I appreciate that, M. I really do. As an organisation, we've fucked up so many times the public has lost respect for us."

With a nod of her head, Shaft felt Marilyn knew where he was coming from.

"I just feel like your contribution shouldn't be downplayed."

"You know you don't have to be so formal around me," Shaft said. "Just chill."

"Just look at me," she said. "I'm chilled."

Shaft was looking at her and from his perspective, Marilyn Okokan was the picture of athletic perfection. Forget how beautiful she was. Dark skinned of Nigerian extraction, eyes flecked with an unusual grey. She was taller than he was, with long powerful legs that were on full display from her tight-fitting gym leggings. Her upper body was just as impressive. Her arms were contoured muscles as if they were lathed from African Blackwood. With her midriff showing her abs glinting like cracked obsidian. Marilyn was superbly confident in her body, but that got in the way of what she was really about.

A good heart and humility.

It was surprising for someone so young to be as focused as she was, then you found out she grew up in Naija but came to the UK when she was much older. A young woman with a good heart using her talents to progress. What more could you ask for? Shaft had been exposed to the baser aspects of human nature too regularly for his own liking, and because of that, he had made snap judgements about some good people. He wasn't proud of it, but he strived to do better. When you come across truly honest 'real' people in the age of Instagram, they stand out.

Marilyn had been a good place to start.

"How is the training coming together?" Shaft asked. "You do look more relaxed than the last time we talked."

"I'm lucky, Detective McFarlane," Marilyn said.

Shaft grimaced at his formal title being used; maybe if he hadn't introduced himself like that in the first place, Marilyn wouldn't have latched on to the idea. But it was habit to announce himself in a situation, even if it was nothing more life-threatening than a severe cramp.

"My trainer has been great; he has given me enough time to heal after my father died. I'll join the training camp in Santa Barbara in a month's time."

She paused, looked down at the display on the treadmill, and then back up to Shaft again.

"I think I'm ready for full training but you never truly know if you don't take the step."

"You'll know," Shaft gave a nod of his head. "I'm no expert, but your passion for the heptathlon, just being around your colleagues, will surely make a difference. It'll do you good."

"I think you're right."

"Of course I'm right," Shaft said, his lips turning up.

Marilyn smiled back, and that grey fleck in her brown eyes shimmered.

"So, are you keeping us Londoners safe?" she asked, her fingers quickly moving over the treadmill's touchscreen display, programming a running scheme that consisted of virtual moors, hillocks, passes and valleys. She increased the speed steadily until she was comfortable. Marilyn was graceful in flight, like a swan treading water.

Shaft raised one eyebrow.

Her relaxing jog was what he would use when he was stretching himself.

"It's a thankless job," Shaft said. "But someone has to do it."

"Your colleagues still resisting change?" she asked.

Shaft snorted.

"That, my sister, is what the Metropolitan police force does. It's their culture, especially the rank and file. My kind of change... " Shaft symbolically rubbed his finger over his wrist, showing his skin colour was unable to be rubbed off, "... Is not what they're comfortable with."

Marilyn nodded with an expression Shaft would have found difficult to do at half the speed but she was able to transmit a note of concern from the gesture.

"I'm a tough cookie with a big mouth, and I have learned you have to make noise to usher in change."

"And you're making noise," she asked.

"I'm making noise," Shaft sang a stanza like a really bad gospel tenor.

Marilyn laughed.

He felt that if anyone could appreciate what he did, she would. But the details of operation Black Book were a closely guarded secret in Metropolitan Police circles, much less something he could share with a civilian. As cool as she was, he could never explain the netherworld so few people inhabited and the dangers to the City of London that were as real as a terrorist threat and as potentially devastating as a nuclear strike. He had been lucky to be introduced to this world of magic and monsters by three supernaturally gifted women ordained with the task of maintaining the tentative balance between good and evil in the city. They had taken him by the hand and sometimes thrown him into the deep end, but Bad II the Bone – the name of their personal protection agency – had become family.

Shaft had found his place in the world, but maintaining it would be difficult, if not impossible because he was straddling two worlds. One of the mundane and the other mystical. He felt he was shit at the balancing act, but his three beautiful mentors were guiding him. If that wasn't complex enough, he was starting to manage some odd feelings. Shaft was never prone to loneliness, but since his metaphysical escapades, he yearned to meet ordinary people. Not professionals from work, not mystically powered humans or worse beings that looked ordinary but were far removed from that. Surprisingly the gym had provided that, and Marilyn was the main outlet amongst a few others. But for all the secrets she didn't know and would never know, just talking to ordinary people was good enough, and Shaft genuinely looked forward to it.

"I think I'm encouraging bad habits, Detective," Marilyn said, watching Shaft's speed decrease. "I don't want you to cool down too much from your run before you finish up."

"You'd make a good drill sergeant," Shaft grinned. "And I can take a hint. What are you doing for the rest of the day?"

She brightened.

"I have a lunch date upstairs in the Dumbbell, actually," her eyes wandered upwards in thought. "After that, I'll be hanging out with some other friends. Then back here for my evening workout."

"You've got it all mapped out," Shaft said, pausing. "I'd tell you what I'm doing, but I'd have to kill you."

Marilyn's lips turned up some more, and she fluttered her eyelashes with amusement.

"You'd have to catch me first," she quipped.

Good Girls Gone Bad

. . .

An hour or so later, Shaft had finished the remainder of his workout, sauna, showered and was heading to the exit when he stopped at the turnstile with an inkling he had left his warrant card in his locker. He made an about turn and ran up the stairs to the first floor, and stopped again. An image of Marilyn popped into his head, and Shaft felt the need to say goodbye. She would still be in the Dumbbell he imagined, and he could wave to her without crashing her lunch date or making things awkward.

Are you falling for this woman? Making excuses to see her?

The blunt question that gurgled from his thoughts did not faze him. The one thing Shaft knew about himself through study and experience was that his errant thoughts were not necessarily who he was. His monkey brain, like most on this spinning mud ball called Earth, was meant to keep him safe. It would do anything for an easy life, and he listened but discounted it's advice when he decided it was talking shit.

Y's the only girl for me, he thought. *I do like Marilyn, but I'd never go beyond my boundaries. Now leave me the fuck alone.*

The Detective retrieved his warrant card and headed up to the Dumbbell. Shaft always thought a restaurant on top of the gym was a brilliant idea. And he'd used the four-star facility before. He was a roaring omnivore, but when he dined here on their vegetarian menu, he didn't miss meat at all. In the throes of delicious food, he'd thought it would be cool becoming a vegetarian, but it wore off as soon as he hit the High Street. At the top of the stairs was the shiny visage of the restaurant, its name emblazoned in chrome and the big two-tone swing doors promising mouth-watering cuisine. Shaft pushed past and stood at the threshold, trying to spy Marilyn in the distance. It didn't take long to spot her laughing with a fork in one hand

and a drink of what could be carrot juice in the other. The Detective stopped himself from attracting her attention. He was being stupid. What more could it be? Shaft could only see the back of Marilyn's date, but as impressive as that back was – black hair cut low, white skin, thick neck, and muscular shoulders squeezed into a form-fitting T-shirt – he was uneasy.

Grow up, bwoy, jealousy doesn't suit you.

But it was much more than that. Shaft couldn't pinpoint what it was exactly, but there was something else. It seemed that Marilyn was having the time of her life, and he couldn't bring himself to interfere.

"Can I help, Sir?"

He took one more look at the couple, his disquiet ratcheting up in intensity as he saw the tattoo reveal itself on the back of the man's neck.

"I've changed my mind, thanks," Shaft said to the Maître d' and left as quietly as he had arrived. He tried to forget the feeling he had for the rest of the day, but he couldn't.

"I DIDN'T THINK YOU'D HAVE THIS DRINK WITH ME," he said, his deep blue eyes welcoming, his accent Eastern European.

There was something about him that Marilyn found very sexy. It was hard to put her finger on it, and she suspected her attraction triggers were busy making connections. All those little actions, habits and mannerisms that made him so damn attractive were making her alarms go off in all the right ways. Igor Romanov was a specimen of the male persuasion. He didn't just look perfectly proportioned from chest to thighs. She had seen him work out, and he was a beast. He induced smiles from everyone he interacted with – not from what he said so much, but more from how he carried himself.

Maybe that was the reason Marilyn was surprised by his question. From her experience of men like him, they possessed an abundance of confidence. Sometimes to the detriment of common sense. Marilyn propped her chin on her steepled fingers and leaned towards her lunch date. He smelled wonderful.

"I'm guessing you must be used to getting whatever you ask for?"

"Not at all," Igor said. His voice was deep and rich with an Eastern European flavour she didn't think he'd ever be able to disguise. "I get rejected too many times to mention."

"I find that hard to believe," Marilyn said. She could feel her voice lowering, getting husky. The skin of her arms was tightening as if a cold chill slivered over them. He leaned closer, and Marilyn's body responded to his proximity by leaning in to meet him.

"Do you know what my secret is?" he whispered.

Marilyn shook her head.

"A thick skin," Igor said. "What people think of me is their business. I'm more concerned about what I think of myself. A really wise man told me that."

"What do you think of yourself?" Marilyn asked.

Igor smiled, his full lips parting as if he was about to respond. Then his eyes glazed, and his smile slipped. And for a fleeting moment, Marilyn saw a flash of something. Something that seemed missing from his persona that was stubbornly difficult to pinpoint. Before she could think more about it, he was back to himself again; his smile returned bright and reassuring.

"I think I'm fortunate to have met you," he paused and lowered his voice as he lent forward to her ear. "I think I'm tired of attracting the fakes. I need someone real."

He rolled his 'R' when he said 'real', and a sound hit her eardrum, triggering a delicious shudder below the belt.

"I could disappoint you?" Marilyn said, her voice level, her eyes betraying her apparent seriousness.

"Impossible," he said, sitting up, his eyes smoothly gliding over her body in one uninterrupted sweep. "Impossible."

Igor watched Marilyn leave, his eyes fixed on her powerful glutes engaging with every step and the confident sway of the hips as she exited the restaurant.

What a specimen.

All the way through his lunch date, he had a raging erection that would not abate and one he had no wish to relieve. A glow of satisfaction overcame him. Not once did he think he was an impostor. He was here because he should be here. What was even more thrilling was her sexiness was only a small part of what made her magnificent.

That thing on the inside made her special.

The Master would be one step closer and very pleased with how he conducted himself. Who would have thought he could come this far, after a hundred years? His stammer was gone. Just as the Master promised. And the pheromone implants gave him the advantage he needed to break through his self-imposed fear of intimacy with women.

A new man.

Indeed, and he had his Master to thank for it all.

Chapter Three

The Kingdom of Luba, Congo 1794

Even for a venerated scientist such as Dr Ulysses Kayanga, meeting the Chief was a privilege or at least he wanted the Royal Court to think he felt that way. His cousin and the 54th Mwamikazi to the throne were essential to his plans, but Antoinette was the real prize. Chieftain N'Debele Ilunga did not make the five-mile journey from his royal court to visit just anyone. Usually, he would travel with his carriers, guards, advisors, ceremonial dancers, drummers and, if the Grand Council felt nervous, a witch doctor.

Not this time.

Even with their history of growing up together in the Royal Court, being family and the sponsorship from his late father, Jonko Ilunga, did not make their meeting a foregone conclusion. Kayanga knew his cousin well and understood the carrot he would need to lure him in. Once it was explained he had gained power that could be useful to the Kingdom from his studies in Europe, the Chief would sing a different tune. Instead of meeting in the Royal Court, his cousin and his betrothed would meet at a secret location. The Chief didn't know it, but Kayanga offered him an opportunity.

Would he take it?

If he was as good a judge of character as he thought, Kayanga knew the answer to that.

IN THEIR YOUTH, THE CHIEF WAS ENTHRALLED WITH HOW Kayanga could explain complex scientific ideas in such a way that clarified concepts the Chief was struggling with in his own studies. But from the squint of his cousin's eyes and the twist of his lips, this particular idea was not so easy to digest.

"And you are serious about this thing? You believe you can do this?" the Chieftain asked.

Kayanga smiled broadly, knowing he had his cousin's attention and made an apologetic gesture with his hands.

"My Chieftain, I won't waste your time on theories. Your father before you sponsored my studies in Europe. He always wanted me to return with knowledge that would strengthen our Kingdom."

"My father did," the Chieftain nodded. "The knowledge he was referring to would help us to be better traders, healthier people and better at defending our borders. Not this preposterous idea of raising the dead. As a man of science, you should know you cannot rewrite the laws of nature."

"These principles could revolutionise our people and our country. Our infant mortality rate would be zero. The things we could do if our population were free from illness and disease."

The Chief took a sip from the polished stone goblet and sighed.

"Why aren't the Europeans taking advantage of this knowledge?" the Chief asked.

Kayanga took a shallow breath, trying to keep his attitude and his tone civil.

"You are the first to be offered this opportunity, my Chief. The scientific institutions of Europe know nothing of our studies or our results."

The Chief gave an uncommitted smile and a shake of his head. He wasn't convinced.

Kayanga bowed, his grimace concealed, his seething contained and his frustration slipping by the attention of his Chief. Antoinette Lukalu, on the other hand, was more sensitive. She sat by the right of the Chief as tradition dictated and had patiently listened to the exchange. Antoinette had always been a good listener and a rare breed of woman. She deserved a powerful man, the kind of man Kayanga was becoming. Their people's traditions, stories and myths weren't just fanciful distractions but what made them strong.

She still believed that, he could tell. And as she always did, she came to his rescue.

"Did you know, my Chief, that there are stories that one of the great band of Kings had been given the secret to life and death in the form of a machine that could bring back fallen warriors?"

The Chief turned patiently to stare into the bright eyes of his beloved.

"I remember the stories, dearest. My father was a true believer, but those were the Dark Ages. That's why he sent me to the best universities to study. To take us into the future." He turned from Antoinette to Kayanga. "A Chief cannot maintain his reign with fairytales. I've been patient with you, cousin, but you have let the Europeans fill your head with nonsense."

"I've tried it, my Chief," Kayanga sounded a little desperate. "I read the old hippo skins your father kept. I followed the ancient instructions of one such skin, and after two months of trial and error, I brought a dead goat kid back to life." His voice rose a notch. "When you were chasing girls, I was discovering the mysteries of the world we live in."

The Chieftain's eye quivered from the barb as if he'd been slapped.

"Have you been sipping on too long fermented banana wine? I think you're losing your respect and your mind."

Antoinette intervened, her voice melodious and calming as she regulated the rising tempers of both men.

"Why don't we let Ulysses demonstrate his newfound power? Wouldn't you want to witness it?"

The Chief peered at Kayanga, whose enthusiasm was reigniting.

"I haven't perfected the process; it will take time to run the tests required, but once I've done the experimentation, then…"

"Enough!" The Chief bellowed. "This is a waste of my time. What has come over you?"

"I assure you, my Chief, this is no jest. I have partnered with an Austrian scientist, the eminent Victor von Frankenstein, and his experiments are groundbreaking, almost miraculous. I wanted to improve on his process by using our ancient technology."

The Chief had lost patience. He stood and reached down to guide Antoinette to her feet but suddenly was uncertain on his feet. He looked around the skin-wrapped dwelling of his cousin's domicile, intending to call his six-man armed entourage to his aid, but there was no one to obey his commands. The mercenaries in Frankenstein's employ made short, silent work of them. The Chief looked back to Kayanga, his vision blurring, his anger having nowhere to go and the question on his lips. Why? Antoinette was already gasping for air like a fish out of water.

Kayanga spoke.

"You don't deserve her; you don't deserve to be Chief." Kayanga's impassive stare seemed to look right through them. "I was unclear at first but now I understand what I must do."

Kayanga took out two vials from his suit and held them up dramatically. "I will take the old hippo skins for my research, and I knew you wouldn't give them to me. I was hoping you would see things my way and these two vials would counteract the poison coursing through your bloodstream and save your lives, but my suspicions were correct. I was offering you power, and you didn't recognise it. Now you will experience that power firsthand."

Kayanga threw the vials to the ground shattering them.

"Burning the boats," he said. "No turning back now. The poison will preserve the integrity of your body but stop your heart. But don't worry, my cousin, my dearest; you will both have life again. I will see to it."

Kayanga stood back and watched the two people he loved most dying on the floor.

Chapter Four

The Realm of the Powers That Be

The rum bar called Miss Mazy's Shack was situated a stone's throw away from the Celestial Sea. It was constructed from the wood of old fishing canoes. Outside there were holes in the planks that let out the welcoming light inside, making the place look like a misshapen Chinese lantern. The waves languidly lapped on the shore, and the small explosion of dominoes being slammed down on tables inside agitated the sandflies looking outside for warm celestial blood. Anancy, the spider God, was proud of this part of town. He should be, after all. Anancy had created it with his own eight hands, or should he say with the elemental forces his kind wielded. Not all of the inhabitants could do the creation 'ting', and neither could he in the beginning, but Anancy was a hustler, a favour here and a favour there. And if you knew the right people, you could upgrade your possibilities. All were welcome amongst the easy-going West African and Caribbean deities. This was his small space in a parallel universe of gods and demons manifested by the combined beliefs of billions of human consciousnesses over human history.

Anything was possible here, but there were rules.

Anancy was playing drafts with the Greek God of thunder, Zeus. Like any other game, there were rules and like all rules the world over, they only applied if you got caught. Anancy was a maestro of never getting caught, a required skill if he was to give his wards – the beautiful and talented Guardians of the Light – a fighting chance against the forces of chaos lining up to disrupt their lives.

Inside the shack were the usual suspects. Aganju, Shango, Big Bwoy, River Muma – gods from Africa and the diaspora. And then there were the honoured guests from Olympus. The main show's two stars were situated in a corner booth, a dish of dry salted fish, fried dumplings and a bottle of white rum between them. Anancy stared carefully at the draughts board and then looked up at the God of thunder's bearded face and dark auburn hair. A thin smile appeared on his dark face, his eyes glinting with mirth, but behind that easy-going façade was the mind of a confident trickster and strategist. With a flurry of hands, Anancy took two of Zeus's players off the board. The All Father grunted and eyed the spider god with suspicion.

Anancy laughed.

It was the kind of carefree, come what may, join me in the celebration of being alive guffaw that was so infectious the bar's patrons couldn't help grinning along with him.

"Big Z," Anancy snickered. "You know you're not playing chess, right? This is checkers, amigo."

Even Zeus couldn't keep a straight face, with Hermes chuckling behind him.

"If I didn't know better," Zeus rumbled. "I would say you enchanted me every time we play these games of strategy."

"Now, that would be an impressive magic trick, Pardee," Anancy said. "Especially as our powers can't work against each other."

"Hmmm!" Zeus said, still trying to figure out how he'd been beaten once again. "What you lack in raw elemental power, you make up for in guile and wit, my friend."

"We've been pardys for multiple millennia, don't be afraid to say the word, big Zee." The spider god was enjoying the look of playful stress on the Greek's features.

The big Greek sighed, the smile remained on his usually austere face.

"Yes, you are a bastion of wisdom," Zeus said.

"Now, was that so difficult?" Anancy asked.

It was even more difficult for the Olympian to admit that other civilisations were just as committed to their deities as the Greeks were in their time. Anancy had a creeping feeling that the king of the Olympians needed to be reminded of that humbling fact from time to time. Maybe that was his way of integrating. Gracing the shack with his presence from time to time, accepting the regular invitations. His entourage had also grown with his attendance. Word had spread that the company was good, and so was the food and drink. Hermes, Hephaestus and Diana had made good friends and were much more comfortable than their leader, who had to keep up appearances. Anancy used that to his advantage. He looked at Zeus and his sombre demeanour that hid a passionate being with a very short temper. His kind did not experience emotions in the same way a human would. Anancy just knew that one of his gifts was being able to get along with almost anyone. And when it came to discourse and information, he had developed ways of getting what he wanted by circuitous means. It was much more fun that way.

"We need to talk," Anancy said, standing from the table, reaching for his trilby and spider cane. He set the hat on his neat Afro head and swung the cane for good measure, its tip igniting the atoms of the air like a wand, leaving a trail of sparkle that eventually died out. Zeus stood with him in a grey pinstriped business suit. His tie was metallic grey, and a lightning bolt tie pin fixed it in place. For his age, the Olympian looked good and carried himself as would be expected of a king. Anancy gestured to the door that led out to the backyard closest to the sea. It swung open on approach. Zeus stepped through, followed by the Spider God. Anancy took out two cigars from his jacket pocket and handed one to Zeus. The Greek took it and, with a sound like popcorn popping, ignited the end with a fingertip.

"What's on your mind?" Zeus asked, taking a pull.

"Let me show you something," Anancy said and walked past kegs of beer and wine bottles, then shuffled alongside a short dividing wall made of coral and seashells. The wall had been eroded to the ground in some places and resembled a demarcation line that ran around the drinking establishment's perimeter, distinguishing the beach from dry land. Both men looked out to the horizon, smoking ponderously on the Cubans. The sea was calm, a dark blue and white hue like a heavenly tie and dye pattern dipped into the inky night sky. In the distance, lightning illuminated the sea and beyond. Angry forks of energy stabbed into the ocean that remained eerily silent, although a light show continued bleaching the indigo sky.

"A storm is coming," Anancy said.

"And you think I have something to do with it?" Zeus's voice raised a notch.

"Not directly," Anancy answered. "But it's ancient history that I'm sure you'd like to forget."

"Enlighten me," Zeus said.

Anancy paused for a moment, took a pull on his cigar and said, "One of the formulas for life the Titan Prometheus gave to man. The one you tried to destroy but failed to. I know it can't be taken back but that...mistake, I'm afraid, will have to be dealt with by the Guardians of the Light."

Zeus listened quietly while Anancy blew animated smoke characters and continued. "I know you've intervened on many occasions to keep the formula out of human hands but there is so much you can do. There is someone walking the earth plane who not only knows the Life Formula but knows how to use it."

Anancy heard the frustrated rumble from the Olympian beside him. He kept going.

"I'm not doling out blame, Pardy. I just need to know that if I need your help, if things get out of hand, I can depend on your... Support."

"You can," Zeus Horkios, the Keeper of Oaths, said.

Anancy clenched his fist in Zeus's direction. The God of thunder did not leave him hanging and touched fists with him too, arcs of electricity dancing around their connection.

Chapter Five

Red Ground Estate, Sussex

Y left Patra and Suzy in the gym as soon as the online spin class concluded. She hurried through the swing doors heading for her quarters through the Georgian-styled country home of the late giant of science and metaphysics, Sir Isaac Newton. The reggae legend John Holt was playing through the in-house speakers.

His mellow voice generated a perfect backdrop for this morning, Y thought.

An easy smile crossed her lips as she mounted the palatial stairs to her room. Would Sir Isaac approve of his summer home bought and run by the ancestors of slaves and indentured servants from the colonies? Thumbs up or thumbs down, she wondered. He had been dead for 300 years, but if he had an issue, his residual energy would speak for him, or he did not care. Y shrugged, jogged along the corridor, opened her door, and spied her phone on the four-poster bed. She snatched it up and headed for the kitchen. Nanny hated when they came for breakfast late and insisted they should share meals together if they were all at the mansion. Y knew their communion had deeper significance to Nanny but she would never say what that was. They knew better not to question it. The beautiful albino woman may seem abrupt at times, but they knew under the prickly exterior, Nanny had their well-being front and centre. It was difficult imagining their home without her.

Y made her way down one ancient stone staircase, then along the cold tiled corridor to the kitchen at the end. She slowed from a jog and finished with a brisk walk. She stepped into a kitchen that centuries ago was where the servants would take their meals and prepare food for the Master of the house. Even before entering, she could hear Patra's raucous laughter. It made her smile too.

"I'm glad yuh come, sis," Suzy sounded playfully exasperated, making come hither motions with her hands to Y to join them quickly.

"Dis poppy show," Suzy explains, pointing to Patra. "Thinks the online spin instructor is flirting with her nympho-self. Please tell her she crazy."

"The bitch is jealous," Patra said almost to herself. "She's je-a-lous." She pronounced the words as if she disliked the taste of the letters.

"You're crazy," Y said to Patra, a mysterious grin on her face, then looked to Suzy. "You know she has this thing..." Y made a gesture of touching her temple and shaking her clenched fists like she was playing craps.

Suzy feigned a yawn.

"Dis has nothing to do with her luck factor, sis. She's only trying to get us onboard wid dis internet sex appeal idea she's been touting on the podcast."

Patra shrugged.

"You bitches may not believe it," Patra said, twirling before her sisters like a catwalk model, surprised she had an audience to entertain. "But it's true."

Good Girls Gone Bad

"Break it down for me," Y asked, flirting with disaster. Suzy rolled her eyes and sighed, having already been subjected to Patra's highfalutin' hypotheses.

"It came to me from our listener stats," Patra said, directing her explanation to Suzy. "You know those little bitty numbers in the columns that tell you I'm a fly chick."

Suzy cleared her throat with exaggerated volume.

"Numbers don't lie," Patra shrugged barely able to keep a straight face.

"And neither do hungry bellies," Nanny added her thoughts to the conversation. "You can measure how sexy you all are after you've eaten."

The ceasefire would last only until the end of breakfast but that was time enough for more important conversations. All three sat huddled together around the huge teak table that could easily accommodate 14 diners. They knew what was coming next and had already prepared their faces for the shot of mystery green juice or green 'shit' as Patra referred to it. Only Suzy accepted the Bush tonic with almost stoic resignation. It was an uncomfortable detail nestled in a fond memory for the Jamaican. It was the only hurdle they had to negotiate before the delicious treats Nanny seemed to pluck from their collective memories. The cook passed out the green juice. Three whiskey glasses clustered together on a tray. Suzy was the first to pull her glass away from the rest and place it to the left of her. They all had their ways of downing the vile liquid. Usually, Suzy would be the first to slide it into her field of vision, then knocked it back. Patra eyed it suspiciously for a few seconds like a stalking lioness on the Prairie and then raised it to her lips in record time. Y, on the other hand, would play with it awhile. Turning the glass on the wooden surface allowing the condensation to pool at the base. Then 'snap!' Like a slash from her famed katana, it was in her mouth and down her throat.

This time she hesitated.

Something had interrupted her morning ritual. And that something purred, rubbing luxuriantly on her Lycra leggings. Y looked down smiling.

"Mei Ling?"

The black Siamese cat with the glistening green eyes meowed. The elegant feline sprang on the table at the mention of her name and strutted over to Suzy. She lay down seductively beside her friend and waited for the inevitable stroking of her ears and tummy.

She purred.

"Gal, what you doing here?" Suzy asked. The cat tilted her head back at the question, exposing her neck and stomach for more rubbing.

"She's been here all morning," Nanny said. "She looked tired from her journeys, an mi give her some milk."

"Thank you, Aunty," Suzy said. "Don't forget her oats and anchovies; deh queen loves that."

The girls gathered around, fussing over her while Nanny placed the breakfast on the table. It was Patra who said what they were all thinking.

"I ain't gonna lie, I love when she visits, but why does some fucked up shit always seem to follow her here."

"She's warning us," Y said. "Making sure we ready for what could come."

Patra tickled the cat's chin.

'You turn up at my crib like you own the place, drinking my milk, eating my fish, the least you could do is give us some more details."

Mei Ling pawed playfully at the air then turned to watch Patra walk back to her place at the table.

"And so it starts," Suzy said cryptically. "Our mystery assassin is deh first domino."

"Mei Ling, God bless her, is the second," Y said.

"And now we wait for the signs and portents as the shit hits the fan," Patra said. "Mei Ling is holding out on us, I think."

Y smiled.

"I'd be satisfied to know how she performs her translocation trick. That would be useful."

Suzy had spent six months in the Shaolin Temple in the Henan province a year ago. Training under Abbott Lee's tutorage. She had made a deep connection with one of the Temple cats. Suzy hadn't imagined the relationship would prolong after her departure. How Mei Ling transported herself from the Shaolin Temple in China to the sticks of rural England may never be solved. And maybe that was the point. They accepted it for what it was. This was their new world, and they should appreciate its mysteries.

"Puss, puss," Nanny called to Mei Ling, whose ears pricked up. "Come for yuh food, gal."

Nanny placed the dish of oats and anchovies near the range cooker, making a song and dance of it. The cat sprang down and bounded towards her breakfast.

No one was talking now.

The only sounds were knives, forks, slurps and sighs of satisfaction.

Chapter Six

Castle Frankenstein, Austrian Alps 1795

The freezing rain and the brutal wind battered the ramparts of the monolith of a castle that had been built into a mountain that generations of the Frankenstein clan called home. It was to be the storm of the century, and Victor von Frankenstein, with his acolytes, was ready to use some of its elemental fury to make a scientific breakthrough. That was, if the Castle could withstand the onslaught of nature.

"Are the energy storage units ready, Mr Fairweather?"

Dr Frankenstein shouted the question over the booming thunder. The Englishman to whom the question was directed was a prodigy, coining new scientific terms and making breakthroughs that would one day inspire the likes of Michael Faraday. That was decades in the future. At this moment he was dressed in electrically resistant boots and overalls, his eyes shielded with goggles. He gestured to the intricate array of energy cells and huge energy storage units he had designed with a massive spanner.

"As ready as they're gonna be, doctor. It was a challenge

constructing your blueprints, but I've done outstanding work if I say so myself."

"And so you should, Mr Fairweather," Dr Frankenstein said. "So you should."

The doctor looked around the Castle, kept partially open to the elements. This portion of the ancient building had been modified brick by brick and repurposed for tonight's grand performance. It had been converted into a laboratory filled with the contraptions of science whose purpose was meant to change the course of history. This was precise work, important work. And no better time to shatter nature's vice-like grip on life and death.

Dr Frankenstein glanced over at the magnificent structure throbbing with energy and built within the Castle like the heart of a Titan. He looked at its creator, busying himself on the final touches to his lightning aggregator. The thing that would trap the mystical lightning in its pure form.

"Ulysses, my boy, can your aggregator withstand the awesome power from the storm of the century?"

Frankenstein teased, grinning from ear to ear like a deranged man. He was so close to achieving a lifetime obsession that the euphoria made him giddy with possibility.

Dr Ulysses Kayanga scowled – the only African scientist amongst the Europeans, and he did not appreciate being called a boy even if he was five years younger than the eminent scientist. His features softened because he could understand the elation Frankenstein felt; he could feel it too. They all could, but Dr Kayanga was just better at controlling it.

The day when men became gods.

"The question, Victor," Kayanga said, his voice deep and cultured but African through and through. "Can you afford to rebuild your ancestral home if it all comes crashing down?"

Dr Frankenstein laughed.

"Are you trying to compare ancient Bavarian civil engineers with the Shaman alchemists from your village?"

"Indeed I am," Kayanga said. "You trust your ancestors, and I will trust in mine."

"We will see," Frankenstein said, gripping a ladder and expertly sliding down to another level of the laboratory.

On this level, there was not as much protection from the elements as there was above, but that's what was required for the third and final member of his society. The Weather Witch hailed from the Scottish Highlands and was a prognosticator of weather conditions and sometimes the creator of them. Frankenstein had travelled the known and unknown world to discover the strange, brilliant talent that possessed the esoteric knowledge required to complete his lifelong obsession.

It had all come to this.

To this moment.

The woman stood on the parapet's edge, the winds screaming around her and buffeting her slight stature with a force that could snatch her off the edge and into the rocks below. Except she wasn't just an observer of the fury roaring around them. She was a part of it, anchored to the flag stones. A part of the process that grew and directed this maelstrom across the mountains and into the path of destiny. It had taken her the better part of the year to lure, cajole and plead with the forces. The Highland woman could not influence it, had no control when it would appear but by adding her essence to the powers that had created this spectacle, she was privy to its comings and goings. Before his quest had taken him around the world, Dr Frankenstein believed with just his superior intellect that he could overcome any challenge. He was a man of science, so combining arcane knowledge with scientific fact was preposterous to him at first.

And here he was, choosing to sideline the scientific method

and pay attention to signs and portents that he could not explain with mathematics or biology.

The soul.

Death.

Afterlife.

Time travel and alternate dimensions.

Telepathy.

Alchemy.

Once, he had believed the natives in the far-off lands civilised by the white man had contributed nothing to progress, but here he was, depending on a Celt and a negro equal to his own intellect. So many mysteries did not fit into the orderly world of Sir Isaac Newton. He had learned his lesson, and Frankenstein was on the cusp of greatness because of his inquisitive and open mind.

"How much time do we have left?" Frankenstein shouted at the weather witch; his words were snatched away by the bluster of the wind. He cautiously moved closer to the woman, his hands hovering over a rough-hewn work bench secured to the floor. The doctor didn't want to disturb her focus but it couldn't be helped.

Frankenstein bellowed.

"Morag! How much time do we have?" The pale figure twitched, the question connecting through the fog of her concentration, and she turned ponderously to face him. Her thick robes were dragging on the wet flagstones. Frankenstein loved seeing the witch like this. Her eyes flashed, red hair dancing wildly on her head, and her alabaster skin glowing. If he didn't know her better, he would have said she was smiling. Even her sombre nature could not contain a smile at the majesty of the powers she was observing. Even the raindrops stopped to look. If they came too close to her personal space they would be trapped in mid-air. Suspended like glistening jewels by the unseen forces that she channelled through her body and vaporised when they came too close. In moments, the blank stare was replaced with intense clarity that sent a chill of excitement up and down the doctor's spine.

"Soon," she croaked. "Stand ready; the finger of the gods will reach out to you soon enough."

"I welcome it," Frankenstein yelled and headed back to his station against the bracing wind with an urgency of a man possessed.

Chapter Seven

Red Ground Estate, Sussex

It was a rainy Monday, and as soon as Y thought she wouldn't be missed by her sisters, she snuck away to the Sir Isaac Newton library. The pre-eminent scientist would be at home here. Except for the Dragon Mist globes that provided light in the vast room floating above her head and defying every law he had proposed in his lifetime. She sat in her favourite leather chair and table, and surveyed the archaic and modern texts on scientific but mainly esoteric subjects surrounding her. Spokes, their benefactor and landlord of this magnificent home, had said the Georgian house had come with some of the books. The rest, Spokes had acquired through various means – legal and illegal – and was keeping them safe. He allowed access to vetted scholars, practitioners and ones whose power he respected. Y wasn't sure she could ever be included in that group of people, but she did know that when it came to feeling a sense of serenity, only the Japanese gardens to the back of the mansion could match this place. Something about the smell of books transported her into a land of fond and comfortable memories.

Her father.

He was the voracious reader, and she was not. The old man had taught her how to respect and cherish books. He had taught her to love the act of writing too.

Pen on paper.

He was old school.

Y pulled her chair up to the old writing desk that had been an item here for over a century and took out a bundle of letters tied with a red, green and gold ribbon from the pouch in her track top. Trapped in the neat bonds of the ribbons was a silver fountain pen. Patiently she undid the binds and spread the letters over each other, revealing the Japanese postage stamps. Her father had left to travel the world when she was young, making that hard decision to leave her mother, who never felt the tug of wanderlust the way he did. Her father ended up in Japan, where he settled and remarried. The Masamune sword that she wielded was given to her by Rupert. She always wondered if he had been told through some mystical means that he was important to her development as a warrior. More than anything, his concern was hearing about her adventures. It was all done through their letters. In the beginning, the idea of using pen and paper to communicate over distances wasn't unknown to her, just not familiar. She grew up with a level of technology that was an integral part of her life. Y's generation grew up on smartphones, web 3.0 and artificial intelligence so what did you expect? Letter writing was another intimate way of communicating that required focus and love. She had a lot to say and a lot of love to share with her old man. Rupert didn't know how much he helped her understand this New World she was involved in and figure out her true place. Y pulled out a drawer on the writing table, the interior smelling like a potpourri concoction and took up three sheets of white parchment paper. She held the sheets over the old school blotting pad, letting them fall to the surface like leaves. They settled neatly in front of her as the mood lights remained an aqua blue.

"What am I supposed to do next?"

The question left her lips and sounded hollow to her ears. Her sisters depended on her to provide some direction. She just wasn't sure she was equipped to do that. Who had decided she should lead them anyway? Ancient texts spoke of her Guardian ancestors a millennium before her. Although their exploits were inspirational, there was no mention of their challenges in accepting the mantle of 'Watunza Mwanga'.

A smile brightened her features and caused the Dragon Mist globes to shine yellow. Maybe her sister's ancestors' view of the world was so different that it was never an issue.

'In our privileged world, we are much weaker'.

The words came as if they had been spoken by someone other than herself. Y looked down at the writing paper and took up the pen. Sensing her affection for her father, the Dragon Mist globes infused her writing area in sunlight.

Dear Rupert...

Y didn't need to turn around when the door to the library opened; her spooky GPS told her it was Suzy. She played this game with herself when Miss Wong was around, which consisted of using her acute hearing to pick up any sound she made moving through the world. But try as she might, she couldn't. Only when Suzy's arms wrapped around her shoulders did she know in actuality her sister was with her.

"One of these days, I'm gonna hear you coming behind me," Y said.

Her Jamaican sister squeezed.

"Yuh know you will get through this, right?" Suzy said, her voice calm and reassuring.

Reflecting off the library's walls was a calming green light from the Dragon Mist Globes. They were reacting to the emotions of both women, translating them into colour.

"Why do I feel suddenly so lost?" Y asked.

Suzy was an empath who could sense the emotions of people around her and could discern the truth from any living soul. She was attuned to the joys and turmoils of her sisters without effort. Usually, Suzy respected their privacy by saying nothing. What Y loved about her sister's gifts was she didn't have to try and find words to explain how she was feeling; Suzy already understood. Y wondered what it was like to never be able to switch it off. Privacy was impossible and you could forget about lying. If they didn't love each other, have patience and an inner connection that didn't allow them to carry resentment, Bad II the Bone could not work.

"Yuh expected dis to be easier than you imagined?"

Y couldn't see Suzy smiling but felt her posture shift behind her.

"Admit it, you thought so too," Y shot back.

"Mama brought me up to be an optimist," Suzy laughed then her voice was soothing again. "But you can't be me, and I can't be you. Deh job you have to accomplish, only you can make it happen."

"So why don't you lead?" Y asked almost seriously, even though she understood the answer to that petulant question. Suzy took pleasure in pointing it out to her for emphasis.

"Yuh were chosen to lead, and we were chosen to follow you."

Y shook her head.

"Next, you'll tell me 'The Powers That Be' don't make mistakes."

"Dem don't," she stated. "After everyting, we've seen, everyting we've done. Nuting about our situation is a coincidence. We have a purpose. You have a purpose. Stop second-guessing deh ting and accept the challenge."

"What if I'm not up to it?" Suzy unwrapped her arms from her sister's shoulders and came around to face her. Even when she moved ordinarily, Suzy was grace incarnate. She lowered herself to her knees in front of Y and bowed her head. Slowly she looked up.

"Sis, if you're not up to it, neither are we. We triumph together, or we fail together."

Y nodded sombrely.

"The only thing is when we fail, people die," Y said.

"Then, sister Yvonne, let's not fail."

Suzy reached out and held Y's hands.

"Mas Spokes is on a Zoom call with us in the next thirty minutes. Him have something to talk about that couldn't wait. I'll see yuh in the Rec. room."

Suzy rose up and almost floated out of the room, leaving Y to her thoughts and an incomplete letter.

Chapter Eight

Castle Frankenstein, Austrian Alps 1795

L ife after death. Dr Kayanga had come into this project, imagining his name would be immortalised because of his Lightning Aggregator – his brainchild and the part it played in changing the course of human history. He knew now, that would not be the case because he had discovered Frankenstein's duplicity. He shivered under the layers of fur – not just from the cold, but from anger and imagined what could have been.

Maybe an African should not be here after all, but that minuscule grain of doubt blew away with the gusting wind of his ambition.

This was his destiny, no matter the challenges.

The Storm of the Century had skimmed the tundra of the Arctic Circle propelling fragments of ice across thousands of miles to the Austrian Alps. The cold bore into his bones, a sensation he would never grow used to. Still, it wasn't only the conditions that made him quiver with excitement but the contribution he was about to make, the legacy he would leave to mankind, no matter what Frankenstein had planned for him. He wanted the world to know what he had done, and he would, but not in the way you would think. Kayanga would not be written out of history, erased by a man he had trusted.

He let out a cloud of frosty air.

He tried to breathe through his frustration and calm his shaking hands. Anger wouldn't benefit him here. He was a gentleman and a scientist. And there was no need for direct recrimination at this time, especially since he had taken steps to safeguard their work together. Once the experiment was complete, Frankenstein would sweep his involvement under the carpet, denounce him and have him ostracised from Europe.

Kayanga had secretly read correspondences from eminent scientists across the continent that the doctor had contacted and never spoke of. The majority of Frankenstein's peers ridiculed him but the ones who were willing to suspend disbelief invited the Austrian to prove his theories to his contemporaries. His breakthroughs were always solo efforts when he detailed his trials and the RSVPs that came his way were always for one.

Victor had underestimated him.

Kayanga had found the doctor's secret journals. All his observations, theories and experiments were meticulously written and drawn in twenty-one thick leather-bound journals. His life's work submitted to paper that one day would be the complete historical testament to a scientific breakthrough like no other. Kayanga had been Victor's guest for many months as they prepared for this moment. He keenly watched the man make copious notes in his notebook and then watched him store it away in his beautiful Renaissance-era puzzle strong box. It stood four feet tall, weighed about a quarter of scheepslast or six hundred kilograms, made from iron, and its façade was black polished metal decorated on its four sides with hundreds of evenly spaced bumps that masqueraded as craft and aesthetics but, in truth, helped complete the puzzle of opening the safe. Bump 97 needed to be depressed. Bump 37 required to be slid from left to right while Bump 57 and 59 were twisted clockwise and anticlockwise consecutively. It was constructed by Italian master craftsmen and used three keys, four of the protuberances needed to be slid, depressed or twisted to reveal hidden keyholes. Kayanga reached out to a safe cracker colleague from the East End of London for advice and then went about the business of memorising the position of the secret bumps and how they needed to be manipulated to show the keyholes. After which, he duplicated the three keys, providing moulds to a master locksmith in Zurich. The extended plan took six months but was worth every frustrating moment.

A drunken evening by the fireplace and Kayanga, not only an engineering and scientific savant had an eidetic memory. He used the moment to open the safe and began the process of transferring Frankenstein's notes to his own journals. The doctor's written account of his life's work would now be expressed in Kayanga's written hand. It was an invaluable treatise on creating life after death through a meandering thougtscape in the mind of a genius. Kayanga congratulated himself for his self-control after reading the doctor's notes on his plans to share his findings with the world. There were speeches written for presentation to The Royal Institute of Science – that would become The Chamberley Societe Technoire ten years later, Academie des Sciences, Academia dei Lincei and The Royal Prussian Academy of Sciences. Not a single mention of his collaborators in his acceptance speeches.

Not once did he admit that he needed to seek knowledge from an African scientist to complete his dream. The good doctor had plans to steal his thunder, and Kayanga had his own plans to survive and thrive from this.

Frankenstein wasn't the only one with secrets.

In the present, Kayanga would remain sharp, even when the air was charged, the wind savage and the rain like grains of sand blasting everything in sight. Lightning ripped the cloak of the night only to see it regenerate, then rip once more as electricity spikes struck the earth in the distance. When Kayanga surveyed the mountain range, the giant fingers of lightning were striding across it and getting closer, the thunder getting louder.

The thunder God Shango had heeded the white woman's call and was attending the occasion with an inquisitive air as mere mortals dabbled with the power of gods. Only time would tell if they rewrote the bedrock of scientific thought or became footnotes in an obscure scientific periodical.

ALL THE PLAYERS WERE AT THEIR STATIONS AND Frankenstein was pleased. Mr Fairweather, having checked and double-checked the energy cells, energy storage units and copper conductors, stood at the ready. All of these scientific breakthroughs would not be available to the wider scientific community for years. Such was the depth of Frankenstein's talent pool. Fairweather peered down at the control board with its rubber-handled racket switches in preparation for his expert handling. Dr Frankenstein stood between the dead bodies of Chieftain Ndebele Ilunga and his bride-to-be. Perfect subjects, courtesy of Kayanga. The naked bodies of the negro and his partner were in superb condition compared to many of

Frankenstein's previous test subjects. The reason behind the body's arrested putrefaction was down to a secret tribal process. Not only did Kayanga choose the subjects for Reanimation, he prepared the bodies for the three months journey from Africa to Europe. He couldn't have done it without him.

Using ancient Congolese methods, he arrested the decay without chemicals or ice. The Chief, who would be treated to the lightning first, was easily over seven feet tall and powerfully built. He had the air of royalty from the set of his reinforced jaw and a solid chin. His face remained handsome with some tribal marks and some scars from the procedure. His eyes must have been ablaze with fire in life and commanded devotion and fear. Away from his Royal Court and Kingdom, tricked and murdered, his eyes were cloudy and lifeless. His corpse was trussed up to a reinforced bench of oak and teak with leather straps laced with copper fibres cinched around his wrists and ankles, waist, chest and neck. Metal probes that one day would be called electrodes punctured the pallid dark skin of his chest, and his bald head, capped with a metal hemisphere and coils of wires shot from its apex, fed into the structure that housed the dead man. The structure was of Dr Kayanga's design and would produce the energies required once the right amount of raw electricity and the essence of the gods was coursing through it.

Frankenstein had learned some of the legends of Kayanga's ancestors, who were said to use the structure to raise the fallen dead in battle. He had never been able to reproduce the process effectively until his path crossed with the African's. And Kayanga himself, from his own admission, may never have resolved the riddle of his ancestor's technology if not for their chance encounter.

That was why he considered their collaboration much more than just the partnership. But Frankenstein could not make their shared brilliance be known. It would show his weakness. A pre-eminent scientist such as himself needing the aid of a native to complete his life's work. He would pay Kayanga handsomely, but he had a feeling that would not be enough. If Kayanga complained about his treatment, Frankenstein would have to insist more robustly than a gentleman should to quiet his protests. As unfortunate as it was, this was the way of the world.

The doctor sighed and kept his eyes on the storm. When the wind eased, and the pellets of water stopped drumming like Japanese kanji drums, Castle Frankenstein became the epicentre of a lightning storm of primal ferocity. The ancient building shook with every explosion of thunder, and night became day as reflections of lightning bolts danced across the slimy brickwork. God's finger touched the array of conductors high above their heads and the vast electric potential was fed into Mr Fairweather's containers. He had ten such vessels, or jars as he called them, and when each was full, the engineer would shout out, 'Jar one full!' Each container tracked the heavenly fire to be used later, flickering in the confines of the reinforced glass like a fiery Jinn. All ten were required for the process to work. And so the countdown began.

KAYANGA FELT THE TINGLE OF A CHARGE FROM THE pocket watch he gripped in his waistcoat as another savage bolt of lightning struck the conductor above them and filled jar ten with its fury.

"Jar ten full!" Mr Fairweather bellowed.

Dr Kayanga tensed, history was upon him. Kayanga was never one to suffer from nerves. He was supremely confident of his genius, but the heat raging in the pit of his stomach was not fear but rage. Rage at Frankenstein for having the audacity to exclude him from this moment. Rage knowing that without his input, none of this would exist. Five dowels would allow the electricity to surge through the structure he had created in specific amounts and at specific times, allowing it to rapidly repeat itself without the aid of a controller. He leaned over to one of the five vacuum tubes, and a serial tongue of phosphorescence flickered inside. It lit his dark features and the wild eyes. He hefted a massive rotary switch under tube one, then reached for the wooden handle of the rotary switch under vacuum tube five. He pulled that towards him with a clunk.

"Release jar one, three and five, Mr Fairweather," Kayanga called out, repeating himself two times above the howling winds. Mr Fairweather gave him a two thumbs up and flicked a pair of protective goggles over his eyes with flamboyant gusto, releasing the contents of the jars and instinctively stepping back to inspect his handiwork or protect himself from a possible power surge. There was a deep-throated thrum, and immediately, Kayanga's structure lit up. You could feel the power, a kind of pull that was far removed from traditional magnetism. This was an organic pull, as if the contents of your cells wanted to merge with the energies being generated, and everyone felt it. Kayanga looked down at Frankenstein on the level below him, who was looking up beside himself with excitement. The two bodies lay stretched on their platforms, and to Frankenstein's hip, a modified surgical table.

Dr Frankenstein held his breath and checked the equipment strapped to the platforms. A colourful array of large thick glass jars were attached to its underside. A steam-powered pump churned away unseen. All were filled with chemicals, and all had capillary tubes siphoning their contents into the bodies above. When Frankenstein was given the go-ahead from Kayanga in the form of a clenched and raised fist, the doctor's broad grin was maniacal. His eyes flashed as laughter he could not contain came rushing from his lips. He turned away from his colleagues to face his creation on the platform. Two ratchet switches were set to his left and right at shoulder height. He grabbed both of the rubberised handles and pulled down. Electricity and magic surged into the body, triggering a string of falling counterweights and the Clink! Clink! Clink! Of chains as the Royal cadaver was hoisted up into the swirling cloud of mystical energies at the apex of Kayanga's structure. Once at the top, it bathed in the swirling whirlpool of what felt like a piece of eternity manifest to every pair of eyes witnessing it.

And it was glorious.

Frankenstein had his watch out, counting every moment his experiment was being exposed. It would do no good to have it overcooked. Releasing another lever and the body began to lower. And as soon as it was on his level again, Frankenstein slammed most switches in place, and the body spasmed violently and then went limp. He slammed the switches again, and the body spasmed again; stored lightning coursing through the cadaver. The doctor was loudly willing his creation to move of its own accord.

"Reanimate you bastard," he screamed. "Reanimate."

How many more times would he keep subjecting the body to this punishment? He didn't know, and he didn't care. Until it was a burning smoking husk if it came to that.

It didn't.

The fingers on the corpse's left hand twitched, and the doctor held his breath, refraining from shocking the body again. All five fingers curled into a powerful fist that tested his restraints.

"It's alive," he whispered. Shuffling along the seven-foot frame to its head. Peering down on the serene and beautiful face. Wispy tendrils of vapour danced out of his lips.

It looked like he was breathing.

The doctor flung his head back and shouted to his colleagues above him.

"He's alive! He's alive!"

That's when Frankenstein's monster opened his bloodshot eyes, looked around its austere surroundings and boomed.

"Why am I bound?"

Chapter Nine

Present Day – Citadel de Camp, Brussels, Belgium

"My gown, please, Igor." Doctor Ulysses Kayanga stepped naked out of the Rejuvenator Pod onto the cold tiled floor of his laboratory. All around him was darkness except for the spot-lighted area he stood in. He was in the near-perfect physical condition and could easily pass as a man in his forties, except he was nearly four centuries old. His black skin glistened from the cytoplasmic liquid in which his body had been immersed. His bald head was matted with a viscous gel that he was combing through with his fingers and flashing to the floor in sticky clumps. Unconcerned by the gory mess, he smiled, and it was as cold as his surroundings. The chiselled definition of his muscles seemed to ripple as the fluids on him began to evaporate. It was a sensuous feeling that made his penis hard.

Dr Kayanga stretched and immediately felt his renewed strength not just in his joints and muscles but the very beat of his heart, in the sharpness of his thinking. The rejuvenator process could locate and swap out damaged or non-performing cells. It made him a new man every time he went through the process but retained his genius and consciousness. Centuries of life kept you in touch with your body and its signals. But he had spent all his long life cracking the code of what most people took for granted. To say the human body was a marvellous machine did not give it justice. Yet, he did not just understand it like some pedestrian biologist but had bent it to his will, sharpening its secrets and using them like a stake to the heart of his enemies. It would be another ten years before he needed a "refresh". His technology was getting better after every advancement. All thanks to Dr Frankenstein's original equipment. At first, the process had taken three weeks to complete, but now he had it down to forty-eight hours. Victor was brilliant. Dr Kayanga could take nothing away from Austrian Frankenstein's understanding of the human body and its functions was second to none – except for himself, that was. Dr Kayanga always wondered if he would have been able to discover the energy that was required to reanimate dead flesh. He would have continued to search for a scientific solution as he had done to prolong life, and come up with nothing. While Victor looked outside of the box and made an intuitive leap, discovering a metaphysical solution and, thus, a platform for technology and the supernatural to work hand in hand. That platform was what endowed Dr Kayanga with his fabulous wealth and success.

Fleetingly he wondered if he could have done it without the Austrian's help.

Yes, he could.

"Sir?"

Standing beside the naked scientist with his gown and towel folded over his arm and a pair of Terry slippers in his other hand was his agent and sometimes confidante Igor

Rakhmanov. Handsome and short in stature. The Russian had been his trusted aide for over a hundred years. Their relationship was a symbiotic one and the reason it worked so well. The doctor had unique requirements that could only make sense to someone with as much to lose as he had to gain. And also to an exceptional individual with a compulsion bordering on madness to discover the mysteries of the universe and themselves. And to someone with the confidence, intelligence and physical attributes to navigate the world as it evolved.

Igor was all these things.

"You look fantastic, doctor," Igor said. "Your calf and bicep muscles are more pronounced."

Igor crouched and came in closer to inspect the curve of the doctor's buttocks and the tautness of the muscles leading into his legs. He then stood and ran his fingers over the muscles of his arms.

"The muscle enhancement process worked."

"Indeed it did, Igor, and now I can go ahead with full production on my Praetorian army."

Igor applauded, his big hands making cracking sounds like a shotgun in the confines of the laboratory.

The doctor slipped into his gown and slippers. Then hung a towel around his neck.

"Have we completed the transfer of our operation to London?" the doctor asked.

"We have. Are you going to work or rest after the procedure, doctor?"

Dr Kayanga thought about it for a moment.

"I'm famished, Igor. Bring me Jollof rice, seabass and roasted organic vegetables." The doctor paused to think. "Also a bottle of Chateau Bourdeaux 1714."

Igor nodded.

"I'll get chef Yves on it immediately."

"One more thing," Dr Kayanga added. "As this will be our last night in Belgium, and before I burn this facility to the ground, I feel like I want to work through the night; bring me my overalls and boots."

"Right away, doctor," Igor bowed and hurried away.

Chapter Ten

Chelsea, South West London

The giant slid effortlessly through the heavy downpour that seemed to be focused on Jermaine Street alone. He was a monster of a man in stature, but even as he projected an imposing figure over 7 feet tall covered in a black waterproof military smock from head to calf, there was a mildness to how he moved through the world. He wasn't slow or ponderous but precise and powerful in his steps. His broad shoulders were held back, and he had an air about him that said he carried the weight of the world on his shoulders but he could handle it. As impressive of a specimen that he was, impossibly, he did not attract a second glance from passers-by hurrying for shelter. The tattoos on both sides of his head were magical glyphs that skewed perception. He was created by man and born to the lightning that had compensated for his disfiguration with unique gifts.

He called himself Kintu, the first man to be created by the gods in Ugandan mythology. He was no longer a man, and his creator was no God. And yet he believed he was the first of something unique, something special with a purpose in the world and maybe the last thing his maker had any hand in creating. They would each prove to themselves who had a greater need to exist. Creator with no heart, creation with no soul, and London would be that battleground. When he was reborn, the question of whether he was just a cursed soulless monster consumed him. What he had come to realise was that his real curse wasn't how he looked but his anger. A kind of anger he wondered if he somehow inherited from the spiteful murderous man who had created him.

Kintu would not let it consume him.

He crossed over to Crawley Street using the pedestrian crossing, just as an Uber delivery rider decided to push past walkers attempting to cross, misjudging the gap he had to squeeze through, his brakes ineffective. It could have turned disastrous if not for the hulk of a man... appearing. Sliding? Running? Teleporting? halfway across the pedestrian crossing, in the blink of an eye, his big hands grabbing the handlebars. The rider's momentum sent him crashing into him but he did not flinch, he simply looked at the rider from under his hoodie. His eyes glinted like chips of charcoal, and his handsome face was scarred, like a rejuvenated, old boxer. The kid on the bicycle drew back with shock and then suddenly mellowed as the spell enshrouding him took hold. The giant steadied the young rider on his feet.

"Sorry, boss," he said, watching the big man cross the road at a human pace and suddenly couldn't remember why he had been afraid of him.

KINTU STEPPED INTO MR AHMED'S CONVENIENCE STORE and stood at the entrance for a moment letting the rivulets of water run off him before entering. He was broader and taller than the door and, for a moment, blocked encroaching light from the street lamps from getting into the confines of the shop. The business was small, with three aisles, but the big man moved through the store with an agile grace, picking up the French biscuits he loved and a bottle of water. He approached the cashier and came face-to-face with a broad smile of the proprietor Mr Ahmed.

"My friend, your money is no good here. Take what you want for as long as you stay in London."

"Mr Ahmed..." Kintu's voice was deep and distinguished, his protest sincere, but Mr Ahmed would have none of it.

"You risked your life to protect my daughter. I'm forever in your debt." Kintu nodded respectfully.

"I don't like bullies," Kintu said. "They were a bad batch and needed a lesson in humility."

Mr Ahmed nodded and grinned.

"You certainly told them," the shopkeeper said.

Something else he had learned from a long life. When you give of yourself, others will return the favour. Mr Ahmed would never be threatened by these lawless thugs again, and he had redirected his bubbling anger into conflict. It was a mutually beneficial exchange for both parties, and his analytical mind would rationalise it, but he knew there was a selfish streak amongst all that.

"Before I forget," Mr Ahmed said. "Your number one fan gave me something for you." The shopkeeper rummaged under the counter and brought a colourful bracelet made from beads.

"Fatima said it will bring you luck."

"You're too kind, Mr Ahmed," Kintu said. "Thank Fatima for me."

The shopkeeper nodded, dropped the bracelet in his huge hands and reached for water.

"Thank her yourself when you see her again...." When the

businessman looked up, his friend was gone, the door just closing shut.

Kintu stood across the road from the derelict Church of St. Michael, the Archangel, that he thought of as Michael the Condemned. The rain had eased, sluicing away the grime from the streets and leaving everything shining, wet and appealing. With his hands in his coat pockets, he stood for a moment and cloaked himself in a cocoon of obfuscation. He then crossed the road to the church, slipping unnoticed through a false section of fence, walking along the length of the church and then down a darkened sweeping spiral staircase that corkscrewed deep into the foundations of the structure. Kintu stood at the reinforced door facing him, his massive feet in a predetermined spot, his preternatural eyesight comfortable in the pitch darkness.

Then there was light.

A flow of LEDs circled the edges of the door, and a voice spoke to him.

"Agent K. Verification complete." With a click, clack, and the whirr of micro motors, the door opened, and Kintu stepped through into his pop-up home and training facility courtesy of the Order of the Mechanics of Jesus. They were a Catholic religious sect founded after a group of Jesuits discovered the connection between magic, science and religion. Kintu was like their patron saint, but he would never agree with that assessment. What he would admit are the facts, not the stories. When he escaped Frankenstein and Kayanga in 1795, he was taken in by the Christian Brothers in Ethiopia, where he stayed for over 50 years. Having an insatiable appetite for knowledge, he travelled to Europe, and while in Italy, he was welcomed by a minor rural seminary. The Jesuits there discovered his true nature and committed to helping him. That was over two hundred years ago, and the Order of the Mechanics of Jesus had kept their promises even if his methods contradicted Christian values.

Kintu walked through the complex, passing brother monks and sister nuns in grey cassocks and habits manning computer terminals and servers, scouring through their mobile library, meditating and praying. They were a committed lot and well-financed, thanks to Kintu's investing acumen. Two centuries of life provided you with certain advantages. The brothers and sisters of the order were his eyes and ears on the earthly plane of existence and that's where Ulysses Kayanga played. Kintu was guided by other forces too and that's why he was drawn to London. Kayanga was here and so too was Antoinette. He could sense the weakening of the bonds that created the equilibrium of good and evil in the city because of the scientist's presence here. Kayanga was here for a reason and Kintu was in hot pursuit of that information like a dung beetle to excrement. This time when they met, there would be no escape from his creator. This time, Kayanga would not be allowed to continue torturing the only woman he loved to satisfy his curiosity. He would rather she die than go through what he had gone through. This was not a threat but a promise.

Chapter Eleven

Petara Barrio, Carracas, Venezuela

"Break! Break!" The convoy leader's voice was controlled and ice cool as he spoke to his driver, tapping his headphones out of habit and feeling the lead vehicle he was in, slow rapidly in response to his instructions.

"Right! Right!" he said as his vehicle veered right, and the rest followed. The convoy, made up of five muscular SUVs, skirted the Petara Barrio at speed. The VIP client was Raphael Hurtado, a Colombian entrepreneur who was being transported from Simón Bolívar International to a high-level meeting and was nestled between two sets of armoured vehicles on either side of him. The black SUVs were all tinted and carrying the BioEnhancement International logo on the doors and bonnet. The security assessment of the route had been carried out two weeks ago. Since then, it had been amended and fine-tuned four times and this final route had been decided on. What Mr Hurtado did not know was that his exact whereabouts had been leaked to his competitors on the Dark Web and a bounty of a million dollars was on his head.

. . .

Mr Hurtado had had three attempts on his life so far, and although this private military company was expensive and shrouded in mystery, their results were undeniable. Even if their methods were questionable from the stories he had heard. Mr Hurtado had asked many questions and had them all answered to his satisfaction. In his head, he had a picture of how they operated. In the front guard vehicle, the convoy leader communicated with the four flank vehicles behind it. The ongoing commentary lets them know when to break, turn left, right or a heads up on road conditions and possible threats ahead. The Petara Barrio was not an ideal route, but was meant to create a smokescreen around their intentions. This was the fourth run of the day and Mr Hurtado was satisfied they knew exactly what they were doing. The SUV's horns blasted from time to time to warn wandering pedestrians, casual mongrels, or goats meandering the roads in dire need of repair but mainly the convoy snaked silently through the ghetto. Even with the assurances and their professionalism, Mr Hurtado was still concerned about factors outside of their control. After all he was driving through a Micro State run by about five hundred armed paramilitaries operating outside the government's purview. He comforted himself with the fact that a mile or two further, they would swing out of the Barrio and connect with the smooth tarmac at Augusto C. Sandino Airport.

Señor Hurtado was on his mobile phone when the convoy drew to a stop. The businessman excused himself from the overseas call and nervously looked out the window. He could see the smoke ahead and the orange flicker of flames on the ramshackle homes of wood and corrugated zinc close to the concrete road. Mr Hurtado was not new to this feeling of imminent danger and possible death. But he was a man of conviction, boundless ambition and the resources to back that up.

"Qué pasa?" he asked; the tremor in his voice was a mixture of excitement and fear. The men he was sandwiched between at the back of the SUV said nothing but one handed him a phone from his inside jacket pocket. The businessman obediently put it to his ear and listened.

"Señor Hurtado," a deep, cultured voice said. "My name is Dr Ulysses Kayanga, CEO of BioEnhancement International. No need to be alarmed."

Hurtado nodded as if the electrical impulses were slow to get to his brain.

Dr Kayanga continued.

"Your convoy has been ambushed by Entere 11. The price on your head has gone up significantly, Mr Hurtado, and yet you had doubts whether my service was value for money. Well, let me demonstrate. If you will kindly look to your right."

The businessman looked right, and the strip of photo chromatic glass surrounding them lightened and became completely transparent. Like a child, he spun in his seat, the mobile phone still gripped in his hand and a three hundred and sixty degree vista now available to him.

"Can you see men with guns coming out of the Barrio?"

"Puedo," Mr Hurtado said.

"Now, quickly look to your left and up into the shanties. If I'm correct, there are more men with guns and grenade launchers, too." Dr Kayanga took a deep breath. "The stage is set, Mr Hurtado; sit back and enjoy the show."

The doors flew open on the SUVs in the back and the front of where the Colombian businessman sat. And as gunfire erupted around him, he witnessed a ballet of violence and carnage he would never forget. Altogether eight men and women exited the vehicles, not with excessive effort but with considered confidence and the kind of conservation of energy you saw exhibited by lions in the savannahs as they approach their prey.

Their bodies were armoured with Kevlar, and their faces were covered with ballistic masks. Señor Hurtado saw himself as a connoisseur of conventional weapons – he had a collection at his home in Bogota – but what these soldiers were carrying left him perplexed. They were equipped with an assortment of edged and stringed weapons, harking back to the mediaeval times of feudal Japan.

Hurtado could not peel his eyes away from a woman – he could tell from her hips and frame that her chosen weapon was a longbow. She vaulted ten feet over the wreckage of a car, hit the ground, rolled back to her feet and dispatched gunmen with arrows firing from her bow like bolts of lightning. As peculiar and amazing as they were to his startled eyes, their strategy was equally amazing. The woman with the bow and arrows was taking out assailants who were on the high ground with stunning accuracy. Neutering what would have been an onslaught of grenade launchers. She was hit four or five times, but she kept going. Her colleagues were getting their hands dirty too with a more direct approach which bordered on suicide. Mr Hurtado was no longer the focus of attention for Enterre 11; instead, they were engaging these crazy gringo warriors who simply walked into bullets and did not bleed. They had a false sense of security at first, brazenly stepping out of their cubbyholes to dish out a hot helping of retribution, only to be met by a wave of flying Shurikens and then slaughtered by axe, sword and arrow. In minutes a silence descended on the smoke-shrouded battlefield. The wail of sirens could be heard in the distance, and the Shadow Warriors, after moving the burning truck that had blocked the road, walked back to their designated vehicles like monks. Señor Hurtado stared at the procession. The last man in the chain was severely damaged. His ballistic mask was shattered, with only a piece desperately hanging from his pallid face. Completely out of character, the man turned to face the Colombian. A carcass stared back at him, bald, scarred and drawn, grey skin and dull, dead eyes. A chill ran through his veins.

"Your money's worth?" Dr Kayanga asked. The businessman had forgotten he still had the phone to his ears. He nodded in the affirmative to the question.

"Si, valió la pena cada centavo."

SCAN ME

Chapter Twelve

Hellfire Club, Central London

After his call to Central America, Dr Kayanga made his way down the candlelit corridor from his lavish suite to a secret room only three people outside of his circle knew existed. The Founders, trans-dimensional beings who established the Hellfire Club, and the Mole Men, bipedal creatures short in stature and gifted construction workers made the labyrinth of tunnels under the club and Kayanga's satellite laboratory. Then there was Mr Toombs, the Maître d', head of the front desk and immortal like Kayanga himself. The doctor suspected immortality was Mr T's natural state. Kayanga's footfalls echoed down the claustrophobic tunnel constructed over 200 years ago from quarry stone dug up from mines in Cornwall and shipped to London via steam train and canal. The Founders had created an establishment straddling the mundane and the supernatural worlds. It was neutral ground where animosity was left outside the oak doors, and any whim was catered for with enough coin or magical currency. The world outside was filled with prejudices, but your colour and creed were insignificant here. You were judged by the power you wielded in dimensions of power that mattered. Membership was open to supernatural beings of all persuasions and moral inclinations. Humans were welcome but required deep connections with the magical realms. What deeper connections could you have than the ability to bring dead flesh back to life? Science and the esoteric had always been one and the same to the doctor; only a few were willing to admit that. And he was one of the few and look at what he had created. Dr Kayanga squinted his eyes from the fumes of the burning torches, eyes that had witnessed conflicts on every continent. These eyes had made discoveries that could revolutionise traditional science but would never be shared. The end of the corridor was shrouded in darkness, his progress lit as torches ignited in time with his steps, and his excitement increased. The doctor slowed his pace as the last two torches lit and revealed the abomination that was the door.

The doctor grinned broadly.

How could he forget his exhilaration at amalgamating a living system with an inanimate object? The door recognised his approach, and across its surface, floating in a viscous fluid, a large accusing veined eyeball protected by a glass shield revolved and stared venomously at the interloper. At the top of the crusty-looking door surface, gnarly-like old leather skin was fed plastic capillaries of red and green liquids running from the surrounding wall.

"Have you been carrying out your duties diligently?" the doctor asked.

The skin split, like a surgeon's scalpel was being pressed against it and the toothless mouth that formed spoke in a slow, considered drawl.

"Always, Master," the door said. "Always."

In its earlier version, it could communicate with modified human lungs, but it was too delicate. Instead, the doctor devised a synthetic voice system. As much as he hated to admit the fact, it was more reliable.

"Having eternal time on your hands, what mysteries have you solved?" the doctor asked.

The Door Thing thought about the question.

"Do you have Time, doctor?"

The doctor thought about it.

"You may be right, Victor. Let us talk later."

The doctor nodded.

Long before Charles Babbage was creating mechanical computing machines, Dr Kayanga was using the computing power of the human brain, moulding the cells and tissues into living thinking creations. Reviving dead tissue and giving purpose again. There was something about the natural mechanisms evolution and magic could create. It had such poetry to it and reflected the sublime rules a supreme being had seen fit to create. Now great minds like Victor Frankenstein's would never die. They would continue their work, and he would learn from their observations. He had never been handed the keys to unlock the secrets of life; for most things, he had to discern for himself and the rest was beyond his intellect to reproduce. So sometimes, he would consult with some of the greatest minds in history. He reached out with almost trembling hands to touch the door that was more mind than metal. Behind the door was an important part of his world, that only he had access to. It was like being transported into a different world, where the same rules he lived by did not apply. The door closed its single eye at his touch and let out what could only have been a sigh. Multiple deadbolts began sliding free. The scrape of cylinders being extracted from the storm doorframe echoed through the rough-cut corridor. The two-ton door swung open smoothly, and the doctor stepped in. Fluorescent lights flickered on with his presence, and he stood in a pristine laboratory in which, at its very centre, a woman floated in a tank buoyed up by unseen energies that sometimes sparked green and yellow.

"Any time now, my dear," Kayanga said and kissed the glass. "Any time now."

Chapter Thirteen

It was the perfect ending to a romantic evening. Igor Rakmanov had organised the date himself and was proud of how all the moving parts fit neatly together. The look on Marilyn's face was priceless when after their walk in the park, hand-in-hand, he escorted her to a horse-drawn buggy that transported them to Luigi's Italian restaurant. Then they had some of the best linguini pasta in London and washed it down with Lambrusco to the soundtrack of Perry Como, Frank Sinatra and Dean Martin crooning in the background. Luigi did not go in for the quaint old-world Italian decor but was more a fashion designer ascetic that may have looked like cold sophistication. But when two people with obvious chemistry shared a table, they carried with them their own brand of warmth. When she spoke, he peered into her molten brown eyes and watched her painted lips move. The words she strung together were intelligent and warm, but he wished he could kiss those lips and in turn she would kiss the one-eyed snake below his belt. Marilyn had slipped off her heels and was using her stockinged feet to massage his crotch, squeezing his manhood and awakening the beast. He was impressed because turning him on wasn't an easy job to do. It wasn't that he found the women with the light inside unattractive. They were beautiful, but he didn't find most of them sexually attractive. However, Marilyn was different. Igor had felt it the first time he had met her in the gym, on top of the other thing he sensed in her, the thing he could just see leeching through her beautiful black skin, buried deep inside. The thing his Master was most interested in and would do anything to obtain. No one else could see it but him, it was his gift.

Marilyn wanted to know where he lived. He had to lie because he never had a place he could truly call home. He was a citizen of the world with his Master. Staying as long as they must in one city or the next, on one continent or the other, fulfiling his Master's harvesting program. Convincing Marilyn to invite him to her residence was easy. She had a great night, she was tipsy, and even if he didn't have ulterior motives, a gentleman couldn't let her go home unescorted. And that's what Igor did. As they walked up to her South London Maisonette, Marilyn had asked him.

"How did you know where I lived?"

"You told me, remember," Igor's confident reply left no room for doubt. She smiled and leaned into him.

Marilyn didn't know that Igor had been studying her for some time now. Before they met at the gym, he had become intimate with her comings and goings. There was no time to slide the key into the lock before there were kissing and testing buttons, zips and clasps on each other. The door eventually opened, and they fell through, kicking it shut behind them.

She tasted like mangoes, he thought as he unzipped her dress and snapped her bra open.

She had released his belt, popping buttons as she dug into his crotch and grabbed his throbbing hardness. This would be bittersweet, and he wished he had more time with her. He kept that to himself because his Master would not like him having feelings for any of his victims. It was a weakness, and a weakness to the Master would not go unpunished.

After, he placed her naked body on the plastic sheeting he carried in his murder kit, sparing the bed from bloodstains. He carefully scanned her dark skin, breasts, the ripple of abdominal muscles, arms and legs and committed it to memory.

Perfection!

She breathed easily, her chest rising and falling; she was fully asleep, a small mercy he never gave to his other victims, but she was special. They had made love passionately and he was pinching himself. Not that sex was strange to him, not at all. It was just this time he wanted to make love to her. He wasn't disgusted by it but elated. Igor didn't want it to end, but it had to. He'd never forget, and as if to reassure himself, he reached into his jacket pocket and took out Marilyn's panties, the ones she had seductively taken off and playfully flicked at him.

Always remember.

Lifting his hand up to his nose, Igor took a deep breath planting his nose into the silky undies and inhaling her musky scent. To think the material had caressed her inner thighs, clung to her pubic hairs and massaged her moistness, made his heart race. He shuddered delightfully, feeling himself harden again. Igor quickly stuffed the underwear in his inside jacket pocket and focused on the job at hand.

He was ready now.

He carefully took out his smartphone and placed it on the side table beside the bed. Igor opened a countdown app, showing four rows of zeros at the ready. He reached down to his feet and lifted a black leather doctor's bag that two days earlier he had stashed in her cluttered front-facing-outhouse.

With care, he laid out his operating tools, all shiny high-carbon steel and keen-edged, from his two-piece scalpel to his bone saw. They smelled of antiseptic and beeswax. He polished them himself after every extraction and was proud to display them. For a moment, he was caught in the broken and distorted image of himself on the metal, like an evil genie inhabiting the tools. A disjointed spirit trapped within, mad with frustration if it wasn't slicing flesh or sawing bone.

Igor blinked and looked down at the rubber gloves on his hands. He needed fingerprint access to his laptop, so he extracted a finger and authenticated his request, bringing up a secure video feed on the screen. There was nothing on it yet, just a holding page. That would change when he switched on the camera and attached it to his forehead. His skin was clammy with excitement as he adjusted the camera and turned to look down at Marilyn's body. It came into sharp focus on the screen. Igor cleared his throat and improved his bearing.

I'm fully prepared, he told himself.

"Are you ready, Master?" he said, speaking into the laptop's microphone. There was a shuffling of clothes and what sounded like sheets of paper. They also seemed like another conversation was taking place even deeper into the background. However, it ended abruptly as the Master answered.

"You may begin, Igor," Doctor Kayanga said, and with a scalpel in hand, Igor made his first incision.

Chapter Fourteen

It was three-thirty in the morning. Shaft parked his E-type Jaguar two streets down from the crime scene and took a leisurely walk back up to the solitary officer standing in front of the yellow and black scene of crime tape. The reserve looked apprehensive, and Shaft could understand why. The young woman didn't have a clue what she was guarding – outside of the fact that a murder had been committed – but he was sure her CO must have scared her a bit with some choice phrases that would have her mind racing a mile a minute.

Shaft had done this before.

"How you doing, Officer..."

"Pembroke," she said, filling the gap.

"Pembroke," Shaft said easily. "I'm Detective McFarlane," he flashed his warrant card. Quick eyes scrutinised it and stood a little taller. "Who's inside?" Shaft asked.

Officer Pembroke looked chuffed that he was asking her for information.

"Crime scene investigators have been here for over an hour now; other than that, it's been quiet."

"Thanks, Officer Pembroke; let's see what's going on."

Shaft lowered himself and lifted the tape over his head. He stood looking at the maisonette with the front door open. Most crime scenes would be crawling with Met personnel, from officers, administrators, CSI and a slew of detectives. It was eerily quiet as only two vehicles stood outside, and as the presiding Detective, he should know what he was walking into. But as soon as officers got a whiff of the paranormal, Black Book was contacted, and the rank and file stepped back. In his eyes, it was unprofessional and downright dereliction of duty, but if it let them sleep better at night, so be it. They knew cases like this couldn't end up in a normal court of law, and they thought they could take the piss with the process. Shaft hoped, for their sake, his department would be around for a long time. Someone needed to clean up the messes that would invariably come and keep the citizens unaware of what lurked behind the curtain.

The Black Book unit was an obscure Metropolitan Police Department. Not entirely secret, but with enough urban legend surrounding it that some considered it myth. Black Book is unique in that it has only one working Detective; most of the top brass who knew of his existence felt that the organisational structure was ridiculous but Shaft didn't think so at all. When the geriatrics at the top of the Scotland Yard food chain found another Detective with the smarts, mental fortitude, and balls to accept the fight against the city's rising paranormal activity, then they could tell him shit. Until then, they had the NWA – Nigga with Attitude, to deal with. Not his words, some smart Alec at Central came up with that one and Shaft thought it was cute, respectful almost. He'd be lying if he didn't enjoy the notoriety and even encourage it. They needed that sense of superiority to get them through the day, and Shaft would oblige. But he'd also like to remind Heads of Departments that what he did was no laughing matter. When they overstepped the mark, he wasn't averse to casting a stink spell or releasing a poltergeist in the admin offices. The perks of this job was knowing individuals with crazy arcane talent. The ones who the Metropolitan Police had decided to ignore for hundreds of years.

Shaft stood at the front door, about to pick up white booties to slip over his loafers, and a chill racked him that was so intense, it was almost painful. It carried with it an undertone of despair that was unusual for him. Shaft stopped what he was doing and composed himself. He never considered himself the sensitive type, especially not in the way the ladies from Bad II the Bone were. But he had his hunches, déjà vu, his gut instincts and even a sixth-sense feeling at times. Nothing unique about that, but this feeling had him unsteady on his feet, and then suddenly, it was gone. He took another deep breath, made sure he was squared away and called upstairs.

"Dr. Aziz Hosseinzaden!"

There was a pause and some shuffling upstairs.

"Will you stop butchering my father's name and come upstairs."

The smart-ass response was what he expected. Shaft tried to squeeze out a smile, but he couldn't.

What the fuck was wrong with him?

He hoped Dr Aziz's affable nature would perk him up, but his mood worsened as he ascended the stairs. Shaft decided to jog up the remainder of the stairs and observed a toilet and bathroom with a small box room across the landing. The main bedroom he was heading towards was lit like a film set. Doctor Aziz was thorough and loved his gadgets. His excuse was that if it made his job more manageable, it was a good purchase, especially if it was on the Met's dime. Framed by the doorway, Shaft stood on the threshold of the bedroom, absorbing the decor and making further conclusions about the person who lived here. Shaft caught himself shivering as his focus fell on the bloody body on the bed. A pale blue hue emanated from the dead body that mingled with the artificial lights.

"Bastard," Shaft spat. "He's not gonna stop, is he?"

He looked over to the doctor.

"Detective," Dr Aziz greeted him in full PPE. His voice was muffled through his 3M mask.

"How did you get here so quickly?" Shaft asked. "And when was it called in?"

Dr Aziz moved closer to him, removing his face mask, his brown eyes glinting.

"A neighbour found the body. One of your team is with her; she's obviously in shock," the doctor said. "We were lucky the window was open, and the neighbour was a busybody; seeing the odd blue light through the open window, she came over to investigate."

"Did they break in?"

"No, she knew where the spare key was hidden."

Shaft nodded.

"Time of death?"

Dr Aziz considered the question with a twist of his neck to relieve his tired spine.

"Five to ten hours." He looked at Shaft, his excitement hard to conceal. "After dealing with three bodies in this condition, you'd think I'd be used to it, but I'm not," Doctor Aziz said. "I came as quickly as I could and let my team get on with it. We're still acquiring evidence, but we should nearly be done."

The team that the doctor had referred to was similarly decked out and consisted of three others of unknown race and gender. One of them cheerily waved at him. Shaft nodded back.

He remembered the first victim and how they nearly called the infectious disease department. Dr Aziz and his team were taking no chances, although they knew what the results would be.

"I did the same battery of tests we did with the other cases, and the glow is harmless; I just can't explain the fluorescence."

Shaft was itching to step forward into the crime scene, but as the doctor gave a running commentary and he made an attempt to get a closer look at what he had to work with, the doctor wagged his finger disapprovingly.

How could he be patient when what he could see was brutal and fascinating at the same time? As the doctor spoke, he relegated the crime scene investigator to a compartment in his mind, but his focus was already in the room. The female body lay neatly in the middle of the bed on blood-splattered white sheets. Her head and feet were covered, but her chest wound stood out. The monster who had done this had cut her chest open, and, Shaft was hazarding a guess, had removed an organ. Even this level of sophistication and brutality would not require his department's presence. The following fact, however, would. A blue glow surrounded the neat incision and emanated from the gaping cavity in the cadaver's chest.

"Are your tests telling you anything new about this?" Shaft pointed to the obvious.

The doctor stood looking at it for a captivating moment with his arms folded and his white jumpsuit bathed in blue light. Shaft wondered what was going through his head.

That's what you get when you demand new challenges in your career, Shaft thought. *Sorry, Doc.*

"Just like the others, Detective. It's not radioactive, chemical, or some kind of bioluminescence. It's obeying none of the normal scientific staples that I'm familiar with."

Shaft breathed deeply and recalled the other cases over an eight weeks span that had a similar MO to this.

"What did he remove this time?" Shaft asked.

"A heart," Dr Aziz said.

"Eyes, lungs, stomach, kidneys and now a heart," Shaft muttered, then asked another question. "Is the process of removing the organs still... incredible?"

"Pretty much," the doctor said. "Like the others, the organs were removed with such precision, as if they were part of a jigsaw puzzle fashioned by a robot with a laser scalpel." He paused. "Was the description too sci-fi?"

"Nope," Shaft said. "It works."

"Good, well I'm nearly done here, and you can come in and do your thing. I'm obviously unqualified to prognosticate on the matters of the esoteric..."

"The 'P' word doc, I like it," Shaft nodded his head in approval.

"Thanks," Dr Aziz said with a straight face. "I need to improve my vocabulary, so I sound like I swallowed the dictionary and trying to use words in my everyday interactions."

"No judgement from me, doc," Shaft said. One of the doctor's assistants was giggling at the exchange.

"I'll have the report emailed to your inbox 24 hours from now when I've thoroughly examined the body." The doctor looked down at his tablet, tapped the screen a few times, and then looked back up at Shaft. "I've just sent you my immediate findings. Keep in mind this is not definitive; my conclusions could change."

Shaft nodded.

"I know, I know, Doc," he thought for a minute, then asked. "What's the DB's name?"

"Marilyn..." he checked the notebook for the surname, "...Awosika."

The name struck Shaft like a sledgehammer to the side of his head. He was still standing at the doorway to the room and suddenly found himself leaning on the door frame for support. Marilyn's name tumbled out of his slack jaw, almost without him recognising he was repeating it. His eyes fogged with tears, and he could hear Dr Aziz from some far-off place, asking if he was okay.

Marilyn!

The smart, sexy woman who made his trips to the gym much more than chores. The woman he had forged a friendship with him was lying on the bed in a bloody heap, murdered by a psychotic serial killer who not only knew highly advanced surgical techniques but was wielding occult powers. When Shaft lifted his head from his chest, Dr Aziz was beside him, coaxing him into breathing deeply.

"Feeling any better?" the doctor asked. "What was that?"

"That was embarrassing," Shaft said, giving him a wan smile. "I've been pushing myself lately. I think I need some rest."

Dr Aziz nodded.

"Once you're done here, I suggest you go home and get some rest. And – that's not a suggestion."

"I hear you," Shaft said. "How long will you be?"

"We are clearing up now. We'll transfer the body to the van, and the crime scene is all yours."

"Can I see the body before you take her away?"

The doctor looked at him strangely and then waved him over. Shaft was conscious of how unsteady he felt and wished to Christ it wasn't showing in the way he was walking. The doctor lifted the sheet from her face, and Shaft stared down at her. His whole body tightened, and he could feel the pressure in his jaw from his clenched teeth. She still looked beautiful, although her skin was pallid from blood loss. He turned away slowly and began walking to the door.

"I'll leave you to it," Shaft said. "I need something from my car."

"Are you sure you're going to be alright?" the doctor asked.

Shaft stopped, turned and looked over at the body. He stared for an uncomfortably long time. He gave the doctor a shaky thumbs-up and left the room.

Chapter Fifteen

Shaft returned to the bloody bedroom with a heavy heart. The many conversations he had with Marilyn were looping through his head as he returned to the murder scene. Her talk of family, passion, and talent for athletics was brutally cut short. This time he could enter the room without authority, and still, he was uncertain. He took a deep breath and stepped into the trepidation he experienced at his first-ever murder scene. This was the first time someone he cared for had been a victim of murder. He wasn't sure how he should feel. Shaft would seek to understand his confused emotions later. This moment required that he remained professional because if he was going to catch the psychopath that had done this, his head needed to be in the game, now more than ever.

Shaft took the rolled-up animal skin from under his arm and kneeled before the bed. This was not standard police equipment but in his world, there were unorthodox options that could help an investigation. He carried the mystical tool that had been loaned to him from the impressive collection of artefacts the ladies from Bad II the Bone oversaw. It carried with it a faint smell of tanned meat. Shaft could never remember how to pronounce its name, but from a loose translation of a long lost tongue, it meant 'A Piece of Yesterday,' as far as Shaft could tell. He was still getting used to all of this. And he was aware he carried with him some baggage that he wasn't proud of. He learned not to embarrass himself around individuals whose perspective was more enlightened than his own by talking less and listening more. He hoped his attention to detail would pay off. Shaft unrolled the animal skin that was shaped like a square with its four points rounded. All over the rough surface were symbols that were first cut into the leather and then highlighted with some form of dye. He had seen the technique used before by a tribe in South America, but this item had been dug out of the tomb of an ancient city in Zimbabwe. The symbols themselves were unique because a written word tradition seemed to have been rare for that period. And yet here it was. The spell was written on the underside. Pronouncing the incantation was one thing; saying it with the necessary passion and belief was another. Once, he had rid himself of doubts that an ordinary man, gifted with no talents or special bloodline, could trigger the magical reaction. It was an incredibly useful tool if the conditions were right. He now thought of himself as a bit of an expert. And could understand how easily power like this could corrupt. Shaft reached up to the bed and plucked up the blood-soaked flannel the doctor had left for him. The detective rolled it into a ball and placed it in the middle of the animal's skin. Sighing heavily and taking a deep breath, Shaft sat cross-legged and recalled the words to the spell.

The incantation bubbled out of his mouth, sharp and clear in an unknown tongue whose meaning was lost in time. If that wasn't strange enough, he could see the transformation in the air surrounding the animal skin and felt it in every cell of his body. Empirically he knew he hadn't moved from his spot on the floor, but it was like he had slipped into an adjoining room, leaving his true body in an identical but different world. In this room, the laws of nature performed in bizarre ways. Shaft picked up the bloody flannel and threw it on the bed, watching A Piece of Yesterday perform. Thousands of points of light appeared in a cloud over the skin, like a heavenly cloud full to the brim with light. Shaft had grown to consider them as little pieces of data that were now starting to recreate the murder scene in the tableau that floated above it. The detective's dark complexion shone with the illumination, keenly watching what was unfolding. The temperature in the room suddenly plummeted. Shaft's breaths misted, and he shivered involuntarily. The only other time this had worked for him – the trick was to use something the victim owned five hours after death; he tried to videotape the spectacle on his smartphone. On playback, the video showed a pulsing spot of light in the middle of the screen and 25 minutes of footage lost. He had to depend on his keen observational skills. Technology didn't do very well interacting with powers unrecognised by traditional science. He reached into his inner pocket, pulled out a notebook, and started scribbling. Once the bits of light had reproduced the likeness of the bedroom, it paused in its work, gathered information from the immediate past, and played it back for Shaft's eyes only. The detective wasn't sure if it was a part of the spell or his overactive mind was filling in the missing pieces of this brutal murder, but he was seeing what was happening above the skin in his mind's eye. The perpetrator was short in stature, about 5 feet six, but he was very strong. The thousands of points of light that made up this kinetic image wasn't able to show detailed facial features but just enough for Shaft to surmise he was white and Eastern European. The man carried Marilyn's body effortlessly into the room and placed her on the bed. They made love. So she knew him. Once she was asleep, he sprayed something on the pillow. Marilyn never woke up. That's when it got interesting. The killer left the room for some minutes and returned with his doctor's bag.

Shaft checked his watch; he had five minutes before the spell dissipated.

The killer set up a laptop for recording or streaming. He laid out his surgical tools reverently beside Marilyn's naked body. He was muttering silent words over his sacrificial altar. He picked up a blade that was undoubtedly not a surgical instrument but an old world edged implement and set it between Marilyn's breasts, applying pressure, and that's when the images coalesced into a single point of bright light and then faded away.

Chapter Sixteen

Y, Suzy and Patra arrived at the Fitzgerald room uncharacteristically early. From the outside looking in, they seem to be three friends bickering with each other unaware of the world they were passing through; but nothing could be further from the truth. Being aware of their surroundings was second nature now, but they were scanning not just what they could perceive through the five senses but the esoteric wavelengths to which only a few had access. Even as they mounted the sweeping staircase and their steps were absorbed by the plush carpets, they observed the three-man team regarding them as they approached.

"Slick is getting paranoid in his old age," Patra said. Suzy expanded her awareness and pictured an ever-expanding bubble with her in its centre, expecting it to ping back with a sensation of threat or calm.

She relaxed.

"Him have reason to be paranoid," Suzy said. "All is not well."

Y walked ahead of them, already knowing from Suzy all

was safe for them to enter, but something sketchy was sharing the space they inhabited. Patra's eyes flicked down to a sigil shaped like the rising Sun made from white and black powder. The granules glowed as they approached. Manning the door were two men and one woman in dark blue blazers and polo necks.

"My sisters and I have an appointment." The security bowed respectfully and swung open the doors.

The Warriors Three entered.

THE ROOM HAD A CAPACITY FOR AT LEAST FIVE HUNDRED people, but instead, at the far end was a huge burnished wood writing desk with a distinguished Wrexham leather chair behind it. An Apple Mac sat on top with a stack of papers beside it, and a gleaming Mont Blanc pen propped up beside the column of documents. To the side of the antique writing desk was a huddle of two women and one man. The older black man broke away from the conversation and headed spritely towards the ladies as they approached.

"Kiss mi neck!" He exclaimed. "My daughter's in deh building." With outstretched arms, he hugged and kissed each of them in turn.

Spokes was the landlord of the elegant and palatial Sussex mansion, but their relationship was much stranger and more convoluted than could be explained from a mere business relationship. The Jamaican had tripped and fallen into a world of gods, Ghouls and Gadgets, pulling the girls with him. His attraction to chaos brought them together in the first place and, in a roundabout way, introduced them to what lay behind the veil of their five sense reality. Three years ago, he was as clueless as they were, but he adapted quickly. And with an eye for opportunity and his Snake Head ring that discerned truth in any person, conversation or thing and with lots of luck or predestination, he left his days as painter decorator to be an impresario of all things mystical. It had been a bumpy, dangerous ride, but the risks were balanced with a fortune of hundreds of millions of pounds reappropriated from a murderous obeah man. The old-school Jamaican was now a connected man in this new world they had discovered together, and with that connection came exposure to the elements of good and ill.

"My little sparrows tell me business is good," Spokes said. "The entertainment business has you on lock."

"We are the best after all," Patra said without a hint of humility. "You of all people won't be surprised to know the world behind the veil is fucking up the hood and the heights."

Spokes nodded.

"Mas P keeping you busy and safe?" Spokes referred to the enigmatic and supremely connected Mr Patel, their business guru and partner.

"Him do him best," Suzy said.

"But we have a job to do, and the threats keep coming."

"I may have something to help with that."

"Pray tell," Y said.

"Remind me," Spoke said. "I need to show you but later."

"I have to say you're looking good, Slick," Patra teased. "Where's that honey that's been on your arm for the last year?"

"I'm keeping her locked away, Miss P. Dis situation has me rattled."

"I miss you, I really do, Mas Spokes, but why, when you come around us, you bring rass trouble with you."

He nodded solemnly.

"It's a gift, Miss Wong."

"A gift and abnormal circumstances we could do without," Y said. "But in our line of business, it seems everything has a hidden meaning we need to understand." Y sighed and looked seriously at the older man. "Who have you pissed off this time?"

"And that's why I love you, Miss Yvonne. Like an arrow straight to the point." He paused. "In business, and especially our business, you cannot function without upsetting one party or another. It's just how deh ting set. You just need to be diplomatic and never leave deh situation unresolved. It's tricky, and I have a lot to lose, but I'm learning."

"Deh, higher deh monkey climb, deh more him expose," Suzy said.

Spokes laughed bitterly.

"Mistress Wong, wiser words have never been said."

"You Jamaicans always have some cute ass words of wisdom for everything," Patra said.

"Pretty much," Y agreed.

"Your grandma must be rolling in her grave, tinking the pearls of wisdom she give you fell on deaf ears," Suzy said. "Yuh too busy playing doctors and nurses."

Patra gave her the middle finger.

Y ignored her sisters and directed her question to an obviously worried-looking Spokes.

"What's on your mind?"

Spokes looked around, and a frown appeared on his face.

"Where is the detective?"

Patra and Suzy started exchanging looks and smiles. They were familiar with this dance of affections between Y and DI McFarlane.

"He's on his way; he'll be coming up the steps in a few minutes," Suzy said.

"Don't mek the man struggle to find his way, go get him," Spokes said.

"Okay, I'll go meet him," Y moved off in the direction of the entrance, and Suzy held her hand.

"Him seem upset," Suzy whispered. "Make sure him okay."
Y left the room.

Y waited ten minutes in the foyer before seeing her boyfriend enter the hotel. DI Winston McFarlane, Shaft to his friends and enemies alike, immediately locked eyes with her in a crowded room. The crazy psychic GPS they shared was on point as usual, and so were the echoes of emotion it carried with it. Y was nowhere as gifted as Suzy but not as pragmatic as Patra. Suzy had been right; Shaft looked sexy in a grey Armani suit, white shirt, complementary tie and loafers. He moved confidently towards her, but she sensed just a shadow of uncertainty. His eyes were dull, and the corner of his lips tugged up with effort to produce a smile. She had not seen him for eleven days and wanted his small talk, his humour and his soft lips kissing her naked body.

"Hey, warrior princess," he teased.

They hugged ferociously, and Y made sure she pressed into him, and he could feel every inch of her. Shaft was a deceptive man, his exterior may look like a cool drink of Guinness, but inside he was an absinthe-laced cocktail. Y found the contrast intoxicating.

"I missed you," Shaft said.

"Not as much as I missed you. I'm worried for you, baby," Y said.

"You don't need to be...." He thought about what he said next, then with the care he said. "Suzy, right?" Shaft sighed. "You know being unable to lie to your woman about anything is creepy, right?" Shaft grinned. "And for the male species, that's damn unhealthy."

Y nodded her head in agreement. She held his hand and dragged him to a seat, where they sat down together.

"What's that aftershave you're wearing?" Y had a way of veering into delicious tangents in the middle of a serious conversation. It was a testament to how the mind worked and the myriad of inputs she received beyond her five senses.

"Creed 1491."

"Hmmm!" Y said, placing her nose to his neck as if she had smelt delicious Jamaican bun baking in the oven. She came close to his neck again, took a whiff and kissed his neck gently.

"Now tell me again, what's going on?"

Y squeezed his hand.

"It's a murder case I have been working on. It hit close to home. It's a project Black Book case, and the serial killer is also a necromancer."

Y suddenly stood, she felt something.

"Let's go talk to Spokes; he has something that I think may be helpful for your case."

"How so?" Shaft asked.

"I'm not sure. I just felt... a possible connection," Y said.

Shaft shook his head.

"So this meeting wasn't just for the old man to catch up?" Shaft asked.

It was Y's time to smile.

"This is Spokes we're talking about, remember," she said. "He always has an agenda."

Shaft thought about that for a moment.

"Yeah, I guess you're right."

They both held hands and headed back to Spokes' make-do Chambers.

THEY ALL SAT AROUND A CONFERENCE TABLE AND LOOKED at the opaque cube that resembled a reinforced aquarium positioned at the centre. Spokes' two female assistants stood a safe distance from the group of Y, Suzy, Patra, Spokes, and Shaft. It was as if they were told a possible explosion was imminent and they didn't want to be shredded by the shrapnel.

"Can you feel the web being spun?" Spokes said and looked at Suzy. "By itself, it looks normal. Your murder brother Shaft, duh run-in my daughtas had with an assassin and now this." He gestured to the cube in the middle of the table. "For whatever reason, when some ting beyond deh norm is brewing, deh Powers that Be, see fit to put all bits and pieces of deh puzzle on the table for us to solve."

And this was where Spokes excelled. He could connect with situations you would never necessarily see, especially if you were in the thick of it. Spokes would sit with the facts at hand, like his long-deceased mother in Jamaica would patiently sit with a ball of uncooked rice on her lap and pick out stones and chaff until the rice was ready for the pot.

"It makes no sense yet," Y said, and the rest nodded.

"What do you think is the connection?" Shaft asked.

"I have a feeling it will reveal itself in due course," Spokes said. "Let's play our hand and see."

Suzy shivered, her eyes never leaving the cube on the table.

"In the meantime," she said. "We go about our business looking out for the connections as dem form."

"What we looking for?" Patra asked.

"Everyting," Spokes said. "Take dis, for example." He pointed to the opaque cube. "I got sent this evil ting five days ago on my arrival to the UK."

"So you've been here awhile," Y asked, her brows raised.

Spokes smiled patiently.

"Long enough that I man could prepare deh surprise I was telling you about."

Y acknowledged the explanation with a sideways nod.

Spokes continued.

Good Girls Gone Bad

"Whoever sent it knew the address of my office in the Docklands and knew I'd be arriving in the country. My ring alerted me to the danger."

"Is not a bomb, or you wouldn't have brought it here," Shaft mused.

"Worse than dat, brother," Spoke said, getting out of his seat and walking into the middle of the conference table. He then reached over to the cube and twiddled a dial that instantly removed the opacity to clarity. Spokes stood back with folded arms.

There was silence as all eyes fell on what was inside.

"Jesus..." Patra murmured, hesitating for a moment before approaching the spectacle. Y reached for the Katana on her back and moved closer.

Suzy's eyes narrowed as she leaned in.

"You're having a fucking laugh," Shaft whispered the words pushing his chair away from the table as he gripped the edge, using his hands to pull him around to a better view. But the 'thing' in the glass case was no laughing matter. A floating child's brain was contained in an armoured housing attached to six articulated cybernetic feet and two wickedly sharp pincers like a scorpion. The armoured brain crawled around its enclosure like a tarantula. It had no eyes but it made a pulsing shriek when Y got too close. Then a click, click sound before it charged the glass with incredible force for its size.

"It was sent to kill me. It had a timed lock that would release hours after arrival, but I jammed the lock closed." Shaft shook his head. "Some bwoy was uncomfortable with the questions I was asking about a cargo." A grim smile darkened his features. He lifted up his right hand, and the Snake Head ring glistened. "Is gonna take much more than that for me to end up on a slab in the mortuary. Much more."

All assembled knew Spokes words were not laced with

braggadocio; the man seemed to have nine lives. Patra had her face so close to the tempered glass her nose was almost touching. The thing was going crazy trying to reach her.

"God damn! What are you?" she asked slowly.

"Give it some space," Y ordered. "I want to see it less agitated."

"Stop antagonising the ting gal," Suzy said sharply. "And maybe I can start answering some questions."

Patra stepped away and came to stand beside Shaft, who stood at a safe distance. Suzy moved around the table, observing the creature from every angle, her diminutive shadow casting parts of herself over it.

"Hmmm," she said as Spokes watched how his daughters worked with fascination. He loved watching them in action and to think over three years ago, they were going about their ordinary lives, not knowing that another side to reality existed, another aspect to good and evil. Nothing should surprise them at this phase of their journey, but that wide-eyed wonderment remained.

Spokes had a lump in the throat.

They always made him emotional. Y watched Suzy walk around the table and joined Patra and Shaft, knowing Suzy would complete her ponderous circuit where they all stood. Suzy finally parked up beside her sisters with a concerned look on her face. She leaned on the conference table with her back to the thing in the glass case and faced her sisters. She glanced over to Spokes, who sat in his seat at the head of the table, watching the drama unfold. Silent communication took place between the three women, a natural mix of body language and a highly developed intuition that bordered on telepathy. Patra nodded, grinning broadly and reached for a silk bag in the pocket of her rough Riders bomber jacket. She took out a shiny metal ball bearing. Without looking at anything in particular,

Patra hurled the four-inch metal sphere across the room. It ricocheted off the metal plate of the door, then off the door handle, changing its trajectory into the chandeliers. Its momentum took it across the ceiling, where it disappeared for a second. There was a tinkle as it bounced off some crystal droppers that made up the ceiling decoration and fell to the conference table below, bouncing off the upturned belly of a teaspoon, the ball bearing smashed into the control panel in the glass box. It switched from transparent to opaque.

"Show off," Suzy said.

Patra shrugged.

A round of applause came from Spokes at the head of the table.

"You could have just walked over to it and switched off the transparency," Shaft teased.

"And where would the fun been in that homeboy," Patra said, then tried to wax philosophical. "It's moments like this that give meaning to life." It took seconds for her straight face to slip. "I'm just fucking with you," Patra laughed, leaving Shaft with a relieved look on his face.

Spokes walked over to their huddled group and asked.

"What was that about?" Suzy leaned off the table.

"The ting in the box is deh product of traditional science, technology, and old magic. Dis is reanimation on a totally different level."

"Only a very few had the secret of bringing dead flesh back to life," Spokes said. "Most thought it had died with Frankenstein, but from what we've just seen, the data is not true."

They all acknowledged his words with nods and shuffles.

Suzy continued.

"Mostly, we are being recorded. Whoever sent you dis ting wanted not just to kill you but do some recon work as well."

Spokes bowed his head to her observations.

"It was taking stock of the competition, considering the threat. Whoever it is knows who we are and what we're about, and that could be a problem."

Shaft looked at Spokes who was silently processing what was being said.

"As freaked out as I am right now, I don't see the connection between this and my serial killer case."

Spokes took the floor for this one.

"It's just too early to tell right now. Whatever powers chose my daughters to be protectors saw fit to entwine our destinies. If dem think that was funny, dem should think again."

"Straight up," Patra agreed. "To be clear, I wouldn't want my destiny to be tied to anyone else in the world but to you guys."

"Yuh too sweet," Spoke said, his eyes twinkling.

Both Y and Suzy rolled their eyes.

"If you think I'm being a dick, tell me, but it's my inner detective calling the shots right about now."

"Shoot, brethren," Spokes encouraged him.

"What if you're wrong this time?"

Spokes gave him a knowing smile, lifted his right hand, and wiggled his fingers, the truth sayer ring on his index glistening.

"For better or worse, I'm connected with this Mesopotamian relic. I understand its language after nuff false starts; the Snake Head ring [A1] has never guided me wrong yet. I can feel this case means a lot to you, so believe me when I say it is all connected."

Shaft nodded slowly.

"Fair enough," he was completely satisfied with the response. They had been through a lot together, and he knew there were some things that he had to take as a given. "I guess I'll have to get on with the investigation and check in with you guys on a regular basis."

"You know that's not gonna fly, Winston," Suzy said. "We've

Good Girls Gone Bad

done this enough times to know when we are connected in a case we have to keep it tight. We need you, and you need us."

Shaft lowered his head and massaged the area between his eyes and the beginning of his nose. He looked tired when he lifted up his head again. He cleared his throat.

"I just wanted the investigation to proceed as fast as I'm able to. I know it's a conflict of interest, but it's personal."

"If it's personal to you, then it's personal to all of us," Y said, and everyone nodded in agreement. "We know how we work best."

"Let's keep with the program," Patra said. "I have a feeling this is going to be a crazy ass ride."

Suzy slapped her arm.

"Gal, just leave deh feeling ting to me. It's not your forte, understan."

"Yes, ma'am," Patra saluted with a dopey disposition.

"We have your back," Y said. "No matter what."

If Shaft believed anything, it was that he wasn't alone. He had to be careful of his ego and remember this wasn't the Metropolitan Police; he was surrounded by family here.

"I appreciate it," he said. "But I need to get back out there, dig some more and see what I can come up with."

"Not tonight, you won't," Y said sternly, getting a wicked smile from Patra. "Tonight, you decompress with us."

Shaft nodded with a tired resignation and felt the reassuring weight of Y leaning on him.

"And while you're here, give mi a breakdown of dis case you seem so concerned about," Spokes said.

"Not before I get this disgusting thing out of the room," Y said. "It knows too much already."

Y moved over to it, gingerly lifted it up from the conference table, and shuddered noticeably.

"Hey Y, I think it likes you," Patra teased.

"What makes you say that?" Y asked.

"Not a murmur from it," Suzy realised Patra may have a point. "Just wait a minute, sis."

Y did as she was told, placing it back on the table as Suzy walked over. She toggled a button on the lower frame of the cube, and the glass became transparent again.

The armoured brain laid on its side. Its electronics looked heat tarnished. In life or, more correctly, in pseudo-life, the folds of the brain had a vibrant pinkish hue. Already the mottled skin was blackening.

"It's dead," Suzy said, looking over to Spokes. "How long did you have it for?"

Spokes thought about it.

"No more than ten hours in the warehouse," he said.

"Okay," Suzy said, keeping her ruminations to herself.

Y picked it up again and rendered it opaque.

"You can leave it with the cloakroom attendant; she looks bored as hell," Patra suggested." And don't forget to tip the bitch. You Brits need to improve on your tipping game."

Y said something, but it was muffled.

By this, Y was nearly through the exit except for her right hand that, hovered in the crack between the frame and the closing door, flipping Patra the finger.

She smiled, shaking her head.

Chapter Seventeen

Monsignor Raphael Lukamba should have rested or at least freshened up after his four hours flight from Vatican City to London, but he had a lot on his mind. His talk at the Westminster seminary was three days away, and he had more important work to do before that. The Church had insisted that he become a guest of the Archbishop of the Diocese of Westminister, and protocol dictated he stayed at the Archbishop's residence. He was off the papal grid for a few days and because of that, the Monsignor made his own arrangements. Two sisters from the Order of the Mechanics of Jesus had picked him up from the airport and had just left him in central London at the corner of Messenger and Profit Street. He stood looking at the imposing but dilapidated St. Michael, the Archangel Church, and could almost feel the history in the old bricks. The Monsignor reached into his long coat, slipped on a pair of glasses, then popped earphones into his ears, quickly concealing his dog collar by buttoning his coat back up.

The glasses felt odd on his nose and around his eyes. He

had never needed glasses, not yet, at least. With his love for scholarly work, it could be in his future, he guessed.

"Safe House location," the Monsignor said. "Monsignor R Lukamba."

Immediately a male voice responded that was more AI than flesh and blood.

"Voice pattern authenticated," it said. "Safe house Charlie, Hotel, Romeo, One, Sierra, Tango, Omega has been loaded to your AR unit, Monsignor."

With a soft murmur and the faint rendition of a Bach symphony, a dynamic map overlay slid into place over the lens of his glasses and in his new augmented reality world, he was guided to his secret home away from home.

It was impressive to see. The facility had become fully functional within two weeks of acquiring the property. And here he was, watching the Mechanics of Jesus, an ultra-secret order functioning like a well-oiled machine. The Monsignor had a few recommendations he would make to the Mother Superior but all that could wait. He was getting impatient as he was being shown the facility layout when he knew where he wanted to be. Still, the Monsignor had to remain respectful; they had taken the time from their busy schedules to welcome him. As a historian, he was constantly introduced to new ideas and his series on Apocalypse Predictions throughout Christendom had made him a minor celebrity in certain circles. He had to restrain himself from not completely being immersed in a room committed to ancient weapons, their functions and their history. He picked up a melee weapon from ancient Romania, blessed and used to battle werewolves.

Fascinating.

He resisted the urge to delve deeper.

"How long has Antiquis Est – the ancient one – been in meditation?" the Monsignor asked his young tour guide.

"Brother Kintu is usually in meditation for at least two hours," he answered. "He prefers not to be disturbed."

"I know," the Monsignor said. "But take me to him anyway."

The young cleric hesitated, then bowed and quickly led the way. He brought him to a doorway where there hung a thick ruby-red curtain that, to the priest's mind, separated the known world from an unknown one. Monsignor Lukamba parted the curtain with his finger and slipped into the dimly lit room without waiting for an invitation. His eyes adapted quickly to the Spartan environment, but there was still much he could not see. Who needed to see his surroundings before witnessing God's mysteries on display? The lonely candles in the middle of the room flickered as they struggled to illuminate the enclosure, or was it the giant of a man crossed-legged, huge hands on his lap bare chested, eyes closed and levitating about 12 inches off the mat. Three colourful juggling balls slowly orbited his head, revolving as they followed their preordained path controlled by forces that the Mechanics of Jesus had been formed to study and use.

The Monsignor had chills.

He never grew tired of seeing it exhibited in the open. Who could ever be? Nobody would have imagined that so many of God's secrets were revealed to one such as him. The Father did work in mysterious ways, after all.

The Monsignor made himself comfortable, took the lotus position and waited, knowing his presence would interfere with his meditation. It took seconds for Kintu to descend to the mat and slowly open his eyes. One by one, the levitating balls came to land on his lap.

"Monsignor Lukamba, what brings you here from the Vatican?" Kintu asked, his voice deep and rich.

The Monsignor smiled bitterly.

"As if you don't know. I may not have centuries of experience and intellect under my belt, but I'm no fool."

"And I'd never imply that you are, Monsignor. It's just that sometimes I prefer a soft introduction before the harsh realities, but I can see that was too much to ask."

"Under the circumstances, it is too much," the Monsignor said. "What you're planning to do could expose us and threaten your existence."

Kintu's back was to the candles, and the Shadow he cast completely engulfed the cleric before him.

"It could," Kintu said. "But over the centuries, you've learned much about the other side of reality. Those lessons will always be known, utilised, and passed on even if the Church were to discover your activities."

"Excommunication would not go down well with your patrons in high places," the Monsignor added.

"And for that, I'm deeply sorry," Kintu looked down at his clasped hands and slowly lifted his head to stare at the priest. "I would not willingly jeopardise what we build here, but some injustices cannot go unpunished."

In the murky light, Kintu's sharp eyes observed the priest again, his scrutiny locking onto the Monsignor's right arm.

"'The struggle continues," Kintu said. "Your arm."

"As observant as always," the Monsignor commented. "Another repercussion we will continue to face if you insist on going down this road."

Kintu reached out to touch the hidden injury to the Monsignor's arm. The thought of his friends being in constant danger made him scowl but it couldn't be helped.

"You need to be more careful, Monsignor; the Knights Templar are dangerous."

"I wonder how much more dangerous they will be if you kill one of their own."

"The Templars have never been good at rooting out corruption in their own ranks," Kintu said. "Since they discovered our existence, it has become an issue the Church has conveniently ignored. What the Vatican refuses to do, I will do for them."

"I'm sure they'll appreciate the sentiment."

"I'm sure they will," Kintu said, considering his next words. "Leave the fieldwork for the younger Mechanics, my friend; we have need of you alive."

The Monsignor shook his head.

"You're worried about my life; what about your own?"

"I'm not sure I qualify as being alive," Kintu's smile was a wry one. "But whatever we classify my existence as, it is mine to give, Monsignor," Kintu said. "I wasn't created in love; I wasn't created in the image of God. I came about from envy, hatred, jealousy and greed. And if that was to be my lot, then so be it." Kintu's eyes flared, and the Monsignor shivered, shuffling uncomfortably in his place.

"I was in love once; did you know that?" Kintu asked. "A beautiful and intelligent woman who was to bear my children and rule my kingdom with me. But that was savagely snatched from me by jealousy and hate." Kintu sighed, and it seemed to come not from his lungs but from some far-off desolate place where hope was a fanciful idea. "I wasn't the best of human beings when I was alive, but my Antoinette did not deserve this. The monster that created me wanted to do the same to her, but he couldn't reproduce the process." Kintu leaned closer to the Monsignor and whispered, his voice gravelly. "The magic was in the lightning." He paused to let that sink in. "On that night, my dead body was blessed or cursed, depending on your point of view, with the power of Shango, Kiwanaku, Indra,

Zeus and Thor. Little did my creator know I would be one in a billion, one in a hundred billion. And all this time, Antoinette is trapped in the twilight zone, calling to me in my dreams." Kintu looked intensely at the Monsignor, his eyes almost pleading.

"Do you think a monster can dream?" He didn't wait for the priest to answer. "I dream. When I close my eyes, she speaks to me. I try to comfort her whenever the connection is strong, but how much consolation can I give to an unfortunate soul trapped in the prison of her own mind for over three hundred years. That, Monsignor, is the definition of hell."

What could the Monsignor say to that? This was truly beyond his remit as a priest. Working alongside forces and players he did not understand but was beginning to appreciate.

"How can you help her if you're dead?"

It was as if Kintu didn't hear him.

"Ulysses Kayanga is colluding with certain high-ranking names in the Knights Templar. I'm sure he's paying them handsomely in coin or kind, but that cannot wash away the stink of that collaboration. I cannot allow that to go unpunished, even if they represent the Church."

Kintu stood. All eight feet of him. The Monsignor's eyes were locked on the scars, gashes and metal tubing that skimmed across the terrain of dark skin. Like artificial veins, the metal tubing burrowed into the flesh of his muscles, supplying his impressive physique with whatever mystical nutrients were required to keep him physically and mentally superhuman. Kintu reached for a towel and covered himself, breaking the Monsignor's spell. The cleric joined him in standing up, looking puny beside him.

"I will go back to our supports and make worst-case scenario planning. I will ask you to consider carefully what you do next."

Kintu nodded and said, "The time for careful consideration, my friend, is over."

Chapter Eighteen

C-Bandit Mines, Democratic Republic of Congo

He had been in worse situations than this before. Situations where the torturer had begun his despicable work giving him no time to mentally prepare. But even when things looked dire, he had a deep-seated optimism in his gut that told him he would come out of it with his balls intact. Whether it was Seal Team 12 or his own resourcefulness that saved him, he believed he would be good.

Not this time.

This time Agent Johnson knew he was going to die here.

The CIA agent wouldn't be the first or the last operative to unrealistically picture themselves retired to a ranch in Texas or fishing on Lake Tahoe.

He grinned grimly.

Who the fuck was he kidding? The truth was being tied to a chair somewhere in the Congo awaiting execution was not too far off how careers such as his usually ended.

He wasn't gung-ho about the fact of dying for his country but dying without knowing why? That was the one thing Agent

Johnson could not abide – this mystery, and his abduction was the most baffling.

In all his thirty-five years of running operations for the Company, this was the first time he couldn't explain through cause and effect any aspect of his mission, including how he conducted himself and the results of his actions. No scenario he could construct was able to explain how he was taken from a reinforced bedroom in the American Embassy – one of the most secure facilities in Kinshasa – and spirited away to wherever this was without so much as a shot fired or an alarm raised.

Who the fuck could do that?

He'd sat in this chair for over sixteen hours in a pristine, almost clinical white room. He imagined how blood splatter would ruin such a beautiful space, but he'd already defiled it with his bodily excretions. The temperature was nice and chilled in comparison to the oppressive heat of Kinshasa. If he was still in Kinshasa.

There were CCTV cameras in the top four corners of the room. Behind him and to his right was contemporary shelf space; embedded ceiling lights were above his head, bathing him in cool LED lights and messing with his circadian rhythms. He had tried to sleep, his training at Langley had taught him to get rest before potential torture, but it was patchy and filled with torment. Maybe it was his unconscious giving back in kind some of the torment he had handed out to others on numerous occasions. Cramp had set in a few times, and shy bladder syndrome was not a thing for him; he pissed on the floor without pride or shame.

As insane as this may sound, he looked forward to knowing who was responsible for his abduction, the how and the why.

The suspense was killing him.

An hour or so later, the door beyond opened and with it, the possibility of some answers.

In stepped a tall suited African man. He moved with confidence and purpose and exuded a noticeable power even from where Agent Johnson sat. Without hesitation, the man approached him, stopping an arm's length away. The American lowered his head in defiance, his chin on his chest.

"Good evening, Agent Johnson. I trust you're feeling uncomfortable?" Dr Kayanga said in a smooth, calm voice.

The man did not answer.

"Come now, you want your last remaining moments to be a game of wits."

The words sank in, and the agent slowly lifted his head and locked eyes with him.

"Much better," the man said, folding his arms." Much better."

"And who the fuck are you?" Johnson asked, trying to lean forward, but his bonds were tight.

The doctor smiled patiently, and Johnson felt a shard of cold fear pierce his gut.

Platinum-grade fear.

Why was this motherfucker spooking him?

Johnson tried to shake it off.

"I am Dr Ulysses Kayanga, the man your department has been investigating for some years now."

Agent Johnson swallowed, trying to maintain a poker face, but the name rattled him. So this was the infamous Dr Kayanga. No wonder he felt the way he did. Some of this monster's aura had telegraphed itself onto him. He recovered as soon as his mask slipped, his training catching the error and smoothly reapplying his façade of unconcern.

What the doctor didn't realise was his file was a thin one, and mainly speculation. The kind of speculation that could give you nightmares, even for a seasoned veteran such as Johnson.

Kayanga came closer and lowered his face inches away from the captive's ear as if there were others in the room eavesdropping on his conversation.

"All the horror stories you've heard about me are true," he whispered.

Every sense was telling him to recoil from the invasion of his personal space, but Agent Johnson did not move. When the doctor pulled away, he was left with his subtle aftershave and the power of the man's gross personal magnetism.

This man was known for having one of the most successful private armies in the world. And in his search for the perfect soldier, the brief reports on torture, experimental amputations, organ harvesting, biological enhancements and genetic manipulation. An actual modern-day Dr Mengele.

The agent took a calming breath and tried bravado.

"You know the CIA are going to take this personally, right?" he spat out. "Do you really want that kind of heat on your operation?"

The doctor seemed to be amused by it all. His smile was thin and cruel.

"I am not concerned about your CIA; instead, they should fear me."

Agent Johnson laughed, his voice hollow.

"You are no different from all the other trumped-up despots in this fucking backwater land you call home. They come, and they go."

"And yet here you are in this backwater land murdering my people, destroying our infrastructure and polluting our soil. You've overrun three cobalt mines so far, and now your attention is on my mining enterprise. But that's where you've overstepped your mark. Here is where your CIA will lose its grip, and you, Agent Johnson, will be the first domino to fall."

"You're delusional," the agent scoffed, his composure

Good Girls Gone Bad

barely holding together. "The Company will get what they want. It's a matter of time. You're in the big leagues, doctor, and when you want shit done, you call for the best and I am the best." Agent Johnson said.

"You were the best," the doctor corrected. "And I admire your candour." Doctor Kayanga reached into his jacket and took out a silver box filigreed with the shape of a coiled dragon then absently he rubbed his thumb over the top of it. "Seventy years ago, your employers and others like them murdered a friend of mine. You may have heard of him Patrice Lumumba, 1936. Brilliant man. He would have created a prosperous Congo. But you took his life." The doctor paused to think. "Do you know what I did, Agent Johnson?" The doctor shook his head and took a deep, ponderous breath.

"I did nothing. I let your overlords get away with it. Now here you are again, causing civil unrest and destabilisation in my country. What do you think I will do this time?"

Agent Johnson shrugged, looking smug, but his mental gears were churning underneath, and panic wasn't far away.

"You are my inspiration, agent. Because of you, I'm even more eager to create my immortal army. The units that abducted you are nothing compared to what is to come. You should be proud; you've ushered in a new era. My private army will give me the means to rid my country of the likes of you, and then, who knows." His eyes blazed with passion. "But before I get ahead of myself, I need some information. Information only you can provide me."

"Go fuck yourself," Agent Johnson spat." You're getting nothing from me."

"I hoped you'd say that. Unfortunately for you, my friend, even with decades worth of spycraft, you've come to a gunfight with a peashooter. You are hopelessly unprepared for the world I inhabit. You will give me what I want."

The doctor opened the ornately designed silver box, walked over to the agent and tipped the contents onto his shoulder. Johnson tried to shrug off whatever Kayanga had left there but to no avail. He couldn't see, nor would he want to. The three grub-like creatures, an inch in length, translucent, peppered with villi for movement, squirmed and wriggled. The creatures sported disproportionately sized chitin mandibles. Wicked things like rotary saws made for burrowing through flesh. After orienting themselves, they began their ascent up his neck while the agent thrashed and cursed.

The doctor headed for the exit, but after five steps, he stopped and turned to face the agent trained to conceal panic but who was smart enough to know nothing would help him now.

"Let me explain what will happen to you, Agent Johnson," he adjusted the cuff of his Victorian-style shirt and jacket. "My neural pupae will travel through your auditory canal and then eat their way through flesh and bone into your brain. The pain will be excruciating at first, but only for a while. They will burrow into your memory, speech and pain centres, leaving you in a state of euphoria, bypassing your reluctance to tell me what I need to know. Once you have answered my questions, the pupae will die, their task accomplished, and then you will die too, Agent, very painfully."

"You sadistic son of a bitch," Agent Johnson hollered, still squirming in his seat, the pupae entering his ear canal.

"But don't worry, Agent Johnson," Kayanga consoled him. "Death is not the end for you; it's only the beginning."

He left the room, smiling as Agent Johnson's horrific screams could be heard through the door and down the corridor.

Chapter Nineteen

University Hospital, East Central London

Patra broke every speed limit London's transport network imposed on her long suffering citizens as she made her way to the hospital. The average motorhead would expect fines to come through their letterbox or into their inboxes after the journey she just had. Miss Cleo 'Patra' Jones would receive nothing of the kind. Every time she broke a speed limit, the automatic cameras would reboot, experience a micro power surge or simply malfunction. Her gift of confounding the laws of probability extended out from her like a magnetic field in times of threat and worry. So as she revved her motorbike, nothing on the road she came in contact with could interfere with her progress.

For the moment, everything was in her favour.

Green lights all the way.

She pulled her bike on the kickstand in the hospital's car park and hurried to the reception desk. Patra was glad it wasn't the weekend because she could imagine the chaos the revellers could cause dragging their drunk and disorderly asses in here, distracting from genuine people in distress.

This evening was far from that.

Three people sat in the plastic pastel-coloured seats waiting for their number to be called. One man in a pinstripe suit was laughing and joking with a receptionist as Petra strode through the sliding doors.

"Ah shit," she mumbled. If Suzy were here, she would have detected this piece of shit way in the car park, but Patra's less-than-perfect sensory skills required her to be up close and personal with these motherfuckers.

The demon stank of tar, sulphur and excrement, but only the sensitive amongst Joe Public would be offended. Patra didn't have the patience or the time for this, but she had a duty, even if it was inconvenient. She tapped the foul thing firmly on its shoulder; the material of the pinstripe suit was exquisite.

"Can't you see..." It turned angrily to face whoever was interfering with its attempts to suck the life force out of potential victims.

Its eye's bugged, and it took two steps back after sensing the institution Patra represented. It bared its teeth, and a low growl like a wolf gurgled from its throat. The receptionist he was talking to looked at him strangely and leaned off the inside counter, straightening up.

"Motherfucker, please. Threats to me?" Patra made a sound like a punctured bicycle tire. Sounding very much like her sister Suzy. "Do you want me to send you back to the pit in front of all these good people, or will you walk out of here, nice an' easy like. Your choice."

"You wouldn't dare," the demon rasped. "There are rules to the game, Guardian, and the ones that required anonymity would be flaunted if you revealed me to these human souls."

"Dawg, I think you have me confused with someone who gives a shit," Patra reached for her back, and the demon flinched and then raised its arms, stepping away from the reception desk.

"Your timing sucks, but that works well for me. If I hadn't turned up, you'd be setting up shop," Patra said, pulling out a vial attached to a gold chain around her neck. The receptionist watched the exchange carefully but was unable to hear the details through the glass that surrounded her. At least the Hell Dweller had the good sense to keep its voice down. With Patra's back to the receptionist, she uncorked the vial and dusted some of the contents on the floor and recited the words:

"We are here; feel our presence."

The dust illuminated for a brief second, and the Hell Dweller shuddered then swore in the tongue Patra instinctively understood.

"Fuck you too," she shot back.

Suddenly the hospital wasn't as welcoming as it was before she had turned up, and the creature wearing the flesh suit of human skin hurried to the exit. It stopped at the threshold, using its foot to keep the door open and turned back to Patra glaring. The lift on Patra's right pinged open. A woman in a wheelchair rolled out screeching, her eyes wild with two more Hell Dwellers by her side just as angry and agitated trying to keep up. The odd trio bungled through the door that was propped open for them by a fellow Hellspawn. The demon doorman remained steadfast; this time, the sudden movements came from Patras left. Some dude was hobbling past her with a plaster cast on his right leg. When he sensed that Patra was the cause of his hasty departure from his feeding ground, he immediately stopped playacting and began walking normally. He gave Patra a wide berth and the finger. The play actor ducked through the door, disappearing into the night. The demon doorman, satisfied all his cohorts had cleared the infected area, shook his head despondently.

"You can't protect them forever, you know that, right," the demon said. "More of us are learning to breach the divide," he offered a phlegmy chuckle. "Resistance is futile. I love Star Trek." The nerve-jangling line continued as the sliding door locked shut.

THE MAN SHE CALLED OG, MR GILES SINTON, LAY ON the pristine white sheets of the hospital bed, tubes in his arms, his chest rising and falling steadily. The monitoring equipment blinking lights produced an almost twilight underwater vibe. The sporadic beeps completed the image of a submariner in his final resting place. OG looked gaunt; his eyelids were virtually transparent, showing the veins running through the thin skin. His jaw was clenched, and even in sleep, he looked like he was ready to tell his stories of how a London boy ducked and dived his way to the top. But here he was, all alone and Patra would be lying if she wasn't surprised by that. She imagined the whole family would arrange an around the clock vigil, so he was never alone.

The patriarch of the family was alone. They were more fucked up than she had first thought.

No biggie.

At this moment, when it mattered the most, Patra was family. She pulled a chair to his bedside, took his hand, and sat. It felt delicate to her touch. Patra stifled a sneeze. At least the family and friends brought flowers and left them on every flat surface. She had bought nothing but her 'Two Long Hands,' something else Suzy would say whenever she went to an event without bearing gifts. All she knew was that OG hated flowers, and if they knew anything about their father and grandfather, they would have known that.

She knew it was stupid, but if anyone could defy old age

because of their attitude to life, Patra believed he could. He was human, yes but there was something bigger than life about him. He had built one of the largest pornographic media businesses in Europe. He was the man who welcomed her to London, gave Patra her first job and became her friend. He was in his late seventies, but he had the spark of a much younger man. He may be down but never out. She wouldn't allow it, even if the code of the guardians forbade direct intervention in human fate through magic. He'd be looked after. Patra would have to get by the old man's family, who were paranoid about where his millions would land when he died. She didn't give a damn, but the old man's daughters were like harpies who despised her immediately when they had met years ago.

Bring it on bitches, Patra thought. She could take it.

They had played many poker games together, smoked cigars and drank expensive brandy, always recounting life and family stories. Patra was confident she knew of all the players in OG's family drama. Patra had done the same for her family in Atlanta. The difference was she had been venting while she liked to think OG was preparing her for a time like this. How he could know something like this could happen to him wasn't clear but the feeling that OG was playing chess, not poker, was evident to her. Patra already knew what things she would do first to help clarify what had happened to her friend. His medical record would be a good start, and then she would allow her Guardian senses to guide her from there. For now, Patra would sit in the dark, hold his hand, talk to him about the future, and hope he could hear her.

Chapter Twenty

Y sat on the edge of the bed and smiled at Shaft snoring lightly beside her. He was a good man, and she was lucky to have him. Sharing her crazy life with someone who understood but cared was a blessing, and she knew it. They were connected and not just by their physical attraction – sex was electric, and that was an almost literal assessment. She was tingling in all of her erogenous zones. Still wet where she should be and harder where you would expect. Her body was tuning like an acoustic guitar, resonating from their bond. She stood and stretched, walking over to the big bay windows overlooking the garden. Her naked silhouette formed on the floor behind her from the display lights artistically set in the garden below.

The night was cool, but it had a sharp, chill edge that Y immediately knew had nothing to do with the weather. Dark clouds were gathering on the horizon. This threat felt different. Or it wasn't the threat at all but how she intended to handle what was on its way. Admit it or not, Y had become the moral centre for their merry band of protectors. Coming to terms with that responsibility scared her. What if the past challenges have been luck or fluke? Did luck even exist? In the world she inhabited, luck could be bestowed – Patra was proof of that. Or was it fate? Even if the Guardians stood outside the forces that affected the average man, could all this be pantomime, and they were its puppets? Their strings being pulled into disaster, and they had no control over it? London was the epicentre for the instability of good and evil and that instability was forming breaches between hellish dimensions and earth. The guardians had their part to play in the bigger scheme of things, and it was that part she felt ultimately responsible for. Y looked over to her Katana on its stand an arm's length from her bed. The gift from her father in Japan had become an extension of her body and the symbol of what she would do to protect her family. Her thoughts drifted to Patra, Suzy, her mom, her dad, the man on the bed, Nanny, and Spokes. Some of the people she cared for. And the ones she couldn't afford to let down. She may not be qualified, or that's how she felt, but whatever presented itself, she would face it. It was uncomfortable having doubts about what she was capable of, but here she was. Y had to deal with challenges all her life. She just never questioned whether anything was possible for her until now. She had been blessed with a strong mother and a wise father. They had guided her, and she had listened. What did it mean in this unusual phase of her life? Maybe the enormity of her situation was just dawning on her. Being exposed to the truth of how the universe works and how close mankind may have come in the past to absolute destruction and darkness may have just sunk in. Whatever the reason behind her newfound trepidation in her role as a leader, Y would continue to perform her ordained duties. As the thought settled, it became clear to her that even her doubts had never yet escalated to anxiety. For all her talk of being alone through this, there was a sense of reassurance that wasn't a mere psychological construct that gave her hope. It was something real that she could put her finger on but at times of crisis like this, it intervened to keep her grounded. She knew her sisters felt it too. It was happening now. Three words popped into her consciousness.

'Know your history. The history of the Wakuze Mwamba.'

As the words prodded her, she was urged to visit the mansion's library. Y didn't fight it. She slipped her feet into her trainers, kissed Shaft's lips as he continued sleeping and reached for her Katana. The blade hummed in her hand and was immediately surrounded by a pale blue umbra.

"Let's learn something of our history," Y said.

Her blade hummed in response.

Chapter Twenty-One

"What if I can't have kids?" Suzy slid the question to the big man across from her like she was a Blackjack dealer. Trevor could either fold from the delicate question or lay his cards on the table. Her small hands were on his big hands, her piercing eyes peering into his unwavering ones. Susan Young to her lover, Suzy Wong to the rest of the world was one of the most gifted empaths on the planet, but the man she loved with all her heart was difficult, if not impossible, to read. From her observations her powers seemed to not work around her lover. Suzy had to rely on unsexy intuition and rudimentary body language to even begin to see through his silent musing. Luckily it was just as effective because she knew all of his tells. Tonight though, he was concealing them well and making Suzy nervous.

They were at their favourite Caribbean restaurant and had just finished a delicious meal. Instrumental reggae was playing in the background, and Trevor threatened to dance with her while patrons ate, making Suzy's cheeks flush red. Her question put a pause to his shenanigans, making him sit down and reach for her hand.

"Yuh okay?" he asked. "Yuh didn't tell me you were going to see the doctor?"

"I'm fine," Suzy said. "Nuthin to worry bout. Just thinking."

Trevor smiled broadly, showing the sexy gap between his teeth. He knew she had been researching the archives at the mansion for unequivocal evidence confirming what she feared but leaving enough uncertainty for hope.

"You haven't answered me."

Trevor sighed.

"Dat's a deep question for it to just come out of the blue like that. What's on your mind, baby?"

It was Suzy's turn to smile, and just as quickly as her serious demeanour had appeared to mask the question, the sunshine of her personality blasted away the prickliness of this discussion.

"Are you trying to dodge my question, Mr Bishop?"

Trevor's big shoulders rose and fell with amusement as he chuckled.

"Would I do dat?"

Suzy rolled her eyes.

Trevor took in a deep breath.

"I'm going to guess you've found out dat having a baby may not be possible for you and the girls? I'm sorry, baby."

Suzy silently nodded, her eyes glistening.

Trevor continued.

"I won't even act as if I understand your world of duppy and obeah, angels and demons. But I do understand what it can be like to be chosen for a higher purpose."

"Your grandmother," Suzy said, having heard the story of

how she was given the gift of third sight and how she was chased out of the little community in rural Jamaica.

"She same one," Trevor said. "After everything that happened to her, she still found love, but the price was high." He considered his following words, finishing the mouthful of Guinness punch in his glass. "I blame myself for running off my mouth about wanting a family, and I won't lie, I do, but family is much more than blood. You know dat?"

Trevor reached over and daubed at the tears in Suzy's eyes with a napkin.

She sniffed self-consciously.

"My rock," Suzy said. "When I doubt myself, you're there to remind me that you have my back."

"We promised to tell each other the truth. I'm disappointed I can't be the one to make you pregnant," he made expansive gestures around his stomach area. "But I can handle dat. How are you dealing with it?"

Suzy sighed.

"I'm not sure yet. I'm willing to pay the price. I didn't think it would be at the expense of my family."

"You've been chosen, baby. And when you are chosen, life nuh play fair."

Suzy looked into the space beyond Trevor's broad shoulders, and for a moment, she silenced the chatter of anxiety residing between that space where there was nothing but time. A waiter came by to leave the bill and broke the spell.

"What if you could have kids?" Trevor asked. "The work you and your sisters are doing is important; how would they manage without you?"

There was a flare of righteous fire in her heart, but as soon as it rose, it died down. There was no threat here, just love and concern. Trevor was right.

"I have so much to give, T," Suzy said, and Trevor nodded

with understanding. "I know more than most what kind of world we live in. I've seen true evil and experienced pure goodness. I'm deh best at breaking the spine of any 'armshouse' who threatens my world or my family."

Trevor nodded.

"I know that to be true," he agreed emphatically.

Suzy sounded thoughtful as she spoke.

"I want to know if I can contribute to a better world without violence. Raising another human being to fight evil by just the example of their life."

Trevor kept nodding as if Suzy's message kept reverberating between his ears, and he had to keep agreeing with it each time he heard it.

"What do you think your old people would say?" he asked her.

Suzy became all misty-eyed, and the expression on her face was faintly sad.

"They want grandchildren, of course."

"And we can give them dat," Trevor said. Suzy looked confused for a moment.

"There are so many children in the world with no one. They need love and family too. Your mom and pops would have no choice but to love the children we have just as we would love them."

Suzy's eyes looked brighter as the idea of adoption blossomed.

"You'd make a badass baby momma," Trevor said in all seriousness.

"And you would be the best baby daddy ever."

He grinned and put his elbows on the table, grasping her hands and staring into her eyes.

"There's a baby out there somewhere that needs a family."

"We could give dem that," Suzy said.

"We could give dem that and more," Trevor emphasised. "You're a Guardian."

Hearing the words from Trevor sent a chill down her spine. And although she was smiling, Suzy couldn't decide whether her reaction was a good or a bad sign. She just knew it was a challenge she would embark on.

Chapter Twenty-Two

Anancy loved being amongst mankind, and for this century at least, London was his city of choice. His excitement wasn't a very god-like emotion, but he didn't know how else to express it. It was a part of his nature, his essence, and so was his strategic thinking, his storytelling and his love of risk. Why else would he be here against the rules that dictated the presence of his kind in the world of men? Of course, it was fun, but he had a purpose too.

He had responsibility.

That made the spider god smile, and he released a cloud of cigar smoke with the symmetry and delicate lines of a spider's web.

What is joke to you, is death to me.

He loved that Jamaican saying. It may not seem as if he was taking his responsibilities seriously, but he had his own way of operating and problem-solving. And it all began with a cup of coffee, a Cuban cigar and a dose of people watching. Not that he needed confirmation. His decision to accept the patronage of the Guardians of the Light was a divine choice if he did say

Good Girls Gone Bad

so himself. But being here on this earthly plane of existence with a storytelling audience of 8 billion souls was sweet. And the spider god wanted to keep it that way.

The Brunswick Café was busy. It was not just a popular spot in itself – surrounded by office blocks – it was spacious inside and out with a mouth-watering menu and seven varieties of coffee, ground and brewed by award-winning baristas. It had that *je ne sais quoi*, an attitude of heart that humankind was so fond of, yet not knowing why. The employees had it, and so did the founder. Even the form Anancy inhabited could sense it, and that vibe would attract those interested in balancing the denizens of darkness formed in the pit or born to a woman. Anancy was on his 4th cup of Blue Mountain coffee and on a first-name basis with the waitress. He wore a cool cream three-piece suit, shades, a Panama hat, and his cane wrestling against his cross legs, its ornamental head propped on the table. An ancient spider anagram was edged into the soles of his leather brogues. Time did not flow in the same way for him as it did for mankind. It progressed here on the earth plane, and he could manipulate it to a degree. Normally he wouldn't, but sometimes he couldn't help himself.

It was the little things.

"Another cup, Mr A," the waitress's melodious voice was proper west London to most, but Anancy had discerned her ancestry six generations back to a quaint village on the outskirts of Accra. She reminded him of a beautiful, talented storyteller he had spent time with centuries ago.

"Make it a hot dark chocolate, like you," Anancy said smoothly, meaning every word...

She blushed.

"When you bring it to me, blow at the steam twice to cool it. A blessing will come your way."

Her eyes flickered as Anancy's words slipped past her

awareness. Still smiling, she turned to leave, and he froze time to admire her. Frozen in time and space, the spider god promised himself he would see her again as a famous poet at another juncture, in another timeline. They would share a bed, and after love making, she'd be inspired to even higher heights. He exhaled smoke from his cigar and broke the spell. Impeccable timing actually as the man he wanted to watch, the serial killer, Igor Rakmanov, walked into the café.

SCAN ME

Chapter Twenty-Three

The armoured truck was being escorted by two armed riders who tried to keep a discreet distance as it left the secure confines of the Biotech facility on Wharton Street. The refrigerated container would leave the city, and at a designated spot in Kent, the riders would hand off the babysitting duties to another security detail that would usher the precious cargo to its final destination. This had been the fourth truck this week, and the process had become rote for the organisers. They had thrown in some variety regarding the routes out of the city and the locations in Kent where the handover took place. But that was the sum total of their creativity. To predict their movements required someone with discipline and patience. It would be difficult, if not impossible, to predict their movements beforehand without time spent surveilling them.

Kintu didn't need to guess.

On this occasion, he would follow the truck where it left the secure facility in the city. And for the fifth time this week, their cargo would reach its destination without incident. Kintu throttled the big Triumph modified to accommodate his frame and weight, pulling behind the convoy and preparing to strike.

A crackle in his helmet comms broke his focus. He flipped up the dark visor and felt the wind in his face; Sister Anastasia was monitoring the situation from their base of operations in London. Over the centuries, the Mechanics of Jesus had learned they couldn't stop the wilful nature of Kintu, so they might as well protect him from himself.

"If I'm correct," she said, her French accent strong. "Their route out of the city may involve a stretch of the industrial road quite far from population areas."

"How far away are we from that stretch of road?" Kintu asked.

"Approximately four point five kilometres," Sister Anastasia came back. "I've just sent it to the heads-up display in your helmet. We will monitor the convoy and let you know if it makes any corrections. But if it remains on course, you will only have ten minutes to disable and inspect it before the authorities are contacted."

"Hum!" Kintu made the sound issue from his throat and nose simultaneously. "That is adequate time for what I need to do."

"Affirmative," the nun controller said.

"I will ensure there are no further surprises ahead of us, and then we will conclude this dry run. In forty-eight hours, we will do this for real."

Kintu flipped down the visor on his helmet, becoming anonymous again and proceeded to follow the convoy at a safe distance.

. . .

The ladies of Bad II the Bone were chilling in the vast lounge of the mansion. Y and Suzy played chess, and Patra had her sound-cancelling headphones on. Even Nanny had joined them, sat in her favourite rocking chair, knitting needles in hand, the ball of wool on her lap, her ageless albino features looking content. Mei Ling, the cat having returned from the temple in China days earlier, lay asleep at Nanny's feet. The 80-inch TV was playing, but the sound was mute.

Y had propped her chin on her fists and surveyed the chessboard in front of her. She loved playing with Suzy because they both commenced a match in silence. It was combative and meditative at the same time. Patra was just too loud, especially if she won. Telling you the steps she took to destroy you was her favourite thing. It wasn't a formal rule or anything, but both women enjoyed it. The silence did something for them both. They would change the rules when it no longer worked for them, but for now, they enjoyed it. Y reached down to move the queen when her mobile phone started ringing. She looked genuinely surprised. Another one of their unspoken rules was when they played, all mobile phones were muted and placed on flight mode. Y knew she had done that, and yet here was the phone ringing again. Suzy sensed something, too, and looked over to her sister's smartphone.

"Yuh bettah answer it," Suzy said.

Y reached over and picked it up and looked at the screen expecting it to be Spokes. He was the only person she knew that could bypass the settings of her smartphone and possibly any other piece of communication equipment. The screen read an unknown caller.

Y shrugged.

"Hello," Y said simply.

"Miss Sinclair?" The voice that asked the question had a profound air to it.

"Who's asking?" Y said. "And how did you get my number?"

The man on the other end ignored the two questions and continued with what he needed to say.

"We met under unfortunate circumstances at the boat club. You and your sisters were impressively disguised, and I had to leave prematurely through a five-storey window."

Y knew who it was immediately. She smoothly placed her phone on the chessboard knocking over the players. She had Suzy's immediate attention when she switched to speakerphone with a deft dance of her fingers. Patra was oblivious to what was going down until Suzy grabbed a pawn and threw it at her. Miss Jones plucked the projectile out of the air without looking at it and flipped her headphone off, readying herself to swear at whoever was fucking with her. She caught on quickly. Jumping out of her chair, she walked over to her sisters on the phone, which had become the centre of attention.

"How did you get my number?" Y asked again.

The voice came again, confident and calm.

"Good evening, Miss Young, Miss Jones."

"Waddup!" Patra said.

Suzy turned to her shaking her head and placed a finger to her lips.

Patra grinned mischievously.

"To answer your question, Miss Sinclair, you're not the only one who has been touched by the inexplicable and because of the horror of circumstance, given purpose."

"And your purpose is murder?" Y asked.

"My purpose is to eradicate men who deserve that blessing. The men who are helping to fuel the imbalance you and your sisters are ordained to correct. Like you, I have no choice in becoming who I am. And neither am I naïve about the world we inhabit. We do not have the luxury to dismiss the ills of the world."

Suzy leaned into the conversation.

"You know so much about us, but we know nothing about you."

The sound of the gurgling fragrance diffuser in the room felt louder than it actually was. The pregnant pause magnified everything around them in anticipation of his reply.

"Forgive me," he finally said. "I call myself Kintu, and I'm the result of morally bankrupt men who wield the power of the gods but lack the conviction of one."

"It sounds personal, G?" Patra asked.

"It is, Miss Jones."

"You know we wouldn't be having this discussion if my sister here didn't think there was something honourable about you," Y said.

"I understand," Kintu said. "And I appreciate your assessment of my character. But whether you think me worthy or not, my mission continues. I just felt it would be prudent for you to realise that we share a common enemy. We may tangle from time to time but remember, our methods are different. And I make no apologies for that."

"And this is your way of an introduction?" Y asked.

"That's correct, Miss Sinclair, but it's also a veiled warning. I will stop at nothing to fulfil my promise. Do not stand in my way."

"What makes you tink we will make you stand in the way of our purpose?" Suzy asked.

He gave a deep-throated chuckle.

"I would expect nothing less from the famous Guardians of the Light."

"Staying out of each other's way may be a good idea," Y

said. "But a better plan would be for you to give us more background on our shared enemy."

There was silence again as the voice on the other end considered the request.

"I can do much better than that," Kintu said. "You will hear from me."

The connection broke, and their introduction ended with more questions than answers.

Chapter Twenty-Four

"I don't know what deh rass is going on exactly," Spokes whispered, his voice harsh and trembling. "But something is brewing, Sister Y, and it feels bad."

Y still had her gloved finger on the text of an old book when Spokes frantic voice on the phone made her stop and pay attention.

"Where are you?" Y sat up, her full focus on the call. Spokes' calm persona was shaken and that was unusual. It worried her.

"I'm still at the warehouse at the Ramsey Industrial estate. I was finishing up my paperwork when deh Snake Head ring start going crazy. I'm seeing red, literally, an my head is bursting. Death is on its way, Sister Y."

"And so are we," Y said, bounding out of the library. "Get your arse to the panic room now. We're on our way."

EVEN THOUGH HE WAS TOLD TO GET TO THE PANIC ROOM asap, Spokes made a detour, and his Snake Head ring did not like it at all. The security control room was manned during the day and was fully automated at night. Spokes had outfitted the premises with state-of-the-art electronic surveillance and subvention breach systems, ensuring his clients' goods were protected. And, of course, some Orisha Guardian magic for anything greater or lesser than a human being courtesy of his Nigerian Shaman. He sat at one of the four chairs and scanned through all of the CCTV cameras around the perimeter of the building. He saw nothing but Tricky, his driver, parked in his space, waiting patiently for him.

"Bloodclaat!" Spokes spat a dark realisation making his heart pound. Whatever was on its way would cross paths with his childhood friend and chauffeur. He grabbed his phone and called him. The phone rang as he paced, urging Tricky to pick up his phone but instead, it went to voicemail. Spokes spun on his heel and headed towards the panic room while leaving a message.

"Listen to mi carefully, Tricky; do not wait for me. Go now, right now, and as soon as you get home, give me a call. Don't wait another second. Call me as soon as you get home."

Spokes stared at the phone for a moment and swallowed hard. Waves of discomfort emanated from his guard ring, screaming in its own way. It was shouting at the top of its metaphorical lungs, pleading with him to protect himself. He thought of rushing out there to warn his driver, but his snake-head ring would not allow it. The force within the Mesopotamian treasure would paralyse him if it felt he was running willingly into danger. If he continued defying its warnings, the ring would hijack his nervous system and frogmarch him to safety. Spokes gritted his teeth. His indecision was becoming painful. How could he leave Tricky out there knowing what was coming?

His eyes scanned the monitors again, focusing on the Rolls

Royce Phantom. He looked away, trying to clear the throbbing pain in his head. Looking back, he saw the headlights turn on, and the luxury car started to edge forward.

"Thank you, God, thank you," Spokes rejoiced. After watching his car depart, he turned to leave the surveillance room. His jangling nerves subsided, and his headache ebbed away as he hurried towards the panic room. He would speak to Tricky tomorrow and pour a few shots from his Appleton Rum collection to apologise. All he had to do now was lock himself away and get comfortable until the girls came calling.

PATRA SWITCHED OFF THE ENGINE OF THE BENTLEY GT and let it silently roll down the shallow hill, then pulled on the emergency brakes. From here, it would be a five minute brisk walk to the guarded entrance into the industrial estate. All three women exited the car in black tactical gear and their favoured weapons. Y had her samurai sword slung around her shoulders, Suzy Wong carried two butterfly knives at the base of her spine, Patra had a telescopic Bo Staff over her back, and her ball bearing pouch on her belt. There was no need for words as Y sprinted towards the entrance. The three noiseless shadows were met with their first sign of destruction that would only worsen as they proceeded. The guard house was damaged from the impact of a fast-moving vehicle in the barrier arm torn from the gate control mount with pieces of the plastic housing and metal parts scattered all over the road. Some tyre marks were embossed on the pulverised debris. Suzy picked something up from the ground, observed it carefully and looked over to Y, who transmitted her findings. Y took a deep breath, squinted her eyes and carefully pulled the Katana from her back. All three nodded to each other, their silent communication crystal clear in their minds, and they sprinted off in three different directions.

Y APPROACHED THE BUILDING FROM THE FRONT AND CAME across Spokes' Rolls Royce Phantom, undamaged but driven off the road. Her breath caught in her throat as she came closer to the vehicle. The white leather interior was splashed with blood. For a moment, she imagined Spokes had tried to escape and was caught, his ring failing him for the very first time. Her physiology may have looked calm as she came around to the driver's side, but the years of being more than an ordinary woman did not detract from the effect violent death had on her. Her shoulders slumped slightly; it was never easy to see, especially if it was someone you knew. Y's chest felt hollow, and cold anger rose up in her. She looked on at Tricky's headless body still in the driver's seat but slumped forward on the steering wheel. On the seat behind him was his head. His mouth was agape, and his eyes wide with horror or surprise. It was rolled on its side in a pool of blood.

"Goddamit, you didn't deserve that," Y said to herself. "Another innocent casualty. Fuck!" She bowed her head, tapped the window three times helplessly with the hilt of her Katana, and reigned in her anger. She spun on her heels, blending with the darkness as she made her way to the reception area.

SUZY'S FINGERS DANCED OVER THE KEYPAD IN THE darkness. There was a Beep! Beep! sound and a compartment slid open, revealing a glowing red cyclopean sensor array that identified her by scanning Suzy's retina. Silently the door that didn't seem to exist a minute ago opened, and Suzy slipped through, butterfly knives in both hands. As far as she could tell – Spokes wouldn't be stupid enough to try and lie to her – the girls had access to every real estate he owned scattered around the UK and the world. He was content in the knowledge they would have no red tape preventing them from fulfilling their duties. Even so, her fellow Jamaican was as suspicious as a man surprised by the sun always setting in the East and not the West. Very few things relaxed him completely, and he gained a perverse pleasure in dealing with the intricacies of the supernatural world that they all shared. From the errant emotions she detected bouncing around the warehouse, this was one aspect of his life that Spokes did not appreciate.

And it was justifiable.

Small tremors of anxiety vibrated in her chest. Something was in here with him. Something with no soul, no emotion, no empathy but single-minded purpose. Spokes had a knack for upsetting powerful people, and he wasn't about to stop now. Suzy moved swiftly through the aisles and well-stocked industrial shelves. It didn't stop her from taking action, but she couldn't completely ignore it either. A bitter taste of gall spread across her tongue, making her saliva glands pump to mask the fowl taste. As unladylike as it was, she spat on the floor while she made her way to the centre of the warehouse.

She stopped abruptly.

Then suddenly twirled both butterfly knives in her hands, fluttering dangerously like the wings of a bird of prey. Suzy kept moving towards the panic room planted dead centre in the warehouse maze. It had normal pretensions of being anything else, other than a reinforced safe that had been modified for human habitation. It could sustain two people for at least a month if required. A circular pattern of Orisha glyphs was burnt into the floor surrounding it; the spell activated when Spokes crossed over it and formed a mystical barrier against an impressive list of threats. Suzy had a feeling the precautions had not been enough of a preparation for the threat lurking in the shadows. She remained alert and held her ground, waiting for her sisters to join her.

PATRA LET HERSELF IN VIA THE GOODS BAY, CLOSING THE big shutter behind her as she entered the darkness. It seemed Suzy had already found a panic room and was emanating a warning that gave Patra goosebumps. She picked up speed as she hustled through the maze of the warehouse. She had a lot to tell them, but in times like this, speaking was so awkward. Instead, she allowed her unspoken observations and sense impressions to be transmitted to her sister through their spooky Wi-Fi. They'd be up to speed when she got to the panic room. Someone had breached the security of the building, but Patra couldn't reconstruct who or what had caused the damage the building had suffered. To her, it looked like parts of the metal skin that made up the superstructure had been punctured by small explosions along the parameter. Patra had counted seven ruptures and debris from what had carried the ordnance in the first place. At first, she had thought it was some kind of incendiary device, but there were no fires, just lingering smoke and the smell of C4. How did she know that? When certain pieces of information were needed, they presented themselves. That's all she could say. Being a Guardian had its perks. And one of those perks was her heightened senses. You would think her fear response would be one of the emotions her talents as a Guardian would see fit to eliminate but no. The ancient instinct of fight or flight stubbornly remained. And if Patra could light up in the dark from the fire of apprehension burning inside her, she would. She was on a razor's edge and frustratingly unable to locate the apparent threat surrounding her.

This was a goddamn trap, and she could do nothing about it. Patra reached the end of a corridor formed from crates and came into the open area inhabited by the panic room. The forms of Suzy and Y were silhouettes standing back to back, weapons in hand, eyes sparkling, and ears peeled. Patra hurried over to join them and form the triad, and immediately they began to function as a seamless unit.

"Let's get him out," Y said, moving over to the illuminated keypad. Suzy and Patra closed in to protect her back as she entered the six-digit number. There's a clockwork- Click! Click! Whirr! Then the Clunk! Clunk! Clunk! Clunk! Clunk! The five titanium bars pulled free from the circular door's reinforced frame. Y pulled the mechanically assisted wedge of steel at the crack. The smell of vanilla wafted out with a glimmer of bright white light triggering mayhem. Blisteringly fast, something darted from the darkness of the ground, leaping towards a gap between the door. Y's reflexes were faster, and her pattern recognition was almost spot on. Almost. She slammed the door shut with a shoulder check, trapping and crushing whatever tried to slip through. The remains hung from the door, and Y could see it more clearly now.

Fingers?

Her mind immediately searched for what the appendages were connected to. Something didn't seem right.

Before she could conclude she was going insane, the evidence that she wasn't came into grotesque view. The memory of the glass cube with abomination of a brain attached to articulated spider legs scarred her recollection. It was the same insane creation, the same twisted mind.

It was a big hairy hand with the manner of a spider. All five fingers acted as legs, and the thick severed wrist had an electronic collar around it, emitting a muffled buzzing sound.

Good Girls Gone Bad

Another of its kin fell from somewhere above and scurried beside the first. Then came a third and the fourth.

"You got to be fucking kidding me," Patra pulled her extendable Bo staff from her back, twisted it and felt the satisfying vibration as it reached its full length in her hand. She twirled it once and pointed it to the creatures. They were not impressed and they attacked.

Bad II the Bone were coiled like springs. They moved out from each other like blooming flower petals, precise but choreographed. An invisible zone of awareness formed in their perception. Anything that breached that bubble was in the kill zone, something the hand spiders would learn first-hand. The attack came in one unrelenting wave. The hand spiders were blisteringly fast, strong and nimble. Suzy took to the air as one of the things fell from above. Her butterfly knives fluttered above her head and her attacker rained down as a gross creamy fluid, severed fingers, electronic parts and the shredded meat of the palm.

Suzy danced away from the deluge but another fell from above and bounced off her shoulder to the ground. Its dark essence and the driving motivation that had been programmed to kill Spokes was like a beacon in Suzy's head. A nasty smudge of depravity she would need some meditation time to remove. She stepped back, readying herself. It hit the ground like a one-handed man trying to clap and turned, lowered its centre of gravity and, with its powerful fingers, leaped back at Suzy. Orienting herself, so she didn't clash with her sisters, she made a micro adjustment and then locked eyes on it, but it was too late; it reached her throat. Suzy slipped her hand between it and her neck and felt the crushing power of the thing. It tried to gain a better grip, a throat-crushing, neck-snapping grip, but Suzy wouldn't allow it. Gritting her teeth, she closed her eyes and imagined the hand was attached to her body and with a subtle twist, pressure on a nerve bundle in the wrist that would immediately make any attacker relent. Instead, this one was animated by magic and science, devoid of nerve impulses but not completely disobeying the laws of biology. Suzy slowly pried its fingers back digit by digit, then flung it to the ground. It skidded and scrambled for purchase, turned and sprang back at her, but this time she was ready. It was sliced and diced in mid-air, its meaty pieces scattering to the ground.

With a cleansing breath and thousands of hours of practice, Y forced some of her Lifeforce into her Katana, making the Masamune sword glow blue. She focused on the ground as the sound of fingernails darting towards her increased. Y fanned her blade as it darted into the path of the esoteric energy and steel. What was human flesh was shredded, and the supernatural elements dissipated violently.

Patra's staff was moving with such speed it was humming, its song only interrupted by smashing into or impaling the Spider Hands. Stepping back, Patra twirled the staff around her neck stylishly, catching it with one hand to grip it in a mantis stance when Miss Jones felt the tingle of her luck factor kicks into play. One of the creatures sprang out of the murk but was caught by the arc of Patra's staff, swatting it into the path of Suzy's butterfly knives and making short work of it.

"Mi count ten a dem," Suzy said, sweeping their surroundings with her senses.

"Yeah, I think we got every one of these nasty motherfuckers. Every one." Patra agreed.

"Let's calm ourselves and make sure," Y said.

They quieted themselves as Suzy reached out.

"Sense anything else?" Y asked, looking at her sister minutes after.

Suzy shook her head, rubbing her neck.

"Nothing that is a direct threat to us," she says.

"Good enough," Y said. "Let's try that again." She keyed in the access code and swung open the big door.

In a moment, Spokes stepped out with a cigar between his lips.

"What deh rass happened? An why are we in deh dark."

IN THE SHADOWS, A CREATURE LURKED THAT SHOULD NOT be able to exist but did. The horrific jigsaw puzzle of human parts scuttled out of its hiding place. Its single eyeball rolled in its orbit, taking in a 360° vista of the violent scene and carefully observing the humans making their way out of the warehouse. It had seen it all. This model was not designed for conflict but for surveillance. The human eye was attached to a cartilaginous stalk riddled with blood vessels and twitching muscle fibres. Locomotion was accommodated by the human hand it was attached to, with a functioning human ear grafted into the back of the hand. The entire skirmish was transmitted to its maker for storage. Its solid-state brain absorbed more data from the carnage, but it would finish its analysis later. It would follow the humans and record more of their activity and conversation. Its maker needed to know more about the enemies taking arms against him.

Chapter Twenty-Five

A corridor of opportunity opened ahead of him, right where the controllers said it would be. It was a perfect stretch of road. On your left was a river, fenced off for the entire length. On its other bank were rows of warehouses from obscure and popular brands. On the right, one more business, similarly fenced, protecting the back of even more business real estate. Kintu accelerated on the modified Triumph and ate up the distance he had allowed between himself and the truck. The aggressive growl of his bike made one of the motorcycle escorts look back. Kintu couldn't see his expression but imagined his horror when he saw another rider all in black accelerating towards him with one gloved hand outstretched with a machine pistol pointed at him. Kintu recognised the micro-expression the rider made; he could see the bunching of muscles as he prepared to warn his colleagues and take evasive action. But Kintu was born of the lightning, and his reflexes were equally rapid. He pulled on his hair-trigger three times precisely. Kintu was looking away before the bullets impacted.

Front tyre.
Back tyre.
Thigh.

A spurt of blood erupted from the rider's leg as he lost control and smashed into the mesh fence. His team took notice, hearing the clamour and realising their number had depreciated by one. Kintu released the handles of his bike for a moment, grabbed the throat of his assault weapon and cranked it. He expertly controlled the motorbike with his left hand and cradled a gun in his right. Kintu veered right and fired once.

Clunk!

And then again.

Clunk!

Two magnetic discs sprang from his weapon, aimed at both escort riders on the right side of the truck. Both projectiles expertly attached to the axle of the wheels. Kintu braked, falling back and veering left just as the twin explosions disabled the other two riders. He wasn't sure if the truck driver knew what was happening because it had maintained its speed throughout. By this, it must have noticed three of its security detail had disappeared and the fourth had ridden away, leaving it to fend for itself. Its journey was about to end prematurely. Kintu revved his beast of a motorbike and hurtled ahead of the truck. A mile in advance, Kintu parked the bike and unfolded a forty-foot rubber-like strip he had wrapped around his huge shoulders and chest like a bandolier. He flung it across the road, anchoring one end of the prototype and allowing the rest of it to cling to the road surface as it automatically blended into the colour and texture of the road. Kintu looked up to see the truck approaching at speed and the driver stepping on his air horn, with no intention of stopping. The giant figure shook his head disappointingly and stepped off the road. He pulled up the sleeves of his tactical jacket, revealing a control console wrapped around his arm.

He spoke to it.

"Arm!" he said simply, and the tyre deflation device suddenly bristled with jagged spikes. The truck driver saw it and obviously knew what it was and stamped on the brakes. Smoke issued from the undercarriage of the trailer, and the squeal of locked tires was ripping through the sleepy industrial estates. Kintu was impressed by the driver's skills as he barely kept the truck from flipping. Tyres shredded, and the trailer had jack-knifed to a stop, blocking most of the road. Before a confused driver could regain his composure, Kintu tore off the cab door, grabbed the driver by the scruff of the neck and dismissively flung him into the fence 15 feet away. The mesh metal fence sagged from the impact, and the unconscious body rolled to the grass verge. Kintu walked to the back of the trailer, his helmet still on and the visor down. He detached the buckle from his belt, another toy from the R&D Department of the Order of Mechanics of Jesus. He attached the magnetic Claymore to the advanced lock keeping the rear doors close to his prying eyes. He twisted it clockwise, making the disc light up with circular LEDs radiating from a central point in rhythmic pulses.

Kintu walked away before it exploded.

Y was getting used to his call.

She was about to step into the shower when her iPhone vibrated on the bed. Unknown Caller showed up on the screen then it began ringing, although it shouldn't have. The giant Kintu had his ways, and a sense of humour as a ringtone always played the finger-snapping theme song of the classic TV series The Munsters when he called.

Y smiled and picked it up.

"I didn't think I would be hearing from you so soon since the last time we talked," said Y.

"Ah, my apologies for interrupting your bath, but I promised you information, and I'm a man of my word. I have attached a video file you should find interesting. It may shed some light on your own investigation."

"What will your information prove?" Y asked. "How can we use it if I am not sure of your motives? This could be a total distraction from what is really going on."

"That is for you to decide. All I can do is provide you with clarity."

"What do you really want, Kintu?"

"I respect your institution," Kintu said. "I've heard stories of the exploits of your ancestors. And they are tales of honour and bravery. I trust what you represent."

"Thank you," Y said. "I think."

"And that is my quandary, Ms Sinclair. I'm conflicted. I know the tsunami that is about to come, and I also know what I'm committed to doing to prevent it. I would be doing you a disservice if I didn't at least prepare you." Kintu sighed. "Consider yourself prepared."

He hung up.

Y took the phone from her ear and rested it on her forehead, deep in thought. Kintu was convincing, but Y would still tread carefully even if Patra and Suzy thought he was cool. She scrolled through her messages and saw the attachment Kintu had sent. Y let the towel wrapped around her fall to her feet. Without looking, she threw the phone on the bed and stepped into the cool tiles of the bathroom.

. . .

"Ow!" Patra complained as she was slapped on her arm by a comb Suzy was wielding. "Bitch, that hurt!" She continued to express her dissatisfaction. This was supposed to be relaxing as she sat between Suzy's legs, her outstretched feet pampered by Y.

But it wasn't.

"Beggars can't be choosers," Suzy said, parting Patras hair into the beginning of a field of Bantu bumps. "If you keep moving about, gal, expect another one. Ants a bite yuh?"

While she was at it, Patra mumbled something about Suzy's cornbread colloquialisms and bad-mouthed Jamaica in the process.

Suzy ignored her.

Y would not be left out of poking fun at their sister's expense.

"You do know I've got sharp implements down here, right?" Y added, sitting cross-legged on the floor at Patra's feet, giving her a pedicure. "Relax and keep still."

"This sucks," Patra moaned. "You'all supposed to make me relax, but instead, you're stressing me the fuck out."

Y laughed.

"I haven't even begun to stress you out yet. Just wait until you see this."

"What?" Suzy asked.

Patra's eyes gleamed with inquisitiveness.

Y took a deep breath.

"Kintu sent me a video that he wants us to all look at." Y stood up from her cross-legged position in a graceful corkscrew and then hurried away. Moments later, she returned with her Apple Mac Pro. Y perched it on the large circular coffee table, opened the video file and pressed play. Patra was about to get comfortable, but Suzy tugged on her hair, the message sent that she was still under the control of the hairdresser from hell.

. . .

THE GIRLS SAT WATCHING THE VIDEO SHOT FROM A headcam and being narrated by Kintu in silent amazement. This shot of the devastation the giant had caused was impressive, but he was focused on the dark interior of the 40-foot trailer. He'd done this before. He reached into his tactical vest, took out, broke and shook some glass ampoules, and threw them into the back, illuminating the interior.

He then nimbly hopped inside.

Condensation hung languidly in the refrigerated interior. The inside was filled with rows and rows of chrome shelves, divided into self-contained sections with their own independent power supplies. There were six rows on each side, and in the central aisle, portable units were anchored in place with straps. Kintu gestured to one of them and felt for a switch on the unit side and flipped it. The large jars in each section illuminated, and floating in a pale mauve solution, in a cloud of bubbles, were human brains. Kintu silently walked through every section, highlighting human organs on display, from kidneys to eyeballs, and they all showed signs of function outside the human body. Kintu casually jumped out of the truck to the tarmac and resumed his explanation of the macabre consignment he had just shown them.

"Our mutual enemy has been transporting a few of these consignments weekly to his research and development facility in Kent. He has the financial resources, the contacts and the henchmen to acquire the body parts he needs. Your friend Spokes tried to interrupt his supply chain by accident, and you witnessed first-hand his disapproval. Why he is collecting body parts illegally is a question for another time. But rest assured, his motives are dishonourable, and if he is allowed to continue, your situation will worsen. We will talk again after you've digested what you've seen and heard; the authorities are on their way."

The video stream pointed to the ground for a moment then it was back up at Kintu in all his scarred beauty, staring at the camera, his brown eyes flecked with ice.

"Be careful, this madman will not stop until his twisted mind is satisfied you have paid for your indiscretion. Do not take him for granted."

The video abruptly stopped.

"What do you think?" Y finally asked.

"I like his style," Patra said. "That nigga came prepared."

"For real," Suzy agreed. "But him have a good heart but driven by vengeance. I really think him want to help; it's just that..."

"What?" Y looked at her sister's confused expression.

"An emptiness," Suzy began. "Every living ting have what feels like a full cup to me, even the more exotic creatures we come across, but he is empty of that. It's just strange."

Patra shrugged.

"As long as it's not bat shit crazy or I want to rip off your head and lay eggs in your guts, strange, I'm good wid it."

"He knows a lot more about what's going on than we do," Y said. "And he has pointed us in the right direction to investigate more for ourselves. It would be rude if we don't accept his invitation."

"I think so, too," Patra said. "Let's poke our noses where they don't belong."

"That sounds like a plan to me," Suzy said.

Chapter Twenty-Six

Bioenhancement R&D Division, Secret Location, London

The musical energy of Papa Wemba filled the autonomous surgical booth with life. But not the kind of life that this place was made for. Six refrigerated surgical booths were set side-by-side with six corpses on metal tables and five sets of robot arms performing delicate surgical procedures. All the units moved in concert, programmed to remove and replace organs that had been acquired and prepared to bring the dead back to life and make them stronger and more resilient.

They did not tire or doubt themselves.
They did not have fear or conscience.
They were perfect soldiers, perfect killing machines.

The music of the gears and servo units formed a backdrop only his ears could appreciate. Dr Ulysses Kayanga was in pale blue surgical scrubs, both eyes looking through 1000x magnifying lenses attached to his PPE, performing the reanimation prep he had developed and perfected from Dr Frankenstein's research and experiments. Kayanga was a man from a different era. Although his genius was unparalleled, he would not pass up any opportunity to test his skill and expertise against machines he had developed. He may not have their speed when it came to pure efficiency – they were second to none. What they lacked was artistry. He held in his hand a synthetic heart that he would place in the chest of one of his soldiers. After connecting nerves and blood vessels to the pump, he made a few minor tweaks that his three hundred years of experience afforded him. He was satisfied that the unit he was working on would be twenty percent more efficient than her other undead comrades. Kayanga noted the model number for a leadership role when he brought this unit to life. All of this was in preparation and no matter how many agents of chaos they sent his way, they couldn't stop him.

These Guardians of the Light did not know what was at stake here. How far he would go to fulfil his destiny. He had learned all he could from Frankenstein himself. His creations, a combination of advanced science and arcane metaphysics that only his genius could reproduce, had reached the limits of their function. His mercenaries could only live for 13 hours, 33 minutes and six seconds. Nothing he had tried could power the body of a reanimated corpse for longer. Whether he used chemical or atomic methods, his creations could not last. This was how it could have ended for him. He'd be transforming the fortunes of the Congo with his army of limitations. This was not acceptable. He couldn't live with defeat like this; that was not who he was. Kayanga was driven and immortality had not dimmed his energy. After centuries of an exhaustive search, he discovered the reason for the limitations of his creations. It was under his nose, all this time.

The Odin storm, as Frankenstein described it. That was the key.

It was the lightning.

He had not understood why the doctor insisted on using

the primal energy from thunderstorms, while the genius of Mr Fairweather could have developed a generator for him even if no such machine existed. Yet, Frankenstein continued with his methods. His notes briefly mentioning the storm's significance, yet Kayanga felt the doctor knew more than he had documented.

That was only the beginning of his issues. Not every lightning storm was made equal. He may not have said it – Dr Frankenstein kept lots of secrets that died with him, but he used his supernatural connections to find a Stormbringer Witch to precisely locate the Odin storm as it formed. Now that Kayanga understood the factors at play, he had discovered his version of the Scottish Stormbringer Witch that Frankenstein had used that fateful night in the Austrian Alps. A South African woman from the Xhosa tribe had sniffed out where the storm would strike. And finally, his warriors would have the life span of gods, and him, the military power to overthrow governments. They would all have to wait in line because Antoinette would be the first recipient of eternal life.

He paused with the laser scalpel in his hand before slicing an artery and recalled it had been over two hundred years since the woman he loved walked among men. She was contained in suspended animation, a process that was both mystical and scientific in nature. Over the centuries, the spell that kept her looking beautiful and unravaged by time required he obtain totems hidden within certain special people. He had created tools to detect the energies these people carried around with them. Then he would harvest the totem which was in the form of an organ with the help of his apprentice Igor. Once found, these organ donors would die in the process of extraction but it was for a higher purpose.

His purpose.

Antoinette was between life and death. Her memories

looped in a head filled with ideas created with nowhere to go. All her normal biological functions were held in limbo. No breath, no excretion, no ageing but only brain function and thought. She had had over two hundred years to think about being with him and no one else. And if that wasn't enough time for the headstrong Antoinette, then he had methods to break her conviction. Whichever version of Antoinette joined him from death, he would get what he wanted; he always did.

Dr Kayanga hung the laser scalpel on a magnetic docking platform to his right. All the operating tools he needed were easily accessible. He required his hands for what he was about to do next. He raised a hybrid heart from the chest cavity, felt its power quotient through his rubber gloves and checked to see if connections were correctly in place and blood vessels modified to carry a souped-up version of plasma to this powerhouse heart. The LED light above caught the odd angles of the heart, making it sparkle. At that moment, with his hands lifted with a miracle between his fingers, Kayanga looked like he was making an offering to the gods. Satisfied, he slotted the unit back into the chest cavity and felt the mild suction pull it into place. He was done. There'd be a preliminary heart function test before her reinforced chest would be fused back into place. Then she would be stored away with her brothers and sisters in refrigerated units until the Shango storm – his new name for the event – came calling.

The Day of Awakening.

That day could not come soon enough.

Chapter Twenty-Seven

The Black Book Division offices were buzzing. All six of Shaft's researchers and analysts were working on the serial killer case and a supposedly related case of organ trafficking. As usual, it would have taken him weeks to discover the connections, but Bad II the Bone had figured out this tangential line of enquiry was an integral part of his mystical serial killer investigation. It would have been good if they knew the fine details, but that was left for him and his team to discover. Shaft was happy with the final iteration of his analyst team – the Witches of Farringdon, as he called them. The analysts that came before were cool but nothing like his current team. And to think it came about from a random thought that blossomed in his mind from seemingly nowhere.

The question he asked himself was, could he find ESP talent in the ranks of the Metropolitan Police force?

Shaft thought that being around his girlfriend and her spooky sisters had dredged up the idea from his subconscious. But whatever the cause, the idea was genius. And to answer the question, yes. He could find talent, and he did.

What was even smarter was how he came to discover the talent in the first place. Shaft had obtained his Master of Science in Anthropology, which wasn't just about understanding tribal societies but human culture on every level. Shaft had committed ten years of his life to understanding the varied facets of police culture. He knew how they functioned. He was a keen observer of a complex society. The rank and file of the Metropolitan Police followed patterns they didn't even realise they exhibited. The institution had high ideals, but it consisted of a bunch of modern-day apes running around with evolutionary baggage.

They were prejudiced, and they feared the unknown.

Shaft looked at personal files that were flagged with reprimands; disciplinary and employment tribunal. Some were troublemakers, but others were misunderstood and therefore targeted. Why it was a hotbed of psychic abilities he had no idea. All he knew was after the unsuspecting candidates were given advanced ESP tests – only the best scores were accepted; he then made up his team.

Spokes was beginning to appreciate why, culturally, witches were vilified and exalted in equal measure while warlocks were ignored. Shaft's ESP tests had discovered some gifted men too. They were less open to the idea of utilising their psychic abilities.

Crispin was the only man on the team and he was their auto visualiser.

You didn't need to be a gay man, artistically gifted or in touch with your spirit, but that seemed to be the profile that worked. That in itself was a study for another time.

Shaft was hunched over his desk, with an area of an otherwise neat and organised surface exploding with printed A4 papers spilling off the desk onto the floor.

"Coffee, Detective?" Shaft looked up at the pretty bespectacled analyst Edwina. He dragged the heavy ball and chain of his thoughts from the world he had occupied for under an hour.

He looked at Edwina blankly, then when his thoughts caught up with him, he said, "You're a lifesaver, thanks."

Edwina had the cup and coffee jug in hand and poured, leaving the cup on his desk. Shaft took a sip and a sigh of pleasure escaped his lips.

Blue Mountain coffee was da bomb.

They deserved it, especially if it was on the Metropolitan Police's dime. They had dithered for years on his request for a paranormal division that would handle the rise in unexplained crimes with a more ethnic bend.

Well, better late than never.

They were forced to take note – and decisive steps – when the supernatural activity began to spill over into the world of Jane and Joe Public. For their reluctance all these years, the least he could do was make them pay through the nose.

Only the best for his team.

It was only on his second sip that Shaft realised Edwina was still watching him at his desk.

"You look tired," she said.

Shaft nodded.

"I know what you're going to say. I'm pushing myself too much. I need to rest."

"Are you?" Edwina asked. "I mean pushing yourself. Because if you are, that's being stupid."

"Don't hold back, tell me how you really feel," Shaft teased.

Edwina smiled.

"Without you, this whole operation collapses. None of us has experience out in the field; we have to rely on you for that."

Shaft could only nod in agreement because he knew she was right.

She was a tall, elegant redhead in her late 50s with 23

years of service in the Metropolitan Police force and her more valuable talents had gone unnoticed all that time. Out of all the ladies in the analyst pool, she fussed over Shaft's welfare more than most. He appreciated it and loved the camaraderie that was developing. They shared personal secrets more easily than most and that tended to bind people together. And Shaft was proud to say it was unique to Black Book.

"We can't help you if you are bed bound because you haven't taken care of yourself," Edwina continued.

"I know, I know," Shaft said. "But I'm so committed to catching this fucker that everything else comes an insignificant second."

"You have doubts you can catch him?" Edwina asked.

"I know we can; I just can't say when," Shaft said.

"So we keep going," Edwina prompted.

Shaft stood up and reached for a chair, sliding it over to his desk. He gestured for her to sit in it.

"Sit with me," Shaft said. She sat, got comfortable and crossed her legs.

"Did you read the report of our last big case?" Shaft asked.

"I read some of it with Donna. Vampires."

Shaft nodded grimly, and Edwina shivered.

"They really do exist," she stated.

"They really do exist. And they're things of nightmare, trust me." Shaft was relaxed as he recounted the memory but had a tremor to his words. "The reports didn't tell you that Miranda Pheare, vampire Queen and mass murderer, got away Scot-free. How do you incarcerate an immortal?"

Edwina made a face.

"You don't think they'll be brought to justice even if the killer is caught, do you?"

Shaft drummed on the desk with his fingers in agreement.

"This time around, things will go differently. I'm going to see to it."

Edwina stood up.

"Your friends, the Guardians, should have some ideas on that."

"They most certainly will," Shaft grinned.

"In the meantime, we have some good news for you," Edwina said.

"Oh!"

"You'll like this. Come over to Narendra's desk."

Shaft slid out of his chair and stood up, walking with Edwina to the other side of the room.

Narendra was on a Wikipedia page reading an entry when Shaft and Edwina came up behind her.

"Edwina, Detective McFarlane," the Indian woman said without turning around. "What can I do for you?"

"Show the detective some of the articles you've dug up," Edwina said.

"Of course," Narendra said and started typing.

Narendra Sethi had come over to Black Book from the narcotics division. Intelligent, hard-working and reserved. Shaft suspected some form of harassment, sexual or racial, had her at his door. And he was so thankful to those cowboy dickheads at narcotics. What had been their loss was his gain.

"I had a feeling about our serial killer after you managed to find out he's Eastern European," Narendra said, still typing away at her terminal. "I couldn't shake it, so I decided to follow up on the hunch with Interpol."

Shaft leaned in, propping his hand on the back of her swivel chair.

"The physical description is vague, five feet five inches approximately and powerfully built, but his MO is distinctive." She paused from typing and turned in the chair to face them. A frown disrupted her soft, beautiful features; long black hair framed her face and intensified her piercing brown eyes.

"I interrogated Interpol's database and came across some obscure CCTV camera footage on some strange murder cases in Paris, Berlin, Rome and Prague."

Shaft started to get animated.

"Have you got anything I can look at?" Shaft asked.

"I'm ahead of you," Narendra said. "This is a case in Prague, five years ago, that involved a victim, Susanna Helotz, who was eviscerated and organs removed. It seemed they had two more cases like it in two weeks." Narendra brought up a video player on her screen and then used her mouse to click the play icon. "This gentleman was seen leaving two of the murder scenes," she said.

Shaft bent down and squinted at the grey and grainy footage. The details of his features were obscured, but the date, his squat physique and the doctor's bag in his gloved hand made him sure he was the perpetrator.

But there was something else.

There were four thick lines tattooed on his wrist. The rest of the design was obscured by his gloves. Shaft vacuumed air into his lungs as if preparing to do battle.

"That's him," Shaft said, tapping his fingers on the desk. "The bastard has been doing this across the continent and possibly the world."

"I think he has," Narendra said. "But to be a jet-setting murderer requires resources. Plenty."

"What compels him to do this?" Edwina asked.

"Get Rosanna to complete that psych profile on him," Shaft said, then paused to think. Something was disturbing him. "Can you send the footage to my monitor?"

Edwina and Narendra looked at each other and smiled at Shaft's lack of tech-savvy.

"Of course," Narendra said, her fingers dancing over the keyboard. "It's on its way to you now."

"This is some stellar work, ladies," Shaft congratulated them. "But what is your ESP telling you? That still small voice you promised to let rip."

Narendra smiled uncomfortably.

Edwina did her nervous shuffle, but both remained silent.

"Forget those fuckers you used to work with before. Black Book is a safe space for your gifts. I want to know what you're feeling."

Narendra cleared her throat.

"When I discovered this lead, my hunch guided me to various European cities. But I felt something else too. It's hard to describe, but it felt like history, like I should be digging further back in the records."

"He can't be by himself," Edwina said. She closed her eyes and cocked her head, breezily taking in secret whispers in the air. "He can't do this alone."

In Shaft's head, he was trying to connect what the girls were investigating and his clues. It was on the fringes of his awareness; it just wasn't coming together yet.

"That murdering piece of shit has been around for years, controlled by a handler pulling the strings." Shaft spun excitedly on the balls of his feet. "Thank you, ladies. Keep digging, keep using your talents, and we'll keep piecing this thing together."

Both ladies nodded, his words obviously encouraging them.

"In the meantime, I want to look through your video footage again, Narendra," Shaft said. "There's something I'm missing."

Chapter Twenty-Eight

This was the fourth night this week that Patra had sat in the twilight of medical machines in the old man's hospital room, keeping vigil with her comatose friend. She always made sure the family left before she snuck in because she knew it would get ugly if they found out she was reading to him. None of this would be possible if not for the beautiful nurse Grace Nkosi. The South African stunner was not just a hottie but a gangsta too. They had met when she walked in on Patra the second time she had sat with the old man. Ignoring her for five minutes, she went about her checks as if Patra didn't exist. Then she asked a single question without even looking at her.

"He means a lot to you, doesn't he?"

"Is it that obvious," Patra had said. A sense of amusement she hadn't known was lurking inside sprang out at that moment, holding its belly with mirth.

Grace gave her a goofy smile and stood reverently listening to Patra reading the boring-arse A Tale of Two Cities by Charles Dickens. The old man's favourite book. The rest was a short and beautiful history. Patra sat quietly thinking about her journey to the hospital and when she was going to tell her sisters about the old man. She wanted to try something first with Nanny's help before she involved them. Keeping up the pretense that everything was okay, especially with the sisters, was impossible. Suzy in particular was treating her with kid gloves because she had detected Patra's pain. But Miss Wong would not intervene until the 'pot runneth over,' as she would say.

Patra wasn't there yet and neither would she ever allow herself to get there. Not with her stubbornness; not with Grace providing moral support. They were alone and the nurse meticulously checked the old man's vital statistics, indicated by the machines at his bedside. When she was satisfied, she scribbled some notes on his chart and hung it up 'old school' at the foot of his bed. Patra sat, arms folded, with her legs stretched out from the standard issue hospital chair that was designed to make your stay brief. Grace came over and sat in Patra's lap. She was petite but well-formed.

Hips and ass for days.

Always neat, her uniform fit like it was tailored and she smelt gorgeous even amongst the lingering antiseptic smells of the hospital.

"I'm gonna get you fired," Patra said, her lips not quite a smile – neither was it a grimace but on the verge of one. Grace shook her head, leaned back and kissed Patra on her cheek.

"You're worried I maybe going too fast, right?"

Patra shrugged.

Grace smiled.

"Relax," Grace said. "I'm a big girl, and I'm one hundred per cent responsible for the direction my life takes. I can't control everything, but what I can control, I will."

"That is gangsta," Patra said slowly. "Most motherfuckers would never consider taking that position with their life."

"I'm not most motherfuckers," Grace said, smiling, the swear word awkwardly leaving her lips.

"I can see that," Patra said, squeezing her around the waist. She wiggled seductively in her lap and stood up.

"I'm going to have to leave you with Giles; the ward is busy tonight. Can you manage alone?" she teased.

"I'll try," Patra leaned back into her chair and folded her arms.

"Any changes in his condition, come get me," Grace said.

Patra nodded and held out her hand. Grace took it, and Patra kissed her fingers. She walked towards the door, straightened her dress and turned to her.

"When are you going to let his next of kin know you've been with him?" Grace asked.

"They not going to appreciate me being here because their bullshit won't wash. I hold them responsible for this. I just can't prove it yet. But when I can, I'm going to bring hell down on their heads. Believe that."

Nurse Nkosi considered Patra's words seriously, then that goofy grin appeared, and she left the room.

Chapter Twenty-Nine

"We didn't do nothin'," one of the suspects with his face planted into the grass verge protested but it was falling on deaf ears. The two-man armed response unit had them on the ground, dragged out of their car at gunpoint after disabling the stolen unit in a short lived high speed chase. One officer covered both men with his MP3 Heckler and Koch while his colleagues searched the Mercedes. A silent strobing police light was on the roof of the SUV. The takedown had been textbook with these two suspects not knowing what had hit them until the unmarked SUV ran them off the road. The two-man police team would wait for backup, but from their self-assured actions, they were sure they had the right men and were going through procedure. The officer rummaging through the stolen Mercedes had discovered a treasure trove of high-end jewellery from Breitling and Rolex to De Beers and Petra diamond necklaces, all boxed up neatly in the front seat.

"Jackpot!" the officer inside exclaimed. "These reprobates

are fucking nicked," he commented. "Caught red-handed because they were greedy morons. You need to see this." He called out to his colleague and then reached down into the well of the second man's side and took out the small black silk bag. It had caught his eye where it lay on the floor. He had a good idea what it was and weighed it in the palm of his hand.

Diamonds.

It was only when the officer slid out of the car that he realised his partner hadn't said a word to him since he commenced the search. The two suspects were still splayed face down in the grass, hands zip-tied behind them but his partner stood staring into the distance, his automatic weapon dangling loosely in his right hand by his side – not standard combat posture, his radio squawking on his shoulder.

"Mick, mate," his partner called out to him with no response. Mick kept looking at something that totally absorbed him in the distance.

"Mick?"

His colleague cocked his head slightly and he saw the blinking blue light flashing at the back of his neck. He slowly walked towards his partner, his finger massaging the trigger guard on his weapon, his senses acute, anticipating a danger he hadn't determined yet. The closer he came to it, the less he understood what he was looking at. Whatever it was, it had attached itself to his partner's neck. His brain was forced to conclude that he was looking at some sort of translucent bat with a blue bioluminescence on its back.

The closer he came to it, the slower he walked.

"What the fuck is ..." the officer murmured, his attention focused on the oddity in front of him and not hearing the fluttering wings getting closer and closer. He reacted to the annoyance by wildly flapping his arms, trying to swat it away but it still landed on his neck.

"Shit!" He panicked and felt the sting. He raised his hand to grasp the thing causing the pain but his arm suddenly stopped in mid motion. With a twitch of his shoulder muscles, an all-consuming pain struck him that travelled from his neck and down his spine. All he could focus on was his body shutting down and soon nothing else mattered. Soon he no longer cared. The body that he once had control over was no longer his, he was now only a passive observer.

"Both biological units attached," Igor said. "The neuroRaptors are in place and awaiting your instructions."

The shadow of Dr Kayanga fell across the monitors and keyboards of the advanced computer station, expertly manned by his Eastern European assistant.

"The police officers are under our control, and the link is stable," Igor said.

The doctor nodded.

"Very well," he smiled. "Instruct them to terminate the target and let me know the results at the Congo charity dinner when it is done."

"As you wish, Sir."

Igor's attention wavered from his Master to the monitors. He hated splitting his focus, especially when the doctor was around. It made him feel his control was slipping. He took a deep breath and wrote a line of code, and left it floating in place. Igor turned in his seat to face the doctor just as he said.

"How do I look?" Kayanga was standing in a tailored tuxedo of dark maroon, white Versace shirt and diamond cufflinks. His black shoes shone.

Igor stood from his chair and adjusted the maroon cravat around the doctor's neck.

"Now, do I look like the Guest of Honour?" the doctor asked.

Igor nodded and smiled tightly. Once the Master had left, his full focus was on the monitors. This evening he would be the puppet master, and he was looking forward to the games he was about to play.

Chapter Thirty

Patra felt the tingle as she brought her growling Kawasaki Ninja to a stop at the traffic lights. She had lived with her preternatural senses for some years now. She wasn't naïve enough to imagine that understanding her gifts in a lifetime would ever be possible but she was an eager pupil. Especially when they were always at hand not just to save her raggedy ass but interpret the dangerous world she inhabited with a fresh perspective a homegirl like her could never hope to understand. Patra looked straight ahead. No vehicles anywhere on either side. She focused on the traffic lights and watched it flicker from red to green, pause a moment and then, just as it was about to revert to red, Patra popped the clutch, wheelied, and sped off. Her adrenaline spiked and the tingle shifted from the back of her neck to the base of the spine.

Oh shit!

Something fucked up was brewing, she could feel it.

That's when she heard the wail of the police siren behind her. Patra slowed and pulled off the road. She dismounted quickly and took off her crash helmet waiting for the police

SUV with the flashing blue lights to come to a stand. The police unit took its time and didn't dim its spotlights. Patra squinted and scowled.

"Punk ass motherfuckers!"

Miss Jones let her gift take the lead in this tango. Altering her environment in imperceptible ways, allowing for the laws of chaos to be less chaotic. The need to know her immediate environment crashed down on her as a sudden compulsion. To her left, two lanes of traffic with the barrier in between. To her right, a grassy area with a bench under a birch tree, a bin, a telecom junction box and two telephone poles. The police SUV just sat there still intent on blinding Patra with its lights.

"What is their deal?" Patra asked herself.

She folded her arms just as the passenger side door opened. The cop that stepped out was unsteady on his feet, tall and fully loaded with Kevlar vest, side arm and his MP4 slung around his neck. The cop was having trouble orientating himself as if he was unsure of where he was. He looked down at his feet then over to the passing traffic then an awkward sweep of his eyes that fell on Patra and stuck. An insincere smile like an opening toadstool took its time to form on his face and remained there. The armed officer started to approach just as his colleague began his slow exit from the police unit too.

Patra stood her ground and watched him approach, every step a meaningful exposé of his frame of mind and it was telling her something disturbing.

"You okay, officer?" Patra called to him not taking her eyes off his spaced-out saunter, hoping he would react to her voice but that peculiar smile remained and a light blue tinge leached from the white of his eyes. Patra held her breath.

The cop hefted the MP4 into his hands and Patra exploded into action. She dove right, her movement a blur and rolled behind the metal box of the telecom hub. There was a pause as her action was so lightning fast, the cop took some time to respond but respond he did. The weapon chattered like it was angrily whispering, high velocity bullets spat into the grass where Patra had once stood digging up the soil in untidy chunks. The cop's eyes registered Patra's trajectory and swung his automatic over to where she was protecting herself. To the untrained eye, the homicidal cops were a bit stiff and awkward but moved perfectly normally when it came to discharging their weapons and tracking Patra's escape. But to Patra, it was as if they were moving through treacle.

As the first cop prepared to strafe the metal box with bullets, Patra had ripped off the door panel that protected the electronics inside. It was to be her shield and discus all rolled into one. She sprinted from behind the metal hub just as it exploded into shrapnel and sparks from the bullets. Patra lifted her shield and scanned the battlefield around her.

The first cop was focused on disintegrating the box and the other cop was walking up to join his colleague and that would not bode well for her chances of survival. As she scurried clear, shield up and making herself a difficult target, Cop Two saw her sliding towards the protection of the bark of the big birch tree. The cop swivelled from his hip and let loose a barrage of bullets in Patra's direction. The shadow of the tree protected her and so did the angle of her shield that ricocheted two or three projectiles.

Patra pressed her back against the gnarly bark of the Birch, took a deep breath and stooped down. Without another thought, she sprang out of the shade of the tree, feet off the ground, the power of a push shooting her forward. She flung her shield with a cry of frustration and a bit of drama. The make shift shield spun out of Patra's hand and the twirling metal struck the park bench, ricocheting off it, correcting its trajectory then smashing into the midsection of trigger-happy

Cop Two. He doubled over, skidding to his knees, his face planting squarely in the grass with a gross slapping sound. Cop One turned on Patra who was out in the open but moving unerringly towards the park bench, her path zigzagging in an attempt to confuse the trigger man – and it did. The park bench wasn't much cover but her luck factor gave her the final push she needed. When Patra's back slapped on the outdoor seating, she used it as a launch pad and exploded herself through the air towards Cop One, who had her in his gun sights.

He pulled on the trigger and the trigger stuck.

Patra's probability nullifying field struck again and she barrelled into the police man with knee and elbow. He was strong, twisting his torso so he had the freedom to swing his weapon up like a club but Patra kept his arm down with her knee and let the hammer of her elbow smash into his forehead.

She did it twice then three times, his eyes rolled back into his head. Nimbly she sprang off him and looked over to Cop Two who was on his hands and knees recovering from what Patra hoped was broken and bruised ribs.

"What the fuck was your deal, bra?" She almost whispered to the cop at her feet. She understood the hunger for power for men like this. Abusing the minority citizens across Europe and the States with impunity. Even for some of these cock sucking, misogynist, racists, trying to murder her straight off the bat was unusual and downright strange. That was not how the game was played. Patra bent and grabbed the unconscious cop by his shoulder and flipped him over on his stomach.

Groaning sounds drifted up from across the grassy knoll as the other cop was attempting to stand on unsteady feet. Patra found herself admiring his grit. She pulled the Taser that was strapped to the leg of the zombie cop she had disabled at her feet. She flipped the power on, felt it humming in her hand, and aimed and fired at his colleague. The electrode barbs hit the cop across from her and fifty thousand volts instantaneously coursed through him, flinging his body jerking on his back.

Patra dropped the Taser and looked back at the cop she had turned over. She easily found what she was looking for and suddenly all this was making sense. The thing attached to the cop's neck made her blood chill. It was like a translucent starfish gripping the back of his neck with a long tail stuck along the vertebrae of his spine, that ended with a smaller version of its head attached to his coccyx. Patra could see the capillary movement of blood through the skin and saw the puncture wounds when the creature took hold. It must have recognised it was being observed and buzzed its wings like a wasp, the blue bioluminescence in its head pulsing.

Patra instinctively stepped back – not feeling less of a warrior but a more prepared one. If this doctor dude was capable of creating these crazy creatures, who knew what other surprises he had up his sleeves. Patra dialled her concerns down and let the situation wash over and around her. There was no immediate threat but she wasn't so sure about its victim. She felt along her right leather trouser leg and unzipped a pocket removing her switchblade. Patra shook her head battling with the decision she had just made but couldn't in good conscience leave the cops in the twin predicament of getting their asses kicked and being under the control of those things' on their necks. She found her leather gloves in another pocket of her rider jacket, putting them on as if she was about to perform surgery. She clamped a small flashlight between her teeth, flicked open the knife and bent down to begin the removal of the creature from his neck.

"Nasty," she moaned as she gripped the deceptively strong gelatinous creature that immediately started wriggling at her touch. Patra thought about the possibility of harming the human host with her efforts, but her sixth sense remained silent as she continued to cut away the fine vessels that had snaked into his skin towards his spinal cord. The holes in the skin were bleeding but not at a rate she was concerned about. It resisted every step of the way. Patra cut it free and flung it to the ground, stamping on it. She hurried over to his partner and did the same for him. At that moment, with the job done, she felt something else. Patra's eyes widened. A dark thought dawned on her.

"Nah! Nah!" She desperately reached for her mobile and started calling Y.

What if the attack wasn't isolated? What if it was planned and orchestrated by the madman to cause maximum damage and confusion? Her sisters' paranormal connection must have been triggered, but she wasn't sure if that was enough preparation for what could be hidden in the shadows for them. Y's phone was ringing without answer. Patra kept trying Suzy as she turned her back on the chaos she had caused, jumped on her bike and rode off into the night, the phone still to her ears.

Chapter Thirty-One

"Deh tings I will do to make a plan come together," Anancy said to himself, looking at the Thunder God seated beside him with a flagon of a frothy alcoholic ginger beer. They had just returned from their adventures, and Anancy had a lot to think about.

The Spider God had never heard of the Lightning Syndicate before; this issue that was developing in his small part of the hidden world of the gods was making him nervous. He liked to have connections everywhere and a little knowledge of everything, but when he realised there was something he knew nothing about, that concerned him. But through his little sparrows, he was beginning to piece together an understanding of what their agenda was. All the Lightning Gods from all the cultures were represented, and they kept the secrets of their powers and dealt with issues that may arise from them. The Realm of the Powers that Be was safe, and so was the Land of the Mortals, but that wasn't the burning issue. One of the secrets that the Lightning Syndicate had kept between themselves had found itself in the hands of men. Men who knew how to use the lightning of the gods and not for the benefit of all mankind either. He needed to know what went wrong. He needed to understand how such knowledge could leave the Realm of the gods and find itself squarely in man's hands. His daughters, the Guardians of the Light, needed to know because they may have to deal with the consequences.

His breddrin Zeus was helpful, but he was weighed down by the ramifications of speaking to someone outside the Syndicate. He needed someone less honourable. The Spider God couldn't wait, his daughters were in danger, and he was required to be the chaperone through the web of threat they found themselves entangled in. He decided to attack another low-hanging fruit with the potential for quick results.

The Norse Gods weren't the easiest people to hold a coherent conversation with, but Anancy loved the challenge, and he also had an advantage none of his kin had at their disposal. Only he knew how to transport himself and others from the dimension they occupied to the earth plane. He considered the possibility of including Loki in his plans but thought better of it. Loki was as sneaky as he was and may have found a route himself out of the realm, but Anancy couldn't deal with his diarrhoea of the mouth and his annoying competitiveness. Anancy had discovered the way and could only facilitate the transfer from the back door.

He wanted this operation to be smooth. And If he was to convince a Thunder God from Earth's history to accompany him to the Lands of the Mortals and have a high probability of having his questions answered, it would be from Odinson. Thor, the blond-headed and boisterous Thunder God, did not believe in keeping his opinions or thoughts to himself. Neither was he a believer in containing his excitement. After getting him to swear secrecy, Anancy had snuck the Thunder God to London, an easy enough task, having done it hundreds of times

Good Girls Gone Bad

himself but it blew Odinson's mind. Once Anancy had softened him up with the many books and comics written about him, the exhibitions and films created in his honour, he was able to start digging for answers to his own questions. Not, however, before he found a pub near the Tower of London and started plying the immortal with cider, ale and bitter. Anancy nursed a bottle of a thousand-year-old rum with cola and used his powers of persuasion to attract other drinkers, especially the ladies, to their table. All evening the God of Thunder regaled his eager fans with tales of adventure derring-do. Once the barrels and tanks were close to empty, Anancy guided his bearded Cinderella back through the wormhole before the metaphorical clock struck twelve. An exciting evening was had by all, and as it drew to a close, both men stood outside Ms Mazy's Rum Bar, watching the waves lap on the shore and listening to Gregory Isaacs playing on the turntable inside. Only then did Anancy pop the question.

"When and where will be the next storm of the century?"

Chapter Thirty-Two

"We popping out to the shops yuh need anyting?" Spokes turned around in his chair, his reverie broken and looked over to see Suzy's bright face peering around one of the large double doors that lead into the extensive library. Even though the room was huge, the acoustics were excellent. Spokes didn't have to shout. He hoped he could disguise his frustration with his new situation but 'dammit' he couldn't.

"I could come and keep yuh company?" He suggested. "I'd stay in the car, of course."

"Big man," Suzy said patiently. "We've been through dis. The safest place for you is here until we sure we can protect you."

Spokes shook his head like he was clearing the cobwebs.

"I know that, but I'm dying here, Miss Wong; it's been a week."

"Hush," Suzy consoled him. "I feel your pain, Mas Spokes, but if I've learned anything from this crazy world, dis is not the end. I know you're grieving, but your driver friend is on his own journey."

"Taken too soon," Spokes muttered.

"Much too soon; that's why him murderer will pay." Suzy paused. "We will get through dis. Now, tell me what I can get for yuh."

Spokes sighed and managed a weak smile.

"Three Dragon Stouts and some plantain chips."

"Yes sir," Suzy grinned and disappeared, pushing the library door closed.

Spokes hated being cooped up, even in a sumptuous mansion, waited on hand and foot, fed mouth-watering food compliments of Nanny and sharing his digs with three extraordinary women. It was just that he enjoyed his freedom and the privileged wealth afforded him, but it meant nothing if you were being stalked by a homicidal genius with the secret to life itself.

Why did his enemies think they could frighten him into submission? Did they think he was a pushover because he was flesh and blood? What they didn't realise was that he enjoyed his abilities being taken for granted. Ever since he was a youth in Jamaica, he had been judged for his dark skin and slight stature. He wasn't the best reader in his class, but he appreciated books and enjoyed trips to the only library in his district. What he did believe he was good at was the creative use of his hands. That had served him well, and when his mother had brought him up to England in the 1960s, he had flourished. But it turned out that books would eventually provide him with his lifestyle and passion, but some things never changed. He was still being taken for granted and others who thought he was a soft touch were still attempting to intimidate him. The difference today was he didn't just have bark but bite.

These few days of isolation from the outside world had not been spent feeling sorry for himself though. He used his time to learn more about the BioEnhancement International CEO. Before Spokes knew that a world existed inside the world he took for granted, he had fancied himself as an import-export magnate. On top of his building maintenance work, he sent barrels, furniture, trucks and car parts to the Caribbean. When his life changed, he became the custodian of one of the most extensive and powerful collections of arcane artefacts in the world, or so he told himself. That fact was like a dam had been constructed across the river of his life, redirecting his flow. Intuitively he knew this was an opportunity of a lifetime and he flung himself into the role of metaphysical impresario and businessman. He surprised himself that it came naturally, even accepting the world of gods and ghosts, monsters and mutants. His new role was not an intellectual stretch for him at all. As a child, he believed the stories he was told by his grandmother and that he read in books. Tales of weird science were his favourite thing. All this was just confirmation of what he already felt to be true.

So why did he think he couldn't make enemies because he was enjoying himself? He should know better than that. At times he seemed to attract a negative energy that tended to stick with him and cause havoc in his life.

This was one of those times.

After all, that was how he met the Guardians.

To be fair, he shouldn't be surprised that BioEnhancement International wanted him and the girls dead; he sometimes had that effect on people.

It was a gift he would readily give back.

He grinned bitterly.

His sterling reputation in the circles that mattered did not exempt him from misunderstandings. But most of his clients understood when he declined to store or freight particular items. He may be a hustler, but Spokes had his principles. That was why he was genuinely surprised when a BEI consignment found its way into his warehouse. He knew about the company and heard about the stories of illegal organ trafficking. So he was already on edge. Then his snakehead ring began to express its distaste. The Mesopotamian relic expressed its discontent by jangling his nerves and messing with his perception until he got rid of it. The only thing he knew for sure was that BEI was inextricably linked with the task the Guardians had to perform. Too many indicators were making themselves known. The challenge, as always, was to unravel the ball of twine that was destiny and redress the imbalance the man in charge of BEI was causing.

Already Spokes was realising this investigation would be a bitch. After three days, his admin team got back to him with as much as they could find on the company and the enigmatic leader, Ulysses Kayanga. His personal wealth was shrouded in mystery, as was his identity; all that was in the public domain was that Congo was his birthplace and he headed a dynasty of biotechnology and mercenary services. He was in the world's top five private military firms, and according to the business journals, he achieved all of that with staff numbers between one and ten. Alarm bells were clanging and Spokes knew there was more to this than was indicated by the facts and figures. This man had one foot in the material world and the other in the metaphysical. And he wasn't afraid to use the latter to advance on the former. Why had he shown up on Spokes' radar? What was he involved in that was causing ripples in the balance? It was safe to say a man like Kayanga would be exploiting his secrets for power and financial gain. All of this couldn't just be about money; there was something more at play here. This personal vendetta against him wasn't just personal. His standard investigations were getting him nowhere, so it was time to reach out to his magical contacts. Spokes would see what they could discern. If there were secrets to be had, he would find them.

Chapter Thirty-Three

South London Coroners, Croydon

Dr Aziz felt good in a suit and tie. His colleague Detective McFarlane looked admiringly at him, used to seeing the forensic pathologist in PPE, not a snazzy suit. Aziz liked to think that if it wasn't for his organised office and his love of visual aids surrounding his profession, you'd think he was a solicitor.

"Going for a business meeting?" Shaft asked.

"No," he grinned. "Actually, I have a TED Talk today at the British Library. 'How thin is the barrier between science and the supernatural'." The doctor gave his voice some bass and gravitas in the process as he said it. "My work with you inspired the title."

"Nice one. If anyone is positioned to break that down for the layman, you're it, Doc. Good luck."

"Thanks," Dr Aziz said sounding pleased. "Now, for the real reason you're here."

Shaft nodded patiently, a knot forming immediately in his stomach. He always had a visceral reaction to this case. It affected him in weird ways that he recognised but had no time to psychoanalyse. The detective made himself comfortable by adjusting his trouser leg and putting on his listening face.

"While I was prepping for this talk about a week ago, an idea struck me, opening up a line of investigation I hadn't thought of," Dr Aziz said.

"Tell me more," Shaft leaned forward.

"What do you know about organ transplants?" The doctor asked.

"Not much," Shaft answered. "I know there's a booming illegal red market for organs. And I know if you have the financial clout, you can jump the queue to find a life-saving donor."

Dr Aziz laughed.

"Always a detective. I meant the science behind it, not criminal implications."

Shaft grinned back at him.

"I'm only familiar with the basics. Transplant rejection is a major hurdle for surgeons, I know."

"Top marks," Dr Aziz congratulated him. "That's exactly where I'm going with this." The doctor's eyes brightened at the prospect of a lesson in medicine. He breathed deeply, a tell which indicated he was retrieving information. "Your body's immune system usually protects you from harmful substances. These harmful substances have proteins and core antigens that attach to their surface. The immune system recognises they are not from your body and attacks them."

Shaft nodded.

"When a person receives an organ from someone else, that person's immune system may recognise it as foreign because the antigen on the organ doesn't match. It can trigger a blood transfusion reaction or transplant rejection."

"You guys have developed meds for that thing, right?" Shaft asked.

"We have, but it's not perfect; your serial killer seems to have succeeded where decades of science failed."

Shaft was nearly at the edge of his seat.

"Are you telling me he's targeting these women based on their antigen profiles?"

"That I am," Dr Aziz said.

"And here I believed the organs were trophies for a deranged mind with knowledge of advanced medical operating procedure."

"If I was to guess..." the doctor said, "...I'd say he was extracting the organs for a specific donor. And I also think if you go beyond this case, all the antigen profiles of the other victims will match."

Shaft shook his head as if it would give him clarity.

"Why would he take an organ multiple times?"

"I'm thinking he may have the same problems we have, and after a while, the organ is rejected."

"Damn! How could he know their medical histories? And more importantly, how could he find out about his victims' specific details without some form of testing beforehand?"

Dr Aziz wiggled his nose and adjusted his glasses.

"I thought about that too. But my conclusion was not very scientific."

"You're forgiven," Shaft said impatiently.

"I think he can somehow sense the antigen profile."

Shaft's eyes widened.

"You're not coming over to the dark side, are you doc?"

"Do I have a choice?" Dr Aziz asked.

"I don't think you do; sooner or later, there will be so much evidence confirming the existence of the supernatural you will have no choice but to accept it." Shaft was enjoying this because he had been in the same position once. "Don't fight it; embrace it," he teased.

Dr Aziz had decided to work with Black Book because of the challenge. He knew the department did not investigate run-of-the-mill cases, and if he wanted to stretch himself, this would be good for his personal development, although not his professional. He had even discounted the stories of Detective McFarlane being a Satanist and reserved his judgement until he met the man. The doctor found him a brilliant detective struggling to explain some of his cases. After working with Shaft for a year now, Aziz was also questioning the authenticity of what he considered the real world. Maybe it was time he adjusted his scientific method to accept the strangeness that he had no choice but to believe.

"You know canines can sniff out cancer in humans," the doctor stated.

"I read something about that," Shaft said. "Some health departments were thinking of training dogs for that very purpose."

The doctor nodded.

"What if your killer can do that and more?"

Shaft looked like that was not something he wanted to consider. He said the words slowly.

"What if you can. My next question would be, who is the recipient of the organs? Organs they've been harvesting for more than five years that I know of. What the fuck does all of this mean?"

Both men looked at each other silently. Dr Aziz opened his mouth; even with his new acceptance of the impossible, he couldn't find an answer to that question.

One step at a time, he told himself. *One step at a time.*

SCAN ME

Chapter Thirty-Four

Y had almost demanded to accompany Shaft to the gym. And no, this was not Yvonne finally revealing an annoying and clingy alter ego and neither was it a cringe-worthy, gym-going ritual they had concocted as a couple. No, this was pure concern for the man she loved and what he was going through. Saying he was fine did not mean she believed him.

What did you expect him to say? He was a man, after all. This case had wounded him. He fought with it in his dreams; she had kissed him back to sleep many nights, and in his waking moments, he was driven. Shaft spent the night with her and woke with a nagging feeling he needed to apply his detective skills to the gym again.

His murdered friend was demanding it in his nightmares.

Y felt like a mother hen but maybe that was who she needed to be. Her responsibilities were becoming clearer to her and she was learning not to fight them. Her role as leader to the Guardians was sacrosanct and so was whoever she decided to share her love with. Y would never presume to think she was as sensitive as Suzy when it came to reading the emotional challenges of the people close to her. But she was no slouch.

Suzy was brooding. Patra had a personal challenge she hadn't shared with the group yet. And Y was worried about her boyfriend and his case. Whether he liked it or not, Detective Winston McFarlane had the pleasure of her company this morning. Bad II the Bone had a security gig to attend in the evening so she had plenty of time to work out and allow him space to work. Y watched her man filling in the necessary paperwork at the front desk of Gold's Gym to get her access. The gym was beginning to buzz with activity and Y prepared herself to see the Hell Dwellers dressed in human skin pretending to fit in. The demons, having slipped into the world from some hellish dimension, were having the time of their lives wreaking havoc in the World of Man. If they were being obnoxious or threatening, Y would call them out but they were small fries in comparison to the bigger picture. Just an unfortunate and less dangerous consequence of the imbalance in the forces between good and evil. Y needn't have worried; the gym goers were all human.

Shaft motioned her over.

"Ready?" he asked.

"Always," she said. "What are you going to do first?"

Y walked through the automatic barrier while Shaft, the gentleman he was, waited for her to go through. He followed behind.

"I think I'll start on the treadmill then see where I go from there," he said.

"Okay, I'll find you." And Y knew he understood. She took his hand and they mounted the steps to the dressing rooms together. She knew why he was so quiet and left him to think. This was the first time he had returned here after he found out about his friend's murder. She had something else on her mind and didn't hesitate in letting him know.

"You were telling me about your dream this morning but big mouth Patra interrupted. It sounded weird but meaningful."

Shaft stopped at the entrance to the men's locker room and looked at her. She could see he was trying to recall the details of the dream but like sand it was hard to grasp and contain.

"I never... well not never but rarely remember my dreams but this was so defined and sharp. I know bits are missing but I still remember the bulk of it."

Y nodded and Shaft took her hand and led her back to the area of the gym that housed a garrison of treadmills.

Shaft pointed.

"I was over here running and Marilyn was running beside me and we were chitchatting about the weather and the news," Shaft said, pointing.

"No sex," Y asked.

Shaft shook his head.

"No sex."

Y looked disappointed.

Shaft continued.

"She was smiling, all comfortable, when I started to feel cold. I noticed we were alone suddenly. All the other users were gone. Then the windows began to ice up. I'm trembling by this but Marilyn is unaffected. She's telling me someone is calling her but I couldn't hear shit. I was so cold but couldn't stop running on the treadmill. Marilyn said she had to leave and that the voice was upstairs. I was begging her not to go and that's when I heard that whispering. If a blizzard could be given a voice it was this fucker. I'm chilled to my core by this but she's happily running on the treadmill while I'm slowly becoming a block of ice. I didn't want her to go but I knew I couldn't stop her. All I remember after that was panicking while I was trapped in a block of ice suffocating and seeing Marilyn skipping her way to the room upstairs, her voice in my ears, in my head. *I'm off to see the Wizard! I'm off to see the Wizard! I'm off to see the Wizard!"*

Y shuddered.

SHAFT WAS IN THE WEIGHT ROOM, NOT REALLY DOING much and unable to shape the memory of the last time he saw Marilyn alive. His recollections weren't helping. He just wasn't sure what he was supposed to do with that information. To his mind, it was interfering with his process. After all he'd been through, he was still uncomfortable allowing his intuition to guide him.

Goddamn it!

He knew that resisting the new world he inhabited would do him no good and yet his old programming had a tendency to kick in and attempt to solve a new world problem with an old world frame of mind. He had to get with the program and begin to embrace new models of operation. If he was to be effective in his role as lead Detective for Black Book or simply as an asset to the Guardians, he had to let go of his bullshit conditioning and embrace the new way of working.

Shaft stood at the entrance to the hall of treadmills, his eyes focused on the one that he preferred to use when he was here. It wasn't different from all the others except for its unusual settings. It was the only treadmill that he could track his distance without showing him how long he'd been running at the same time. He didn't know what it was about watching the timer that made his running session seem longer but when he focused on distance, he felt less pressured for some reason. Machine 24 did that for him. As he looked at it again, a petite older lady walked briskly on the machine beside it, the music of

Sean Paul pumped through the speakers all around. He recounted his last minutes with Marilyn, not knowing it would be his last. In a set of mental pictures, he could feel himself in conversation with her again. In his mind's eye, he followed Marilyn as a misty spectre from his dream as she made her way upstairs to the juice bar.

I'm off to see the wizard, she said.

Shaft's imagination pictured her pushing the door to enter the trendy juice bar. He imagined her sitting down and smiling at a man waiting for her, a cold cucumber mint juice in front of him – no idea why he thought of that.

I'm off to see the wizard.

Shaft leaned off the archway that led to the treadmills, his vision blurring momentarily, his heart pounding, his brain churning out possibilities that were suddenly meaningful.

"She went upstairs to meet a killer," he muttered to himself. "He was here; the bastard was here, all along."

There was a sinking feeling in the pit of his stomach, but he made no effort to alleviate it. He was wholly immersed in the horrendous possibility of having been in the same building, at the same time as the monster that murdered his friend. Shaft shook his head for clarity, his features grim but his heart heavy as it continued to race. There was no need to question what he had stumbled upon. Every sense, every fibre told him it was true; he just needed to prove it empirically. Somewhere within these four walls, there was something he could use. A lead would help him stop this maniac once and for all.

Chapter Thirty-Five

Red Ground Estate, Sussex

The sound of checkers Jumping four of his black players on the draught board made Spokes wince. "Goddamn it!" He moaned.

"Will I ever beat you at this game?"

Mr D. Godden, fruit and veg trader extraordinaire and immortal, slurped at his Earl Grey tea before laughing heartily.

"Mate, you've got to roll out of bed on a Bank Holiday to get one over on me."

"Yuh think you're slick, but I never give up. I will beat your rass one of these days. Mark my words!"

Mr Godden stroked the spiky protrusions on his chin contemplatively.

"Do you mean your children will beat me? Or maybe even your children's children."

"Funny," Spokes said. "One more game, and let's make it interesting."

Nanny breezed into the kitchen, where both men sat across from each other.

"Do you enjoy losing money?" Nanny asked Spokes casually. "Because when you do, I will not listen to yuh moaning after Mr Godden leave?"

Spoke shook his head. His dirty draws hung up and seen by all. He laughed at how callously Nanny threw him under the bus.

Mr Godden laughed too, his gold tooth glinting.

"And Mr Godden' Nanny continued. Thank you for the fruit basket; it's been a while since I've seen such a wide display of Jamaican fruit. They make my kitchen smell real good. Like a real Jamaican kitchen."

"Anything for you, my dear,' Mr Godden took off

his flat cap and bowed at the beautiful albino woman. "You know you do the best cup of tea in the world?"

She waved him away, blushing.

"Guh, easy on him, Mr Godden."

"Don't worry Constance, I will."

"Constance?" Spokes mouthed the name with incredulity and shook his head. When he thought Nanny was out of earshot, he said.

"How deh rass, do you know her first name. She protects dat fact wid her life."

Mr Godden tapped his nose twice and grinned.

They were ganging up on him, but he was glad his immortal friend had come around to see him and shoot the breeze, having heard about the threat to his life. Spokes also knew that as concerned as his friend was for his welfare, something else was brewing for him to leave his business and his three dogs in London to see him in Sussex. Spokes wasn't sure if he had been given some helpful advice on the protocol of dealing with beings who lived five to six human lifetimes, but he knew enough about his friend and how he thought many moves ahead in business and life.

That's why he was so dominant in Draughts, and this visit

was one of his moves. Spokes automatically switched his perspective when he had dealings with his friend, allowing him to take his time to get to a point or reveal some critical information.

Their perception of time was starkly different from how humans perceived it.

They had all the time in the world, and their communication style made that obvious.

Like most humans, Spokes was impatient but learning to go with the flow. He had nowhere to go and nothing better to do.

"Before I take the last shackles out of your pockets,' Mr Godden said. 'There's something you need to know." Spokes sat up and breathed deeply, focussing on what the Fruit and Veg man had to say.

"You may be interested in one of my customers,' Mr Godden said.

"Yeah,' Spokes leaned towards him. "Who dat? A business contact?"

Mr Godden shook his head.

"If I'm not mistaken, the same geezer whose trying to kill you."

"Yuh serious?' Spokes asked, sitting up, his attention fully engaged.

"As a heart attack?"

"That fucker has a lot of payback coming his way. Yuh know where him a hideout?"

"Breathe, mate," Mr Godden said. "There's good news and bad news; choose your poison."

"Good news," Spokes decided with a twist of his lips.

Mr Godden nodded.

"I know where he's staying."

"How?' Spokes immediately looked surprised and elated at the same time. 'your man has a love for Volcanic Salmon

Bananas. They are rare - I have a contact in Hawaii, and only I supply them to a small clientele, mainly witch doctors from Africa and the Caribbean.'

'From that, you knew it was him?' Spokes asked, interested in how he came to the conclusion that made sense to a mortal. Mr Godden's lips stretched thin with amusement. 'Easy? he said. 'The doctor was the only one in that small group who wanted the fruit and not the banana sucker with the fruit. I think he's making Kasiksi - a Congolese liquor.' spokes nodded, impressed with his reasoning. 'And deh bad news?' Mr Godden shrugged before answering. 'He's a guest at the Hellfire Club.'

'Him protected,' Spokes said simply, unable to hide his disappointment.

He looked up at the white man who outwardly looked in his late fifties, flat cap, a twinkle in his eyes and a pristine white apron and wondered out loud. 'Don't you feel a conflict of interest because you provide the Hellfire Club with food, but yet yuh provide me with information."

"No conflict at all, my old China. They have their rules, and I have mine. I have never stayed at the Hellfire Club, and I never will. Immortals have the ability to go with or against Eternal rules. You just have to be willing to pay the price, whichever way you decide?"

"What was your price?" Spokes asked.

Mr Godden sniffed, flicking his thumb across the tip of his nose.

'Let's just say I can only transact business with the club, not use its lavish facilities."

Spokes shook his head. With an expression of disgust. 'Dem ever try to squeeze yuh?' 'A few times the centuries, but if you've lived as long as I have, you learn to be resourceful. Ducking and diving."

"Be careful,' Spokes said. 'If dem catch wind of our link, they could try to cut off yuh livelihood."

Mr Godden shrugged.

"Bollocks to them. They will do what they have to do, and I will do what I must do."

"Spoken by a man who has options," Spokes said.

Mr Godden smiled knowingly and then became serious.

'I love this city, always have. When I was asked, before my being became three-dimensional, where I wanted to be, who I wanted to become. You know what I said?"

Spokes nodded.

"I wanted to be in London. I wanted this timeline and this section of the multiverse. There was no hesitation. This is home for me, and I will never sit back and allow the poxy Hellfire Club to do it an injustice?"

'I hear yuh and I owe yuh,' Spokes said.

"Protecting the city, that's pay enough,' he paused, and a twinkle returned to his eyes.

"Now let's get back to me taking your money."

Spokes laughed.

Chapter Thirty-Six

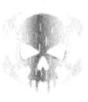

Y knew they would eventually meet in person; she just didn't realise it would be so soon. The memory of chasing him through the newly renovated halls of the hotel as he tried to escape from a potential murder scene was fresh in her mind. The enigmatic Kintu had arranged to meet with the crew and promised to divulge his knowledge of their shared enemy and something about himself too. Suzy and Patra were impressed by him, which was good enough for her, but she still maintained a sliver of doubt. They had agreed to meet him at a location of his choosing, and as uncomfortable as that was for Y, she acquiesced. And the giant's choice was a beautiful and peculiar one at the same time.

The meetup had transformed into a road trip that made Y yearn for more time out of the city. Their burden that was palpable to all three of them lifted when they crossed the M25 on their way to Coventry. With Patra at the wheel of the Bentley, they made their way into the heart of the UK and almost forgot who they were and what they were ordained to do. They stopped at the Lion and Anchor Pub in Rugby, had a sumptuous meal, laughed, and drank Red Stripe beers.

The seriousness of their responsibilities came rushing back to remind them as they stood looking at what once was the Catholic Cathedral of Coventry but now was a restored shell after being bombed in World War II. In its glory days, it must've been a magnificent structure. Now it was a memorial to the lives lost from the relentless pounding of the city by the German Luftwaffe in the Blitz of 1940. The three women stood looking at it in silence; Patra popped the bubble of their reverie.

"It looks like it's closed. What time you got?"

The question was directed to Suzy.

"Seven twenty five," Suzy said without taking her eyes off the building.

Y took the lead.

"Kintu doesn't strike me as a man who would let out of hours affect his plans. Let's go in."

Y walked up to the elegantly designed wrought iron gates, and they swung open on her approach. All three stepped through and followed the gravel path up to the old cathedral, neatly manicured grass verges and beds of fastidiously arranged flowers on either side of them. Multicoloured spotlights positioned around the perimeter of the building shone on the walls giving it a feel for the dramatic, almost a Hollywood film set allure. Drones that looked like they were packing heat buzzed above them, keeping eyes on the old cathedral and the streets around it. Y wondered if Kintu was worried about them or their mad scientist friend. A set of stairs ahead of them would have decades ago led into the central area of worship through oak or birch double doors. Today instead, the guttered interior would look more like an architect's life-size floorplan, and the ornate floor tiles had been replaced with grass. As Bad II the Bone came up the stairs, they saw two large men in tactical gear and dog collars covering the large double doors into the open space beyond. They didn't carry weapons openly, but Y knew they had weapons concealed.

"Miss Sinclair?" A sweet, resonant voice coated with a sexy French accent came from the shadows on the right. Y stopped and turned to face the approaching voice. It belonged to a dark-skinned athletically-built Catholic nun. Y was taken aback.

She was unlike any nun Y had ever seen. The colours and the vibe were all wrong but in a good way. She wore blue combat trousers with a utility belt around her waist. Her top was made of camouflage material, with short sleeves and with what looked like a ninja pen in her sleeve pocket. A silver crucifix was pinned over her left breast pocket, and the habit, the only giveaway to her religious associations, covered her hair and matched the colour of her paramilitary ensemble. She held her hand out and came up to the women shaking Y's first.

"Miss Sinclair," she said again. She bowed. "Miss Wong, Miss Jones, my name is Sister Charlotte Achu. I'm so honoured to meet you."

"Thank you," Y said.

What was it about religious figures that were so disarming in the most tense of situations, Y thought. She was still working out her feelings regarding Kintu and his mission then he went and associated himself with the church. A killer, combat trained, and obviously occult-powered. Back in the day, he would have been burned at the stake, and they would have been excommunicated. The church wasn't her favourite organisation, and was no bastion of virtue, it had done some God-awful things in its time, but like any institution run by men, even the ones who claim they have direct contact with the Divine had managed to do some good despite themselves.

"What order do you belong to?" Suzy asked.

Y wasn't surprised by the question; her sister had gone to a Catholic school in Jamaica. And even with Y's limited knowledge, Sister Achu was dressed unlike any nun she knew of.

The sister smiled, her eyes twinkling with amusement.

"Come, come," she ushered them towards the double doors. "Brother Kintu will explain everything."

The big dudes at the doors stepped aside to let the Guardians and the sister through.

Chapter Thirty-Seven

It was just as Y had imagined it. The interior was made up of benches that replaced the original pews, and the polished Sicilian tiles were now a patch of grass and gravel with parts of the bombed architecture evident on the ground like a floor plan. Other sections raised like stalagmites erupting from the ground, the original walls shattered by German bombers. In the distance where the altar would have been stood a tall amorphous and shimmering silhouette that even Y's enhanced eyesight could not discern clearly. Sister Achu still led the way calling out to different people; to other nuns like herself and male versions on the ground and to the teams on the scaffolding that were constructing an interior framework around the shell of the cathedral. There were bundles and bundles of wires snaking through the scaffolding and into obscure pieces of equipment nestled around joints like nodes of some sort. On the ground, the root-like wires that carpeted the floors led into over twenty generators that she could see, all throttling away with a subdued power muffled by sound-dampening panels. Y thought it was overkill for the few lights surrounding the structure. She filed the thought away, expecting an explanation before the night was done. Her more immediate questions required answers. The figure in the distance that formed the nebulous undulating shadow coalesced into a tall, strapping black form as a small group of four approached him.

Was it an obfuscation spell or camouflage tech? She would have to ask Suzy.

Kintu had his back to them, speaking to the group. The contrasting height between the man and the group was stark. He was easily over seven feet tall. Y remembered questioning how a man that big could move so fast and be so agile.

And here he was in the flesh.

The women of Bad II the Bone stood on one side of the table, and Achu rushed around to the other side, stood beside the giant and tugged on the sleeve of his black gown like a child seeking attention from her father. Immediately Kintu paused, knelt and leaned back so Achu could speak in his ear. She hurried back around to the Guardians and smiled at them.

"Brother Kintu will be with you in a moment," she motioned to the seats with the grand sweep of her hand. "Sit and make yourself comfortable."

She hurried away, but the girls stood, waiting for their host to greet them. The group of nuns and seminarians who had been attentive, even enraptured, by him dispersed quickly, and Brother Kintu turned to the Guardians.

"My guests," he said, his voice deep and rich. "Welcome."

His force of presence blew on the girls like a mild gust of wind. He stood without body language, his hands in the black cassock, a hood over his head, submerging his facial features into shadow. For a moment, Y imagined they would go through the entire evening with him maintaining distance between them, but she was wrong. She was wrong about many things that concerned the mysterious Brother Kintu. He came around the thick oaken wedges of the huge table and let his hood drop to his shoulders. Before they could react to his visage, he bowed, took Y, Patra and Suzy's hands, and kissed them in turn before stepping back.

Kintu was even more magnificently twisted in the flesh than he looked presenting his findings to them on video. He possessed a face the grandmasters of a bygone time would have fallen over themselves to render in a storm or on canvas, but nature's masterpiece had been tainted by the hand of man. His prominent African features remained, however, even after the horrific injuries that Kintu had obviously been subjected to. He had short neat hair – Y wondered who his barber could be – with a network of large and small metal tubing burrowing into the muscles of his exposed neck. Deep furrow-like scars mapped his face, ear to lips, forehead across his eyes and down to his cheeks, from the chin and across his throat. His skin retained its dark complexion, but there was a waxy consistency to it. Strangely, Y pictured a corpse washed up on the shore with the waves lapping on it slowly, tide after tide. All that did not matter when you stared into his eyes. They were limpid pools of intelligence and power, devoid of malice but filled with righteous indignation.

Y cleared her throat.

"Thanks for inviting us," she said.

"Appreciated, Kintu," Patra said. "Can I call you K?"

Kintu bowed.

"Respect," Suzy said. "I hope all of this isn't for us?"

"Yes and no, Miss Wong," Kintu answered cryptically. "This is an experiment I wanted to show off to you. Something I've been working on with the scientists of the OMJ."

"The OMJ?" Y asked.

"The Order of the Mechanics of Jesus," he said. "Please,

sit," he motioned to the comfortable chairs. "I promised an explanation of who I am and what this conflict is about. What I'm about to show you next will explain with the clarity you deserve and prove a theory I have long been postulating."

"Two birds with one stone," Suzy said. Kintu closed his eyes, hearing her words. The corner of his fleshy lips twitched upwards.

"I was in Kingston in 1919, then I stayed in Haiti. My collection of Vintage rum began from then. The Caribbean could be magical, but the Europeans took our people from Africa, supplanted us in the islands and then scarred and traumatised us."

"The slave trade was no joke," Patra said. "You look good for your age, K?"

Kintu nodded, his eyes opened again, and the clarity in them almost took her breath away.

"I have a secret," he said.

"Care to share it?" Y asked.

"Lightning," he said matter-of-factly. "Let me explain."

Kintu turned away from them, reaching for something they could not see. He slipped a communication rig over his head.

"Nigga has style," Patra whispered, leaning over to Y. "I like him."

Y nodded.

"He's a perfect host, that's for sure, but is he being manipulative?" Y looked over to Suzy, who was in her own world. She smiled.

"I feel like dis is the safest place for us to be outside Sussex mansion. Him cool." Suzy pronounced. "You can relax."

Y's shoulders lowered, and she breathed more evenly, taking her Katana off her lap and leaning it on the table. Sister Achu came over quickly with a bottle of their favourite tipple –

Asti Dulce Spumante. She poured into their glasses without invitation.

"Now that's what I'm talking about," Patra said.

"Enjoy," Sister Achu said, her voice low and Y figured she wasn't just referring to the wine but the upcoming entertainment. The giant returned from his position around the table to where the ladies sat – in the old church that would have been the nave. His movement was silent and effortless. He turned to face his guests with a tablet in his big hands and the communication rig over his head. He paused for a moment and looked down at his feet. Mei Ling, the cat, was rubbing herself on his legs and purring. He reached down and picked her up. The cat looked comfortable in his arms.

"Is she yours?" Kintu asked.

"In some kinda way," Suzy said, smiling. "She's her own boss. But she likes our company."

"A special creature," Kintu said.

"Very special," Suzy agreed, and Kintu placed the cat on their table. Mei Ling strutted over to Suzy and lay down in an unladylike fashion in front of her, tummy up. Suzy rubbed her stomach.

"What mi tell yuh about meeting strange men?" Suzy whispered.

Mei Ling ignored the advice and got comfortable.

"My guests, Miss Sinclair, Miss Wong and Miss Jones," Kintu began, his voice amplified through the speakers.

"Not many people know of my existence outside of the Order, and although our motivation will be opposed at times, I respect the ancient institution of the Guardians of the Light." He looked away from his seated guests and stared down at his extra-size tablet. He tapped his finger on the screen three times quickly and ran his finger across it. The lights in the cathedral dimmed, and Joseph Bologne Chevalier de Saint George's violin concerto began playing in the background. He spoke again.

"All places of worship were designed to create the ultimate religious experience through your senses for anyone who entered. The architecture was created so you could directly experience the invisible possibility of heaven."

All around them, thousands of violently vibrating beams of light emanated from light sources attached to the scaffolding that surrounded them. The colourful laser beams were moving so quickly your eyes could not follow, but there was mathematical precision to their movement. And soon, the Guardians began to see that a hologram was being woven, beautifully reproducing the interior look of the old cathedral before its destruction. From stained glass windows, Gothic arches, and pews, to altars and vaulted ceilings.

"Wow," Y whispered.

Patra whistled, trying to touch the images closest to her, and Suzy gasped with eyes wide.

"Once you cross the threshold..." Kintu continued, "...you left the real world behind. You were in a virtual environment that instilled a sense of belief and sensory experience through sculptures, prayers, songs and religious rights. And just like the virtual environments of today, it was a database of information; it just wasn't connected. I found out how to make that connection possible."

The violin concerto was reaching its peak, and the classical orchestration was almost setting the tone for what was to come next. Kintu's finger flashed over the screen on his tablet, making him look like a digital conductor of a composition of light, sound, and soul. The spectral images appearing were walking into the cathedral with their families. A choir appeared singing noiselessly, then disappearing to be replaced with a class of children in Sunday school. Multiple phantom priests took their positions at the pulpit, speaking to a congregation long dead. The astral choir boys swinging thuribles, indicating the beginning of a celebration, incense pouring out of the outlets of the censers.

"All you see here being replayed is the data embedded in the ground and the remaining brickwork. The memories, if you will, of this place. Everything is recorded. Not just here..." Kintu touched his skull, "...but here." He made a grandiloquent sweep of his arms that took in the entirety of the space they inhabited. "You just need to know where to look for the enhanced emotional data and how to extract it."

"Memories," Y whispered to Suzy as they watched the apparitions that had come through the doors of this building for over a hundred years and were replaying what they had done.

"Duppy," Suzy said. "A technology can manifest deh history of a building or an inanimate object touched by a human soul. Dis is amazing."

"Damn! No magic either," Patra said. "Pure science. Bre's a smart cookie. I'm impressed."

"Now you've experienced for the first time my Entelechy Projection System," Kintu went on. "As I promised, I want to tell my story."

Kintu drew two fingers across the screen of his tablet, and the walking memories suddenly disappeared, leaving behind the ethereal hologram of the church's interior, glowing blue.

"You will be the first and last to see this. Tell my story as you tell your own."

The ladies of Bad II the Bone held their breath as one, their eyes focused on an area between the virtual pulpit and the lectern. The conflagration of colourful laser lights was slowly beginning to make some sense to their eyes.

"I was a king 300 years ago. A king, murdered with my Queen-to-be, because of jealousy. Because of family and the avarice of a madman." He paused; the visual representation of his thought process was still nebulous as he drew on his recollections, and the virtual jumble of memories began to clarify itself. "The real story began in the Congo, but my resurrection took place in the Austrian Alps."

Kintu walked past their table, and Patra had a dopey grin plastered on her face; as she crossed and uncrossed her legs, uncomfortably.

Suzy looked at her suspiciously.

"Yuh feeling okay?" she asked.

"Top of the world," Patra said. "I knew I was going to like this guy but not as much as I am now."

"What you talking 'bout gal?" Suzy asked. "Spit it out."

"I know you can feel it," Patra said. "The dude is like a walking generator."

Suzy nodded in agreement but still looked at her sister blankly. Even Mei Ling was waiting for the punch line.

Patra continued squirming and giggling.

Y was being drawn into it too.

Suzy looked at her darkly.

"Chill bitch," Patra said, her explanation thankfully taking on more pace. "You know my piercing? The one I had done in Camden. The one downtown." She winked and pointed to her crotch.

Suzy shook her head and groaned, regretting she had asked.

"The gold and platinum alloy vibrates like crazy when he's within range. The closer he comes to me, the more it vibrates."

Y was holding back laughter.

"What can a girl do?" Patra said with manufactured sincerity.

"Walk away and squeeze," Suzy said.

Patra shook her head.

"That's the difference between me and you, Miss Wong. My mama didn't raise me like that."

"Yuh poor mother tried an' yet here were are," Suzy said.

Y broke up the scuffle.

"You two need to pay attention," Y said. "And P, squeeze."

All eyes were back on the coalescing image above their heads. They could begin to make out mountains and a Castle precariously perched on the craggy rocks. The seconds ticked by, and the scene became clearer, but the foul weather of sleet and lightning obscured the view. The image faded to black and then they were looking at a scene inside with all the players of the unfolding drama present.

The Guardians were hooked.

Chapter Thirty-Eight

Anancy couldn't decide what suit he should wear to the opera tonight. His sense of colour, style and mischief was telling him to be flamboyant and multicoloured, but he needed to reign in his godlike ego and focus on the job at hand. He stared at himself through the window of a department store in central London and grinned broadly. He undid the buttons of his banana-yellow zoot suit and did a twirl. Today banana was his favourite colour, but he would make an exception for his daughters and change to dull black. Anancy pulled on his braces and let them go with a twang. He needed to get his head in the game, even if he was going to see his favourite performance. Arm-in-arm, a couple walked past him and must have been wondering at his antics in front of the shop display.

"Nice suit," one of them called out to him.

"Thank you kindly, Rachel," Anancy said, tipping his trilby at them and absorbing Rachel's wonder and surprise that he knew her name.

"Have a good night, yuh hear."

Anancy was feeling excited.

There was always something thrilling when he was involved in the Guardian business. He wondered if the other gods in bygone eras felt the same way about their charges as he did. He may never know because the details of such things were hidden from even the gods themselves. A dirty grin brightened his countenance. No deity had ever or would ever get as involved as he had in his daughters' affairs. Others may have been chaperones in name only, but he had a genuine love for his charges and would not see them fail if he could help it – within the Rules of Engagement. Of course.

"Of course," he answered himself, the grin still solidly in place. Anancy tapped his gnarly cane three times, sparks issuing from the tip and the ancient words and images carved into the wood suddenly animated. They swirled about the wooden shaft telling stories, casting spells, creating worlds in a self-contained maelstrom that burst from his stick into the real world in a flash of light leaving the Trickster God in a dapper blue tuxedo with matching trilby.

He adjusted his bow tie.

"Not bad," he said. "Not bad at all. Just you," he looked down to the black Oxfords on his feet. "You letting down the team. Give me some star power."

He touched his shoe with his cane, and the leather immediately became a transparent barrier to some far-reaching galaxy – twinkling stars, shooting comets.

"Nice!" he said, shaking his head. "Very nice."

Anancy couldn't be a hundred percent sure that he had to solve the riddle of the Prometheus Code and the lightning storm, but he must be close. He had investigated three possible humans who somehow had the ability to unlock the secret to life after death. He looked into a historian who was a fellow at the Faculty of Human Sciences at Oxford University. He was a nice enough man who didn't have a malicious bone in his body, but Anancy's professional opinion was he didn't know his ass from a bedhead. The Prometheus code, to him, was more of a metaphor for scientific development in the eighteenth century.

A German archaeologist at the University of Bonn, Herr Muller, was so close to understanding the code but could not leap the scientific chasm between life and reanimation without discovering much more of Frankenstein's documents. His failure was because he felt there was something missing in the puzzle.

Ulysses Kayanga, on the other hand, was different. He actively used the secrets on himself and profited from them. He believed it was his legacy and took offence to anyone he felt was against his ambitions. That had been the case with Spokes and now the Guardians.

He certainly knew how to keep a grudge. Maybe his perception of time had changed with his ability to live forever. He had used some of what he knew to extend his own life.

He stank of the Prometheus Code.

This man understood the code's intricacies and the part the Lightning of the Gods played in raising the dead.

Anancy needed more.

Tonight, would clarify some details he was unsure of, and then he would need to find a way to prepare the Guardians.

He would follow the Rules of Engagement set by the Powers That Be aeons ago. All he could do from here was hope they could discern the meaning of the signs and symbols he gave them. His physical gifts were limited to just one item of significance at a time. That had played out well with the vampire Queen. He thought about what it would be this time.

Anancy reached for a Cuban cigar in his coat pocket and watched his ride pull up to the curb. The black Rolls Royce turbo glided to a stop, its powerful engine idling and its bodywork and rims gleaming. The door popped open. He touched the tip of his cigar with his fingertip, and it flared red as he pulled on it gratefully. He slipped inside, and the door closed behind him.

"Mr Nansi," the driver said jovially. "Where to, Guv?"

"The Royal Opera House." He paused. "And Pete, tek yuh time. It's a sweet evening for a cruise."

"No problem, Mr Nansi, a cruise it is."

Chapter Thirty-Nine

Royal Opera House, Bow Street, London

Dr Kayanga may have seen Aida one hundred and four times over three hundred years but the performance still brought a tear to his eyes. And this was especially significant to him because it was a majority black cast and never before had the lead been played by an Ethiopian soprano. It was a sublime performance and he hated mixing business with pleasure but he couldn't miss this performance and neither could he miss the conclusion of a long overdue project.

Being an arts patron of the Royal Society, they provided him with a meeting room where he could finally conclude this piece of business. He would slip out of his box close to the end of act two, scene two as the Grand March proceeded and his negotiations should be complete by the end of the intermission. The doctor mouthed the words of a memorised exchange between Aida and the pharaoh with the same passion the performers did. He leaned back in his plush seat surveying the seats far below him and then the stage. The doctor couldn't get too comfortable as he would soon be leaving the world of ancient Egypt for a less romantic world that he unfortunately was all too adept in navigating. His skills of adaptation in this New World were second to none but he still wished he had lived in simpler times. With his intellect, he would have been considered a God in the true sense of the word a thousand years ago. He sighed and stood in the darkness of his box, immediately the two praetorian bodyguards that had accompanied him to the event and who had merged with the shadows came to life and positioned themselves on both sides of him as he strode out to the empty corridor. The doctor walked briskly towards his private meeting room, his footfalls echoing off the walls while his chaperones moved like ghosts beside him.

"What do you mean, there will be delays?" Dr Kayanga asked, his voice boomed deep and threatening. The two representatives from Compass Point Engineering tried to explain their dilemma but the doctor cut off their excuses with a decisive sweep of his hands. He looked keenly at the architectural drawings they had brought in for him to look over, ignoring the cowering engineers. Dr Kayanga had invited these two partners to the opera, making sure their evening would be a delightful one and giving them the impression he was anticipating a progress report in the positive.

But he knew it wouldn't be. He had been keenly following some supply chain issues and their causes that the company had been having. This was a performance for his subordinates to see how he dealt with disruption and wilful insubordination.

The doctor ran his manicured fingers along the lines and curves of his original drawing, modified so this firm could construct the apparatus he had designed to capture the raw energy of the lightning. He had acquired the lighthouse in Cornwall with some resistance but that was to be expected. The doctor had forcefully manipulated the council representatives and the owner of the property itself. His Neuroraptors had attached themselves to the nervous systems of the influencers and the most powerful decision makers in the town. His creations made them suggestible to his every demand. Nothing could be allowed to slow the progress. The fruits of this event would allow his business to ascend to the very top of the privatised military industry pecking order. His homeland of Congo would be the first to benefit. The mines controlled by these blood-sucking foreigners would be liberated first. Then the Congo would be returned to the hands of the Congolese and he would provide oversight to the government. Then the new threats that foreign governments didn't have the stomach to face that his army would be able to stamp out and clean up. He would eradicate all the threats from the end of the Cold War – at a cost of course. The doctor's eyes flared as he looked at the engineers.

"Did we not discuss the timing of this project was of the utmost importance?"

The female spoke first.

"We understand, Sir, and everything else has been completed but we have been let down. I'm so sorry. We just can't get the shipment from any other country in time."

There was a glint of levity in the doctor's eyes.

"You are still having issues with the original source, yes? The rare metal trader from Congo, if I'm correct?"

The man in the engineering duo cleared his throat nervously.

"'The Zairean gentleman in question was our source for the Niobium metal. He took the downpayment for the order and then decided to hike up the price at the last minute. I thought we could negotiate but he wouldn't budge. He has the order ready, all we need to do is get him to ship it. It's been three weeks."

"I know," the doctor said his words measured with menace. "That is why I have decided to intervene on your behalf."

"Sir, we've tried..." the engineer said but the doctor insisted.

"Call him. Mr Augustin Bemba will be pleasantly surprised to hear from you." The engineers looked surprised that Dr Kayanga knew the man's name. "When you connect, put him on speakerphone."

Dr Kayanga was already on his phone speaking quietly to someone on the other end. He finished quickly and placed the smart phone in his jacket pocket but not before checking his Richard Mille transparent watch. The female engineer had her phone to her ear, listening to the ring tone. She nodded and then said:

"Hello Mr Bemba, this is Florence Wyck from Compass Point Engineering. How are you?"

There was a shuffling in the background.

"Ah, Miss Florence from the UK. How are you? Ready to do business?"

Florence looked over to her client, who did not miss a beat.

"You should have taken the first offer given to you by my employees, Mr Bemba, and you would have been so much better off."

The new voice in the telephone conversation threw the Congolese business man off his game. Mr Bemba cleared his throat and composed himself.

"Who is this?" the Congolese trader asked. "Do you think your threats will make me reverse my decision?" He laughed and it was a hoarse phlegmy rattle as if he had just recovered from a bout of 'flu'.

"Oh no, brother," Kayanga said. "That wasn't a threat, that was me stating fact."

"You must have powerful zuzu to be threatening me from the UK?" Bemba kept laughing.

Dr Kayanga checked his watch again.

There was a pounding noise from the African end of the call, making Dr Kayanga grin devilishly.

"My associates are accessing your office as we speak."

Splintering crack and thud made Mr Bemba scream. A heavy door crashed to the floor, heavy footfalls came next, a wet crunch and another scream.

"You will release the cargo to me under my employees' watchful gaze. Do you understand?" Kayanga demanded.

"Aayyii!" Mr Bemba's version of yes was filled with terror. Dr Kayanga nodded, satisfied, as the man's gibbering howls echoed through the device speakers.

"Take it, take whatever you want," Bemba bellowed. "Just get these evil things away from me, please."

The sounds of Mr Bemba's pleas rose and fell, punctuated with sobs and hitches in his breathing. Both engineers stood riveted to the spot, almost afraid to breathe themselves. Back in Kinshasa, the listeners could hear the keyboard being nervously used.

"Are you done?" Dr Kayanga asked impatiently.

"I... I... I'm done," Bemba stammered, his tone short.

Dr Kayanga made a hand gesture to one of his bodyguards who marched over from his post. He handed the doctor a spectacle case that was stitched into the tactical jacket the hooded man was wearing. The doctor slipped the smart glasses over his eyes and could see what his mercenaries were viewing half a continent away. The flat-screen monitor sat on a lavish desk in a room decorated with pictures of Mr Bemba's rich and famous contacts. Kayanga speed read the export document, his eyes locking onto the digital signature.

"Well done. I'll leave you to consider how next time you should best deal with paying customers. Au revoir monsieur Bemba," he said, satisfied with the paperwork,

Dr Kayanga checked his watch and started to exit the room. He stopped between the two man mountains flanking him and turned to the engineers, still standing in shock.

"No further talk of delays," he said flatly.

"No further delays," they both said together in a mixed up, overzealous reply.

"Good," the doctor said. "Very good."

The black and white spider that looked like it was wearing a dinner suit slowly lowered itself on a single glistening web and landed amongst the schematics; the humans in the distance let out a sigh of relief and began a nervous conversation as their client left the room. In the comfort of his eight-legged arachnid form, the Spider God had seen it and heard it all. Dr Kayanga was a dangerous man. And Anancy understood what was going on but still needed to see what the good doctor was building on the scenic Cornish coastline of England. Anancy took his time to crawl over the papers and absorbed the words and pictures into the setae covering his legs and abdomen, storing them in his sensory systems for immediate recall. But not before he finished the opera. Once that was done, he would find Leroy's Shebeen in Ladbroke Grove, smoking a few Cubans, sipping on some Dragon Stouts and making sense of it all. Then would come the strategy, and he couldn't lie; that was his favourite part. How would he pass on whatever he learned to his daughters? How indeed?

The two engineers had finally composed themselves and returned to the table to retrieve their papers. Anancy was done and he spun a web and leapt off the table as he paraglided to the ground. His mind was racing as his spider mandibles tried to twist into the semblance of a smile because he knew the party was about to begin.

Chapter Forty

The Witches of Farringdon had finally identified the killer and coined a name for him. With some old-fashioned detective work coupled with their ESP skills they had accomplished something, they were beginning to doubt they could. The department's forensic sketch artist was creating a likeness of the Surgeon from Spotters – ESPers who could track his psychic signature once they picked up his scent. Shaft stood watching from a distance as the image came together, snatches of his appearance merging through Consolidators – ESPers who could identify the facial features of a target, if they too had some significant psychic anchor. The bastard's physical dimensions compared precisely with the enhanced silhouette the Piece of Yesterday had shown him in Marilyn's bedroom.

Now Shaft knew the identity of his killer; his next steps needed to be precise. His every move would be under scrutiny. He couldn't afford to be discovered. This operation was nothing like working with Joe Public. These villains dealt with using supernatural powers in one way or another. He could be human using mystical implements, but he wasn't going to take that risk. He had a mixture of talented ESPers and civilian contractors who he had to depend on to keep him in their sights but hidden.

Shaft hadn't thought twice about putting The Surgeon under surveillance, but from a manpower perspective, it was challenging. Black Book had a generous budget in comparison to other departments of the Metropolitan Police but it wasn't enough. The sums Shaft had to play with required him to find creative ways to get the results he was looking for. He called in favours, used subterfuge, stole or borrowed as he preferred to call it – Metropolitan Police parlance, a touch of applied blackmail when necessary and developing a closer relationship with London's mystical denizens through Spokes' assistance.

After discovering The Surgeon's MO, Shaft and his team still did not understand why he was doing what he was doing. Was the pathology of a supernatural serial killer any different from a mundane, run-of-the-mill serial killer? He was knitting the bizarre details together to make sense of them in the new world of crime he inhabited. Forget about the impossible... the 'I' word meant nothing here.

Anything was possible.

He let the facts of the case coalesce at the front of his mind and then lined up some pertinent facts in an order he could try and make sense of.

First, The Surgeon targeted victims with a particular antigen profile and extracted specific organs. And secondly, he favoured his victims to be of a certain fitness level and had been targeting gyms in the west London region. He had no actual pattern to his visits to the fitness facilities, but Shaft was hoping if he found another victim, his attendance levels would go up for that particular gym.

It would seem he found another victim.

The killer had visited the same gym six times in the space of a week. Someone had piqued his interest, and whoever that was, they were in grave danger. Shaft was confident The Surgeon's reign of terror was drawing to a close, and he wanted to be the one to end it. He needed to make sure he covered all his bases. Whatever evidence he would attain needed to be indisputable, and that took patience, attention to detail and a methodical nature. Shaft may not be patient but he wasn't fucking about either. He would do whatever it took. If it meant sacrifice he was willing to make it.

THE DETECTIVE STOOD ON THE OTHER SIDE OF THE BUSY Knightsbridge Road and looked at the imposing structure of the Hellfire Private club. If anything, this mysterious place was the bane of his existence. It was here vampire Amanda Pheare had spearheaded her reign of terror.

And now this.

There was a pattern developing. And Shaft knew there would come a time he would have to confront this issue. He would pick his battles because this war was for another time. They were too connected.

He had lived in London most of his life and heard rumours of this place. Only now he understood that anybody in the occult realm with clout in London could stay here. It was an invitation-only establishment. The good, the bad and the ugly. Not even the Metropolitan Police could access it. He had tried.

After getting into the face of the top brass, the Chief Constable for the City of London grudgingly introduced him to a repository kept for the police by the Bank of England. Only a few chief constables and the Commissioner of Police knew of its existence. It was a very interesting place and answered just a few of the questions he had always asked himself, including the hands-off treatment the Hellfire Club was receiving. It seemed there were a few pages missing from the Magna Carta. One of those pages outlined the protection of an organisation established by a Baron with supernatural ties. The Hellfire Club was his legacy and served as a neutral ground where beings that visited or resided on this plane of existence could do so without concern. If that agreement was to be dissolved while the nation had a reigning monarch, there would be hell to pay, literally. And as fate would have it, this is where his killer resided.

At least Shaft knew where he was when the time came; as soon as he left the confines of the private club, he would be nicked. For now, Shaft and his team were watching him around the clock. There was an electronic crackle, and Shaft looked down at his hand gripping his police radio tightly. He had almost forgotten he had it in his hand. He listened carefully over the drone of the traffic.

"The vultures coming in for landing. Are you in position?"

Shaft keyed the radio.

"I'm in position standby," Shaft casted his eyes across the road, cursing as traffic suddenly began to slow. Shaft skipped through the moving cars to the central island halfway between opposite sides of the road. An Uber pulled up, and the killer stepped onto the sidewalk. He was short and muscular, handsome and well dressed. He had a mane of dark hair, sharp Eastern European features and a ready smile. Was it his charms, or was there something else at play? Shaft decided it was both. His most deadly weapons were his eyes. They betrayed him. The detective thought that was why he wore Ray-Ban sunglasses night and day, but the few times Shaft had seen him without his shades, his eyes were dark pools with a spellbinding intelligence and a threat that lurked below the surface. Shaft understood the attraction. The Surgeon's animal magnetism was as deadly as a sharp implement in his doctor's bag.

"Vulture is still at the front of the establishment speaking with the doormen," Shaft reported, his binoculars irritating his nose. "I'll stay with him until he says good night."

"Roger that, Detective," his teammate responded. "I'll hang around with you. I have eyes on him from the corner of Clarion Street."

"That's his best side," Shaft said. "Make sure you take some flattering pictures for our file."

"Roger that," surveillance team two said.

SHAFT TOOK THE BINOCULARS FROM HIS EYES, SMELLING the rubber from the lens protectors and scratching the side of his nose. He looked down to the pavement absently, then looked back up to see a limo pull to the front of the Hellfire Club. As vehicles arrived, Shaft's binoculars were back to his eyes again, watching his killer almost stand to attention on the vehicle's arrival.

"ST two, this is ST one."

"ST to receiving."

"I think this could be his kill partner rolling up. Take pictures like it's his birthday," Shaft said.

"Got it."

It was hard for Shaft to see what was going on, but he guessed his killer had opened the car door for the person or persons inside. Two men stepped out first, and they were huge. He could see them above the SUV, hooded and in black. It was unclear who the new player was until the party was mounting the steps into the Hellfire Club, and he could see the back of the man's head.

"Dr Frankenstein, I presume," Shaft whispered.

The dark-skinned man in a tuxedo had the bearing of a high roller, flanked by the two giants who matched his steps like shadows and beside them was Shaft's killer in animated discussion.

"SD2 to ST1," Shaft said.

"ST1 receiving."

"Did you get that?" Shaft asked.

"Oh yeah. We got it," ST2 said, sounding elated.

Shaft made a fist.

It was time to start putting names to faces.

Chapter Forty-One

The Tree House, Willesden Green, North West London

Getting out felt good. Spokes stood with his hands in the pockets of his suit trousers, teasing the material with his fingers. It was something that he did as a 'bwoy' when he was in deep thought.

The habit never left him.

Birds chirped in the trees around him.

The impresario rocked on the balls of his feet, once, twice and then back to being flat-footed. The house at Willesden Green that had his attention was one he had bought three months ago. Eight bedrooms, detached, high fence and spacious. The neighbours minded their own business and this part of north-west London was hassle free. You could expect some raised eyebrows when residents saw 'ethnic people' not just walking the streets but having the financial clout to push their own keys into a multi-million pound home. They would get used to it or they could go fuck themselves.

In a life before all this, he used to work on homes of this calibre. Homes he never imagined he'd ever be able to afford if he lived three lifetimes. He had afforded his rich clients with the kind of respect reserved for holy men. Back then he was confident in his work, proud of his skills but not his self worth. Everything changed in a moment of chaos. To say he had a seismic shift in his fortunes was an understatement. Not to mention his business, his responsibilities and his calling.

Ah, his calling.

If not for his undead breddrin and the ladies of Bad II the Bone, he wouldn't know he had a calling at all. Did people like him have callings? Before fate intervened in his life, he wouldn't have thought so, but he was oh so wrong. Once he was introduced to a world that existed beside his own, with millions of pounds of financial assets at his disposal and not to mention the powerful artefacts he was left to take care of, Spokes took to his new responsibilities like a duck to water. Formal learning was never his forte. He was good with his hands. Little did he know there was so much more to him than he had imagined.

Look at him now, soaking up this New World like a sponge. Amidst everything, the weirdness, the power, the arcane knowledge and his new skill set, none of this would have been possible without the ladies. He may not voice it enough but his respect for them drove his exploration and his constant pursuit of knowledge. He would do whatever it took to help them in their sacred duty. After all they had helped him find his own.

SPOKES FELT A STRONG ARM SNAKE THROUGH HIS OWN AND the petite but strong figure leaning on him. He glanced to his left, seeing the beautiful dragon tattoo on Suzy's arm.

He smiled.

"Penny for your thoughts," Suzy asked.

He patted her arm.

"Just thinking 'bout how far we've come, Miss Wong."

Both of them stared at the building, its presence having an inexplicable allure especially for Suzy.

"This better be good, Slick," Patra said, interrupting the magic. "I just left a steaming bubble bath with my name written all over it." Patra sucked on a lollipop looking at the building in the same way they were. Y walked past all three of them and stood waiting at the wrought iron gate, her fingers running over the words shaped from iron.

The Tree House.

"Aren't you going to let us in?" Y asked.

"Yeah, man, of course." For a moment, Spokes sounded perplexed then the faraway look in his eyes sharpened and he was himself again. "My apologies," Spoke said. "Come ladies, come."

He took a key fob from his jacket pocket, pressing the small remote nestled amongst the keys.

There was a chirp and a green light from a module on the gate clicked and ponderously swung open.

"Bring the car around Miss P, I'll open up."

Patra spun around and jogged over to the Bentley parked on the curb as Spokes, Suzy and Y walked up to the impressive front door in the distance. The front yard was pristine. The driveway landscaping was made of black granite blocks with flecks of quartz, matching edging slabs that gave off the wet effect that made the regimental green shrubbery running alongside stand out.

"I love what yuh did to the place Mas Spokes, very nice," Suzy said.

Spokes touched his heart and bowed.

"It needs to be, Miss Wong, it hold something of great importance."

"I can feel it all the way out here. Some powerful energies at play. It's a sum neutral force. Neither good nor evil."

Spokes nodded in agreement.

"You've been working on this for months now," Y said. By this time, they were standing at the big double doors. "Patra's been badgering you to tell her what you've been up to and you resisted. That takes guts."

"You telling me," Spokes smiled turning the key and pushing the door open. "Miss P can be very persuasive."

"And very annoying," Suzy said.

"I heard that bitch," Patra said having parked the car and jogged over to catch up with them. "I'm just inquisitive," Patra corrected the misconception. "I love to know shit."

"We know," Y said. "And yet we still love you."

"What's not to love?" She countered, already attempting to mount the sweeping staircase. Suzy grabbed her arm, pulling her back in line like a wayward child. Spokes was heading towards what was a set of elaborately carved wooden doors and a possible lounge beyond.

"This is beautiful," Y said, her fingertips trailing along the intricate characters and scenes, masterfully etched into the wood from the top to the bottom of the door. "Can you hear that?" Y asked, her question tinged with excitement. She put her ear to the door, a pine bouquet from the ancient wood drifted up to her nose, transporting her to Epping Forest with her father. She could almost hear the sounds of birdsong, insects and the wind blowing through the trees. "It's singing," Y said.

Patra came over, touched it tentatively, and put her ear to it too.

"Sounds like a chant," she said.

"You are right," Suzy said. "It feels like a protection incantation."

"As far as I know," Spokes added. "The doors are protecting itself and the contents from the wrong kind of influence. The chant is spoken in the tongue of the first Cameroonian people. No idea what it means, all I know it's protection." Spokes leaned into the door and pushed it open. The hinges did not protest as you would expect from a door as ancient as this. It swung apart smoothly. The perfume of exotic flora and the woody scent of vegetation wafted outwards to greet them. Fluorescent lights flickered on as Spokes waved them inside.

Y passed over the threshold first, Suzy next and Patra at the rear. The American made a funny face expecting some kind of reaction to her entry but none came.

"Suh yuh do have a good heart after all," Suzy teased.

For her kind words, Patra gave her the finger.

"Damn," Spokes nodded his head satisfied. "It's grown."

"What has?" Y asked.

"My seed," Spokes said and took in a deep breath, releasing it with a tremor of excitement.

"That was a seed three months ago?" Patra asked.

Spokes nodded.

All four of them were looking at a leafless tree, ebony bark, whose craggy branches spread wide more than up to the ceiling and across the width of the room. Thick roots bore through the wooden floorboards and claw deep into London's soil. If that wasn't breathtaking enough from their angle, they were looking at a huge spider's web that could not have been generated by a spider that nature intended. The webbing was too white and as thick as thread, and unlike a traditional web pattern, the lines did not extend outwards from a central point. They looked like a roadmap. Whatever had woven the pattern sat inert on a branch on the fringes of the web.

It looked mechanical.

Suzy pointed it out first.

"What's that?" she said.

"Dat my dear is deh spider," Spokes paused to let it sink in.

"It's an enchanted mechanical ting that creates a web that represents the fractures between our reality and the others across London. The more the balance is disturbed the more cracks in barriers between worlds and the more our little spider will weave."

Suzy took two steps toward the tree, stopped, peered at it and looked back to Spokes, pointing to a high branch.

"Tell me that is not what I think it is?" Suzy asked.

Spokes laughed. His chuckle was throaty, he looked relieved.

"Well spotted, Miss Suzy, you are a Jamaican after all. It is what you tink."

Y looked puzzled.

"It's a beehive," Suzy said raising her eyebrows and shrugging.

"Hell no!" Patra said. "We need to fumigate that bitch."

"Not a good idea, Sister P," Spokes said calmly. "The bees are a part of deh process," he paused to think. "I'm just beginning to understand what deh pictographs in the tomb were trying to seh."

"Tomb?" Patra's question went unanswered.

"It didn't come with the spider?" Y asked.

"As far as I can see, these are ordinary bees, attracted to the web, that are somehow able to detect the fractures and tears in reality then carry the information like pollen back to the tree."

"And deh tree takes the data and compiles a working map," Suzy added.

"Something like dat," Spokes added.

"How the hell did you find this?" Y asked.

"That is what I do, Miss Y," he chuckled." It was found in the tomb of a chieftain in tenth century Cameroon who had similar problems to us back in the day. The tribal elders allowed us to use it."

Good Girls Gone Bad

"I'm going to go out on a limb and say there were no detailed instructions on how it works," Y asked.

"You would be right, Miss Y. Just the basics," Spokes seemed to rummage around in the attic of his memory before he continued. "The oral tradition kept by the elders, surprisingly was still in place after hundreds of years. It was enough to recreate the tree after scrounging some other bits and pieces. There may be some gaps in our knowlege but I can reach out to some authorities..."

"No," Y said. "Let's keep this to ourselves. You've outdone yourself. This is great. Thank you." Y hugged him and the others joined in the huddle.

Spokes beamed.

Chapter Forty-Two

Suzy couldn't help herself. She had left the adoption agency with tears in her eyes. The empath was filled with sorrow, fear, confusion, apprehension and a glimmer of joy. Trevor held her hand all the way out of the glass foyer into the chilly London afternoon. The piazza they walked into had seats surrounding a fountain with an exuberant metal phoenix made from beaten blades of steel, not rising up from a lake of flames as it should but from an algae-rimmed pool. Trevor took a seat and guided his girlfriend down, so he was staring directly into her brown eyes.

"Are you alright, babe?" Trevor asked, still holding her hand.

"I'm fine," Suzy said, wiping her eyes. Her expression was as if she had caught herself being silly. "I'm just feeling a little overwhelmed," her voice was low, and she looked genuinely surprised by the effect looking at the children would have on her. Together they had looked at 30 children, and even through cyberspace, Suzy had felt their fear, sorrow, and some joy but mostly confusion, especially for the older children. It had hit her hard because she hadn't prepared for it. How can you prepare for something like this? Suzy wanted to tell herself it would never happen again; next time, she would know what to expect. But she honestly wasn't sure and the thought dragged down thick curtains of sorrow around her.

"How do we choose?" Suzy asked. "Dem all need a home and a family."

Trevor smiled and patted her hand, knowing that gesture always annoyed her. She felt old when he did it.

"I can't believe I'm telling you dis, but we can only go with our hearts. What other way is there?"

Suzy smiled weakly.

"You mek it sound so easy, but after dem emotional energy imprinted on me, I can't separate my feelings from their little hopes and dreams."

"I'm sorry you had to go through dat babe, but in the fucked up way, you will appreciate even more what we're about to do."

"Feh real," Suzy agreed. "Is more than just another adoption but a covenant."

"I like that because it's true," Trevor looked up at the slate of grey skies. "Are we ready?" he asked.

Suzy leaned forward and pressed her lips to his. He reached around her small waist and pulled her into him, the electricity between them crackling, and for a moment, questions and doubts felt insignificant. Reluctantly they broke from their passionate kiss.

Suzy's eyes twinkled.

"You know we won't be doing this alone. We have a family who will have our backs no matter what we decide. We need to be doing this for the right reasons."

Trevor nodded.

"What better reason than to raise a family, create a legacy and give back something positive to society."

"You have been thinking about this," Suzy said.

"I have; that's why I want us to be sure. Let's chill for two weeks and get back to this then."

Suzy thought about it for a minute, then agreed. They both stood and locked arms. Trevor opened up his phone and deftly dialled the number with his free hand.

"My yard?" he asked.

"Your yard," Suzy said.

Chapter Forty-Three

Margaret was a worrier, and Y respected her mom for that. Growing up with her, she had a knack for seeing the worst-case scenario in everything that related to her daughter and that had them at constant loggerheads. As an older teen, Y began to appreciate her mother's protectiveness. Y was her only child, and Margaret wanted the best for her daughter in a cruel world.

Y may never fully understand the ever-present fear you have for your children's welfare, no matter how old they were. The closest thing Y had to knowing where her mother was coming from was how she felt about her sisters. She felt ultimately responsible for them in the dangerous world they inhabited, even though Suzy, Patra, Shaft and Spokes were the most competent people she knew. If that dread feeling when they weren't around her was anything to go by, then she could appreciate why 'mommy' was the way she was. Some of it had obviously rubbed off on her.

Y folded her arms as she stood on the threshold of a newly installed panic room in her mother's house. The new leather smell with aromatic wisps of paint and metal grease imprinted on her consciousness. Whenever there was an emergency, and she thought of safety for her mother, those smells would assail her first.

"What do you think?" Y asked. "Cosy or what?"

Margaret, who was standing right behind her, gave a non-committal shrug.

"It's cosy," she said. "But there's no windows."

Y sighed.

"There is not supposed to be any windows, Mom. It's self-contained." Y continued to sell it. "It has every modicum you need even though I don't expect you to be in it for more than a few hours in an emergency anyway. Although you could survive in it for a week."

Margaret made a face and nodded.

"I like those symbols on the floor around it. What do they mean?" She pointed.

"I'm not sure," Y lied. "Something to do with the company's founders."

"I still think this is excessive, Yvonne. TV, toilet, comfy bed sofa, fridge. How can you afford it all?"

Y pursed her lips knowing exactly where her mother was leading with her questions.

Margaret sighed.

"You had the house renovated to accommodate this metal box. You hire a crane to lower it in through the roof, and then how you convinced the council to allow that is beyond me."

"Your daughter has connections," Y said, smiling.

"Lawd, the neighbours were having kittens," Margaret continued. "That ugly one who lives beside me, I know she contacted the council to complain many times."

"Let them," Y said.

"Come to think of it, nobody has mentioned it in a week. That's strange for these busybodies around here."

Y spoke under her breath.

"That's what happens when you have a well-placed 'forget it' spell constructed by a master warlock."

"What did you say, Hon?" Margaret asked.

"Nothing, Mom," Y said quickly.

Y stepped back in line with her mother and hugged her around the shoulders.

"Do you trust me, Mom?" Y asked, her voice low and serious.

"Of course, honey," Margaret answered without hesitation.

"Well, trust me that this is just a precaution if there's blow-back from my work. I want you to be safe."

"Safe from what?" Margaret asked.

Y seemed to think deeply about the question.

"Keeping you safe from everything."

Margaret looked at her daughter strangely.

"You've never taken the easy route, have you? That adventurous spirit you inherited from your father. And that sword. Do you go anywhere without it?"

"Nowhere," Y said, smiling. "It's a part of me and is not a sword, Mom; it's a Katana."

"I stand corrected," Margaret said. "Just be careful with the police. A black woman and a... Katana... is not a good combination."

"I'm not worried, Mom. They're the ones who should be worried."

"'That I can believe," Margaret said. "You haven't changed." Her eyes flicked to the gallery of framed photographs on the wall. A young Yvonne wearing her numerous karate belts adorned most of the images. Her posing with a Bokken at the head of her martial arts class was especially striking.

Y was also drawn to the photographs. They transported her back to the passion she felt learning to control her adolescent mind and body through martial arts. Little did she know it was all in preparation for this period in her life. Y had a sense it was how it was supposed to be.

"I was worried you wouldn't stick with it, but I'm glad you did," Margaret said. "Did you ever think to give it up when it got hard?"

"Never!" Y said. "I couldn't have done it without you, Miss Sinclair."

"You did learn from a good teacher," Margaret gloated. "A good mother is forced to be that and more for their kids. But there was one thing I could never teach you, that was patience." She smiled wryly.

"When it comes to the ones I love, patience goes out the window, Mom," Y said, kissing her on the forehead. "While I'm here, let's go through the process to access your state-of-the-art panic room."

"I hope there are no keypads. I hate trying to use keypads. They wreck my nails."

Y rolled her eyes.

"No keypads, Mom, you like this." Mrs Sinclair [A1] nodded, thinking about some random point that was bothering her.

"I think they should call it another name instead of a panic room."

Y's eyes widened.

"Okay, Mom..." Y said.

"Spread its appeal," Margaret continued.

"Any ideas?" Y prompted, trying to keep her mind off what would come next.

Her face brightened.

"Peace of mind lounge," she said. "I like that."

Good Girls Gone Bad

Y laughed – the kind of laugh only her mom, sisters and her lover could extract from her.

"I promise I'll look into rebranding the panic room business after I show you a few things," Y said.

"Are you being disrespectful?" Margaret asked, feigning strictness.

"I wouldn't think of it, mother dearest," Y said, taking her mother's hand and placing it on the scanner integrated into the reinforced door. "Now, don't move. Let's allow the system to map your palm print."

"How long will this take?" Margaret asked.

"Patience," Y said, enjoying her mother squirming.

Chapter Forty-Four

University Hospital, East Central London

Nanny stood in the hospital's private room, making clucking sounds of disapproval as she spoke with Patra.

"Dem was trying to poison him..." Nanny paused to make that statement sink in, "...slowly. If him never get admitted here when he did, you'd be attending his fineral."

Patra shook her head, dislodging some errant tears from her eyes.

"Those backstabbing, money-hungry, heartless motherfuckers," Patra spat. "That man lying there has given his life to making his family comfortable, and this is how they repay him? Gotdamn!"

They both looked at the peacefully sleeping patient with Mei Ling curled up beside him, her black fur stark against the white sheets.

Nanny sighed, her eyes piercing in the dimness and her alabaster skin glowing from the light of the monitors. For the last two days, she had been administering a pipette full of herbs and bushes she had concocted from her garden in the greenhouse at the mansion.

"Him tek well to the herbs I prepared for him. They will flush out the poison and begin healing any damaged organs. His aura was weak and fractured, but I shared some of my own with his. It will rejuvenate in time. Let him rest; tomorrow will be a better day."

Patra nodded.

"I don't know how to thank you, Aunty; you saved him." Patra hugged the Albino woman fiercely, and she reciprocated. Her beautiful, ageless face showed her happiness only in her eyes and a small wrinkle at the corner of her mouth. She straightened her coat and clasped her hands together. Patra couldn't help but picture her as a Caribbean Mary Poppins.

"How you getting home, Aunty?" Patra asked. "Do you want me to book you an Uber?"

"Nuh need," Nanny said. "I'll mek my own way home." She paused and looked over to the much too comfortable cat. "You coming, puss?"

Mei Ling looked up, green eyes glistening, swished her tail, meowed and stretched, working her claws into the sheets, sheathing and unsheathing them. Her weapons tested, she leapt off the bed and gracefully bounded to Nanny's feet. The woman bowed and glided effortlessly towards the door and, without looking back, said:

"Say good night to your lady friend Grace for me." Nanny opened the door allowing the cat through first, then she followed and disappeared.

Patra laughed.

She should have known better than to think she could keep secrets from Nanny.

SCAN ME

Chapter Forty-Five

Overtime Nightclub, Leicester Square, Central London

Shaft stood outside the nightclub and, just for a second, regretted telling Y his plans for apprehending The Surgeon tonight. In a parallel world, he would be her protector and it would be completely out of the question for her to tag along in an operation like this. Then he would remind himself that his girlfriend was no ordinary woman and worrying about her welfare was not the best use of his emotional energy. He was old school, and the gender roles had shifted in his life. He welcomed the change; it just took time for him to adapt. Shaft looked around and wondered if he'd done enough to pull off the look. He couldn't do much about his age – he guessed the majority of people standing in the queue were mid to early twenties. The detective decided he had the attitude but not the look. Superficially he projected an easy-going and amiable attitude as he stood in the queue to get inside the world-famous Overtime nightclub.

He wasn't ringing any alarm bells that shouted 'Cop', which was good enough for him.

Except deep inside, there was a turmoil of emotions as he

prepared for the possibility of The Surgeon being arrested. In the space of two weeks, he'd been in this position twice, and he had left the covert operation empty-handed. The Surgeon was meticulous and seemed to have an early warning system that kept him on the right side of the law. But for how long? He was obviously stalking his prey from the gym, getting to know his victim from his regular jaunts to the fitness studio on Beckton Road. Shaft had him on surveillance both psychically and using standard police procedure. It was only a matter of time before he struck again, and Shaft wanted to be there to put the cuffs on when he attempted to murder his next victim. This was the part of the job he hated. You needed patience and focus at this stage of the operation, especially when you could almost see the finish line. If that wasn't enough challenge for him as the team leader, he was the one responsible for the budget and the allocated resources. To be fair, the unit's budget was substantial even if he had to strong-arm funds from the old heads at the top. It wasn't limitless, and The Surgeon's case was stretching his finances. They were still in the black, but he was beginning to wonder how long he'd be able to keep up this intensive surveillance.

No matter what though, Shaft would remain composed and go through the motions required for a successful conclusion to this stressful operation. In about twenty minutes, he wanted to have eyes on The Surgeon with his next unsuspecting victim Rosalind Pike. Bad II the Bone were in the building with two undercover coppers he borrowed from Vice. Outside was crawling with plainclothes police. He thought he was well and truly covered for backup. But he also knew what could go wrong, would go wrong.

The detective would remain fluid.

. . .

Shaft breathed deeply as he stood in the nightclub's foyer; the music's vibration was reaching out to him not just through the air but through the soles of his feet. He rotated his head until it made that comforting cracking sound. He was now ready for anything that could go down. Shaft walked into the main area and immediately began assessing the space he had to work with. Exits, toilets, bars, seating, DJ booth and a few extra things to be aware of. A fountain and a very impressive fish tank were focal points. If it wasn't such a packed night, and due to its circular design, he'd be able to see across the space from any elevated position. But that wasn't going to be possible. This was going to require him to stay close, but that made Shaft uncomfortable. He didn't think The Surgeon realized he was being followed. He hadn't altered his patterns.

Predators survive because they have an acute relationship with their surroundings. The more aware and tuned into the hunting grounds they become, the more efficient killers they become. They usually get caught when they start to discount all the vital data they had internalised that made them such exceptional monsters. Once they began to think it was their intelligence that made them superior. That was usually the beginning of the end. The Surgeon suffered from none of these misconceptions, and so far in his reign of terror, he had not taken a wrong step. It had already been decided that if they apprehended this monster, they would have to catch him in the act. Shaft couldn't afford to just go through the motions because who knew when his killer would decide to strike. Shaft took in a deep breath, the sound of Hip-Hop artist Busta Rhymes reverberating in his chest, and he let his detective awareness slide even further into place before he joined the throng.

. . .

Igor Rakmanov saw himself as a lover, not a fighter. His Master was all about the battle. Creating the perfect form and function to prevail in varying combat situations. The Master's creative genius and his love for warfare made him suited for what he did. Similarly, Igor's skills were suited to what he did best. Using his body to make women happy, he took the light they had inside and shared it with someone who was more deserving of it. He would never consider himself a killer. That was a vulgar term for someone who took life for no rhyme or reason. He had a duty.

One such a giving soul sat opposite him in the crowded nightclub. Igor placed his hand over her delicate one, using his finger to gently tap to the music playing over the speakers on her soft skin. They shared a table with a nearly complete bottle of champagne and two empty flutes. Igor leaned forward with his legs apart underneath. Rosalind had her right foot in Igor's crotch, her bare feet massaging his balls and cock, which by now were impressively erect. Igor had a self-assured smirk on his face, not just because he was getting his jewels fondled, but the light inside her was so bright he was glad he was wearing shades. He was always surprised that only he could see it. It was like he had the power of X-ray vision, allowing him to peer through skin, muscle, and blood vessels to the incandescent fruit of a one-of-a-kind organ pulsing inside. His vision was one of his gifts, and everyone had gifts. He could see it and know when it was ready for harvesting. Rosalind was ready and tonight was the night. She was so kind to share a part of herself with him. The beautiful Rosalind would never know who her kidneys were benefiting. All she needed to know was her sacrifice did not go unrecognised. Dr Kayanga had her name amongst the hundreds of others who made the ultimate offering so that one day his Antoinette, the woman the Master had kept alive for hundreds of years, would walk amongst men again. It was an honour for Igor to play a part in such a glorious love story.

"What are you thinking?" Rosalind asked, interrupting Igor's romantic musings.

Igor smiled.

"I can't wait," he said, his voice husky. "I have something you need."

Rosalind looked at him quizzically then it dawned on her what he meant as his penis hardened even more. Her smile broadened, and both stood reading each other's thoughts. Igor leaned over to her ear and whispered what he had in mind. It seemed to excite her because she moved in closer to him, his aftershave expensive and intoxicating. Rosalind reached for the massive bulge in the front of his pants and squeezed. Ideally, she would need both hands to fully hold what he had, but she made do. Igor grunted with delight, his heightened senses discerning her racing heart and the dampness of her crotch. Igor grabbed her hand, and they started to make their way to the nightclub dance floor on the other side. Dance music was playing and every inch of the floor space was occupied by skanking and gyrating clubgoers who were adding to the soundtrack of Buju Banton with their own voices. Igor loved the energy and the contact as he waded through the human bodies. He could swear he was absorbing some of their excitement into his body, soaking up the sexual electricity. Rosalind gripped his hand, feeling the energy too. It tingled over her skin, making Igor proud that her last moments would be filled with grace.

Soon it would be over.

SHAFT HAD SURREPTITIOUSLY REACHED OUT TO HIS TEAM. Y and the girls pinged him before he could see any of them. He didn't think he would ever get used to that. Shaft was a node in the psychic network of the Guardians. Through some process he was never privy to, he could sense them when they were in proximity. The detective even knew who it was from the unique tingling sensation in his groin and abdomen. When Suzy or Patra came into his field, they introduced themselves as tingles in his head and heart.

Go figure.

He could only imagine Y getting a good laugh at his expense whenever she told him she was around. He felt so much better they were here. His concern was with the sophisticated communication equipment that could be undependable at times when it needed to run smoothly. It was just so loud and frenetic in the club. That's why the detective always ensured he had eyes on The Surgeon.

A wave of bodies glided past him.

In one moment Igor and Rosalind were kissing.

And the next.

They were gone.

A runaway train of panic hurtled down the track but never got far. Shaft immediately put the brakes in place and composed himself. Not allowing himself to think, Shaft approached the crowd in the direction he hoped The Surgeon was heading.

"Has anyone got eyes on The Surgeon?" Shaft's voice was measured but nobody came back to him with an affirmative. "Find him, people; I want to know exactly what he's doing and where he is."

"Got it!"

"We'll find him."

"And when you do," Shaft said. "Report back."

Shaft was slipping into the psyche of a madman, utilising everything he knew about him and his MO; the detective did this every time his quarry moved in a particular way. No matter how innocuous it may seem. As far as Shaft was concerned, there was a meaning behind it. Nothing he did was insignificant.

Nothing.

Shaft picked up the pace through the revellers; his heart was pounding, and this did not feel right. The Surgeon had been missing for five minutes, and he knew the damage he could do in such a short period. As audacious as even he was, The Surgeon would not commit murder in the open. He needed some kind of cover. Something that would shield him. As these thoughts came to the forefront of his mind, Shaft had begun to push clubgoers to one side; he was running now, shoulder-checking anyone in his way and brandishing his warrant card to the ones who saw him coming. There was no turning back now; if his hunch was wrong, his cover and the benefit of surprise would be lost. The Surgeon would know he was the subject of an extensive operation and would alter his tactics to suit the new circumstances. Months of work up in smoke.

That was if he was wrong because if he was right, this could be so much worse.

The nightclub had four sets of toilets situated around the circumference. With a crowd like this and with drinks flowing from three bars, foot traffic would be heavy. He had one choice out of the four WCs, and then he had to decide whether he would enter the male or female restrooms. Shaft would allow for that decision when the moment required it. He let his intuition and what seemed like logic guide him, opening up himself to the force around that impacted human decision and praying he could influence it in some way. The sea of bodies parted. Shaft growled his way through them, his warrant card producing force of respect that made them skitter away. And before he could take a breath of preparation, the toilet loomed ahead of him. Shaft didn't hesitate; there was a tightlipped scream from a female punter as he barged into the ladies' toilets. He pulled his Browning automatic from his shoulder. And held the nozzle down, his finger inches from the trigger. Two young women skittered by him. He shuffled deftly as part of the floor was wet and slippery but kept his stride wide as he approached five cubicles. Three were empty, and two were occupied. Again, he let his intuition guide him, and he slammed the flat of his foot to the sliding latch on the inside and felt it buckle under force. The door flew open, revealing a woman on the throne, panties around her ankles, head thrown back, screaming at the top of her voice.

"Fuck!" Shaft spat and reversed. His sole focus was now on door number two. He planned to use his shoulder, this time bracing himself to lunge at it when the door swung open.

He paused for a beat.

Shaft lifted his weapon and peered into the cubicle. His brain took moments to interpret what he was looking at, and still, he was uncertain. Rosalind flopped on the toilet seat, but Shaft couldn't see her completely, as if he was looking through a shifting opaque barrier that was momentarily blocking his view of the woman. In a second, he saw her torn dress from her midriff, blood seeping through the material. Then he couldn't see that detail again; it had disappeared like a mirage. Rosalind's eyes fluttered in a state of agitated unconsciousness as parts of her image appeared and disappeared like a flickering computer screen. Shaft barged into the cubicle attempting to grab her out, and that's when he felt it.

Flesh muscle and bone.

Something invisible was posted between Rosalind and himself that shrugged off his advances into the cubicle, sending him sliding back out. With his weapon still pointed forward, regaining his posture, Shaft took two steps back, trying to calm his breathing and pounding heart. With wide-eyed incredulity, the invisible someone began assembling one pixel at a time into a figure in front of him.

The Surgeon.

The killer, who was utterly invisible a heartbeat ago, was slowly becoming opaque. Grinning madly with the ceremonial knife raised high in his right hand. Shaft raised his weapon.

Time seemed to work differently for The Surgeon because as Shaft's finger wrapped around the trigger in a practised movement, as the bullet exploded from the barrel, The Surgeon twisted away from the projectile like his upper body had dematerialised into an evasive position. The bullet that should have drilled into the killer's chest exploded the toilet's cistern behind him. It happened so quickly Shaft wasn't able to reacquire his target. The Surgeon barged through him, slashing his throat as he flew past. Shaft leaned back as the blade flashed past his jugular, losing his balance. As he turned to look back, gun in hand, the short, stocky figure burst out of the toilet and into the nightclub.

"Fuck! Fuck! Fuck!" Shaft scrambled to his feet and ran over to the woman in the cubicle. A quick life signs check, and he was happy she was alive but bleeding. A sudden feeling of disappointment threatened to crush him as The Surgeon made his getaway. The Metropolitan Police teams would grab him, surely. What if he tried that invisibility shit again? Could he evade them?

A bitter smile unfurled on Shaft's lips as he dashed out of the toilet in pursuit. He may not have the privilege of an old-fashioned police collar, but good luck trying to get past Bad II the Bone.

Good fucking luck.

. . .

Good Girls Gone Bad

THE CLUB WAS IN PANDEMONIUM AS THE SURGEON FLED, causing as much chaos in his wake as possible. The music coming from the speakers couldn't drown out the screams that provided an audible trail Shaft could follow. The problem was he couldn't follow where it led because of the human traffic between him and The Surgeon. He was swimming against the tide but couldn't stop. He looked right and left, searching for an alternative route, and that's when he saw the two-man police team that had followed him to the toilets; they had obviously given chase, and The Surgeon had tried to stop them. He had slashed one of the officers in the face, his colleague trying to stymie the blood flow with his shirt. Shaft could only make eye contact and keep moving. The bastard was dropping bodies in his path as he made his escape. Shaft dodged arms and legs in a confused motion, dragging up a few people who had stumbled to their feet. Nipping in the bud the potential for a stampede.

His altruism did not slow him down.

He wanted to be there when they took him. He wanted to see the anguish and disappointment in his eyes as his reign of terror ended. Shaft wanted the satisfaction for himself, his team, Marilyn's family, and this monster's victims.

With that fire raging in his gut, he desperately kept moving against the crowd.

Y WAS ON A HIGH, SURVEYING THE NIGHTCLUB FROM THE first-floor balcony, when The Surgeon burst out of the toilets. Her heart lurched as she immediately thought of Shaft. Her psychic connection with her lover may not be as acute as with her sisters, but it was good enough. He was agitated but unhurt. She sighed with relief but held her breath as the two man undercover team tried to apprehend the serial killer. They had mingled well with the clubgoers, and as soon as he burst out, they sprang into action, but The Surgeon, as surprised as he was, reacted to the threat with lightning swiftness.

Y wanted to confront him then and there, but there were too many people under her. She would be too late as The Surgeon effortlessly brushed off the hands trying to grab him and sliced air and flesh in a frenzy of exploding blood and skin. The officer screamed, the sound louder than the music, and held his ruined face as he fell to his knees, blood seeping through his fingers. Y grimaced; a chill ran through her, and so did righteous anger. The only thing she could do was wait for the floor below her to clear.

Without hesitation, she sprang off the balcony into the air, swung from a gantry and took the 40-foot plunge as if she had just walked off her porch. Y hit the dancefloor in front of The Surgeon and stopped him in his tracks as he saw the woman standing from her crouch. He was surprised and flustered, but he recovered quickly, lunging at Y with his blade. The Surgeon was preternaturally quick and strong. He tried to slash her throat, chest and abdomen in one fluid and lightning-fast 'Z'.

The move was faster than the eye could follow. Y was just as quick, shuffling backwards, agilely evading slashes. But The Surgeon pressed forward, spinning like a top, lowering his centre of gravity reminiscent of circus performing Cossacks. He obviously had training in some martial arts Y did not recognise and one he was adept at. Y moved in close and blocked the slashes that were coming thick and fast. The Surgeon changed tack again, from attempting to cut her stomach open to lacerating her legs. She danced away, and he followed like a human-powered guillotine, altering his angular momentum like an ice skater. His balance was exceptional. For the first time, Y reached for her Katana on her back, and The Surgeon, seeing an abrupt end to his assault, used his powerful legs to rocket himself into a crowd heading to the fire escape but not before slashing Y's thigh and disappearing into the crowd.

Y swore and grimaced.

The Surgeon's blade was mystical; it had cut through her Kevlar leggings like butter, and the minor wound was stinging. Her consternation did not last as a smile blossomed on her lips.

He's coming your way, she thought. The message was transmitted through the ether to her sisters, loud and clear.

Igor Rakmanov burst through a rarely used fire exit situated at the nightclub's rear. It had been designed for staff at the back of house to escape in the event of a fire without traipsing through the club to get to safety. Igor didn't know all of this, but he knew that it was out of the way and would provide his best chance of escape.

He was mistaken.

Igor came to a screeching stop.

Suzy and Patra stood glaring at him, arms folded, blocking his exit.

"Is this the white boy?" Patra turned to ask Suzy.

"Yeh man, a him dat," she said.

For the first time, Patra turned away from her sister and looked at him with unshielded disgust.

"So, you enjoy murdering women?"

Igor grinned a perfect grin and took a step toward them, his blade drawn back, a few stragglers squeezing by him on his left and right, having been turned around in the confusion.

"My Master spoke of you... The Guardians," he said. "You have been interfering in his business. You should have left him alone."

Patra narrowed her eyes with frustration and looked at Suzy.

"I know Y said not to kill him but I'm going to fuck this cracker up."

"Be my guest," Suzy said stepping back. Patra reached into her shoulder bag and took up three large ball bearings that she balanced in her right hand using her fingers to deftly keep them revolving in the centre of her palm.

"It looks like you were in a hurry motherfucker," Patra said. "Don't let me stop you; come on."

Patra beckoned him forward.

Chapter Forty-Six

South Cornwall Coastline, Grimwall Lighthouse

Dr Kayanga lifted the two-ton block of machinery and held it up for a visual inspection before placing it neatly beside the ever expanding mound of other equipment. He appreciated the power he felt when he used the RX710-Z exoskeleton. It wasn't just about amplifying his strength 50 times, but the freedom it gave him to work on his more labour intense projects without involving his legion of engineers and technicians. This kind of work was meditation for him. No need to call on his scientific expertise or vast knowledge to wrangle the solution to a sticky problem. Here it was, muscle alone and his thoughts were left to percolate in the background.

Igor had received a delivery of power modules still packed in huge wooden crates. Within 45 minutes, he had removed all fifteen modules and stacked them together for his team to access them easily. He had thought of training select team members to use the exoskeleton prototype but decided against it. Such a powerful tool in the hands of subordinates would be a lapse in judgement. The possibility of traitors within his team was remote, but why stack the odds against yourself?

Forklifts, pallet jacks, side-loaders, and AVGs would have to continue without the technological leap forward provided by the RX710-Z. It was a morale booster as well. Seeing him stride across the floor, lifting and moving equipment, while the various engineering groups went about their business, knowing he was there, watching, correctly and disciplinary if the need arose.

Satisfied that he had completed a high-priority job on his checklist, the doctor decided to get more hands-on with his quality control checks.

MOMENTS LATER, KAYANGA WALKED THROUGH THE NEWLY constructed facility carrying a tablet and wearing a hard hat. The 40 disconnected parts were situated in rows of five, and as the tech teams finished the installations of his design, he went about his business of making sure everything was perfect.

"You!" He snapped his fingers, pointing to a young female employee, his voice filled with authority and a little threat. The technician stopped what she was doing and hurried over.

"There's a hairline crack on the quartz glass of pod 27. Have it replaced immediately."

"Yes sir," her squeaky voice was earnest. "Right away, Sir." She scurried away, leaving the doctor to continue his quality assurance checks. Kayanga reached the end of aisle four and looked through a magnificent arch of photo chromatic glass that framed the transformed Grimwall lighthouse in the distance. Thick sheath copper strands snaked from the base of the lighthouse along the chalky ground some two hundred metres from the building he was housed in. The magical energy he captured would then be siphoned in measured bursts into the pods.

Antoinette would be bathed in the celestial fire first. He looked down to the tiled floor from his elevated position, and dead centre of the vista in front of him was an up connector socket embedded into the industrial grid tiles. Antoinette's containment pod would be connected right at the intersection, and she would benefit from the transformation first. Just as it should be, with the savage waters smashing into the coastline as a backdrop. Very fitting for his ultimate act of creation. He imagined the glorious scenario in his head for a few seconds when his mobile phone rang. The caller ID appeared as an augmented reality image courtesy of the doctor's contact lenses. The call was coming from his legal team in Canary Wharf. This was the great-great-grandson of the legal representative he'd had for over a hundred and fifty years. Smyth, Cruickshank and Duckworth.

"Yes, Mr Smyth," he said coolly. "How can I help?"

"Dr Kayanga, it's good to speak with you. Your colleague Igor Rachmaninov has been detained by the Metropolitan Police for murder."

"Hmm." The doctor considered what he had just heard. "Where?" the doctor asked simply.

"New Paddington Green high-security facility. I'm about to dispatch my best team to the location to begin legal proceedings."

The doctor smiled crookedly, a twinkle in his eye.

"Don't bother Mr Smyth. I'll handle it from here."

"Doctor?" The solicitor was about to protest, but the doctor had decided.

"Thank you for your continued discretion, Mr Smyth. It will not be forgotten."

Chapter Forty-Seven

Knights Templar Safehouse South West London

Retired Major General Rupert Pemberton made his wedge of Angus steak issue a rude sucking sound as he pressed his knife into the succulent meat on his plate. It reminded him of tight vaginal muscles and moist sex. Further reminding him that after his solitary meal, he'd be making those exact sounds in a luxury flat in Knightsbridge. It had been a challenging week for him but nothing that a bottle of Château Cheval Blanc red wine couldn't remedy. The meal of finest moist sirloin steak, creamy Maris Piper potatoes, blanched mushrooms and seared asparagus was what the doctor ordered. He would thank the chef as he always did because his kitchen staff genuinely believed only the best was good enough for their discerning membership.

Of the four safe houses the Knights Templar had in London, the Sloane Square residence was his favourite. The security was second to none and the facilities for higher ranking officers were exemplary. There was even a cleric at hand to cater for your spiritual needs if required. The Major was feeling frisky so before he immersed himself in the communal bath whose waters were provided by an underground spring founded by his brothers in the 16th century, he would sharpen his shooting skills in the firing range. He was eager to try out his new custom designed Glock. Until then his focus was on the exquisite meal in front of him. And chef Rene kept the standard consistently high.

The Major took a sip of his wine, swirling the liquid around in his mouth, feeling the fresh and fruity grapes explode over his tastebuds. He looked down at his blissfully silent phone and suddenly wondered why he hadn't heard from the security detail outside. Yes, they knew not to disturb him without cause but they would make encouraging sounds beyond the door to reassure him they were doing their jobs. The Major took a mouthful of asparagus between his misgivings and then hovered his hand over the sensor under the table to summon one of his security detail who he guessed were languishing outside. There was a conscientious knock on the door and it swung partially open. His security did not come in to show himself. The door remained ajar with no sign of his men, no sound but the tick, tick of the grandfather clock in the hallway. The Major felt the hairs at the back of his neck stand on end.

"Flagstaff?" he called, placing his knife and fork neatly together beside his plate.

"Hastings?" Even out of his own mouth, his voice sounded concerned and he chastised himself for that. It wasn't becoming of a retired major in the Royal Marines – who had seen action not only in the Falklands but on clandestine missions for the Knights Templar – to be concerned. You were either prepared or dead.

The Major's breathing became steady and measured, his eyes never left the door. Motes of dust floated through the crack, the mood light beyond reflecting off the particles. The old soldier felt his ears warm as he engaged his hyper audio training. Visualising a pulsing mandala, reducing some tolerance and increasing sensitivity in his ears. He had nothing but a white noise reflected back at him except his sixth sense was pulsing like a klaxon. His fingers cautiously walked over to the new gun he'd rested on the end of the dining table.

As his flesh touched metal, a liquid shadow moved from the hallway with such rapidity and absence of sound the Major only felt the air part, his skin prickle and the huge figure stood before him. His reflexes were sharp for his age but he could only manage to grip the Glock's butt before his size 48 custom made combat boots slammed down on his gun hand and swatted the weapon away. The Major heard and felt his bones break and as he filled his lungs to scream, a hand covered his mouth and most of his face.

The shock had made him hyper-sensitive and he felt a cold metal point in the palm of his hand. Before he could scream again, a Damascus steel blade had pierced his palm like the tender beef he had been eating and kept going into the old wood of the dining table, skewering him in place like a butterfly on display.

The Shadow stepped back observing his handiwork or keen to see the man's reaction. Watching the Major in shock, still trying to remove the knife from his hand and table made him smile. The Major grunted in frustration, standing up, sitting down and swearing. Either his food had been drugged or magic was at play because the Shadow was becoming discernible – first its huge chest down to his legs. The Major needn't have seen anymore to know that he was in the presence of a legend. The bane of the Knights Templar and the most wanted man, beast or entity on their most wanted list.

The giant was fully visible in black tactical gear, its face covered in the ballistic mask. The Major frantically pulled on the custom-made Bowie knife attaching him to the table but with muscles taut, the sounds of struggle trickling from his mouth, it was an impressive attempt – but useless.

"You must be wondering why no blood? Why no pain... other than your broken hand that is?" Kintu said.

The Major was taken aback by the deep bass of voice and the cultured inflections of the creature that spoke to him.

"We have a lot to talk about," Kintu said. "And I want your full attention."

"You abomination!" The Major spat. "In the name of the holy Trinity and everything we hold dear, I rebuke you foul beast."

"Childish," Kintu said shaking his head in what could have been amusement. "You have no choice, Major, and that is why your organisation is irrelevant and not fit for purpose."

"You'll get nothing from me," the Major threatened. "My brothers and I are willing to give our lives for what we believe in." The Major flexed his jaw trying to bite down on an implant in his tooth.

"Honourable but not necessary," Kintu said. "'The fast acting poison in your false molar will not activate while my blade is through your hand. The spell on the blade won't allow it."

The Major roared with frustration.

"You and your ilk can continue believing magic is evil or doesn't exist all you wish. Tell yourself otherwise when the spell within the blade forces you to tell me the truth."

"No!" The Major wailed jumping to his feet, his eyes wide, breathing erratic. All his training out the window at the prospect of being manipulated by the one thing his order considered satanic at the worst and an aberration at the best.

"Major, how many good people have you murdered or excommunicated from the Church because of your prejudice and outdated beliefs?" Kintu asked with such earnestness it felt as if he wanted to pull up a chair and listen to the man's explanation.

The Major squirmed, he tried to respond but his tongue felt heavy and unresponsive. All that came out of his mouth were grunts and mumbles.

The spell was taking hold.

"You call me abomination," Kintu said. "And yet you and your organisation supply military cadavers to a madman with no questions asked."

Kintu walked over to the doorway, effortlessly dragging the bodies from the hallway into the room and then gently closing the door behind him. He turned back to the Major.

"I need to know everything about your operation with Dr Kayanga. Leave nothing out."

The old soldier's eyes glazed over and he swallowed with difficulty. With trembling lips he let slip secrets only he knew. Secrets he would pay dearly for divulging.

Chapter Forty-Eight

The Residential Area Surrounding New Paddington Green Max Security Detention Centre

The black Mercedes panel van pulled up on Gant Street, its engines idling. The back door opened, and a dense wall of freezing fog hid the contents of the darkened interior from prying eyes. The van rocked from side to side as whatever was inside shuffled around, the shocks straining under the weight. Two black-clad figures stepped out into the night carrying something heavy and machinelike. They lowered it to the sidewalk activating four explosive clamps that fired bolts deep into the concrete, securing the mystery machine to the spot. The two figures re-entered the van and closed the door behind them, leaving wispy tendrils of fog to dissipate in the night air.

They drove away with three more drop-offs to make.

The New Paddington Green Maximum-Security Detention Centre had been built over the old Paddington Green police station, which had been a functioning holding cell for over a hundred years. As it stood now, the Max had been upgraded to take in the new breed of threat, international and home-grown, to the United Kingdom. Securing them in short-stay facilities before extradition, sentencing or transfer to more permanent housing. Secretly billions had been spent on the construction of an intelligent building. The structural design of the Max had been constructed to withstand missile impacts and protect the infrastructure from seismic events. Tempered glass was used for the administrative portion of the building above ground, which was 12 storeys up. Cutting-edge bioterrorism prevention systems had been implemented to mitigate all known threats. The brain of the building situated in the sub-levels was fed large parcels of data from military and intelligence sources. The Max may look like a glorified holding cell, but it was a node in the vast intelligence network that could analyse signals and warnings, detect connections and recognise critical moments in seemingly isolated events. Accessing the Max compound was done through armed checkpoints. Vehicles were scanned, IDs confirmed, and canine teams made regular sweeps. Entering the main building as a staff member or guest was a seamless process that was a testament to the advanced facial recognition systems, x-ray scanners, metal detectors and human/AI profilers that all worked in concert. The developers had considered everything, or so they thought.

The Mercedes van's door flew open as the west London neighbourhood of Paddington went dark. The team had deployed and activated four large-scale EMP generators around the Max simultaneously. All electronic devices within a mile radius were dead, some cars were inoperable, data stored on disks fried and a portion of the power grid was disabled. The Max had its own generators, but the electromagnetic pulse would have fried them too, allowing access for the shock troops who were stoically waiting in three vans. The dead soldiers stepped out of the fog-shrouded interior like automatons, all in black tactical gear and Kevlar body armour. Their faces were shielded with ballistic masks. They carried sharp-edged weapons on their backs and bags of equipment. They had helix grapnel – REBS compact launchers, rope control devices, flexible wire ladders, Atlas powered ascenders, explosive hook equipment, coils of rope and blocks of C4 explosives. They stood silently in rows of three as if they were toy soldiers arranged by an unseen hand. In the dark, they looked straight ahead with dead eyes. Unmoving except for the twitch of a finger or the flex of a shoulder.

No nerves.

No breath issued from their mouths in the cool evening; their chests did not rise and fall with exertion. But they were alive in a twisted subversion of life. And soon, they would be fulfiling the duty they were created for. A message was sent by their puppet master, and they all came to attention, moving into three separate groups. Then with preternatural speed, they sprinted away in the darkness; chaos and destruction were on tonight's agenda.

Chapter Forty-Nine

Paddington Green Maximum-Security Detention Centre

Igor sat in the Spartan bed, his back to the cell door and continued his deep breathing. He had been here for four nights and was beginning to develop a ritual after the mundane process of being booked, which consisted of a strip search, photographs, attempts to ID him – which failed – cursory questioning that was met with silence, and a medical check for his bruises and swellings after the tussle with the Guardians. All of this done under the cold gaze of armed guards. He was chained and dragged off to his new accommodation after that. Igor was housed in Cell Block Omega amongst the serial killers, terrorists, and gangsters. As far as he knew, he was one of the first inmates with magical or related magical powers. Igor had a feeling he would not be the last. His new digs comprised a Spartan concrete box whose walls were a sickly yellow colour that was supposed to improve mood, but Igor didn't need it. Wherever they had placed him, the matter of his mood and his emotions were firmly under his control. The bed was actually a ledge, jutting out from the wall and on top of that was a waterproof mattress. The authorities had tried to sanitise it, but Igor's senses could still smell the piss, vomit, and cum within the fibres. Disgusting, it may be for some but not him. He was comfortable around the human body's secretions, ejaculations or expulsions. They made up the grand machine, which was the human body. Igor wondered how long he had here to ponder such things.

He had met his match.

And as much as that hurt his ego and body, the sexy American woman had battered him as her equally attractive friend watched. His enhanced strength had not helped him, nor did his blade. She was quick, strong and skilled, and he was beginning to appreciate why his Master was so concerned with these Guardians. Igor could only hope they would meet again so he could return the favour.

In the meantime...

It was a waiting game as far as he was concerned because his Master would find a way to release him; he always did. Prison wasn't for such as him, he had been told. They were above that. His incarceration gave him an opportunity to test his mental resilience, his patience and his meditation skills. He was determined to understand more about himself when he left this place than when he entered. Wasn't the idea of living about discovering yourself even if you were over a century old?

Igor brought his focus back to his breathing. Every intake made air whistle through him like a turbine. He caught the rhythm, cleared his mind and let his breath take him away from this place where time didn't matter.

There he would wait for the Master to come for him.

Chapter Fifty

Black Book Offices Farringdon, London
Four Days After Operation Kilo

"So this is your secret weapon," Y said over the subdued music. "They're making you look good, Detective." Shaft was across the room with a drink in hand, looking over to the voice and meeting it with a broad welcoming smile.

"And so they should," he shot back. "So they should."

Y broke away from her sisters, who were all smiles. She headed into Shaft's arms while Patra made a beeline for the hors d'oeuvres and sandwiches. Shaft introduced Y as the leader of their merry band. The title wasn't as uncomfortable as it had been in the past.

One of the witches – Y wasn't sure she could call them that quite yet – was a tall woman with blonde hair, an expressive face and intelligent eyes. She approached the couple with a Prosecco in hand.

"Hi, I'm Edwina, team leader. I've heard so much about you."

They shook hands.

"If he told you I snore in bed," Y said. "He's lying."

Edwina smiled.

"What he didn't tell me was how beautiful you are. Your entire crew, actually."

Shaft shook his head.

"That's kind of a dick thing to say when you're talking about your girlfriend, don't you think?"

"No!" Patra and Suzy said the word together, grinning like kids with food and drink in hand as they pulled up to the group.

"He's deh shy type," Suzy said. "Yuh have to pry compliments out of him."

They laughed.

"Not true," Shaft said matter-of-factly. "I just feel beauty is in the eye of the beholder. I know what I see, but others may not share my opinion."

"You know that's bullshit, right," Patra said, popping food in her mouth.

"Stop digging," Narendra joined the ever-growing group and introduced herself.

"You're not what I expected," she added.

"People tend to say that a lot," Patra said. "What did you expect?"

Narendra hesitated, unsure of whether she was overstepping the mark. She looked over to Edwina, who nodded to her.

"Scars, bruises, limps. You know, the kind of thing you get from conflict."

Patra was laughing raucously.

"You were expecting some Shrek-looking bitches, wearing some of that Xena Warrior Princess shit."

Then Narendra was laughing too.

"The thought did cross my mind," Narendra said.

"We saw the pictures of The Surgeon after you captured him at the nightclub," someone shouted outside the circle, obviously listening to the conversation. "From his mugshot, it looked like he was hit by a bus." Everyone laughed.

"Not me," Suzy said, looking at Patra.

"The motherfucker tripped and fell," Patra said seriously.

"But you don't look any worse for wear," Edwina said. "You still look gorgeous."

"Thank you, sugar. You look gorgeous, too," Patra said. "We heal quickly, but the pain takes way longer to disappear in more ways than one."

"All I can say is what you did was amazing," Narendra raised her glass, and everyone followed suit.

"Hey!" Shaft protested. "They only did the sexy bit."

"But we do it all so well, don't you agree," Y said to him. Reluctantly Shaft mumbled something and raised his glass.

"We can't hear you, Slick," Patra said.

"Okay! Okay! You do make it look good," Shaft said.

There were cheers, and it took Shaft a few minutes to calm them down. The mischievous twinkle in his eye disappeared, and a more serious air surrounded him.

"Let's give a thought to Officer Joel Sullivan, who nearly lost his life in the line of duty. He is recuperating in the hospital but will suffer life-changing injuries because of Operation Kilo."

There were words of solemn agreement all around.

"Thanks for everything you've done, team. We wouldn't be celebrating tonight if it wasn't for all of your hard work. Enjoy; we have plenty to do tomorrow."

"Slave driver," somebody shouted.

Shaft accepted the barb and shook his head, smiling. He got a kiss on the cheek from Y. The girls huddled in a little bit closer.

"Where's Spokes?" Shaft asked.

"We left him on the phone with one of his Honies," Patra said.

"It looked like him couldn't pull himself away. Him safe, though."

"So when are you ladies going to fill me in on the relationship between The Surgeon and this Dr Kayanga brother you've been pursuing?"

With his arms still around her waist, Y addressed the question.

"What's your schedule like, Detective?"

"It's always open for you ladies, you know that."

"Compliments will get you everywhere," Patra said.

"What about midday tomorrow at the mansion?" Shaft asked.

"I think he is trying to tell you someting," Suzy said, her smile broad.

Y caught on immediately and lit up, but Patra, obviously needing to inject herself into the lovers' business, called out a possible issue with Shaft staying over the night.

"You're not going to just waltz up in my crib like a boss, sleep in my beds, beating up the coochy all night and not make your special Spanish Omelette in the morning. You know that, right."

Shaft raised both hands in defeat without firing a shot to defend himself.

"I wouldn't dream of doing that," Shaft's voice rose an octave. "If Nanny gives me permission to use her kitchen, then we're good to go."

"Mek sure," Suzy said as if to confirm. "Or tings could get messy."

"Scout's honour. I'm in the kitchen bright and early tomorrow morning," Shaft winked at Y and felt his pocket vibrate. The detective took the phone out of his jacket pocket and looked critically at the screen. The call was from the Max facility at Paddington Green.

"Excuse me, ladies. I need to take this."

Shaft moved out of earshot. His face flushed darkly.

Suzy looked surprised.

Seconds later, all their mobile phones were ringing off the hook.

Chapter Fifty-One

Red Ground Estate, Sussex – Ten Minutes Earlier

Spokes had missed the opportunity to go and see Shaft at his offices. He wanted to meet the team and congratulate him on a job well done but Spokes' girlfriend required attention, or so he wanted her to believe. He was still under house arrest, so any opportunity he got to leave the mansion, even if it was with the ladies escorting him, he should jump at the chance, but his queen came first.

He would speak to the detective at a later date.

Spokes smiled and wondered how his forty-five-minute marathon call to Charmaine in Los Angeles had gone so quickly. She was pissed because the Jamaican girl, thirty years his junior, was disappointed the European cruise they had planned to take had been cancelled. You would think that being told you were a mystical impresario who did business not only on the earthly plane but with denizens from the multiverse would be a deal breaker for most chicks. And that was one of the many differences between the sexes. Men were accomplished at ignoring the reality in front of them. Especially if it contradicted their view of the world. While a woman will most likely want to hear the truth no matter how crazy and fucked up it could be. Once you've come clean and they haven't run screaming out of the room or considered you crazy, you're at stage one. A black chick from the hood would give you a sideways glance and a body language scan as she assesses your style, and you're good to go. That's how it had been with Charmaine. If Spokes was honest with himself, he had expected the dreaded burnout would have struck their relationship already – as his legion of ex-girlfriends were a testament to. But no, she was still firmly committed after all she had heard and seen. Spokes smiled to himself again.

She could be the one for real.

Charmaine did like to talk, though, but he was never tired of hearing her speak; even when she demanded more time with him, he always left their conversation feeling enervated. His throat was dry, and he thought of asking Nanny to bring him a drink. Then decided against it. It's just that it would be herbal tea, and he wanted something stronger. He walked over to a trolley with a large globe of the world on top of it. He flicked at an entire section of the planet and watched the northern hemisphere slide underneath the southern, revealing six bottles in the globe's core, ranging from rum to Scotch. He took a glass and dropped three ice cubes, hearing them tinkle and dance before he poured the Johnnie Walker. He held a mirror up, remembering his slain driver when the Mesopotamian snake around his finger tingled and started screwing with his perception – its way of communicating with him. His vision tunnelled, and he held onto the trolley to maintain his balance. Spokes looked around his plush surroundings; his world had gone topsy-turvy. Experience told him his Snake Head ring was trying to tell him something, and he thought he knew what. The 80-inch monitor of the Sony TV was the only segment of the crazy tableau generated by his ring that looked normal.

"Yuh want me to turn on deh telly?" he asked.

Spokes retrieved the remote from a coffee table, ensuring his focus remained on the widescreen.

"What now?"

He started to flick through the channels suddenly, his mouth filled with saliva as if he was about to bite into the sweetest Julie mango ever, just as Sky News made an appearance. His tastebuds registered caramel and milky toffee, and he knew he was on the right channel.

He stared at the screen and listened to the excited tones of the newscaster.

"And now for the breaking news," the newscaster made a furtive look at an off-screen monitor. "The Paddington Green Maximum-Security Facility has been attacked." The screen changed from the newsroom to video footage of a building. What seemed like part of the structure had been bitten off by something vast and ravenous. A massive explosion exposed the infrastructure, with debris still raining down to the sidewalk below.

The thought that this was where The Surgeon was being kept blazed like a neon sign in his head.

"Jesas!' Spokes whispered, shaking his head, grabbing his phone and calling the girls.

"Jeesaas!"

Chapter Fifty-Two

DRC Embassy, Kings Cross, London

The gates of the service entrance to the Democratic Republic of Congo Embassy slid open, and a convoy of two black Terradyne Gurkha MPV armoured vehicles rumbled through and along the reinforced concrete underground driveway that led up and onto the main road. Bulletproof oversized tires squeaked on the ramp, and powerful V12 engines roared, their sound echoing in the confines as the vehicles prepared to merge into London evening traffic. The lead driver must have felt something because instead of gunning the engine to power the armoured vehicle up and out, he slowed, and a vast shadow stretched ahead of him. The driver's reflexes were acute as a thousand foot-pounds of pressure locked the wheels, bringing both vehicles to a sharp stop. The yellow garbage truck that had blocked their exit expelled air from its brakes and, like a mechanical hippopotamus, settled itself in position. The lead driver leaned on his horn, but the burst of sound made no difference to the predicament ahead of them. Shrill female voices could be heard coming from the muscular garbage truck. Doors opened and slammed shut.

Then footsteps.

"Didn't I tell you this would work," a voice said.

"Shhhh!" Said another.

"I hope yuh feel deh same way about yuh plan when the police come knocking."

"Fuck the Po-Po."

"Very mature."

The bickering ended abruptly.

Bad II the Bone walked into the headlights of the lead vehicle as if they were on stage and about to perform the greatest hits.

Y glared at the convoy and spoke first, a voice clear and decisive.

"You didn't think you were the only one who knew how to locate someone you really, really wanted to find? We don't take kindly to threats, but when they're given, we respond."

Y took a breath, considering what she would say next. "Whatever you plan to do, Doctor, we are obliged to stop you, using everything we have at our disposal."

Patra couldn't help herself. She butted in.

"She being diplomatic and shit," Patra said, her voice carrying menace without strain. "I'm not the forgiving type. You tried to kill me using those zombie cops, remember? But I'm going to make an exception for you. Pack up your shit, and leave dodge," Patra thought for a moment. "You've got some bad juju, and it's fucking up our town. You've got to go, man."

The laughter that echoed off the walls was sharp and mirthless as if it didn't quite understand the purpose of the act.

"I read some historical texts about your ancestors. All women, all impressive." Dr Kayanga stepped out of the armoured vehicle, adjusting the sleeves of his jacket. Immediately he was surrounded by a barricade of four Kevlar-clad men and women, who had exited the lead vehicle and positioned themselves around the doctor like visual interference against possible snipers. "What you fail to understand," Dr Kayanga continued. "You have met a man with a purpose, and unfortunately, history will not look on your exploits favourably this time. You see, I have a grand destiny, my country must be taken back from the Imperialists, and no one will stop that from happening. Not even you."

"We have a grand destiny, too," Suzy said. "And that is to stop your rass. We can't tell you where to go, but London is under our protection."

"Do you really want to bump heads with us after all you've read about what we are capable of?" Patra said, a perplexed look on her face.

"Your reputation may precede you ladies, but you've never come across anyone like me," the doctor reassured them. "If you decide to continue along this path, prying in my business, then your blood and the blood of all you hold dear will spill."

Patra tensed and stepped forward, but Y held her hand and squeezed. The subtle communication was understood but not appreciated. Patra took a deep breath and swore under her breath.

"Do you think you have seen the limit to the nightmares I can create?" Kayanga said. "Well, think again."

"I guess we'll be seeing each other then," Y said. "You will need more people in your army."

Dr Kayanga laughed heartily and disappeared into his armoured vehicle.

Chapter Fifty-Three

Red Ground Estate, Gymnasium/Dojo Training Space

The skipping rope felt good in Patra's hands as it slapped on the gym floor to the rhythm of her own making. The sound echoed throughout the auditorium, and she danced on the spot, dripping sweat and cocooned in a strobe cloud of swirling skipping rope. Nothing mattered outside of the creeping fatigue in her arms and legs after 20 minutes of full-on jumping rope. Her enhanced stamina and coordination were breathtaking, even though Patra would not think so. She upped the spin rate, the rope whistling through the air, her feet tapping on the wooden floor, and Hip-Hop legend Nas reminded her over the speakers that this was a 'QB' bitch. The door to the gym pushed open, and Y stepped through; Patra wondered if Suzy would join them having the same dream she had.

In the meantime, Nas seemed to have a message she needed to hear, as she kept skipping.

. . .

WHEN THEY CROWN YOU, AND YOU RISE UP TO YOUR position, carry on tradition.

When they knight you, and you go to fight, go to war, don't petition, carry on tradition.

When you rep what we rep, you carry on tradition.

SUZY WALKED IN NEXT. THEY OBVIOUSLY COULDN'T SLEEP either but knew what was required for peace of mind. Both her sisters were kitted out in gym wear. Patra saw the determined look on their faces from the mirrors that positioned themselves around the gym/dojo training space. Patra slowed but did not stop her skipping, keen to see what her sisters were up to. Both women strode purposefully towards an equipment locker and reached for something that made her smile even under the circumstances.

Y WAS IN THE MIDDLE AS SUZY AND PATRA TWIRLED THE long rope at either end with blistering speed. Double Dutch, the way they did it not only tested their strength and reflexes but had a way of elevating their consciousness through movement. They all took turns to be in the centre because, through a combination of silky-smooth reflexes, stamina and strength, that's where the sweet spot of transcendental calm resided. When their preternatural gifts were pushed, they seemed to transcend into an altered state as they performed the acrobatic movements, the rope whistling above and below them. They would perform this ritual to exhaustion when life became too much and tough decisions needed to be made. All three were on their backs, looking up at the ceiling, breathing heavily. The sisters were silent for a while there then Y said:

"Hot tub!" The final phase of the ritual was convening in the Jacuzzi to talk strategy.

Patra jumped up.

"I'll meet you there in five."

"And I will fire up deh tub," Suzy said gracefully coming to her feet.

"Sounds like a plan," Y was up, too and followed them out the door.

When Y stepped naked into the bubbling hot tub, Patra and Suzy were already comfortable. Y slipped under the warm fragrant water, not caring about her hair getting wet and slowly emerging up to her breasts. Patra and Suzy were already talking, but Y immediately became the centre of attention.

"How deh detective holding up?" Suzy asked, having already felt the waves of disappointment from Shaft after he found out what had happened at the Max facility. Even though she knew this, she wanted to hear Y talk about it.

Y blew water from her lips, making them flap like she was braying.

"He's disappointed. The Surgeon spent four nights in prison. The man is still a mystery, and with his connections, namely Kayanga, he was able to escape."

"Shaft did him job," Suzy added.

"He can't blame himself for that," Patra said. "But that Dr Frankenstein motherfucker has balls, man. Springing his homie and blowing up a jail to get to him. That was some Assault on Precinct 13 shit."

"The good doctor may think it's over, but it's not," Y said. "We know something he doesn't."

Y smiled grimly.

There was silence between them as the bubbles of the hot tub gurgled.

"I take it we all had the same dream," Y asked.

"I think we did," Patra said.

"Him finally decide to reach out," Suzy said.

"What slow jam were you dancing to?" Patra asked, smiling. "Mine was Luther Vandross's Dance with my Father."

"Beres Hammond," Suzy said. "Rockaway, my favourite tune."

"Omar," Y added. "There's Nothing Like this, club classic. Whoever he is, he certainly knows his music."

"Feh real," Suzy said, using her hand to disperse a clump of bubbles clustered creatively together. "Him wanted to keep him features hidden."

"We were too close together; my head was on his chest," Y said, then hesitated. "...That perfume, though."

"I'm still buzzing from it," Patra said.

"Not as much as what him seh," Suzy placed her hands behind her head and stretched. "We now know what all dis means."

They all recalled the whisper as he spoke in their ear while the music played, and they danced. It wasn't just words they heard but scenes that played out in their dreams like sensory movies.

"We need to plan, and I think our plans need to include Kintu."

They both agreed with Y.

"Deh big man should be able to contribute his experience, expertise and resources to deh effort."

"Hell yeah," Patra sounded excited. "Kay would be ready for a piece of the action."

"Him have a bone to pick with his cousin Kayanga."

"He's angry. It may have been a few hundred years ago, but

what that monster did to him and his woman is raw. I'm not sure he can keep his composure?"

"Nah!" Patra said. "Kay got this, you'll see."

They both looked at Suzy.

"Him know what's at stake," Suzy agreed. "If him nuh play him hand right, he could lose his woman forever."

"I'll reach out to him," Y said.

A goofy smile suddenly appeared on her face.

"Couldn't sleep, babe?" Y raised her voice to speak above the gurgling sounds.

Shaft shook his head as he approached the hot tub in a bathrobe and flip flops, the garden path lights lighting up his steps as he made his way towards them. Y turned in the tub to watch him.

"Miss me?" she asked.

"Of course," he said. A smile appeared, but the gesture wasn't committed, it turned tail and disappeared. "Space for one more?" he asked.

"Of course," Y said.

"Come in," Suzy said, and Shaft mounted the wooden steps.

"Dude!" Patra shouted, stopping Shaft in his tracks. "You know the rules man."

Suzy and Y giggled.

Shaft shook his head and looked to the stars above. He dropped his bathrobe and his drawers.

"Better?" Shaft asked brazenly with his arms out and turning to show his tight arse and substantial tackle.

"Much better," Patra said, sounding more relaxed. And they all wolf whistled him as Shaft sank into the bubbling hot water and joined the circle of trust.

Chapter Fifty-Four

Kintu sat patiently on his modified Triumph motorbike, waiting patiently in the darkness for the vehicle he would tail to drive out of the private car park of Compass Point Engineering. He was alone and only had his Mechanics of Jesus communication hub patched into his whereabouts, using the energies that kept him alive – at least their understanding of it – as a means to track him. His surveillance of Kayanga and his operations had led him to this engineering firm based on the eighth floor of the Reinhard building near The Shard in London. The mechanic's analyst had researched the young company, and Kintu was impressed. The start-up was manufacturing turnkey superconductivity quantum computers. Their solution was built on designing intelligent manufacturing processes that provided researchers, developers, institutions and governments access to technology that would normally be out of their reach due to cost or complexity. They had a small research and development arm that handled hardware and software, and Kintu knew Kayanga was taking advantage of this. The puzzle was laid out before him, and whenever a new fact or a piece of information was presented, more of the solution became clear. The doctor was obsessed with finding the process that could reproduce the likes of Kintu – their only successful creation. And for all his missteps Kayanga must have discovered what Kintu had always known. What made him who he was had nothing to do with the brilliance of Dr Frankenstein or Dr Kayanga. They provided the vessel and made sure it functioned but they could not breach the threshold of immortality. All they had was brain and the body of a dead man that, after thirteen hours, would begin to rot even with higher form magic and technology at play. They could never create the reality that was Kintu, only the lightning could do that. The essence of Shango, Thor, Zeus, Raijin or Tonatiuh, had to be in the storm clouds, in the thunder and rain. Kayanga not only wanted to create a private army but resurrect Antoinette.

Only the lightning could do that.

Kintu flexed his gloved fist around the throttle.

It was unthinkable, but Kayanga knew when and where the storm would hit. There was no other explanation. Kintu flipped up the visor on his helmet.

Even at this time, central London was still bustling, the humans going about their mundane business unaware of what was happening to their city and oblivious to the threat men like Dr Kayanga posed. Kintu didn't need a human heart to feel for the human family he was once a part of. These people sleeping on the streets, leaving the pubs, or standing at the bus stop needed him. He felt responsible for them, and his long life of service was a testament to that, even if there had been episodes of bloodshed. Such was the path he had decided to take. And along that path was a dream of freeing the love of his life from eternal bondage. And if he died in that pursuit, it would be worth every agonising moment. That's why he would be here all night if that was required, then the next night, and the night after that.

THE BLACK SUV PULLED OUT OF THE MULTILEVEL CAR park just after two in the morning. An OMOJ agent had placed trackers under all six of the company cars Compass Point Engineering owned. This vehicle was on loan from Kayanga and his company and from surveillance reports, there was a driver provided around the clock. Kintu switched his bike into stealth mode. The sound of his revving engine was cancelled out as his active noise control kicked in. His bike and the motorcycle leathers he wore were riddled with microscopic image sensors that recorded his surroundings and transmitted them back on the surface of leather and metal. At night he blended into his environment perfectly, keeping a discreet distance, patiently following the SUV out of London to the Cornish coast. Four and a half hours later, the SUV pulled up to the well-lit facility with a lighthouse at its head, perched precariously on the craggy rocks. Kintu pulled back off the road, parked his bike and found a vantage point to observe them from amidst a copse of trees. His enhanced night vision allowed him to see clearly over the distance. The area was surrounded by a seven-foot chain-link fence with signs everywhere stating it was electrified. The only way in via land was guard-posted by armoured security teams. He could not see over the cliff, but he would imagine there would be beach patrols or speedboat patrols in the choppy waters. He saw the work being done to a building not far from the lighthouse. Kintu surmised the construction work would continue 24/7. A new shift would replace the team of engineers and construction workers, and the work would continue until it was done. Kayanga had a deadline to reach and Kintu would be there to disrupt and destroy it. He had a lot of work to do and he wanted to begin this very moment. Backing up on his hands and knees, Kintu retreated and when he thought he was at a safe distance, he stood and began walking back to his bike.

That's when he felt it.

The inherent charge of the environment around him shifted. His relationship with the electro-dynamic nature of the world was so acute he felt discomfort if the balance had been disturbed. He may not have understood exactly what had changed but he knew it was dangerous. He reached out to the mechanic's communication hub through his headset.

"Ugly Duckling One to Base Camp," his voice was gravelly.

Sister Josephine's calming tones did not respond to his transmission. He tried again and heard nothing; his own unease persisted. His signal was being jammed. He tensed his body, preparing for what came next.

Snap!

As the sound reached Kintu's ears, he was already taking evasive action but whoever was participating in this attack was able not just to mask themselves in their environment but mask the echoes of their humanity too.

The first harpoon made a whooshing sound as a high-powered pneumatic system spat the sharpened rod at the speed of sound. Kintu picked it out of the air before it could skewer him through the neck.

Kintu examined it.

The metal spear had a spring-activated claw at the tip and was attached to a metal-weaved rope that, even with his great strength, he couldn't snap.

Instead, he pulled.

Its owner flew out from his hiding place into the clearing, wedging himself between tall trees. Kintu grunted and pulled again. He heard the gratifying snap of bone, but the expected cry of pain did not come. Kintu swung around, still holding the harpoon in his hand, hearing the Whoosh! Whoosh! of two more projectiles heading his way. He evaded one with a twist of his torso and let it splinter a tree behind him. The other he swatted away, metal clashing with metal as it hit the ground uselessly. Movement was coming from around him now, and as much as he could process multiple threats preparing to incapacitate him, he wasn't confident he could evade them all. His theatre of conflict looked like a metal spider's web. All the harpoons that had missed him were lodged in trees or in the ground.

It was just a matter of time.

The first harpoon that pierced his shoulder burst through bone and muscle; the tip spring loaded, opened into a claw on exit, sending an explosion of pain that his mystical physiology processed and discarded. Kintu roared, pulling the attached rope and its wielder into the open. The man was strong, but Kintu was stronger. With four huge pulls, he dragged the man on the end of the harpoon gun out into the open. Dressed in black tactical gear his head and face were covered with a ballistic helmet and a mask that was askew from the struggle, showing pallid skin and lifeless eyes. Kintu understood why he hadn't sensed their ambush.

They were inferior versions of him.

He snapped back to the here and now as multiple whistling harpoons hurtled towards him, slicing through the air and pinpointing his neck, chest and thigh. He disappointed his attackers by leaping into the air and twisting mid-flight out of the path of two, but the third pierced his thigh in an explosion of blood. The harpoon kept going, anchoring itself into the ground, pinning itself and dumping him back to earth. Gritting his teeth, he jumped back to his feet, tethered by two harpoons, and more were streaking towards him. His speed was impaired by being speared into place, but he still danced away from most of the lethal barbs directed at him. His attackers were more brazen now, stepping away from the line of trees, overpowering him with numbers. His body was already compensating for the damage being inflicted on it; but as he continued to struggle, he kept causing more damage to himself. One more harpoon drilled through his thick upper arm, its tip borrowing into the soil, his blood trickling along the metal rope. Kintu looked like he had been trapped in a giant spider's web as he thrashed to free himself but couldn't. The ends of the harpoons were no longer in the hands of the attackers but tethered to pneumatic spikes in the ground with power leads snaking off into the distance.

He was trapped.

The more he struggled, the more he ripped his flesh. Kintu knew what to do, although it was a procedure he had not called upon for over a hundred years, but he would do so without pride or regret now. He wasn't afraid of dying; what he could not abide was dying without righting this wrong. Kintu psionically sent out a distress beacon and prepared for what would come next.

High voltage electricity coursed through the wires.

He spasmed wildly, his muscles locking and releasing, his jaw muscles following suit. A cyclical surge of electricity ran through the metal ropes spearing through Kintu's frame, disrupting the elements in him that were magical and short-circuiting the organics he shared with humanity. He tried to hold on, continuing to struggle, to fight, but he was shutting down, rebooting himself. He closed his eyes and let the darkness come. All he wanted was to live to fight another day. He deserved that at least.

The Triumph motorbike was parked away from the commotion, almost unconcerned that its rider had been captured. A psionic alert had been received and a protocol put in place. After a while, a fissure opened up in the rubber plug at the end of the throttle, and Beetle One squirmed out and climbed up under the steel clutch, testing its functions like a real insect, cleaning its mandible and legs. It was about three inches long, created by a 17th century French alchemist. It was 90% mechanical with some 21st-century modifications by the Mechanics of Jesus.

Batteries not included.

This creation was all spiral springs and gears unaffected by signal-blocking technology. Beetle One took to the air, its tracking beacon sending out a distress call as soon as it was out of range.

Chapter Fifty-Five

University Hospital, East Central London

Patra sat on the hospital bed beside Giles Sinton with her arm around his scrawny shoulders. The old man had lost weight, but that could be rectified. He was alive and recovering and Patra was glad for that. The old man was sitting up in bed, his cheeks rosy and temperament upbeat. He was free of the monitors hooked up to him, and his eyes were bright and full of life. It was a stark contrast from a week ago.

"I could kill for a cigar," Giles said, testing the boundaries of his very attractive but impatient convalescent nurse.

"Are you fucking kidding me right now," Patra said, shaking her head in disbelief. "You, Mister, are gonna take it real easy. Slow it all the way down, you hear me?"

Giles nodded with a wry smile.

"I'm just pissed off, disappointed, and bored."

"I feel you," Patra said. "This shit is going to be uncomfortable, but it's got to be done. Blow off steam with a couple of these," Patra handed him a plastic cup of green Jell-O. Giles looked at it like he wanted to throw it across the room.

"Thanks," he said glumly. "It wouldn't happen to have nicotine in it?"

"Not funny, G," Patra looked seriously at him. "You need to chill. When the family turns up, I'll leave you to trash it out with them."

Giles gave a harsh bark of a laugh.

"No, you're bloody not," his voice croaked. "You're going to sit right here and have my back when the bloodsuckers turn up."

"You sure about that?" Patra asked.

"Very sure," Giles said. "I have a surprise for them."

Patra didn't feel great telling her friend that his family was trying to kill him. From the many talks they'd had on family and every other ill that largely affected the world over cigars and Johnnie Walker, she knew a lot about the family dynamics of the Sinton's. She understood more than she would like to admit. Her family in Atlanta was just as complicated and fractious. But Patra couldn't help but think that this murder attempt was more to do with the imbalance of the forces in the city. The same forces she and her sisters were struggling to keep in check. It had an adverse effect on London's inhabitants in ways they did not quite understand; all of this could be a result of the unseen currents that have a far-reaching impact.

It could be making people crazy.

Hell, OG was alive because of her gift. It had altered the outcome of the event in her favour by small, almost imperceptible amounts. She couldn't say for certain, but her luck factor may have been the deciding factor of his survival. Could this be a creeping corruption that was a result of the skewed imbalance the city of London was experiencing? A chill like electrical static crackled across her skin, and Patra let the thought slide.

There was a knock at the door.

"Come in, come in," Giles said, and in stepped a well-dressed older gentleman; his bearing said legal representation.

"Harry," Giles said. "This is family."

The lawyer had droopy eyelids, but his liquid blue pupils were sharp and alert. Harry nodded with a smile at Patra.

"Harry," Giles continued. "You two need to get to know each other better. I'll make the arrangements."

Patra looked over at him quizzically and then leaned over the bed to shake Harry's hand. It was firm and safe.

"Now, let's get this circus on the road. Harry?"

The solicitor had already removed a ream of papers from his attache case and laid them out in neat piles on the side table. The lawyer looked down at them and then at Mr Osborne.

"Are you sure about this, Giles?" he asked with a south London accent that made Patra imagine that these two had grown up in the hood together.

"I've never been more sure of anything in my entire life, mate," Giles said. Then he seemed to consider something, and with a wry smile and a twinkle in his eye, he said:

"I, Giles Sinton, being of sound mind and body. Do hereby declare this to be my Last Will and Testament."

"Aww shit!" Patra burst out. "You adding me to your will?"

Giles laughed, his head excitedly hinging up and down on a scrawny neck from weight loss, his returning exuberance bouncing off the walls.

"Welcome to the family, Miss Jones."

SCAN ME

Chapter Fifty-Six

As soon as the message came through from Sister Charlotte that Kintu had been captured, Spokes and the girls had already known. Suzy had detected the SOS, and immediately Bad II the Bone was on war footing. They all headed to the Tree House in Willesden Green, a priority message sent out immediately.

Everyone was in attendance.

Spokes was like a fly on the wall as it all came together. The main room that housed the tree was where Nanny set up tables and chairs. She had prepared food and drink, and they all shared in it. The church delegation consisted of Sister Charlotte, two other sisters and the Tech seminarian. They all sat together. Shaft had invited two members from his trusted Witches of Farringdon to observe proceedings. The Metropolitan Police wouldn't admit they were involved in the operation that was to come, but Spokes knew the detective had informed all the top brass. The room was cold; the tree somehow lowered the temperature slightly. Spokes daubed his forehead and returned his monogrammed handkerchief to his jacket. He was an awful backseat driver. Knowing the girls had to go out and face the danger while he waited never sat well with him, and this time was no different. He'd be no good in a firefight, but he couldn't help himself from worrying. This meeting would iron out the details, and whatever they concluded at the end would be the plan of action. Spokes had watched the girls brainstorm strategies to stop this madman Kayanga and rescue their friend. Their physical prowess was a given; they were incomparable warriors. He did not give them enough credit for their organisational skills. Being amongst Bad II the Bone may seem chaotic as they threw ideas around, took the piss and bumped heads. But at the end of the banter, jokes, amateur dramatics, and their love for each other came usable solutions from what looked like a hot mess. Spokes was feeling butterflies fluttering in his stomach as he imagined how Y would pull together these diverse groups who may not realise they had so much in common. Would they see it her way?

He had faith in the girls and sat in the corner as it seemed Y was getting ready to address her audience. A shot of J Wray and Nephew rum would have been welcome, but he resisted. Nanny glided over to join him. Elegant as always in her signature long floral dress, head wrap and classic beauty, she crossed her legs, showing her sandalled feet and squeezing Spokes' hands for reassurance. Her voice was husky as she whispered in his ear.

"Dem know exactly what dem doing, Mas Spokes. Don't you worry?"

Spokes smiled at her, and they both watched as Y came to stand in front of the spiderweb tree.

"He's not dead!" Y looked at Sister Charlotte comfortably seated in front of her with a cup and saucer in her hands. "So don't lose faith, even if you can't contact him. I'll explain in a moment why I know he's being held hostage."

The nun bowed with a wan smile before she took a sip of tea sweetened with honey from the tree. "Thank you, everyone, for coming under these circumstances. We've all been impacted by one man who thinks he can execute his plans without paying the price. He thinks his plans are only known to him, and that's where he's wrong."

Y looked at Suzy and Patra.

"My sisters and I had been given the authority to maintain a cosmic balance weakened by Dr Kayanga and his plans. The damage is significant but could be irreparable if he's allowed to continue."

Y pointed to Shaft.

"Detective McFarlane is here because of another – related – case, which comes back to what this is all about." Y backed up and turned towards the spider web tree. Her animated presence seemed to bring the ominous-looking tree to life. The glistening obsidian bark was dusted with hundreds of grains of light from the trunk to the branches. The huge spider web hanging from the tree glowed from the thousands of light sources behind it, showing the fracture lines that were present across metropolitan London. Most were small and thin tendrils of the web, inconsequential lines that the mechanical spider excreted to represent naturally occurring imbalances that were never a cause for concern. The thicker, darker thread demanded attention and ran across the city like a tectonic fault line. It showed what was possible if Kayanga wasn't stopped. Smaller webs that were not as thick branched off the main line like lightning bolts, with the potential to cause untold damage. No one in the room had any idea what physical effects an event like that would have on the city. The only thing anyone knew for sure was it had a few historical texts that spoke of it, and the overwhelming sentiment was a fissure of that size would be very bad. Biblically bad. Y pointed to the thick silk thread that ran through the web.

"This line represents the worst-case scenario for everyone, and we didn't understand why. A reliable source cleared the whole thing up for us, and we owe him a debt of gratitude. Now we know where, how, and why." Her smile was a grim one. She sighed.

"Kayanga wants to replicate something within Kintu, and only through the upcoming storm can he do that."

Sister Charlotte raised her hand as if she needed more clarity for an algebra question she was unclear of. The nun stood. Y nodded over to her.

"When last we spoke, you briefly mentioned this storm, so I took the liberty of consulting a renowned meteorologist and her team in our Order. They haven't been able to detect any weather patterns that could lead to the storm you talk about."

Y smiled.

"Kintu said you were thorough, Sister Charlotte."

The nun bowed curtly, and Y interpreted that as a vote of appreciation.

"You won't be able to detect this storm when it comes," Y said. "It's a supernatural event outside of science and religion. I'm not going to stand here acting as if I understand it because I don't. All I know is, it's going to happen and we need to be prepared. I know you're used to doing your own thing with a vast network behind you, but this time, you'll have to step out of your comfort zone. Can the Mechanics of Jesus do that?"

Sister Charlotte sat, leaned back in her chair, daintily holding the teacup between two fingers, her eyes sparkling, the mind under the habit was sharp and focused.

"You are the Guardians of the Light for a reason," she said. "We may share an understanding of your World because of

Brother Kintu, but this is *terra incognita* for us." Sister Charlotte sat up a bit straighter in her chair. "Kintu is not just our brother and my friend but the de facto founder of our Order. God willing, I want him to continue in that capacity." Her eyes shone with emotion. "You have my support, and all our resources are at your disposal."

"Thank you," Y clasped her hands with relief. "I have some ideas I want to run by you."

"And we have some suggestions, too," Sister Charlotte said. "I'm sure we have strategies that will help."

"Oh, I know you do," Y said. "But first of all, I want you to know the kind of man we're dealing with and the powers he has at his disposal."

"Don't you have a file on this piece of shit?" Shaft chimed in for the first time, immediately regretting his choice of words. "I'm sorry, Sister," Shaft apologised.

"No apology required, Detective," Sister Charlotte shrugged. "I'm a bit embarrassed to admit that Kintu had an encrypted secure file that he did not share with anyone. I could have insisted, and maybe he would have relented, but I didn't."

The nun lowered her gaze.

"Don't worry, Sister, we've got your back. I just thought you had some more Intel to add to what we already have." Shaft looked across to his colleague. "Edwina, when we're finished here, make sure you provide the sister with everything we've got. We can do his psych evaluation and a profile of his serial killer friend."

Edwina nodded.

"Okay then," Y announced. "Let's get down to business."

"Amen!" Patra said.

Chapter Fifty-Seven

When Kintu opened his eyes, his first conscious act was to control the surge of anger that was building in him after realising his predicament. It would be a bushfire if he did not snuff it out now. There was no place for it. He could only hope there would be a time to release it later.

He had faith.

Kintu was spreadeagled like a Vitruvian man, looking up and encased in a modified Iron Maiden. His legs and arms were bound, and he barely had enough space to move his head from left to right. It was claustrophobic and airless, but Kintu was not affected by either. His chest rose and fell out of habit, but he only needed air when he spoke. There was a viewport in front of his eyes that gave him a perfect view of a sterile white ceiling. Kayanga was knowledgeable enough to isolate him from any system that required electricity. He was naked. Stripped of his jumpsuit and gadgets. They had gone to unusual lengths to make his modified Iron Maiden free from electrical power or anything with an electronic signature. Under different circumstances, he may have played the role of an intrepid investigator assembling the pieces of a complex puzzle and giving himself the breathing space to come to a conclusion.

There was no need for that drama.

Ulysses Kayanga had finally caught up with him. It was a relief, a conclusion to centuries of cat-and-mouse clashes that were simply in preparation for the storm to come. Kintu reached out beyond his prison to sense his surroundings and realised he was not alone. The aura of an individual coloured the otherwise sparse room.

"Where is Kayanga?" Kintu bellowed, the sound of his voice booming in his metal shell. Whoever was in the room with him had reacted to the sound coming from his containment shell by hurriedly leaving to report what he had heard. When you lived for hundreds of years, time did not have the same meaning. What may have been hours elapsing for most felt like moments for him. Kintu, as he wrapped himself in his own inner world, was performing mental experiments to spice up his stay. He recognised the aural signature as it entered the room, and his self-control slipped. A gurgle of disgust surfaced in the back of his head, a repugnant stench that was not a smell but an all-over feeling. It was shame. Shame for hating one man so much.

Shame for hating family.

Dr Ulysses Kayanga approached the viewport and looked down on Kintu through the glass, shaking his head. His smile was tight, and his eyes glistened with satisfaction. There was a grating sound as metal latches were pulled free in the section of the Iron Maiden around Kintu's head and shoulders.

It cracked open on its hinges.

"Cousin," Kintu said, glaring at him. "You must be feeling pleased with yourself."

That irritating smile appeared again.

"In fact, I am," he paused to think. "The last time we spoke was in Paris at the Château Dillue hundred and ten years ago, or was it a hundred and five years? You were on one side of a wall of flame hurling obscenities, and I was on the other." Kintu pictured the memory with perfect clarity. He had been so close to freeing Antoinette from Kayanga's clutches that he could feel the relief even now.

It was not to be.

Kayanga had trapped him and fled.

"Where is she?" Kintu asked, each word carrying weight and venom, demanding much more than a response but an explanation.

"Safe and sound," Kayanga said. "She's always with me. Always."

Kintu licked his lips, his eyes looking beyond Kayanga's image and the white backdrop.

"How have you kept her alive all these years if you haven't been able to exploit the lightning?"

Kayanga's smile was a broad one. He laughed.

"Once a scientist, always a scientist. Where's your heart, cousin? You two were lovers, after all. And here you are, wanting to talk shop. Where is the righteous anger, the vengeance?"

"Stop playing games, Kayanga, and tell me what you've done," Kintu spat.

The doctor became serious. Looking deeply into himself, recounting his process. It felt good. Outside of Igor and Frankenstein himself, he had never had a need to truly explain his process to anyone. They would neither understand the science nor condone his motivations; the latter, he didn't care one way or the other about, but to talk with his intellectual equal – that was a pleasure. Especially one who had straddled the worlds of the physical and metaphysical; even he would be stupid not to partake.

"I nearly lost her a few times," Dr Kayanga began. "The reanimation process without the mystical lightning had its limits, but I didn't know that at the time." He turned away from Kintu and folded his arms. "If you were alive, I could extend your life indefinitely with a few tweaks, but if you're dead..." He shook his head. "Let's just say I haven't been able to break through the time barrier that restricts the process. Reanimation lasts for 13 hours, 27 minutes and 15 seconds. I knew someday I would find a solution to the problem, but until then, I used a cryogenic preservation process that I developed from studying Alaskan Tree frogs."

Kintu raised his voice in an attempt to show his lack of interest in the details.

"Did you solve the issue of lethal ice crystals forming in the tissues?"

"Of course I did," Kayanga said, shaking his head. "I've been using nanotechnology hundreds of years before it was discovered."

"So you managed to resolve that issue; what about..." It was Kintu's turn to be brusquely interrupted.

"I know, I know," Kayanga said. "You're so predictable, cousin. You want to know of your lover's soul. Will it still be intact?" The doctor pursed his lips and shook his head melodramatically. "Her soul was more elusive to find and maintain, so I sorted out the mystics and necromancers to aid me. I stumbled across a process that required the transplantation of organs from a special and rare group of people. What makes them unique is they capture and store residual Lifeforce in specific organs. They have no idea that they are walking around with a repository of concentrated energy that was ripe for the picking."

"More innocents to be slaughtered for your goals," Kintu

said, his voice clear, although his words may have simply been thoughts that slipped out into the world.

"And that is the precise reason why you don't deserve her. I am willing to do whatever it takes. And if it takes removing organs from these witless cattle, then I will continue to do so without remorse."

"The strange murders in London were you all along," Kintu said.

"Igor, actually. He did a fantastic job of acquiring the organs over the years. We did what was required, and Antoinette is in good health. When she stands beside me physically, mentally, and spiritually whole, all of this will be worth it."

"Standing beside you?" Kintu scoffed. "Wake up, man, she never loved you, and she never will. Can't you see that?" His words were meant to sting, but Kayanga was too far gone to care what anyone thought of him.

Dr Kayanga shook his head and sighed.

"All these years, I've been searching for a way to bring Antoinette back, and you cousin, you were the solution all along."

"You're delusional," Kintu spat. "You were the one who murdered her, murdered me because I didn't back your plans. I was your cousin; your Chief, she was your friend, and look at what you did."

"You poisoned her against me," Kayanga's voice had risen an octave. "I should have resurrected her instead of you, but Victor insisted. I should have had her by my side when I free the Congo from the imperialists. Instead of soiling my hands with the likes of you."

"And yet here we are, the monster and the deluded," there was a snort of amusement from inside the containment shell.

Dr Kayanga clasped his hands, placing them into his chest as if he were praying, his patience departing.

"Let's see how amusing you find it when I begin the process of sucking the Lifeforce out of you and transferring it to her."

"You are even more pathetic and misguided than I thought," Kintu said. "If you think the force that created me can easily be manipulated, then power has truly driven you mad."

"You underestimate my genius. Can't you see?" Kayanga scowled. "There will never be another you; you're one in a billion freak. I don't need to understand it; I just need to be able to use it. But all I need is the substance that fuels you. The mystical energy that's contained within the lightning that now runs through your veins. I will force that same energy out of your cells and use it how I see fit."

"You're welcome to it," Kintu snapped. "If my journey ends here, so be it."

"You may not carry fear, my friend, but I know you're filled with regret. Regret of what could have been. What you could have done if you were more resourceful and more prepared. Think about it."

Kintu remained silent, having said enough.

Kayanga smiled broadly, clasped his hands behind him and tipped on his toes with satisfaction.

"Two nights from now, this will be all over, and the legend of Kintu will come to a close. All you have built, the relationships you have nurtured, the allowances you have made, all worthless."

Kayanga shook his head with an air of false disappointment.

"One of the greatest scientific discoveries, disappearing with no fanfare or accolades. It would be a crying shame if you asked me. A crying shame."

The doctor sighed and fixed Kintu with a disingenuous look.

"So much to consider. So little time." Kayanga slammed the hatch shut, closed the viewport on Kintu's containment unit and, with relish, slid the two bolts on either side of his captive's head in place.

Chapter Fifty-Eight

The monster storm came from nowhere, baffling climatologists as it raced screaming from the Atlantic Ocean to clash violently with the Cornish coastline burdened with sleet, rain and electricity. Storm Siegfried had appeared without the usual markers and quickly established itself as one of the worst category seven storms in the past ten years. It was the kind of meteorological anomaly that had been witnessed and reported sporadically throughout history. Above average rainfall and extremely intense electrical activity were its prevailing characteristics, but its pattern of occurrence would elude and confound scientific minds. It would be studied and cited for years to come, but only the arcane circles would understand its true significance. Sheet lightning lit up the belly of the clouds, and the wind expressed its fury.

Kayanga stood with his hands clasped behind his back and looked over to the rolling Atlantic Ocean from the safety of the observation deck. Behind him was the Weather Witch looking down on a trellis table. For one so young – the South African woman was in her early 40s – to have such arcane knowledge required a full human lifetime. She was nowhere near that age requirement. Luckily for her, the traditions of her ancestors were downloaded directly into her unconscious. She contained many reincarnated aspects of her ancestors throughout history, her consciousness trapping all the many women who possessed the Gift in the past. She had been a well-kept secret, but there was not much in the world of science, sorcery and necromancy that he couldn't discover. She came to this once-in-a-lifetime event wearing traditional Xhosa attire. She favoured black and brown beaded fabrics, and her Doak – Xhosa head wrap – took its influence from her elegant skirt and top. Kayanga was not the only one who would mark this day as significant. She may be South African, and he Congolese but Africans were not afraid to show how much something meant to them by the quality of clothes they wore.

And she did look magnificent, staring at her table draped with animal skin and crystals scattered over its surface. A fine layer of sand was scattered over the scene. She was chanting in Xhosa, both her arms making sweeping gestures as words left her trembling lips, sometimes in a whisper, sometimes in a staccato growl that sounded almost canine. Her table was a representation of the environment outside. An animated ecosystem that, through magical means, echoed the prevailing maelstrom and the structures outside.

The Weather Witch had no control over how the storm impacted the environment, but she could lure aspects of it through her spells, and she could track where it went with enough accuracy that her sponsor could take the necessary steps in advance. Dr Kayanga held a picture of this vast operation in his head, and as he stood watching nature's savage onslaught outside, he ran the mental model in his mind's eye.

While the operation proceeded, outside Igor was his eyes and ears.

Every thirty minutes for the last five hours, the Russian called with time-sensitive information. Like a jigsaw puzzle, the pieces were locked into place, and the final completed masterpiece was in sight. Igor would join him when the lightning storm was at its peak. For now, he was content with watching his brainchild evolve and revelling in how disparate elements came together so seamlessly. That was why perimeter security was directly under his control, and he would absolutely not leave that responsibility to anyone else. Kayanga had no misconceptions that the cavalry would come, but the Guardians were out of their depth.

They were women, after all.

And then there was the Order of the Mechanics of Jesus.

They were a joke.

How could an institution with such deep pockets have a prize such as Kintu in their midst and not take the opportunity to explore his gifts by subjecting him to a suite of tests or a barrage of experiments. The only man brought back from the dead with gifts that far surpassed his original human state.

What a wasted opportunity.

In this weather and with his minions patrolling the compound the religious order could only stand and watch as he made history. The doctor looked down at the electronic gauntlet attached to his left arm. Dispassionately he looked at the animated LED readouts and the colourful symbols and numbers dancing before his eyes. Kayanga could see the integrity of the electric fence surrounding the compound and the sensors on the cliff's edge. He knew the position of his reanimated soldiers and his spider hands. He had considered his airborne 'neck huggers' as a further deterrent to anyone stupid enough to try, but the weather put paid to that idea. The communication rig on his head vibrated and immediately, Igor's confident brusque tones and AR features came into view.

"All forty-nine cadavers are in their containment pods and hooked up to the power supply. Only Antoinette and his cousin are not in their appropriate positions."

"Well done, Igor," Kayanga said, his voice even, revealing nothing of his excitement. "I've considered my position. I will oversee their connection after all."

"Good, Master. I'll await your arrival."

The connection went dead.

The doctor turned away from the elemental violence outside and mentally prepared himself for his tasks in building 'A'.

As he shifted, two shadows peeled away from the wall. Following the doctor as he moved from the window, they flanked him on both sides. His reanimated bodyguards would protect him at all costs, and so would their brethren, who at this very moment were ready to repel whoever or whatever tried to interfere.

The doctor glanced at the Weather Witch.

"Is our timing the same?" Kayanga asked. Without looking up from her skins and the miniature twirling sands of her magical ecosystem, she said, with a sweet South African burr: "The timing will remain the same."

"Good," Kayanga acknowledged. "Very good."

Chapter Fifty-Nine

Kintu could feel the isolation as he lay in the Iron Maiden torture box that had been placed in a concrete room with no light and no life. Still, he searched beyond his confinement, but no living thing was in range, and he suspected that's precisely how Kayanga wanted it. The lightning that had given him life after death had seen fit to connect him with the electricity of all living things in his surroundings. He could sense the traditional speed of life – not magic – by their electromagnetic signature. Kintu had taken this awareness for granted for centuries. He was ashamed that it took his confinement to truly understand its importance. Not eating for 72 hours was easily bearable; his metabolism was adept at adapting to the harshest conditions. He could go without food for ten days without concern; that was how much control over his bodily functions he had. He could switch them off at will. The celestial lightning made him a biological contradiction that should be a rotting organic shell with synthetic parts thrown in for good measure.

Good Girls Gone Bad

And yet here he was, concerned about his lack of connection with living things and his weakened state as a consequence. Their natural electromagnetic glow bathed him when he was around humankind; animals and plants all added something special to his own vast internal generator. Casting his mind back, there was never a time he was utterly divorced from the life force of nature.

Never.

Except for these last days, and it was exacting a creeping price he had to pay. Not much longer, he thought, according to his nemesis, and in forty-eight hours, he'd be seasoned enough for Kayanga's experimental procedure to work. Kintu was about to submerge himself into deep meditation when he suddenly felt a shift in the tapestry of electromagnetic energy. It wasn't artificially produced; this was emanating from a living thing. He immediately felt it acting on him, warming his muscles and sinews, clearing his thought processes and elevating his mood.

Who was outside?

Someone had been able to breach Kayanga's heavy security and, more impressively, had done it without alerting the guards on 24-hour sentry duty around him.

"Tell me who you are?" Kintu asked, his voice echoing inside the box.

The identity of the saviour remained a mystery until he heard scratching above him and then two sounds.

"Meow! Meow!"

Kintu focused, squinting in the darkness, not quite believing what he had heard. In moments it all made sense when he saw the elegant Oriental short hair cat peering down at him through the viewport, her breath fogging up the glass.

"Mei Ling?" Kintu said. "How?" He then caught himself.

Mei Ling was no ordinary cat, that much he knew. The feline purred, licking the glass and using her paws to swipe at him as a means of saying hello or encouraging him to play. When she realised he was unable, she meowed her frustration and lay down over him, feeding the life-giving energies he needed and, like a sphinx, watching and waiting.

Chapter Sixty

South Cornwall Coastline, Grimwall Lighthouse

The beach under the lighthouse was being lashed by wind, rain and wave. The darkness that had gripped the landscape would depart as a crackling lightning bolt licked across the dome of the sky, igniting the angry clouds for seconds at a time, like a napalm bombardment from above. Nature's flash photography showed a barren landscape of rock formations devoid of life and a lonely lighthouse atop the cliffs, its light strobing across the seas.

On the pebbles far below, there was a rhythmic beeping that could be heard only if you were crazy enough to be on this windswept beach with your ears literally to the ground. A gloved hand seemed to appear from amongst small rocks like a land crab, but on closer inspection, the hand wasn't appearing through the stones but on top of them. The beeping suddenly stopped as Y, Patra, and Suzy switched off their timers and emerged from under the camouflage storm canopy that had blended seamlessly with the environment. They came together in a huddle, using each other as anchors against the powerful winds tugging at them. They were still in their wetsuits, having scuba dived from a trawler hours before the storm front had moved into position and hunkered down using amazing camouflage technology designed by the Order of the Mechanics of Jesus. They had to shout over the howling winds to hear each other.

"We all having a good time?" Y said, her bottom lip trembling.

"It's as cold as a motherfucker," Patra announced. "My muscles and joints are stiff; I need to move them before I freeze up."

"Stop deh moaning," Suzy teased. "Just picture kicking deh Surgeon's rass; that should help."

Patra thought about it for a moment as the winds wailed around them.

"Damn, you're right, sis, that does work," Patra said, lifting her face up to the sky and licking her lips as rainwater sluiced off her head to run down her wetsuit.

Y checked her luminescent watch, and they threw arms around each other's shoulders, forming a circle. The promise of battle and the sisterhood they shared in intense situations like this sometimes triggered an altered manifestation of the Guardians' power that was inconvenient and uncontrollable. A pale blue aura surrounded them, making their skin prickle and their location evident for the wrong eyes to see. It was like a reminder to them that their connection was not only skin-deep but soul-deep. A link in the chain of the collective unconscious that stretched back a millennium or more and could be displaced by death but never severed. They had each others' backs no matter what, and, it needed to be said, on a subatomic level where it was all about energy and magic. They silently absorbed its power and waited patiently for the luminescence to die down and then disappear. They kept the scrum in place, grinding their feet into the pebbles for purchase, clasping each others' shoulders for balance and being whipped and buffeted by the wind and rain. With a crackling boom overhead, the thunder reverberated through their bodies showing nature's spectacular power and, for a second, bringing night to day.

"We all know what we're doing," Y shouted over the din. "I'll scale the cliff first, making sure it's all clear. You'll know if I run into trouble. I'll move on to let Sister Charlotte and the team in. Decide between yourselves who will disable the power supply and who will lead the assault on the main building." Y nodded at each of her sisters, licking her lips to taste the sea salt. "Whoever can help secure Kintu after our main objectives are achieved, go for it. The Surgeon is a bonus, just don't kill him."

"Be careful," Suzy yelled. "I can feel Kayanga's creations roaming about up deh. An murder deh pan dem mind."

Y nodded.

Suzy placed a thick circle of rope around Y's neck and over her Katana. Next, Patra placed the climbing equipment holdall over her shoulders, ensuring it was secure.

"See you up there," Y said, and they touched fists. Y turned on her heels and ran towards the cliff, disappearing in moments as the darkness and its fury swallowed her whole.

Chapter Sixty-One

"Are you having a fucking laugh?" Shaft mouthed the words, looking through the rain-splattered window of his vintage Jaguar at a spectacle that should not be possible. The interior was comfortably warm, and lover's rock tunes were slowly grooving through the speakers, trying to soothe him, but they had a difficult job on their hands.

Now, this.

Shaft quickly looked down at his silver Thermos and wondered if something contraband had been slipped into his aromatic coffee. He looked outside again at the foul weather, one click away from the madman's compound and saw that the well-dressed black man in the natty suit and fedora hat was still standing there. As you would do in a torrential storm, the man had stopped to light up a cigar about fifty yards from where he was parked. Amazingly he looked unruffled amid the gale-force wind, his suit and hat unaffected by the elements as if, everywhere he went, a protective bubble of calm followed him. Shaft was betting he couldn't light his cigar; even when he was witnessing the sheer impossibility of what was happening, he still made a stupid bet with himself. A delicate flame sprung from between the man's fingers and didn't as much as flicker as he pulled gratefully on the cigar tip, flaring a crimson red. The mystery man gave a smile as he released the smoke from his lips, and like everything else about him, it too wasn't affected by the tumultuous weather. The smoke danced around him, forming fleeting symbols that made Shaft wonder if he imagined all of this. He recognised Yoruba, Ashanti and Amharic characters from his anthropological studies in Africa. That was life before the Metropolitan Police that had prepared him for the extraordinary life he was leading now. Shaft caught himself with his forehead pressing against the cool glass; the music was layered back in his awareness, and he had been transfixed with the strange man's antics. Shaft shook his head to clear the fog; the dapper man outside, untouched by the elements and utterly unconcerned with its ferocity, looked over at him.

They locked eyes.

Even from that distance, a sudden feeling of insignificance wormed its way up from Shaft's ancient unconscious. The detective shivered.

It was not so dissimilar from his life flashing before his eyes, but this was an ancient part of his brain which was bringing his mortality front and centre. Throwback to times when men met gods and immediately knew their place in the world.

Shaft swallowed with difficulty.

He couldn't move for a second and felt the pressure on his eyeballs being pulled in the direction of the stranger.

"I love your taste in reggae music, Detective Mac," the voice came from the speakers in his car, crystal clear. "I'm particular for Beres Hammond. I even helped him with a composition. That man is a genius."

It was him.

The detective's eyebrows arched, wondering how a man

standing in a lightning storm could compromise the Bluetooth connection between his smartphone and car stereo.

The benefactor, Shaft thought. Who else could it be? The mystery man who was always on the fringes, never showing himself in real life but, according to Y, turned up in their dreams. He gave them tools like someone from Greek mythology or a quest computer game. And he was obviously concerned about their well-being because here he was, again, unable to sit back and let them face danger without his aid.

What did he want from him?

Shaft stared at the stereo, unsure if he was to speak into it or use some other means he wasn't familiar with to communicate.

Fuck it.

"It helps me to relax in stressful situations," Shaft said, leaning forward and feeling like an idiot speaking to his stereo.

"Relax, Detective Mac, I know this is unusual, but hanging around my daughters, I'm sure you're familiar with the unusual."

Daughters? Shaft thought, then understood immediately. It was a term of endearment his Jamaican grandfather would use. Y had told him that when he communicated with them through dreams, they experienced him differently. He looked the same but spoke with an accent or dialect like an observer. Shaft suspected some of that ability was at play here.

"Can a human ever be familiar with someone like you?" Shaft asked, looking out of his car's window to the being standing outside. He tipped his hat at him. The cigar was still hitched between his lips; his response did not require vocal cords or sound. He was comfortable communicating through other means. He blew another cloud of cigar smoke.

"Dat is why I love humankind, not just because you are who you are but because you are so adaptable. Survivors," the man said. "And there are no better survivors than my daughters, but even they require help."

Shaft nodded in agreement, about to make a smart comment but thought better of it.

"The bigger heads have rules that govern my intervention. And as smart as I am, there are some things I have no control over. But you, Detective Mac, you can move amongst men, being one yourself."

Shaft took in a deep trembling breath.

"I'm not sure you're talking to the right man," Shaft said.

The mysterious stranger laughed, and a hint of coconut and sea spray infused the interior. For a timeless second, Shaft found himself transported to bacchanal, music, and sun, and then he was back in the grey, raining, here and now.

"Detective Mac, who could be better? Miss Yvonne thinks the world of you, and you think the world of her. In dangerous and tricky situations, you have each other's back. I don't get to oversee love stories a lot, but this one will be epic!"

"It doesn't feel like that now, she's in there, and I'm out here."

"Don't worry," the mystery man said. "You will be in that evil place with her soon enough."

"And you. What can you do?" Shaft asked.

"I've done all I can do, but I have a favour to ask of you."

Shaft listened.

Soon the conversation would disappear from memory, leaving only a compulsion to find Bad II the Bone in the chaos beyond the fence and give them something they would need.

Chapter Sixty-Two

Y did not hang around the cliff's edge after securing the rope and dropping it down to her sisters on the beach. Her job was to reduce the numbers of whoever and whatever was roaming the grounds, support the sisters from the Mechanics of Jesus to acquire their assets and help shut the place down. Y checked her diving watch and a shudder rippled through her even as she crouched in the darkness and the pouring rain. Y recalled what she had been told by their benefactor in the dream. Thirty minutes for the window of opportunity to open. And the plan was to have her sisters up from the beach attacking the complex before the window opened. The elemental forces that created Kintu would perform ballet on the stage of the sky tonight. Dr Kayanga had about forty-five minutes to manipulate the energies in the lightning and produce life after death for his own ends. Enough time for his actions to rip the balance of good and evil apart in the city, renting gaping holes in the fabric that separated the earth plane and the infernal dimensions. It had happened before in the historical accounts, and the outcome was stomach-churning chaos. Civilisations had been wiped out because of it, and Y could not allow that to happen.

She could not allow it.

Y spun in the pooling water like a figure skater who had abandoned ice for its temperature-challenged counterpart. The lighthouse was to her left, with the sheer cliffs to her back. Just beside her was her bungled-up wetsuit. She was in her black woven Kevlar jumpsuit with her Katana fitting neatly into a tactical scabbard on her back. A satchel was around her neck and chest with some Mechanics of Jesus treats and other paraphernalia inside. Ahead of her were the T-shaped prefab buildings and, beyond that, the perimeter fence. There were regular security details that she could see, and immediately that rang alarm bells. Y reached back to touch the Katana's hilt with her fingertips in readiness for an attack. Her sword responded by kissing her fingers with a delicate surge of energy. She smiled.

They were both ready.

She slowly pulled it from its sheath. Even with the rain, Y's grip was tight and unyielding. Her Katana gripped back completing the bond. She kept her enhanced eyes sweeping the terrain ahead, feeling the anticipation. There may be nothing she could see, but that did not mean there was nothing there. Y would not make the mistake of underestimating Dr Kayanga and what he was willing and capable of doing. She plotted a path in her head and looked to where the trajectory would end. Her destination was the door set just beside where the two buildings connected. She reached into the bag of tricks provided by the Sisters of Mechanics of Jesus and let her fingers grasp a glass sphere that sat amongst the other goodies. Depressing the north and south poles of the globe, she launched it along the ground in her intended direction. It broke up into thousands of beadlets that carpeted the ground as far as she could see. Y waited before she followed the Yellow Brick

Road. Her patience paid off. A sizzling sound erupted from below ground, then the electronic Pop! Pop! Pop! of components frying all along the strip of ground. Satisfied that her route was now free of detection devices, Y hurried towards the door, her Katana trailing behind her.

WHEN THE BULLETS STARTED FLYING, SUZY AND PATRA were ready. They both came up from the climb, breathing hard and just in time to see what horrors were about to show themselves. Suzy's early warning system was shrieking, and even though she had no idea what the threat was or where it would originate from, the empath knew it lurked within striking distance.

"Yuh ready," Suzy shouted, her words snatched away by the wind. But Patra knew.

"Ever!" She responded by opening up the telescopic Bo stick with a flick of her wrist and a WAP! WAP! sound. She twirled the extended stick and smoothly moved into a battle stance, fully focused. Both stood unmoving, water rivulets streaming down them. Above them, the jagged bolts of lightning rendered their poses into silhouettes like some classic ancient reliefs.

Once.

Crack-kak boom.

Twice.

Crack-kak boom.

The earth vibrated from the force, but there was something else causing the ground beneath their feet to shift. That was when the ground came alive. Like a crop of scrofulous seeds pushing up from the depth of hell, bad seeds germinated from a madman's imagination, eagerly clawing their way to the surface. They were hands unattached to bodies reanimated and given cruel intelligence by Kayanga's weird science breaking ground. If their presence alone did not make you hesitate and question your sanity, then what they saw next would. They had been modified.

Some hands were strapped to ballistic weapons. Others were armoured, their nails sharpened claws. All were scuttling towards the women like the march of land crabs.

"Shiiit!" Patra hollered. "I hate these motherfuckers."

As the words were uttered, the hands pinpointed their positions with a click-click of weapons engaging. Patra hit the ground, leaving her stick to be retrieved later; her hands dug into her drawstring bag on her hip, and five steel ballbearings appeared in the palm of her hand. She released them in midflight, sending them hurtling towards the army of weaponised disembodied hands. The ones who could open fire did, their numbers depleted by Patra's projectiles. While Suzy's butterfly knives were a blur as she swatted bullets, altering their trajectory, and with Patra's probability altering power, they were redirecting them at the ground or back whence they came. Patra was an agile moving target, bullets ripping into the soil near her or slamming into her Kevlar jumpsuit. She ignored the pain and kept moving. They could not pinpoint her even with wet and digital hardware processing the information. But these things utilised magic too, and Patra knew it. She manoeuvred herself back to where her stick sat unused. Executing a twirling backflip, Patra snatched up the telescopic Bo stick and swung it back in the direction she had come. The connection with some of the horrors that had been chasing her was true, knocking them in the path of a swordswoman with no remorse. As far as they could tell, the hands had no means of verbal communication, yet they screamed as thrice-folded steel forged by the Shaolin monks of Henan province, cut through dead flesh and bone. The five-fingered nightmares continued to scream their frustration as their prey outmanoeuvred them. The women kept slashing and stabbing at their attackers until there was not much left but twitching appendages in various states of butchery. Suzy and Patra stood breathing heavily in the downpour, chunks of gore being washed off them to the ground.

They silently overlooked their handiwork.

Patra flexed her shoulders.

"Ouch!" she said, poking at impact points on her Kevlar jumpsuit. Suzy looked her sister over, ignoring the gashes on her own exposed body. The bullets may not have penetrated flesh, but the bruising from the bullets would hurt for some time. She then squeezed Patra's upper arm.

"Yuh feel dat?" she asked.

"Son-of-a-bitch!" Patra grimaced. "Yeah, I feel it."

"You'll live, gal. If yuh haven't noticed, we heal quick, so suck it up. Tings are building; I can feel it."

"No shit," Patra said. "Let's go."

Both women sprinted off in the direction of the main building.

Chapter Sixty-Three

The lightning display was getting more intense, and Dr Kayanga smiled. The Reanimation Chamber was like a great maze, and he had front-row seats. From his elevated position, all of the pieces in this creation game were in place, patiently waiting for a flame to ignite the sticks of dynamite. Igor stood beside him, watching the lighthouse in the distance through binoculars. The tall white building was the focal point of the maelstrom raging above, a point of concentration that attracted the primal electricity contained within the clouds. The Weather Witch had poured magnetic feral fluid around the perimeter of the lighthouse. It possessed the power to alter the polarity of the ground to the opposite of that of the thunderclouds above. Making lightning strikes inevitable and predictable to a degree. The lightning strikes had begun frequently at first, touching the copper lightning rod like the finger of God. An hour ago, the frequency had increased, but the number of lightning strikes required within a specified period was not quite there yet. Kayanga was unusually calm as he waited. He knew this part of the process was beyond his control, and just this once, he was content with that. In a moment, he would walk down to the workstation that had been set up beside his cousin's containment pod. The process of life beyond life for his 45 volunteers would be automatic, but the doctor's unique skills would be required to tease out Kintu's secrets, which meant a more hands-on approach. The energies he would unravel would then be used in conjunction with the lightning to produce his army. No more limitations. His troops would be immortal killing machines which would do his bidding around the conflict theatres of the world. With that thought, a glow of satisfaction warmed his cold heart. For the briefest of moments, he basked in that outcome.

It was not to last.

His gauntlet was vibrating wildly, and so were the compound's proximity alarms. They had been breached, and he didn't have to guess who it could be.

Y HAD DECIDED AGAINST BLOWING THE LOCK ON ONE OF the doors leading into the main building, allowing one less task for her sisters to undertake to gain access. But she resisted the urge to tweak her plan of action because she knew the most significant amount of resistance would come from inside that hornet's nest, and Y also knew they would need help. Allowing the sisters from the Mechanics of Jesus into the compound would remain her priority. Y slowed her pace as she approached the main gate. The entrance had a guard house at each side with automatic gates in between. Two lone silhouettes stood in the elements, unconcerned almost. Y knew there was no further need for stealth when the alarm started blaring around her, and the blinding security spotlights began illuminating the pools of darkness that had been her friend. Y stood up from her crouch, speared to the spot by a beam of light, her Katana gripped by her side. She sighed and blew against the rivulets of water running down her face. The sentries saw her immediately but made no attempt to attack. Instead, they pointed at her and from each guardhouse ejected three security personnel, dressed in tactical gear from head to steel-tipped Dr Martens. They all carried high-tech batons, dashing her way, splashing through the puddles of water, their screams silent, and their vacant eyes were only seen as the world brightened between lightning strikes in the heavens.

They were human but programmed.

Kayanga had them under his control. She could sense it. Y would have to make sure they returned to their former lives and families bruised, battered, definitely beaten but alive.

That was all she could promise.

They came attacking all at once with machinelike organisation, predictable and, as far as martial arts training would philosophise, flawed. A wave of three launched at her from the first quadrant of the crude circle they had formed around her. The shock batons crackled through the air as they swung the weapons high and low in tight arcs, Y's eyes tracking them. The Guardian apologised to her Katana because the blade was not created to be used in the way she was about to use it, but she was sure there would be time enough for it to draw blood.

Y spun like a Spanish torterra in the bullring. Using their own momentum against them, she ducked from one, shoulder-checked another and used a flat blade like a whip to the neck of the third. They stumbled away just as three others sprang forward. Y felt the electric charge of a baton close to her cheeks but slipped away from one, then grabbed the arm of another. With the speed and power that must have surprised them, Y guided the captive arm with the shock baton, rammed it into the neck of the third and held it there. The smell of burnt skin wafted up, and for a moment, the receiver of forty thousand volts glowed in the dark and then crumpled to the ground.

They kept coming.

One down, five to go.

Chapter Sixty-Four

Sister Charlotte knelt at the fringes of the tree line. The electric fence surrounding the compound fifty metres away was sizzling as energy coursed through the metal links and raindrops evaporated on impact. She couldn't see all of them because of the advanced camouflage gear that rendered her squad invisible in darkness and heavy rain, but forty-strong Mechanics of Jesus operatives were at her back waiting for her command. She wasn't depending on the Guardians to overpower the sentries before they would enter but was using the frequency of the lightning-storm as a metronome to countdown to when to commence the breach. The idea of attacking Kayanga just as he was occupied with his nefarious reanimation process came from Nanny of all people. It was a brilliant idea that played on Dr Kayanga's need for control. He would never delegate that task to anyone else if the files about him were correct. If they had an opportunity to free Kintu and destroy what this madman was doing, it would be then. Brother Ignatius and Sister Gertrude were tasked with observing the weather conditions, mainly the frequency of the lightning strikes. Sister Charlotte could picture the younger nun's mathematical mind plugging value variables into an equation she had constructed just for this situation, and it was all done in her head. Sister Charlotte may not be a genius with numbers like her peers, but she could sense it would soon be time. She unzipped a pocket in her tactical jumpsuit and unfolded a gold and wood rosary, swinging it on her finger. She centred herself amidst the rain and lightning and then began to recite the Acts of Contrition.

KINTU COULD FEEL THE PULL OF THE LIGHTNING AND listened as it whispered to him.

It wanted to embrace.

And it felt like they had never been apart. A friend who you haven't seen for years but knew your paths would eventually cross again. Kintu's containment chamber was propped up at an angle inside the purpose-built grand room his cousin had constructed for the reanimation process. Kintu recognised how important he was to this procedure due to where he was positioned. He was dead centre in the space, and all around him were high-tech glass sarcophagi – the units of the refrigerated dead bodies prepped and ready for a second life. To his right was a control station that was suited for one person. And Kintu knew who that one person would be. Kayanga wanted to be close when he drained him. He wanted to gloat at their centuries-old feud and how it had ended with him being the victor.

Did he know that could just as likely work against him too?

The power conduits that fed into the building came from the sophisticated lightning collector that was the modified lighthouse in the distance. The power of the heavens would be siphoned through the superconducting coils of the Sub-Zero

Good Girls Gone Bad

Magnetic Resonance Filter and then through Kintu. His essence would be extracted and then directed to Antoinette just behind him. Then his soldiers would share the remainder among themselves. Kayanga's pride and God complex obscured his adherence to the scientific process. This entire procedure was based on large doses of supposition born from desperation. The only time the doctor had utilised the mystical lightning had been with Frankenstein almost three centuries ago, and Kintu had been the result of that collaboration.

Why would you presume the same outcome from a source of power no one knew anything about? The variables were too numerous to comprehend, but Kayanga was willing to take the risk. He had boasted about the machine he had been working on for centuries. And as he spoke, Kintu surmised what his esoteric engineering had designed. Kayanga was working off the theory that lightning was infused with neutrinos and cosmic rays. The Sub-Zero Magnetic Resonance Filter would isolate and strip the cosmic rays of the neutrinos and bombard his body with particles, hoping to release and unravel the energies that made him and then siphon it into Antoinette and Kayanga's undead army.

Was all of this love or ambition?

Who could tell? Kintu knew it could go awfully wrong, or Kayanga's suppositions were correct. He had no choice but to wait and see. Kintu's strength had returned thanks to the cat, but escaping his containment unit without aid would be impossible, even with his renewed vigour. For all his outrage, he could do nothing. His heart was heavy. He had imagined introducing Antoinette to a new world after her centuries of imprisonment. Holding her by the hand as she reacquainted herself with the heat and the sun of their beloved Africa. All he had suffered and sacrificed would be worth it if he saw her reaction. Kintu could not remember the last time he had succumbed to anguish. His work had been barbaric and morally questionable at times, and he moved within the dirty cracks of society, being judge, jury and executioner for beasts born human but who chose to become evil, twisted and corrupt versions of themselves. And even as he rubbed shoulders with the dross of this world, he became adept at reframing his experiences.

He had faith.

A Christian concept that had come to his aid many times before and promised him forgiveness for all he had done. But tonight, faith had abandoned him. The monster with no soul began to wonder if it had ever existed at all.

PATRA AND SUZY HAD SPLIT UP SO THEY COULD COVER more ground as the clock counted down. Suzy remained in the foul weather, having lost a rock-scissors-paper duel. She should have known better. Instead, she flung some choice Jamaican swear words towards her sister, who would be making her way into the warmth of the building. Suzy made her way towards the lighthouse while Patra played with the explosives given to her by the Mechanics of Jesus.

Suzy smiled when she heard the double pop-pop as the shaped charges obliterated the lock, allowing Patra entry. She wished her sister luck, catching herself and realising if anyone needed luck, it wouldn't be her home girl. Suzy marched towards the lighthouse; the need for stealth had passed as the compound was lit up like a stadium from the security lights. The rain was relentless, but Suzy was blocking out her trivial concerns and focusing on what was in front of her. She breathed evenly and did a final check of the equipment attached or hidden in her jumpsuit. Satisfied, she gripped both butterfly knives, the dangerous-looking spikes on her knuckle guard glinting savagely. The figures in the distance were not perturbed by her approach at all. They stood like parade ground soldiers, almost oblivious to the rain, wind and lightning. Even with so much atmospheric interference, Suzy could feel the stationary figures emanating waves of emptiness. The magic that went into creating the human being was absent from the group. Suzy approached them confidently, knowing what came next was inevitable. She tried to find some shared emotion that she could exploit but gave up after a moment. They were functional and more physically accomplished than the average man or woman, but they were not alive in the truest sense. Horrible facsimiles of the human condition.

Miss Wong shivered like the cold she was experiencing was not outside of her body but inside. There was something about the idea of reanimation that was unsettling. Mindless zombies were mere puppets in the hands of a master sorcerer or Voudon. What Kayanga had created was far worse. Soulless, enhanced mercenaries able to take and follow orders with the ability to be taught. What was even more unsettling was as she got closer to them, she could sense the fleeting memories and wispy convictions that had not been completely expunged from memory floating around in their consciousness. Suzy felt the dissidence, and with some effort, she discounted it. Three lightning bolts struck the lighthouse in front of her, one after the other. It was beginning, and she had to disrupt the process. The air was charged, the hairs on the skin were standing on end, and the smell of ozone brought back memories of thunderstorms in Jamaica. Her Dragon Tattoo felt as if it wanted to crawl off her skin. All memories and all feelings were squashed and stuffed into a corner of her mind, where she could retrieve them later. This moment required absolute focus because the creatures staring back at her would punish anything less.

Chapter Sixty-Five

"Can you feel it, cousin?" Dr Kayanga's dark face was lit up from the backlight of the monitors embedded in his workstation. His eyes sparkled, and the shifting colours dancing over his skin were an indication that the machine built and powered by sorcery and science was working. His hands moved expertly over dials, knobs and slides. The temperature was cool, almost refrigerated in the Reanimation Chamber. A laboratory, it may be, but it was also a morgue. Looking down on the floor plan from his perch, Kayanga observed how it reminded him of the Grim Reaper's flower. The petals were dead bodies found inside the shiny containers, cables like veins running to the central stem. The ovary was the filter, and Kintu and Antoinette formed a barrier. The sinuous black stems were thick cables from the lighthouse that fed into the chamber, and Kayanga was the sunlight. The source.

He shook his head.

The scientist had gone for an analogue interface because the vast mystical and high power output involved with this process would interfere with the more subtle laws of physics that computers depended upon. It was all vacuum tubes, thermionic valves, cathode ray tubes, triode tubes and copper energy storage units. He didn't realise how much of an impression the technology of the early 19th century had had on him. The hum and the burnt dust smell of the operating valves were comforting. It was helping him to relax, and why shouldn't he? The doctor knew they would come for him. They would try to stop what cannot be stopped. He lifted his head from the instrumentation to the majestic lighthouse in the distance. The spectacular panoramic view through the tempered and reinforced glass 50 feet across that occupied most of the frontage of the building was smeared with rain but still showed off the lightning strikes clearly and regularly. He checked his watch and glanced around.

The Reanimation Chamber was safe from interlopers.

Igor was outside managing his forces, and his more mindless creations were programmed to incapacitate or kill whoever was unfortunate to stumble across them. Even if they could find a way into the main building, this chamber was like a nuclear bunker that was protected, just as the lighthouse was protected by his soon-to-be obsolete reanimated legionnaires.

Nothing would disturb this moment.

He would be the one to watch his beloved take her first steps and see his undead army unshackle themselves from the time restraint of thirteen hours twenty-seven minutes. They would become his immortal army soon enough.

The lightning was striking the lighthouse more frequently now like the precision bolts were being thrown by Shango himself. As close as he was, he could almost feel the effects of such power. He looked down at his instrumentation and made some adjustments. The doctor looked over to his cousin's containment unit and smiled broadly.

"For your service, cousin, I salute you," his grandiloquent pronouncement was riddled with mock respect.

A switch was thrown without and within. The lightning strikes were coming at a consistent explosion of energy like a Titan's heartbeat, the huge lighthouse resistors finally allowing the electricity through Kayanga's infernal circuit. He had the final say as to when this complex process would begin. He flipped three toggle switches in sequence and smashed the glowing green button in the centre of the instrumentation panel with the palm of his glove.

Energy surged through the thick coaxial cables that ran into the Sub-Zero Magnetic Resonance Filter. Thick roiling mist emanated from the cooling copper coils, like a witch's cauldron, tumbling to the ground, forming a carpet of fog. His instruments lit up even more as the circuit completed itself, the multicoloured lights glinting off the surface of his protective goggles and a maniacal grin on his face.

Chapter Sixty Six

All of Kintu's senses were alight as if he was an exploding star in the firmament of dark space. There was no pain; instead, he became connected to everything. He could feel it all, see it all, taste it all. In a small corner of his consciousness, he wondered if the good doctor had imagined this would have been a possible side effect of the process.

He didn't think so.

And yet here he was, his essence out in the world in a hyper-charged version of astral travel. He could see the Mechanics of Jesus and the Guardians fighting outside of the laboratory, all at once, reading their frantic individual thoughts. Then he was back in the laboratory but not the real one. This was a copy, a possibility, and he was standing beside the slab Antoinette was laid out on. Behind him was Kayanga, fixed in a moment, the temporal seconds moving forward at a snail's pace while the energies he was trying to wrangle were interestingly having unforeseen offshoot effects on Kintu, his guinea pig. In what felt like an eternal second, he stood looking at Antoinette, who was no longer lying on the small granite slab but sitting up, her slender legs swinging, her shoulders back, her eyes intense and beautiful. Her lips parted to speak, but no words came forth. Kintu intuitively felt wherever this place was, it was for him to speak and for her to listen. And he had to do it now because the sands of time pouring into the hourglass, the last remaining grain, would return him to the reality of the here and now.

That he knew as fact.

Back to the horrors that awaited him, an almost inevitable extinction.

"Release me," Kintu said. "Set me free."

Antoinette's eyes blazed, and she smiled.

Pop!

Y's shoulder dislocated as the ball joint of her arm pulled away from the socket of her shoulder, such was the power of the blow that caught her off guard. The pain hesitated; then, like a gust of wind igniting a flame, it erupted. She gasped, her eyes prickled with tears, her left arm went numb immediately and her senses flaring red. Y flew forward from the force of the strike from behind. She rolled on the damaged shoulder, screaming at the pain, her momentum carrying her back to her feet and into a Yasumi stance.

She grimaced, grinding her teeth.

Y took a moment to breathe through the pain and assess. Below her awareness, her sisters were transmitting complex sense impressions of their personal battles. Everyone learning from the others experience like a hive mind. They were evaluating what was working and what was not, and the tapestry of information that would help them take advantage of an enemy's weakness by filtering through to all three sisters was on point. She had dealt with the flesh and blood attackers without much concern. They would suffer broken bones, gashes and concussions. But the three reanimated soldiers were something completely different. She had managed to decapitate one. It was on its hands and knees at that moment, crawling around in the mud, hoping to continue with the fight after it reattached its head. The other two, carrying a sword and a two-bladed axe, were damaged but kept coming. They did not experience pain the way she did. The lithe blond man had used the metal knob of a sword pummel to cause the damage she was cursing her way through. The big female swinging the axe had come close but had never connected with the blades, or she'd be looking at broken bones and severe lacerations. The Mechanics of Jesus had breached the electric fence but were being attacked by what looked like roots shooting from the ground, decimating their numbers. Y needed to help, but she had to incapacitate these two first because they were actively blocking her route to them. Never taking her eyes off the two reanimated warriors, Y backed up towards an empty guardhouse. Once her spine touched the cool steel frame, she turned and slammed her dislocated shoulder, once, twice, then three times into the frame. She couldn't hold back the scream and fell to her knees. The bone head had slotted back into the arm socket perfectly but her torn rotator cuff required her accelerated healing to knit muscle fibres back in place. Y took a ragged breath and got back up to her feet and suddenly, rotating her shoulders, grimacing again and looking over to her adversaries.

"Okay, let's try that again," Y said.

She lifted her Katana, and it glowed deep blue.

SCAN ME

Chapter Sixty-Seven

Patra stomped down the central corridor, the three-piece staff swinging around her neck, a string bag filled with ball bearings beating a rhythm on her hips and leaving a trail of bruised, battered and unconscious bodies behind her.

All roads lead to Rome.

Patra knew she was getting warm by the density of bodies getting in her way. She was heading in the general direction of the sea. The entire building was designed as a point of focus for the lighthouse on the cliffs. The construction of the building had one purpose and one purpose alone – to facilitate the smooth functioning of the antechamber. And within those reinforced doors was what they were committed to destroying. The three corridors that Patra had stumbled across all connected to the nerve centre she was yet to see. If she had been given the freedom to move at her own pace, she would have been there already, but roving bands of humans were hellbent on frustrating her as she marched towards whoever was pulling the strings. Dr Kayanga was sending them as human cannon fodder, concerned only with results at any cost. The puppet master was hoping she would unleash her frustration and cut them down in cold blood.

He didn't understand what the Guardians stood for.

Patra had seen those nasty mind-controlling creatures from her run-in with the motorcycle cops. Their slimy tentacles were attached to the back of the neck of every man and woman that had attacked her so far. Their strength and reflexes were enhanced by these creatures, and their aggression turned up a few notches. Given an opportunity, they would rip her throat out or pepper her body with bullets.

Fuck you! Her thoughts were directed at the mad scientist. *You'll never get me to do your dirty work for you.*

No way.

Patra came around the final corner and could see an assembled group of figures in the distance. Behind them look like the mother of all doors. But before that, another group of humans had seen her, and there were hurrying Patra's way, guns drawn and shock batons ready, the creatures on their necks acting for them. She charged them without hesitation. Patra folded the three-piece staff in her left hand and, with her right, dug out four thirty-millimetre ball bearings. Sprinting by this, multiple bullets whizzing by her, she leapt to the corridor wall, angular momentum allowing her to make five good steps along the surface before gravity topped her back to earth. Patra had already released two ball bearings before her feet touched the ground. Without further thought, she let her luck factor do the rest as she focused on the chick with the big ass and the dude with a face like a horse. Unravelling the three-piece staff again in both hands, she went to work. By this time, the ball bearings had done their job, giving a concussion to two gun-toting security personnel and dumping them in a heap on the floor. The three remaining guards were in for a painful treat. Patra wanted to get to that big arse door ahead of her, but these three were standing in her way. She started twirling the three sectional staff overhead, to her left side and to her right. As she edged forward, the three-piece-staff a blur, they attacked, only for hard cherrywood to go smashing into heads, arms and shoulders, breaking and dislocating bones. Patra stepped over two crumpled bodies and moved towards the remaining combatant, who was looking unsure of himself. She took one step and then hesitated. A prickly itch at the base of her brain signalled danger. Her perception suddenly shrank to a focus point. Everything around her slowed to a crawl except for the bubble she occupied. Every sense was heightened for however long she remained in the temporal zone. Instinctively Patra measured the duration in fractions of a second.

She became one with the threat.

A trigger pulled, metal rubbing on metal, an explosion of gunpowder, the sound of the bullet travelling down the barrel at the speed of sound, shockwave expanding into the atmosphere.

Then there was a whiff of cordite that wasn't so much a physical smell but an extrasensory perception.

Still in the zone, she had a fraction of a second warning to adjust, to take action.

Just enough.

Patra leapt back, twisting in midair.

The high-velocity bullet slammed into her, taking her down and out.

"Did you get her?" Igor asked.

The undead soldier nodded and stood from his prone position with the enormous high-powered sniper rifle in its big hands.

"Is she dead?" Igor's tone was impatient, excited.

The soldier looked down on him with dead eyes and expressionless features. In his former life, he was a handsome man who had committed his life to King and Country. His new duties were committed to a visionary with similar methods to his once sovereign. The soldier was a big man, but his words were precise, the amplitude regulated just above a whisper.

"The kill shot was unsuccessful, but the target was hit and incapacitated."

"I wanted her dead. How did you miss?" Igor asked.

The soldier did not answer. He seemed just as surprised as Igor was, but he didn't have the range of emotions to express it.

"Send two of your men to retrieve the body from the corridor," Igor commanded.

The soldier looked back at him blankly.

"Forget it! I'll choose them myself."

Chapter Sixty-Eight

Kayanga stood riveted. He had his hands on his head and eyes filled with tears of joy as he witnessed his envisioned process come to its glorious conclusion. His dark skin was a screen of exploding colours from the many reflections of the equipment surrounding him. The platform he stood on rotated so that he faced Antoinette, positioned just behind him. He carefully monitored her vital statistics, and he became increasingly elated with every brainwave spike and rise and fall of her breasts. She would be his masterpiece, a seemingly living – she was far beyond that – breathing, heart-pumping human being, unlike the one who donated his energies to her.

It was working.

The intellectual leaps he had made, the theories filling in the gaps and his outlandish mental models.

It had worked.

Any second, Antoinette would open her eyes as if she had awoken from a restful slumber, some of her mystical crutches replaced by human biology. He wanted to gloat. He wanted

Kintu to see he was right and his cousin was wrong. Kayanga shifted his focus from Antoinette, and as he revolved on the platform, he hurried over to Kintu's containment unit. The viewport on top was open, and inside, a flickering light show was bursting through the reinforced glass. He adjusted the photo chromatic safety goggles over his eyes. Of the interior, he could barely see the outline of his cousin, thrashing about and enveloped in a pulsing kaleidoscope of light. The doctor's smile was a broad one as he looked away, satisfied. He turned back to Antoinette, the most important part of the complex dance that was occurring in the Reanimation Chamber, but he didn't complete the movement. A jagged bolt of pain stabbed into his head, and the world went red. A segment of iron pipe was swung and connected with malice to the back of his neck. The doctor twisted as he stumbled forward, glimpsing a makeshift club coming down again, his consciousness ebbing. The doctor looked up through blurry lenses before the dark tides of unconsciousness tugged at him. A double vision of Antoinette standing there with an iron bar raised high; the gleam of madness, or was that anger, in her eyes. Kayanga weakly raised his hand to protect himself, but the pipe came down once more, and this time his world went dark.

SUZY GASPED, FEELING PATRA'S PAIN IMMEDIATELY. HER eyes welled up with tears, the stabbing pain in her side was short-lived, but the wave of numbness threatening her joints would continue for as long as her sister was in distress.

Suzy gritted her teeth and compartmentalised the emotions. The numbness emanating from her sister's dilemma in the other building was not as easy to ignore. It was slowing her down, and that was dangerous.

At this very moment, she was being chased.

Suzy was sprinting up the winding stairs of the modified lighthouse, her frantic footfalls echoing off the metal stairs. Behind her, two reanimated soldiers were in hot pursuit. Who said getting out of the rain was a good idea? The luxury of dryness had a price to pay, and she was paying it. Suzy had whittled down their number by one. Suzy had chopped off both hands of the unfortunate soldier. The loss of limbs hadn't incapacitated it at all. It was still fully active but unable to hold a weapon. Not satisfied, Suzy had tried to decapitate it but had to forgo that plan to barge into the lighthouse and try to dismantle the operation of the structure from the inside. Four well-placed mini bombs, courtesy of the Mechanics of Jesus, blew off the entrance door, giving her access. Her pursuers didn't want that to happen. They were relentless, and even with her advanced physiology, she could feel the raw edges of muscle fatigue creeping into her thighs. They did not seem to have such concerns and were gaining incrementally.

Suzy could sense them and could also sense she was not too far from the top. She had an overwhelming feeling to look back and down, even if it would reduce her speed. Suzy stopped abruptly, sensing something. She suddenly leaned back. A swirling blur flew over her, coming so close that she could feel the air part above her jumpsuit as it embedded itself into the brickwork with a reverberating thwack! The burly female had flung the two-bladed axe out of frustration or strategy. Either way, it was too close for comfort. Suzy started taking the steps three at a time.

THE TENTACLE CURLED AROUND Y'S ANKLE AND SQUEEZED, sending other fleshy tendrils to secure her arms and then try to incapacitate her, but it wouldn't get that far. She shuddered; the touch of reanimated flesh that was moulded in a vat and being used by Kayanga as a weapon was disgusting to her, but Y didn't let her squeamishness detract from slicing and dicing. She shrugged violently, then lowered her centre of gravity, her Katana a pale blue blur like a hot iron cutting through the octopus-like protuberances that kept erupting from the ground, slithering along the ground and then rearing up as a Cobra would. Y kept her overwhelm in check as the psychic information from her sisters came flooding in. As concerned as she was, she had a job to do; no matter how bizarre it was or its effects on her psyche, she could not buckle. The creatures had caught the Mechanics of Jesus off guard, and they had suffered casualties. Y had helped to turn the tide of the battle. The regenerative power of the tentacles was diminishing, allowing Y to cut her way through the wriggling flesh to Sister Charlotte, who looked like she had been to hell and brought some of it back with her.

"I'm glad you made it through, Sister," Y said, both women instinctively joining back to back. The nun sighed heavily. It wasn't exhaustion but grief.

"How are your sisters?" Sister Charlotte asked breathlessly, expertly using her two daggers to skewer, and then cut into a probing tentacle, its fluid splashed at her feet.

"Not so good," Y responded. "That's why your team needs to get to the laboratory now. We haven't been able to stop Kayanga's process, but we need your numbers to handle the possible fallout."

"Can you handle this while we fall back?" Sister Charlotte asked, just as Y thrust her Katana with both hands into the thick mottled bud of meat that had reared up to attack; she thrust down, grabbing the dull end of the blade and, with a grunt, opened up the tentacle into neat halves that flopped to the ground twitching.

"I've got this," Y said.

Sister Charlotte pushed away from her, and with a shrill

whistle, her remaining team, a disciplined unit, disengaged and started to fall back.

"Use the bombs," the nun called back to her, and with the Ninja-like fighting force at her back, Sister Charlotte led a dark stream of bodies towards the laboratory.

Chapter Sixty-Nine

The two dead soldiers marched down the corridor on Igor's instructions, kicking the bodies out of their way with their big feet and cutting a path through the chaos towards Patra's body. The woman they were supposed to carry back to Master Igor lay on her side in a pool of blood. His instructions may not have been logical, but they didn't question them. The soldier with the long sword slung around his back was the one who reached down to pick up the body. He elected to uncemoniously lift the woman by the scruff of her neck, his fingers effortlessly circling her throat. And that was when a hand clamped on his hand.

The dead man's version of surprise shone through his eyes. He awkwardly looked down at the woman's hand holding his and, with a cock of his head, tried to pull his hand free but couldn't. The woman dug her fingers into his flesh, slowly tearing through the ultra-tough epidermis and into muscle. She matched his strength as she lay on the floor and slowly began to use his power to pull herself up to standing. The blank stare on the dead soldier's face did not allow for surprise that was not programmed into its facial repertoire, but something about his uncertain body language spoke volumes.

Why was the woman smiling?

Patra stood strong, staring into the eyes of the reanimated soldier. The stomach region of her jumpsuit was moist with blood, and her supernatural metabolism was already repairing the damage of the high-velocity bullet that had pierced her side and exited her body cleanly. The shock wave that had not just shaken her internal organs but disrupted their function began to settle down from the pressure wave, and that was when the pain came like crashing waves on the shoreline. Every breath was prickly, the movement of her diaphragm was sending rivulets of pain like molten lava trickling up and down her abdomen. Tears welled up in her eyes, and her lip trembled with the effort, although the unnerving smile remained.

Patra stood strong, knowing her next burst of energy would wipe her out completely. Instinctively she called on reserves from her sisters, who were in better shape than she was and the psychic conduits of thought energy connected between them immediately. She felt her body go warm, some of the pain dissipating and intuitively knew this was a band-aid on a gunshot wound.

Fuck it, she thought. *Beggars can't be choosers.*

Seconds had elapsed from when she was picked up from the ground and had grabbed the dead soldier's wrist. The other soldier analysed the situation quickly and moved in. The sword slid from the scabbard on his back like shit in olive oil. The soldier who had tried to pick her up tried to pull his hand free, especially after seeing his brother-in-arms attacking, but Patra held on like a recalcitrant dance partner. The soldier swung at her and didn't seem to care whether an errant blow struck his partner or not.

Patra was counting on it.

He came at her again with a two-handed swing. Patra skipped away from the steel, the air parting, wrangling her reluctant dance partner to follow her lead.

Then suddenly, she stopped.

The soldier swung his sword again with a wide arc but this time, instead of evading it, Patra approached her attacker, lifting her conjoined arm and placing it in the trajectory.

Metal sliced through flesh.

It was a smooth cut that did not bleed and took the soldier's hand clean off at the wrist, sending it spinning away. He looked surprised, grabbing at the missing appendage but before he knew what was happening, she had grabbed his neck, wedging her staff into the ground and smashing the soldier's head down onto it. The force was such that the staff's tip punched through his throat and into his brain with a crunch. Patra stepped back and pulled the staff free with her boot and let the body fall to the floor.

Something must have snapped behind the eyes of the remaining reanimated soldier because the growl of his attack was guttural. Patra's staff was once again three sections, and she stayed out of the big sword's way as it sliced the air around her. Force for force, her staff was no match for forged steel. And Patra knew she had to end this quickly. Her fingers dug into her thread bag, the tips of the fingers recognising the new ordnance gifted to her by the Mechanics of Jesus. She pulled out two between her fingers like a magician. The soldier came in close; if Patra didn't know better, she would have thought it was frustration, and his frustration had made him more creative. Instead of his usual tactic, he wanted to be close and personal, using the pommel and hilt of the sword like a sophisticated battering ram.

It looked like he had places to go, and Patra was standing in his way. She used her body to block the hard edges of the sword, deflecting his arms and knowing if any one of those blows directly impacted her, they would break bones at best or put her down for the count at worst. Patra slipped past every one of his powerful swings, nimbly depositing the modified ballbearings in the utility pockets of his tactical trousers and top. She ducked before she could be hit by a stray fist and danced away from him. He lumbered towards her again, but for the first time, Patra wanted distance between them. The ballbearings were a surprise, and the timer had been synced. She turned away and covered her ears, not knowing how loud it would be.

There was a Pop! Pop! Pop!

When she turned back, the soldier was in three bloody smoking pieces.

"God damn," Patra grinned.

"Three would have done the job," a voice behind her said. She didn't turn around.

"No fun in that, sister," Patra said. "What took you so long? Did you bring the crew?"

"My Sisters are always with me."

Patra looked unsteady on her feet.

"Shall we take the laboratory?" Sister Charlotte asked.

"Hell yeah. I thought you'd never ask."

Chapter Seventy

The double-edged battle axe sliced through the air where Kintu's neck had been only seconds before. The force of disturbed air made it whistle before it embedded in the machinery, sparks erupting into the ceiling. Kayanga's bodyguards had attacked in concert from the floor of the Reanimation Chamber once they realised what Antoinette had done. They bounded on the walls, grasping hand holes in the architecture and nimbly swung themselves up to the platform where their adversary stood. Kintu did not move from where his feet were planted. Instead, he shifted his upper body left then right, like a boxer making himself a blurry moving target that evaded the attempts to cut him in half. That strategy had worked, but the doctor's second bodyguard would not make the same mistake his brother-in-arms had.

Neither would Kintu.

He had squandered the opportunity he'd been given as Kayanga's bodyguard tried to extract his axe from the metal; the second guard ran forward, his blade held parallel to his body, intending to skewer him through. Both metal bar and

Damascus steel clashed, and Kintu used some of his momentum to guide the weapon away from his body and then planted his size fifteen boot into the other's knee as the axe was pulled free. He heard a satisfying crunch, watching the reanimated soldier contort noiselessly, expressing pain in the only way it knew how and dropping the axe in the process. Kintu scooped it up in a heartbeat, just as the sword man came back around with a sweeping swing of his blade. Axe in hand, Kintu brought the savage weapon up and into the jaw of the man he had taken it from, feeling it crack the bone of his mandible and gouge into his neck, synthetic circulatory fluid spewing. Still attached to the axe, he swung his newly acquired puppet around so that the blade that was meant for him hacked into his flanks. Kintu let the body fall and pulled the axe out of the body with a wet, squelching sound. Even with the soldier's damage, he was down and not out. Kintu knew there was only one thing that could make it inevitable. He planted his boot into the chest of the thrashing man like an executioner and let the sheer blade of the axe come down on the man's neck. The blade's edge was keen, and the head rolled away; Kintu spun to face the threat he had sensed was upon him and brought his axe up to stave off the attack. His attacker was seconds away from splitting his chest open, but the metal of his axe and the steel of his rival was between them both; for a moment, they were at a stalemate, blades locked. These facsimiles of him were strong, resilient and dependable, but they were not him. He was the original, the one-in-a-billion progeny of the lightning. Until this moment, he could not be reproduced, and if he had anything to say about it, he would never be duplicated. Kintu snarled, threw his head back and delivered a head butt like a thunderclap. The first head-butt was to get a measure of his rival, but the second and third, he put his neck and shoulder into it. The reanimated soldier staggered back, his eyes twirling in their sockets, and Kintu took to the air, stamping him in his chest with his boot, the force taking the soldier over the railings and into a silent plunge.

Kayanga had been too confident, and outside of the two soldiers Kintu had dispatched, he was alone. The original Frankenstein's monster stood surveying the Reanimation Chamber. After what he had been through, his energy returned with the swiftness that amazed even him. Kintu was standing outside of his containment unit with Antoinette in his arms and Dr Kayanga on the floor at his feet. Antoinette had clubbed him well with the steel pipe, and the doctor was injured but alive. The ordeal must have been too much for her, and she collapsed. All he knew was she had saved him.

She had saved him.

Somehow his pleas in the alternate dimension had not gone unheard. His beloved had acted.

It pained him to think it, but Kayanga's theories were right; Kintu had added something of himself to Antoinette and the dead soldiers below. Kintu had considered this was the end for him; he had accepted his defeat and prayed for deliverance. But Antoinette had pulled him from the jaws of annihilation. He would not waste the opportunity. He looked at the woman in his arms. She was beautiful. The doctor had done well. Almost three centuries ago was the last time he saw her smile, listened to her words or felt her spirit. And here she was, as vibrant as if their previous encounter had been a day ago. Seeing her sprawled on the ground, he had thoughts of disaster steamrolling through his mind. But having touched her supple black skin with its sheen of health, he knew she was okay. Her aura was strong, and her collapse was more exhaustion than any chronic malady. He gently laid Antoinette beside his cousin and quickly grabbed the pipe his beloved had used with such Congolese ferocity on the doctor's hard head. This time it was about to be used for an even more glorious purpose. Destroying the doctor's life work. Kintu began swinging the iron bar into Dr Kayanga's platform. The metal felt good in his hands as his returning strength made him understand the damage human men could cause. He tore through the control panel, revelling in the burn of the electricity coursing through the machinery. He reached the guts of the monitors crunching cathode-ray tubes between his fingers and yanked out circuit boards and tendrils of wires.

It wasn't enough.

As Kintu looked down onto the floor below, the containment units changed from red indications to green as his extracted Lifeforce created the monsters that would do Kayanga's bidding.

That was unacceptable.

He couldn't do this alone. Kintu paused from his destruction; a wave of good feeling assailed him. His people were here, their Lifeforce strong. He would return but his beloved needed to be safe, first and foremost. Kintu gently picked up Antoinette and balanced her on his broad shoulders. Looking down at his cousin, he shook his head and grabbed the doctor by his boots, dragging him through the debris by his ankles to the secure entrance of the Reanimation Chamber.

Chapter Seventy-One

Already the Mossberg shotgun was slick with sweat in Shaft's hands. The rain had stopped, and the lightning had been relegated to an impressive illumination in the belly of the battleship-size clouds above. Shaft almost wished for the rain as he made his way through the nightmare scene that stretched out ahead of him. If he didn't know better, he would have said truckloads of offal from an abattoir had been dumped around the inner parameter of the compound. But he did know better and shivered with every step he took. A raw, fetid stench rose from the carnage that made his eyes water. He attempted to breathe through his mouth, but that did not help. His loafers were fucked, crusted with mud and unrecognisable gore.

Why did he ever think that he would remain on the sidelines for all of this? It's not that he didn't want to be directly involved, he really did, but he was also a realist. And he knew what was inside this compound required 'tenderising' before his frail human arse could stand a chance in conflict. He did feel like a bit of a pussy, and he knew Y would be pissed to see him without giving the all-clear message, but he didn't give a shit. He had an excuse to break the promise he had made to her. It was a goddamn order from a being with Old Testament power and Shaft had a feeling that even if he wasn't enthusiastic about being the Courier, a being he considered a God could compel him to do what it asked by uttering the right words.

He didn't feel compelled. What the hell would being compelled feel like anyway? All Shaft knew was what he had to deliver to the girls would conclude this horror show once and for all. He patted his breast pocket to confirm that he still had the object he'd been given. Relieved, he kept high-stepping through the carnage, shuffling past twitching and flapping pieces of blackened meat that hadn't been hacked or blown up but smelt like burnt rotting flesh. Shaft was glad he was on their side. The girls had dropped the hammer on this place, and the resulting fallout was not pretty. He tried to picture them handling this nightmare, and his exhausted mind could not appreciate the enormity of it. Were they okay? Shaft stepped off what could have once been a manicured lawn, but instead, it looked like a tractor had run amok over its surface. As unsafe as he felt, Shaft took the time to make the sign of the cross over the broken body of a nun. Instead, he focused on her face, which was untouched except for some droplets of blood on her cheeks. The rest of her body was mangled beyond recognition. His heart was heavy as he kept walking. The detective felt much safer when he stood on a concrete path, away from open ground and the possibility of whatever those things were erupting from the ground and dragging him down to the depths. He hurried along it to the black building in the distance, his mind racing, his senses on high alert as he swung the shotgun from side to side, his finger not straying from the trigger guard. He was thinking how exposed he was when an explosion of sound and heat made him lose his footing. Looking up and over to the direction of the blast, a small cloud lifted skyward from the top of the lighthouse raining brick and steel to the ground below.

"Fuck!" Shaft hoped no one he cared for was in that structure. He thought about investigating but kept heading towards the imposing black building.

Compulsion or free will?

Who gave a fuck.

He kept moving forward.

IGOR WAS AN OPTIMIST; HE STILL THOUGHT HE STOOD A chance. He had seven reanimated soldiers at his side whose energy would deplete in hours. The Reanimation Chamber to his back. Ahead were the Sisters of the Order of the Mechanics of Jesus and the bitch from the Guardians he thought he had killed. Igor still imagined his chances of finishing the job were good. And felt a rush of elation when the circular five-ton blast door began its symphony of lights and sounds behind him, heralding its opening sequence. The Master had succeeded where all had failed, and Igor couldn't help a glow of pride filling his chest like a shot of vodka warming his insides. If they were respected before now, they would be feared and revered. The door swung open slowly and noiselessly. Igor turned to congratulate his benefactor; the sounds of machinery and electrical discharges inside insistent.

The giant stature of Kintu stepped out.

His long shadow crept forward, freezing Igor's expression in a mask of incredulity.

"Where is my Master!" Igor croaked.

But before he could protest, all hell broke loose.

. . .

Y pulled the emergency door open and hesitated. A wave of awareness made her skin prickle and her wound-up muscles relax. She paused and slowly turned to see Suzy hobbling towards her, beaten, in pain but not defeated. The smouldering wreck of the lighthouse in the background looked like a chimney that had blown its stack. The relief that her sister was no worse for wear was palpable. How Miss Wong managed to survive the devastation would be a story for another time.

Both women scrutinised each other.

Some of Suzy's long hair was burnt, her eyebrows singed, arms and face dotted with minute craters formed from explosive ash. Her complexion was much darker now from layers of soot.

Y, on the other hand, was slick from biological waste; small chunks of viscera still clung to her as she sported a bloody nose.

"Yuh look like shit, sister," Suzy eventually said.

"So do you."

The two women hugged ferociously.

"You smell like you were sitting on a barbecue," Y said.

"It come close," Suzy agreed. "I'll live to fight another day." She looked down at Y's blood-soaked leg. The Kevlar material below the knee had been ripped by what Suzy imagined to be one of the doctor's nightmare creatures. The wound had stopped bleeding, but the gash was still obviously painful.

"You need medical," Suzy said.

"We need to fight," Y said. "It's not over yet."

"Why did I know you'd say that?" Suzy said shaking her head. "Just promise me one thing."

Y nodded.

"If it gets intense, lean on me. I'm here for you. Always."

"I know," Y said. "I know."

They grasped each other's hands and marched into the foreboding black building.

When Shaft came around the corner, he stepped into an unusual mediaeval battle zone. Broken bodies lay scattered in the corridor ahead of him. A fine mist from ruptured air-conditioning units carpeted the floor. The signs of a pitched battle were evident everywhere. He knew why his detective senses had deduced this to be unusual. Minor evidence of gunshot exchanges and controlled explosions scarred the surfaces, but from the discarded weaponry and the hacking damage to the walls and floor, the preferred means of attack had been sharp-edged weapons. Not something you usually see at a crime scene.

Shaft looked down at his shotgun, wondering if he was appropriately armed, and decided he would stick with his modern equivalent. Ahead of him, he could hear the sounds of battle without being able to discern the combatants through dust and smoke. Metal banged on metal, and the sounds of exertion and pain bounced off the walls to his ears. He hurried forward, picking his way through the debris, stopping at the sounds of explosions and then continuing, his shotgun sweeping ahead of him from left to right like a flashlight. He heard scuttling sounds through the mist that made him stop and focus more – if that was at all possible. His eyes picked up quick darting movement at his feet. Shaft stepped back, looking around, praying for the mist to thin so he could better look at what was stalking him. It was like he was in an echo chamber because the scuttling sounds were coming from all around him. One minute it was to his left, then the next behind him and all his inadequate eyesight could register was the tail-end of something serpentine slivering away. What was worst, Shaft knew his mind wasn't playing tricks with him. If he was correct, Patra had told him about these things, which scared him shitless. Having no control over his faculties was one of Shaft's biggest fears. For that reason, he had never been drunk, and the thought of something controlling his actions while his consciousness was imprisoned gave him panic attacks. He decided to pick up the pace, his senses alight like a bulb, his bowels stuffed with ice. Something wriggled through his feet; if he didn't know better, he would have thought it was trying to trip him up.

There it was again.

He stumbled but caught himself before he fell to his knees. Shaft gripped the shotgun even tighter and swung it at a sharp ninety degrees angle, pointing to the ground in front of him. His tired mind was sure the sting or the bite would come from there but it didn't. Instead, he punished himself with the thought of a quick-acting designer venom that the madman Kayanga could have concocted in his nightmare creatures.

Shaft needn't have worried.

A blur of movement through the air registered on his right, and the detective reacted with uncanny swiftness fuelled by fear. He swung the butt of the Mossberg just in time to swat away the thing that sprang out of the mist towards his throat. It made a splat sound when it hit the tiled floor, and Shaft, for the first time, could see the organism in all its gross glory. It was translucent like a jellyfish, its inner working visible, obviously capable of flight, and its underside a complex system of biting or probing organs it used to enslave you. Once it regained its orientation, the thing pivoted from its spot like a cobra and sprang back towards him. Time slowed, and Shaft's muscles bunched as they prepared to swing his shotgun like a club.

Then...

Pain erupted in his shoulder blades, and Shaft rocked forward as something organic slammed into him.

Organism two had just shown up. There was no time to think. The thing would be making its way up to the back of his neck, puncturing the muscle to reach his spinal cord, and that would be game over.

The detective stiffened and fell back; gravity tugged him; he pulled the trigger twice on his shotgun as the first organism flew over him. He watched with satisfaction as the evil thing exploded as his back hit the floor. There was a squeak as the second creature on his back took the brunt of his fall. What came next wasn't pretty as Shaft thrashed around on his back like he was on fire; when he thought the creature was sufficiently stunned, he jumped up, his back battered and bruised, pointed his shotgun point blank range at the floundering thing and pulled the trigger.

"Fuck you!"

SHAFT SUDDENLY BROKE THROUGH THE DENSE atmospherics, his view unencumbered and the relief showing on his face. The life forms of the Mechanics of Jesus were spread across the entrance to a room protected by the most enormous door he had ever seen. Something from a bank vault had been transported here to protect something significant. The vault door was partially open, and beside it was another first for him. The tallest man he'd ever seen.

Shaft immediately knew who that was and realised the girls had not exaggerated his presence. He was impressive. Even more impressive was the sight of the trio of Bad II the Bone looking battered and bruised but very much alive. Seeing them alone gave his stress-pickled body a boost of energy. Shaft started to jog towards them furiously, waving his free hand to catch their attention. Suzy looked over first and smiled broadly, seeing him. Y followed suit looking surprised, her eyes sparkling their incandescent brightest and, if it was at all possible, looking sexier than the last time he saw her. He may be in the doghouse for this, but she would forgive him.

Don't hate the player, hate the game, Shaft thought and smiled.

Chapter Seventy-Two

Kintu gently lay the unconscious body of Antoinette into the awaiting arms of a sister from the Mechanics of Jesus.

"Keep her safe," his voice boomed as they hurried her away.

Sister Charlotte was front and centre, eyes giving away her relief at seeing him alive and well.

"We were worried," she said.

Kintu nodded and put his huge hand on her shoulders.

"I was worried too, but it seems for the moment I still serve a purpose on this plane of existence."

"God is not done with you yet, Brother Kintu." Sister Charlotte motioned to two sisters who were carrying a large canvas bag between them which they deposited at his feet.

"A gift?" he asked.

"I thought you'd feel unloved if you were unarmed when all about you were 'strapped' as they say."

One of Kintu's eyebrows arched, surprised at the nun's choice of words.

"So you brought my favourite weapon's project all this way. You are indeed a woman of faith, sister," he said.

"And prayer," Sister Charlotte added. "Where is the good doctor now?"

Kintu pointed to the Reanimation Chamber while eagerly unzipping the bags.

"I don't need to tell you that without the doctor in chains or dead, this is not over."

Kintu nodded again, strapping the harness around his chest and the power pack on his back.

"This will end one way or another," he said, his eyes never leaving the vault door. He slipped his hands into the gauntlets and secured the laser units of his wrists. Touching an activation switch in the centre of the harness, the power pack came to life and thick strobing coaxial leads leaving the power pack and feeding into the gauntlets of both hands indicated readiness. Kintu lifted his right arm and the glowing blue shaft of light extended a foot from his wrist, shaped like a cutlass, humming from the outlet of the gauntlet like it was powered by a swarm of angry wasps.

"Station the sisters at the entrance with orders to destroy anything other than me that steps out of the Reanimation Chamber," Kintu said.

Sister Charlotte bowed and watched him fire up the other gauntlet and step back into the Reanimation Chamber, closing the massive doors behind him.

Y THREW HER ARMS AROUND SHAFT'S NECK AND DREW HIM in. Her lips were warm and soft. Her tongue met his, and they did that delicious dance that would invariably result in fireworks, but this time it was more contained. Shaft smiled and took a breath.

"I missed you too, baby," Shaft said. Still in each other's arms, Y peered into his eyes and said:

"I'm mad at you. You promised."

"I know, I know," Shaft said. "But someone demanded I get to you, and he was very persuasive."

"Who?" Y asked, stepping back.

Shaft's eyes hinged up and a question mark formed on his features. He shrugged and shook his head.

"You know, that is a very good question. All I know he's not human, and he feels very responsible for you girls."

Y smiled with recognition, and her excitement immediately got the better of her.

"You met him? In person, I mean."

"In a manner of speaking," Shaft said. "He wanted you to have this," he handed her the rough spherical object that looked like an odd seed. "He said you'd know what to do with it."

Y held out her hand, and Shaft dropped it in her palm. She closed her fingers around it, triggering imagery that flashed behind her eyes. Y looked distant for a moment, and Shaft took the opportunity to thoroughly survey his environment. The heavy-duty door was now closed, and the giant of a man had disappeared. A Mechanics of Jesus unit was stationed there, weapons brazenly unsure and all aimed at the vault. Whatever or whoever stepped out of the Reanimation Chamber needed to be RSVP'd beforehand, or the reception would be bloody. His eyes wandered over to the activity on the left. A battle had just ended. Blood and bodies were strewn in a concentrated topography of conflict. Shaft couldn't see clearly through the milling figures but glimpsed Patra and Suzy at the head of the cadre of Mechanics sisters. As soon as his eyes hovered over both women in the distance, they seemed to sense him and locked eyes with a nod and a pained smile. Suzy enthusiastically waved him over. "I think they have something for you," Y said, looking pleased with herself.

Intrigued, Shaft wandered over to the gathered bodies, excusing his way through the sisters until he was beside Patra and Suzy. Reanimated soldiers who had the misfortune of dying twice sat like decommissioned marionettes. Some had been respectfully covered with sheets, being offered absolution by a nun with a rosary, while two others were being examined by a sister, the complex mobile lab strapped around her shoulders. As interesting as all that was, the man pacing along the wall like a cornered animal caught Shaft's attention. Igor Rakmanov held his blade up, marking the air with its keen edge as a warning to anyone who dared to approach him. Madness shone in his eyes as he prowled up and down. Patra and Suzy had no need to speak; Shaft could succinctly express the overall sentiment.

"You're a slippery bastard, aren't you," Shaft growled. "It seems your time is up, and there's no getting away this time."

"Do you want me to tenderise his arse?" Patra asked.

Shaft looked at Patra's bloodied clothes and her pale skin. He smiled at her weakly. Shaft shook his head slowly, keeping his eyes on The Surgeon.

"I wanted to give him some licks before handing him over," Suzy added. "But I'll leave it to you, brother."

The detective dangled his handcuffs from his finger and then threw them over to him.

"Put them on," Shaft said.

The Surgeon walked over it and took a step towards Shaft.

The Detective swung the shotgun around to his back and reached for a stun gun in the waist of his trousers. He pulled it, aimed and without hesitation fired. The three barbs attached in a neat triangle on Igor's chest, and Shaft pulled the trigger. The standard issue Police stun gun delivered Fifty thousand volts, but Shaft had his armoury adapted. One hundred thousand volts coursed through the wires and directly into The Surgeon's body. An ordinary man would be dead in moments, but Igor was no ordinary man. When the oscillating voltage slammed into him, it sent him to his knees, with his head back, his teeth gritted, and his entire body locked in a spasm. Shaft released the trigger and cut off the electricity.

"I'm not fucking about, Igor. Put on the handcuffs."

The Surgeon was on his hands and knees, breathing heavily and glaring at the detective.

"I can do this all night," Shaft said, pantomiming the action of pulling the trigger on the stun gun. He must have seen the determination in the detective's eyes. Igor Rakmanov shook his head and reached forward to take up the cuffs.

"You are under arrest for multiple murders, including Marilyn Abiola. You do not have to say anything, but whatever you do say..."

Chapter Seventy-Three

After handing off Antoinette, the supposedly unconscious doctor was gone. His slippery cousin had disappeared back into the Reanimation Chamber.

No matter. Kintu was laying waste to his equipment just the same. The plasma blades attached to his arms were slicing through machinery and circuitry, marking the structure of the building with their intense heat and his anger. He was one with the destruction he was bringing to Dr Kayanga's brainchild. Sparks flew everywhere, tendrils of smoke coiled around him, explosions erupted as delicate machinery crashed and massive energy systems failed catastrophically. Noxious yellow fumes formed from spilt chemicals reacting with electricity and drifted waist height throughout the complex. The thrum of overhead fans kicking into operation to scrub the atmosphere did not interfere with his mission. Kintu was the Destroyer personified, but even with his tremendous strength and righteous anger, he couldn't do this alone. He may not have been able to stop the transference of energy to the awaiting soldiers below, but he could stop the process from proceeding further.

Only Kayanga could help him do that, and only with the required 'persuasion' would he have the slimmest chance. He needed to find him first. If he knew his cousin at all, he would have redundancies on top of redundancies, with every possible eventuality considered and a solution in place. The only reason why he was not face to face with him right now was because he was brewing something. Kintu stopped his rampage and looked over his shoulder at his handiwork. The destruction he left in his wake was impressive, but it didn't satisfy him. In truth, he was disappointed with himself. He felt pride in what he was doing, a cathartic release he should be ashamed of. The fragments of selfish humanity he had left inside never ceased to amaze him. He gestured with his thumb and forefinger on both hands, and the plasma blade shrank into the gauntlets.

"I know you're hiding in here, cousin," Kintu's voice boomed in the interior.

"But it's no use. The battle is over, your troops have been defeated, and there is nowhere for you to go."

His voice echoed uselessly.

"It's all over, cousin; let's end this now."

The pause was followed by heavy footfalls and, with it, a voice amplified through speakers.

"I wasn't hiding, cousin," Dr Kayanga said. "I was preparing for the final act."

Kintu spun to face him, his plasma blades unsheathing, humming as the air surrounding them shimmered. The doctor stood nearly ten feet tall, ensconced in a metal exoskeleton, its massive hydraulics flexing with potential power and its pilot at home with its controls.

"You didn't think trying to destroy my plans would not

meet with the greatest of resistance?" Kayanga said. "You should have disappeared when you had the opportunity."

"And miss my chance to humble you?" Kintu said. "Never."

Kintu ran at him with a guttural roar, arms and legs pumping like a locomotive, his powerful thighs launching him into the air, the plasma blades pointed towards Kayanga's lumbering mechanoid. Flesh and metal clashed.

"Son-of-bitch," Patra said. "He went back in."

Y nodded her head in grim agreement.

This had to end now.

Kintu had gone back into the Reanimation Chamber, dissatisfied with Kayanga being loose inside. They couldn't leave him there, there was one last thing they had to do to conclude this sordid chapter.

"We've got to get him out of there," Y said.

"I can feel his anger from here," Suzy said. "But it just fizzled out a few minutes ago."

"I don't like how that sounds," Patra said. "Do you think the doctor fucked with him?"

"I do," Y agreed. "So let's get in there now and pull him out while we can.

They hustled towards the vault door, and as Y drifted through first with her Katana drawn, they could hear her say in their minds like an echo.

"Eyes wide."

Suzy and Patra followed close behind.

Chapter Seventy-Four

A scream rattled his insides, like the screamer was realising the horrors from his nightmares were real. Fear was reverberating in his head like it was an empty cavern. Kintu did not recognise himself. Fear had always been his constant companion, not his torturer. Only then did he realise that the silent scream was coming from him.

He was on his back, looking up at the ceiling of the Reanimation Chamber, unable to remember how or why he was here.

Helpless.

Klaxons were blaring. The smell of ozone permeated the air as the overhead lights flickered. The blank space in Kintu's mind throbbed like the cursor on a computer screen for a second, and then the reboot of his consciousness began. In moments he was aware but could not move. His muscles were locked from his neck to his ankles, and he recalled with crystal clarity what had just happened to him.

"...My control," the voice said.

The words echoed in his head with no significance.

Then the pain flared like a brush fire.

The increasing pressure, like a vice on his chest, accelerated the retrieval of his short-term memory, and so did the voice towering over him. Dr Kayanga was strapped into the RX710-Z exoskeleton rig with his size thirty reinforced steel boot on Kintu's chest.

"You are under my control," Kayanga said again. "Did you really think that when I created you, I wouldn't embed a redundancy system for my protection?" Kayanga laughed. "It's a cliché that the creation turns against the creator. Your brain was reprogrammed through neuroscience and sorcery. You cannot harm your creator once I trigger the subroutine that shuts you down."

In his head, Kintu could only thrash and scream, but in the real world, he was silent and unmoving.

Kayanga had the upper hand once more.

"Where is Antoinette?" Kayanga asked, knowing no answer would be forthcoming. "No matter, I'll just have to find her myself," he paused to think. The articulated joints that formed the exoskeleton frame he was embedded inside flexed like it was preparing to move. Kayanga lifted one gigantic foot and slammed it down on Kintu's chest again. His cousin's arms and legs flew up almost with comedic effect from the force. Kintu felt and heard ribs snap. The pain did not hesitate to make him aware he was being broken and he could do nothing about it. Kayanga continued to torture him with his words.

"Do you think this is over?" he raved. "Defeating my army outside will not stop this. Were you paying attention to the green lights on the pods?" He paused. "They are the reason this is just the beginning. And only because of you. Never forget that, cousin. All because of you."

With the sounds of servo-motors engaging, Kayanga's exoskeleton lowered itself so he could be closer to the condemned man.

"I'm glad we could have this final moment together," Kayanga said. "Dying in that containment pod did not suit the warrior persona you have adopted over the years," he chuckled. "It's the least I could do. No need to thank me."

The doctor lifted his leg, and so did the RX710-Z, the feedback loop lagging by a second or two. He let the pile-driver of a foot drop. A blur of mechanical power and precision engineering slamming into flesh, bone, and metal.

Boom!

He peered down at the soles of his mechanical foot to see the pulp of what was once Kintu on it.

There was nothing there.

Kayanga lifted his mechanical foot from the crater of deformed metal he made from the force of the stamp. He whipped his head around within the exoskeleton and saw what he had somehow missed. Kintu's body was being pulled away by two of the bitches that called themselves the Guardians. For the first time, he wished he had weaponised the unit, but its raw power would be sufficient to crush them underfoot. He strode towards their position with three bounds, his footfalls reverberating off the metal grating as he moved with a kind of loping grace. He caught up easily, looming over them, when something dawned on him. There were always three guardians, and he had only seen two pulling Kintu's body.

Where was the other? The Asian.

Kayanga felt the breath on his cheeks and the keen blade at his throat, and he grimaced.

How?

The woman was contorted through the framework that made up the exoskeleton without him hearing or feeling her presence until now.

"Tek it easy, big man," the woman said. "One more step,

and I'll take your head and introduce it to your feet. Yuh understan mi?"

Kayanga shook his head, his mind racing but unable to see a way out of the bind he found himself in. He helplessly watched as his cousin was dragged away, the effect of his neural trigger diminishing with distance.

"What do you propose the next step will be?" Kayanga asked matter-of-factly as if he was in a business negotiation.

The woman with the Butterfly knife at his throat laughed a bitter chuckle.

"Yuh choices are limited to none, doctor. It depends upon you."

"Oh!" His interest peaked, but the woman didn't want to hear his opinion and pressed her blade closer to his throat.

"Yeah, man, we are going to destroy all of dis..."

Dr Kayanga tried to interject, but the woman tilted the blade's keen edge upward towards his jugular, breaking the skin and silencing him again.

"Everyting you have created will be dust. You can stay and disappear with your life's work or suffer the consequences for your actions and leave with me now to the outside."

Before the doctor could express his defiance, the woman was gone.

And whether he knew it or not, the countdown had begun.

Chapter Seventy-Five

When Suzy reached the fifty-ton door, it slid open, and Y was there to meet her. They clasped arms. "Did he accept your offer?" Y asked.

Suzy sighed and looked over her shoulder, squinting through the smoke and shrugged.

"His fineral, sis," she paused, her defiant words hung in the air, almost feeling like she was giving him more time to change his mind. "Let's end dis," Suzy said, squeezing past Y without looking back.

Alone, Y stood between the Reanimation Chamber and the main building. The enormous circular vault door cast a cold shadow into the smoke-shrouded landscape of the chamber's interior. Y opened her hand to look at the peculiar object in her palm. She peered into the swirling smoke, electrical sparks raining down from the ceiling, explosions and the sheer destruction. The doctor's decision to stay would prove fatal. Y threw the seed into the chamber and took one step back. The air seemed to change as it made contact with the metal floor. There was a sound like ice rapidly forming on a surface. A smell of heated metal. The reaction took a deep breath, and when it exhaled, it did so with a roar. A crystal growth exploded outwards from what she considered the seed, expanding at an exponential rate and destroying everything in its path. The mechanically assisted vault door swung closed in time, followed by a resounding boom from the inside that shook the foundations. Everyone stopped and watched apprehensively as tiny crystals formed between the door's seams and the housing surrounding it.

It held.

A wave of relief and exhaustion washed over the battle-weary warriors. It was palpable, the relief radiating from the group, etched on their faces, in their sighs, in the slump of their shoulders.

This was done.

The question, unspoken but no less potent, hung in the air: had they won the battle but lost the war?

Chapter Seventy-Six

Sky Garden, East Central London, Four Weeks Later

Y stood with a glass of Champagne in a glittery little black dress, looking proudly at her immediate and extended family mingling. They were all here. Everyone she loved and cared for. Shaft had left her to get drinks and must have been Shanghaied by his team from Project Black Book. Her mom had brought a date with her – Y was still trying to process that revelation. A toy boy, ten years her junior, and she had kept it a secret from her only daughter for months.

They needed to have a long, long talk.

Suzy was here with Trevor, and Patra had brought her girlfriend, nurse Grace. She, too, had kept that quiet for a while but eventually came clean after the events on the Cornish Coast.

Y was still puzzled. Mr Sinton's family wanted him dead but was thankful Patra had discovered the plot and saved him. The entrepreneur was back in good form if the catwalk model on his arm was anything to go by.

The peals of laughter made Y look over to another group who were having the time of their lives.

Alcohol?

She didn't think so.

Spokes, who always cleaned up well, was in front of four sisters from the Mechanics of Jesus, cracking them up with one of his catalogue of humorous Jamaican stories.

Y shook her head in amusement.

Sometimes, when in the thick of things, she forgot there was more to life than their duty to protect this great city. They still had the challenges many ordinary people had and would continue to have them. Her family constantly reminded her of that.

A pair of warm hands touched the skin of her exposed back, adjusting the criss-cross straps of her dress and ensuring her stunning look remained stunning. The hands fluttered up to squeeze her shoulders and then disappeared.

"Yuh look beautiful tonight," Nanny said, not stopping but leaving behind an aroma of honeysuckle in her wake.

"Thank you, Auntie," Y called after her. "You do too."

Y was taken aback seeing Nanny glammed up in her long skirt, slippers, satin jacket and head wrap, her alabaster skin glowing. She shouldn't be surprised by what this beautiful albino woman did. Nanny was magical in more ways than one. A woman of hidden depths and undetermined age. And Y was glad they had her in their corner. She didn't see her smile as she walked away, but Y felt it.

Pondering magic, Y's eyes drifted to the kind of spectacle she should be used to by now but felt she never would. In the rooftop garden, away from the music and food, the stunning woman stood in a cloud of butterflies, her dark skin gleaming from the diffused sunlight and her smile beatific. Around her were more than a thousand species of exotic plants cascading over steel and concrete, gurgling water features and ponds filled with Koi and spotted turtles. Where the woman stood barefoot, surrounded by adoring butterflies, was a fragrant hotspot of smells from lavender, peppermint, rosemary and wild strawberry. Y could hear the soothing hum of bees pollinating flowers that may have gone unnoticed to most because of the music, but Y knew Antoinette was absorbing it all.

Mr Patel's extensive contacts came good again as the entire 15th-floor Chisholm Building was booked for the evening. Kintu had expressed a desire to expose Antoinette to the New World she found herself in. When he had recovered, Y arranged this family affair as a thank you. The Spider Tree was not showing the massive fault lines that had appeared as a thick web segment before they clashed with Kayanga. That had disappeared, and with it, the further weakening of the balance. Disaster averted; it was time to take a breath and prepare, but family bonds needed strengthening. Y knew without it, no matter how significant the stakes for mankind were, it would all mean nothing. She watched as Kintu joined Antoinette, and she placed her small hand in his huge one. A few brave butterflies alighted on him, but the majority stayed within Antoinette's gravity.

Y smiled and felt the presence that she recognised immediately come to stand beside her.

"I never got to thank you for all you've done," Sister Charlotte said. "Even with our resources, I'm not sure we could have brought Brother Kintu back without you. Your gifts are amazing."

"I'm flattered," Y said. "I'm glad we're on the same side. You've got a formidable group of people behind you too."

"I know," Sister Charlotte said, bowing. "It's a challenge keeping ahead of the Vatican and the forces that want to destroy us, but we have powerful friends," the sister nodded at her.

"And our secret weapon is Brother Kintu; of course, he gives us an advantage. We have thrived for over 300 years. We will continue to do so."

"So, what's next? I mean for Kintu and Antoinette."

Sister Charlotte breathed deeply, straightening her tunic over her camouflaged combat trousers and turned to face Y for the first time.

"We will return to our HQ in Ethiopia and continue our mission. We did not find Dr Kayanga's body, and we know how resourceful he can be. If he's alive, he will come for us sooner or later, but the Mechanics of Jesus will be ready."

Y nodded slowly, recognising the steely determination in her words. Y hoped for Kayanga's sake that he really was dead.

Later in the evening, Patra hobbled over to where Y and Suzy stood, dopily placing her chin on Suzy's shoulders.

"Gal," Suzy said, annoyed. "Are you a puppy?"

Patra grinned.

Y couldn't keep a straight face.

"You know this is bad manners leaving our family, friends and lovers to fend for themselves while we chat," Y said.

"Shit," Patra said. "They used to it by now."

"They betta be," Suzy said.

All three looked on in comfortable silence for a moment.

"Do you think the man in our dreams is watching us?" Patra asked.

"You know," Y mused. "I think he's been looking after us from day one."

"I'm glad he's around," Suzy said.

Patra nodded, .

"Me too."

Ms Jones wore a pants suit with a low crop top exposing her muscular stomach. The mark left by a high-calibre bullet that had punched through her side was gone from her skin, but the internal damage would take more time for her magical metabolism to heal.

Y and Suzy could feel her pain.

"Yuh know you could have stayed home, right," Suzy said. She was rocking a glamorous red dress with matching shoes and a split showing her toned legs.

"And miss all this free food and drink?" Patra said. "Are you shitting me?"

Suzy shook her head, exasperated, then went back to watching the rest of their extended family enjoy themselves.

Y hugged them both.

"I'm glad we did this," she said. "We needed it. They needed it."

"We've put them through a lot," Patra said.

"And there is a lot more to come," Suzy added.

All three looked over at the glittering city of London from their vantage point of thirteen stories up in the Sky Garden. From here, the place they were ordained to protect was vibrant and alive. They wanted to keep it that way.

"Can we keep all this together?" Patra asked.

Y turned to look at them both.

"Who else will?" She sighed. "We were never given a choice, but we have come to realise we were born for this. London still needs us, and things could get worse before they get better," Y said, looking to Suzy, who nodded. "In the meantime, we'll be here to patch up the cracks until the imbalance can heal itself."

Beside them was a table with glasses and a half bottle of

Champagne. Y poured the liquid into their glasses, taking one for herself and giving her sisters one each. Y raised a glass.

"For the challenges to come," she said. "Bring it on."

"Bring it on," they shouted in unison, clinking glasses, their voices drifting over the city they were born to protect.

Chapter Seventy-Seven

One Day After the Lighthouse Explosion, 1 Mile Off the Cornish Coast

The seas were much calmer after the freak storm of the night before. And the people in the rowboat were benefiting from languid waves and easterly winds, not that it mattered. The man rowing the boat in the swells had a powerful, unrelenting stroke and had not flagged for the last four hours. They must have been 100 nautical miles from the point they had taken to the water, and the rower seemed as if he could keep going forever. The other two crew members sat in silence to the metronomic slap of the oar on the water. A muscular female had her arms protectively around the shoulders of a man covered in a reflective thermal blanket, shivering. The figure under the thermal wrap was a grotesque landscape of burns and lacerations. Under his skin was a multitude of compound fractures, including a punctured lung. But the doctor understood his body with the intimacy of a molecular biologist. He was so in tune with his physiology he had self-diagnosed his own injuries and controlled some of the more life-threatening trauma he had suffered. An ordinary man would already be dead. Even with his superhuman metabolism, the good doctor would eventually succumb to his wounds if steps were not taken as quickly as possible. He moaned in time with the excruciating waves of pain that smashed into him and imagined himself immersed in the cold life-giving nutrients of his rejuvenation pod. He tried to smile, but his broken, lopsided jaw prevented that, only allowing a painful pout. Kayanga had been bested, and that hurt more than his injuries. In the arms of his surviving progeny, he reassured himself that from these two would spring his army.

Then he would return with Antoinette at her rightful place beside him.

That was for another day.

Today he would recuperate, take stock and make plans. After all, he had all the time in the world.

THE END ...FOR NOW

SCAN ME

About the Author

Anton Marks is a dynamic and trailblazing writer with a passion for speculative fiction. Anton cut his novel writing teeth on a Jamaican crime thriller - **Dancehall** but immediately wrote the futuristic gems of **In the Days of Dread** and **69**. Anton's supernatural series **Bad II the Bone**, is captivating readers, while his young adult Sci-Fi/Fantasy series **Joshua N'Gon: Last Prince of Alkebulahn**, written under the name *Anthony Hewitt* is enchanting a new audience. With a fresh perspective and eclectic style, Anton Marks is an exciting addition to the world of speculative fiction. Join him on his writing journey and become the best you can be by subscribing to his weekly email - www.antonmarks.com.

Printed in Great Britain
by Amazon